CW00495167

A SCANDAL OF SECRETS

J.F. HOWARD

A SCANDAL OF SECRETS © J.F. Howard, 2023

J.F. Howard has asserted his rights under the Copyright Designs and Patents Act 1988 to be identified as the author of this work. This book is sold subject to the condition that it shall not, by way of trade or otherwise, be lent, resold, hired out, or otherwise circulated without the publisher's prior consent in any form of binding or cover other than that in which it is published and without a similar condition, being imposed on the subsequent purchaser. This is a work of fiction and any resemblance of the fictional characters to real persons is purely coincidental and non-intentional.

ISBN: 978-1-7391652-9-1

Cover Design © Graeme Parker at Provoco Publishing
Provoco Logo ©MJC at Provoco Publishing
Edited by Jane Murray

Provoco
PUBLISHING

Table of Contents

Prologue

He didn't want it to end this way! In his own eyes, he was the hero of this tale and heroes don't get mercilessly slaughtered by their enemies inside a burning barn; a place that had provided so many wonderful memories for the young Anthony Crawford. Despite the gravity of the situation and, of course, an urgent need for him to get out of there before the whole place was ablaze and he was trapped inside, his mind took him backwards in time. He began to think not of his escape, but of his past, and the events which had led him to be there, trapped, facing his own imminent demise. He crouched down in the farthest corner of the barn, away from the flames, head bowed. Hadn't he read somewhere that there is more oxygen nearer the ground, or there were less fumes and smoke at any rate. Charlie Chaplin came into his mind and Crawford had to laugh, despite his current situation. He supposed it was a fitting thought. After all, the many hopes and dreams he had at his young age, were inspired by Chaplin, one of his screen idols. He was arrogant enough to believe that he, like Chaplin, could conquer Hollywood one day, with his own unique brand of humour and vision of the world.

His hero, too, came from humble beginnings. Chaplin was a London boy with a talent for performing, who would settle in America, take the film world by storm, and revolutionise cinema with his storytelling. Crawford saw many similarities between him and the man who was the screen's biggest draw. Also born to humble beginnings, the loss of his father to the Great War had paved the way for his impoverished mother to marry a man who walked amongst the elite and was a true embodiment of the high society of the era. Hence, here her son was, trapped in a burning barn!

Crawford's mother, Jane, had worked hard to escape the shackles poverty placed on her and her boy. 'Working your fingers to the bone' wasn't just a saying, Crawford thought bitterly, remembering the sight of his mother's bony hand, the paper-thin skin stretched across little more than a skeleton. He had felt frightened whenever he looked at her hands, a symbol of how hard she had to work to ensure young Anthony had everything he needed. Luckily, perhaps, her financial worries were no more when her boss at one of the factories where she worked had suddenly decided that his affection for her was true love, and matrimony was both the logical and romantic next step forward. Jane had married Philip Crawford not thinking of him, but of his wealth and what that would mean for her son. Anthony had been adopted by his mother's new husband, who had given him his name and the benefits of education and wealth, but there was no love, no affection. It was as though, in order to gain the love of his wife, Philip didn't have any left to give her son. A place in his business was not earmarked for Anthony, something his stepson was very resentful of. Anthony had not shown massive interest in Philip's business affairs, but as a young boy, he had often felt a sense of loss when looking for the man who would provide the security of hope, guidance, and affection; the things he had enjoyed when his father was alive. This only served his want of joining the family firm, as he felt it was his only way of earning the praise and adulation of being perceived worthy enough to be Philip's heir.

His stepfather had provided a roof over his head, food on the table, and money, but remained indifferent to the boy, although he had to concede that Anthony was relatively quiet, and never too much trouble, although that somehow irked the mighty Philip Crawford. He would have liked the boy to have displayed some sort of passion about something, anything, which they could have shared, but Anthony did not muster the emotions about the interests his stepfather needed from him and consequently, he was deemed worthy of little attention, a mere by-product of the woman Philip had wed. Anthony brought little shame to the door but, in turn, was hardly a worthy heir to the throne. At least, the former was true until this evening!

What should have been a Christmas soiree, the envy of all who didn't receive an invitation, had turned into an eruption of scandal that, for Anthony Crawford, ruthlessly highlighted the hedonistic and hypocritical life that the elite had been living for a number of years, or perhaps since time began. Yet he, too, was a hypocrite. A socialite who completely embraced the hedonism of the ruling class and all the trimmings that went with it. A man who would happily wreck a home and use servants for his selfish pleasures, whilst all along living on the charity of Philip to enjoy his wine, women, and song. Of course, Chaplin was the one who would cleverly mock the social norms and inequalities, which inspired Anthony to be the constant critic of the societal elite. A master of disguise! One who knew the many scandals and secrets of those around him, whilst all along living amongst them and playing them like a fiddle. However, there was a nasty plot twist in this production which had led him into a burning barn and made the chances of a happy ending to this tale highly improbable. Not that he was sure what the happy ending looked like for Anthony, but it certainly wasn't this.

Plus, of course, he was still, in all likelihood, going to perish in a fire!

The heat was stifling. A barn that had seemed so huge to Crawford a few years ago was now unbearably claustrophobic, clouded with smoke and as dangerous as the fate that surely awaited him. An area capable of comfortably accommodating at least a dozen horses and at least one hundred bales of hay, was being devoured by flames. Searingly hot bolts of amber, ochre and scarlet greedily consumed the air, the hay, the old, sturdy wooden structure. Thank goodness the horses were turned out, Crawford thought, although God knows why the safety of a dozen or so polo ponies sprung to mind, with he himself in mortal danger. And not just from the fire, he thought, as the sound of gunfire rang inside the recesses of his mind.

His face and shirt were stained with dirt, smoke and blood, his fair hair thick with sweat and his lungs filling with smoke. The huge barn cackled as the flames destroyed the very walls that had once provided him with both safety and sanctuary. He was unsure how long he'd been there, although it couldn't have been long. Seeking refuge in the barn had been a smart move, he'd thought, although now he was beginning to wonder! He'd felt he had eluded his protagonists when he had charged out of the French doors, amidst the chaos that had erupted inside the bedroom of his stepfather's Oxfordshire mansion. Had they followed him out to the barn, those who wanted to see him perish? That was the only rational explanation, Anthony reasoned. It would be perceived as an unfortunate accident. A houseful of guests, people wandering about the estate, smoking, and drinking. A drunk, young man of privilege overly indulges on the fine claret on offer at the soiree before taking a walk outside, with an oil lamp providing the only source of light. His inebriated self, coupled with the soft ground conspires to see him fall and set the place ablaze. He could almost read the obituary notice in The Times now! 'The result of a tragic accident, the family of the late Anthony Crawford are desperately saddened to announce…' and whoever was out to kill him, would have had their work done for them, literally!

Well, even if they had set the blaze which seemed destined to claim him, they wouldn't be the only ones guilty of something, Crawford reasoned, in between gasping, wracking coughs as the flames leapt around him and the smoke-filled air became thicker. He too was guilty, although it was a fine time to be thinking of such things, as the acrid clouds choked his throat, and it was getting harder to breathe. He had no choice but to go outside and confront whatever lay in wait, reasoning that being shot would be a better ending than being burnt alive or suffocated by smoke inhalation. Espying a route of escape, he knew his nearly six-foot, athletic frame was still strong enough to make it outside! Time to act, Crawford, he thought, while allowing himself a brief moment to reflect on the few, wonderful, and heady months of life he had recently experienced.

Coughing, gagging in the heat and the smoke, Crawford was suddenly bitten by guilt. This actor was the one who had the moral high ground; a character that was meant to be of higher morality who had come from the working-class hardships – something that made him better than those around him, Jane aside. Anthony's production was meant to be something that highlighted injustice and shone a negative spotlight on those pretending to be something they weren't, using marriage merely for convenience or a stepping-stone for greater power and status. His character was flawed, needed a rewrite. For all Anthony's criticisms of lies and deceit, his sexual urges had made him part of something he despised. It was like Chaplin mocking someone for being short yet feeling a sense of hurt when taller, richer characters physically and emotionally abused his diminutive stature. The smoke stung Anthony's eyes along with the guilt of his actions. He had to face the fact he had contributed to the loss of life, multiple heartbreak, and irreversible scandal from which many would never recover.

Indeed, if he didn't get out of this burning barn, he would not recover. He would be dead! Crawford felt like his flesh was cooking. His own face was too hot to touch, and his skin seemed to be crisping like the Christmas goose he and the family enjoyed for dinner each year. Now, he was in the oven and was desperate to turn down the role of roasted bird, with his only escape through the huge and heavy wooden doors and into the unknown. He knew something was waiting, and he knew it wouldn't be pleasant. Sensing this could be the final moments of his tale which was now entering the realms of tragedy, before he made one last desperate dash through the flames, towards those heavy, wooden doors, Crawford could only think one thing: this really would make a great film!

Chapter 1

"My, you do look smart, Anthony," remarked a proud Jane Crawford upon paying close inspection to her smartly dressed, well-built son.

The dinner jacket did look good on young Crawford, and he was more than happy to allow his proud, yet worried mother, who just happened to be passing his room ahead of an 'important' social soiree the Crawford's were hosting, the chance to pass such a compliment.

Crawford stood at the foot of his mahogany, four poster bed. It and his writing desk were the only two dark pieces of furniture in a predominantly white and somewhat austere room. There were no fancy frills on the plain and simple bedding, no pictures or photographs adorning the stark, pale walls. It was as though the young man did not entrust anyone to know any more about him than was absolutely necessary. Predominantly white and plain, the room's huge window provided a beautiful vista of the Oxfordshire countryside and, more importantly for Crawford, a horizon to where he wanted to be and would, one day, get to.

Sitting himself down at the mahogany desk, where he would often pen short stories and scripts for roles that he was sure Chaplin would approve of, afforded Jane a chance to indulge her motherly instincts and perform some last-minute maintenance on her son, quickly slicking down a few rogue hairs that protruded from his sharp parting on the left side.

"This new *Brylcreme* all of you young gentlemen are wearing is frightfully strong in both smell and hold; your hair is looking wonderful, darling." Since marrying her second husband, some four years ago, Jane Crawford had spent countless hours refining her speech and adopting what she thought were upper class words and phrases. Anthony winced whenever he heard his mother speak but didn't have the heart to tell her she sounded ridiculous and that there was a faint, yet undeniable East End twang to her voice.

Losing the father of her child in the Great War, she'd worked hard to better herself, taking cleaning jobs and utilising her ability to sew to make ends meet, and eventually, she had managed to buy an old typewriter and taught herself to type, which had proved fortuitous for them both, as a position at Crawford's, one of England's finest makers of women's clothes became available. The investment of a shilling for the typewriter had turned out to be one of Jane's more canny decisions, as Philip Crawford had fallen in love with his secretary and after a brief courtship, he had married her, much to the amazement of his few true friends and the wider, monied and aristocratic social circle in which he moved. Himself a lonely widower, he agreed to take her young son as his own, bestowing the family name upon him, as well as the benefits of a London house, moving Jane and her son from the fringes of East End poverty to the privileged environs of St John's Wood, access to seemingly limitless money and the huge Oxfordshire mansion, where they spent much of the summer (London being very unfashionable in hot weather) and the Christmas season. The large country estate came with yet more servants (Philip keeping a full staff at both residences), endless rooms, and grounds so vast it required a team of gardeners and ground staff to maintain it. Philip had told the mother and son, upon their first weekend at the house, that His Majesty, King George had been entertained there.

"'Mother do stop fiddling with my hair,' Anthony replied. 'If the bloody *Brylcreme* is so strong, it doesn't need you messing with it! Look, you've got the stuff all over your hands. You'd better wash it off in the sink.'

Jane looked crestfallen, but obediently went to the sink and rinsed her sticky hands under the taps. Anthony watched and gave her a smile. His mother's face suddenly transformed; the anxious expression she habitually wore melted in the approval of her son.

Anthony was grateful. He'd seen his mother struggle, he remembered her worries about finance and whether they would eat today, and he knew their circumstances had prematurely aged her soft features. Her face displayed more wrinkles than it should at the age of forty but now was once again playing host to a smile. Small in stature, her slim figure looked resplendent in her flowing, black evening gown, while her light brown, shoulder-length hair was tidily arranged in a chignon. Crawford loved his mother and was glad that her marriage enabled her to live a life of the sort of luxury he had only previously read about in newspapers. He did not pause to consider that he, too, was afforded the same benefits of wealth and privilege, and he enjoyed both greatly.

With education ending for him upon his father's death and the abrupt halting of the two shillings and sixpence pay he had been entitled to as a corporal of the Royal Engineers, Anthony had to be the man of the house; the dirty, inner city ramshackle hovel they called home. He and his parents had occupied two rooms of the squalid, three-storey building, which had housed another three families. Their rooms were in the basement. Dark and dingy, and always frigidly cold, at least they had a fire when they were able to afford a meagre few lumps of coal. He'd got a job at a butcher's shop and had been proud to be contributing to the household, at last. The job, of course, ended before the union of his mother and stepfather. Philip Crawford had then taken the boy in hand and provided an intense amount of private tutoring both in the basic subjects of Mathematics, English, History and Science but also, he had paid for elocution and deportment lessons, whilst instructing Anthony himself in the ways of the rich and elite high society in which the boy would now move.

A role in the family business was something Anthony craved, but Philip Crawford could not see a 'perfect fit' for his stepson in his empire, preferring Anthony to pursue a military career.

"Made a man out of me, boy," Philip would often tell him. *"The finest armed forces in the world, just look at The Empire! Gentlemen of bravery and valour, it would certainly make a gentleman of you."*

Determined to push back from what Anthony viewed as a version of hell, particularly due to the fate of his own father, had seen the cold and insensitive Philip grow increasingly impatient with the young man living under his roof. He was used to getting his own way and was hell bent on Anthony being embarking on a career deemed worthy of the status he had inherited, just as long as he wasn't part of the family business. This had often confused Anthony and helped build resentment. Surely a place within Philip Crawford's empire would be the easiest option all round.

The most ardent defender of his wishes and happiness, his mother frequently went into battle for her child, often enduring many verbal blows on behalf of Anthony from her husband, whose exasperations often ended with the phrase: *'I only have his best interests at heart, life is not all about daydreaming and is certainly not a film!'* Jane would often find a way to protect and cushion her son and he would often be allowed to live his highly comfortable and relatively responsibility-free life.

So, Crawford enjoyed an allowance and spent his days writing letters, walking, running, or simply dreaming about following Chaplin to Hollywood and making his fortune. He had few friends and had learned his lesson when engaging in conversation with the servants, something his stepfather took a dim view on and had no issues with letting him know.

"They are not your class, at least not now, anyway," Philip Crawford had told the boy, who was often reduced to a small child by his stepfather's cold stare. *"I expect certain standards that will be met. I make no allowances for anybody, is that understood?"*

From that day Anthony had been careful regarding over-familiarity. He refused to talk down to anyone, but his loquacious nature had been tempered, or at least hidden when around his stepfather or any other member of the society he was part of, but massively at odds with.

His private tutoring had unearthed a talent for the written word, but Crawford was only interested in the cinema. He was convinced his look, demeanour, and engaging personality would soon take the silver screen by storm. His flair for the written word would come in useful for screenplays and direction, the latter of which he also knew Chaplin was also adept at.

Although exasperated by his stepson's 'obsession' with cinema, Crawford Senior had, on occasion, taken his adopted offspring to the odd matinee production at the local theatre.

Sporadic though they were, young Anthony had enjoyed his stepfather's company; Philip would remark on the athletic prowess and ability of Douglas Fairbanks, even suggesting that the boy had similar tools in his locker. It had greatly surprised Anthony when Philip had spent the afternoon with him in the cinema, and though the younger Crawford suspected he'd probably explored every other avenue of getting someone else to take Anthony, it was a childhood memory that the young Crawford cherished and maybe the exact point he knew that he was destined for the big screen.

"This dinner tonight, Anthony. It is very important to your father," said Jane, her words sharply bringing Anthony back into the present day. "The Fords are wonderful people and also hugely influential."

Gazing into the wide mirror adorning the white, painted wall, to check her appearance for what must have been the hundredth time, his mother continued. "They are a charming couple and I'm sure it will be a right go -, rather splendid evening, I should say."

Correcting herself was a daily chore. Now part of high society, one must live, act and most certainly speak correctly!

Her son could have corrected his mother on the fact that the cold, business-driven man who was her husband, was not his father, but he had learned to bite his tongue for her sake. Also, Anthony was well aware of the relatively easy life he enjoyed since gaining a stepfather whose reputation was known throughout the land and whose creations had even been rumoured to have been graced by celebrities and socialites, including Mary Pickford and, most impressively, Queen Mary! Hard work had brought Anthony the lifestyle to which he was becoming accustomed, although he had yet to make the connection between the two.

"I will do nothing to let the name of this house down, Mother." said a solemn Crawford, who would do his utmost to not disrupt what was a life of ease and security for the woman who had given him everything she possibly could, even when she had had little to give.

He would not have to do a lot. Merely sit in silence until

spoken to, if at all, and remember his manners when required; something he felt he was good at. Good manners were not an exclusive property of the elite, although his own had become somewhat more refined since his stepfather had insisted upon the elocution and deportment lessons Anthony had despised. However, the etiquette, on the other hand, was different. Crawford wondered whether his struggles to fit into the upper-class echelons in which he now lived, was a subconscious objection to a group that he was now part of, but could never truly accept, or be accepted by. He was unable to recognise that his subliminal inability to accept his new status led to those he was now mixing with rejecting him on the basis of his own aloofness.

How he wished Harry Hewson-Greaves was here providing one of his jolly pep talks. His only real friend since becoming a Crawford, Hewson-Greaves was born into wealth, privilege, and opportunity; he subsequently knew only one life - the one Crawford had been introduced to through his mother's marriage.

The only son of an exceedingly wealthy pioneer in the automotive industry, the twenty-two-year-old had excelled at school and was already being fast-tracked into his father's empire. Hewson-Greaves was a kind, humble individual, who downplayed his ability and seemed mildly embarrassed by his status. With Philip Crawford and Hewson-Greaves Senior mixing in the same social circles, friendship between the two boys had been encouraged, in the hope that Anthony would learn and develop into the man his stepfather wanted him to be. An organic friendship had soon developed between the two. Harry loved Philip Crawford's stepson's imagination and free mind, while both enjoyed sport and the silver screen.

His mother's small hand rested on her son's broad shoulder. Their brief moment of togetherness was interrupted by a voice that caused the young man's hairs to stand up on his neck.

"Darling, I was wondering where you had gotten to."

Philip Crawford entered Anthony's bedroom without knocking and moved with purpose towards his wife. Giving his stepfather a terse glance, which luckily Philip didn't notice,

Anthony wondered how it was that his smart, black dinner jacket with incredibly shiny lapels, and crisp white shirt were perfectly tailored and incredibly expensive, yet he felt cheap when in the presence of this man.

"Is all well?" Philip enquired to his wife without so much as a second glance to her son, who was now up out of his chair and doing his best to adopt the correct stance.

"Of course, Philip," came Jane's nervous reply.

"Our guests will soon be arriving," he told her. "We should be downstairs to greet them."

His eyes now fixed on Anthony, he continued, "All of us."

Turning on his heel, Philip swept out of the room, with his wife's shiny, high heels tap-tapping on the wooden floor of the hallway as she hurried behind him. Anthony gave a deep sigh and followed a few paces behind. Walking swiftly along the huge landing, with its wooden panelled walls providing a backdrop for the dozen paintings that were on display. A fan of John Constable, Anthony would often stare at the images of Dedham Vale, often citing the artworks as one of his inspirations for his stories and scripts. He was always overwhelmed by the fact that the paintings were originals. The lead up to Christmas would see festive decoration adorn the house but Philip forbade any tinsel going anywhere near his impressive collection of art. It wasn't that he feared damage; in truth Anthony's stepfather hated Christmas. Much more receptive in the early years, his tolerance for appeasing his wife and stepchild had waned as time drew on. Anthony would often refer to Philip as *Ebenezer* after reading *A Christmas Carol,* much to the humorous delight of Harry. Anthony recalled reading the novel for the first time and actually changing the character's name to Philip as he felt it a perfect for his curmudgeonly attitude.

"Are there no prisons! Are there no workhouses!" Anthony allowed himself a smile whilst recalling his rather poor attempt at imitating Philip's voice, although Harry's howls of laughter never minded the poor quality of impression.

Anthony snapped out of his daydream upon realisation that he was close to walking straight into the master and mistress of the house, another thing which would have been met with Philip's disapproval. He shortened his stride and walked more slowly than usual, not wanting to catch up with, or overtake the lady and gentleman of the house. His hands behind his back, he moved along in a style that was reminiscent of a slow march at a military funeral.

He studied his stepfather, begrudgingly admiring the physical grace and stature of the older man. Ruthless and calculating, only snippets of Philip Crawford were known to Anthony, who would never enquire further. From early on, Philip had made it clear that he was not a man for nurture or small talk, but rather a stalwart of business, standards, discipline, and rules.

Widowed for ten years before he decided to make Jane his second wife, Anthony often wondered if his stepfather considered marriage along the same terms as a business venture, and why he had married his mother, a woman so clearly beneath him. What had Philip Crawford's first wife been like, thought Anthony? Certainly, different from his mother. He strongly suspected the man who had begrudgingly adopted him had perhaps endured a first marriage that had not gone all his own way. The original Mrs Crawford, who'd fallen victim to scarlet fever, had come from wealth and may have been a bit too independent for his fiercely traditional stepfather. And while unions between the classes was still frowned upon in some quarters, a meek, mild-mannered dependent such as Jane obviously suited Philip perfectly.

Born into wealth, Philip Crawford had worked hard to contribute to the success of the family business and was the only real successor, possessing a sharp mind for the industry and a ruthlessness to take on, and defeat, competition at all costs. His mother had died when Philip was just five years of age and his father had been tough while raising both he and his younger brother. Philip's younger sibling had been his father's favourite but had died in military service during the Boer war. Anthony wondered if this little snippet of his stepfather's past was one of the reasons for Philip Crawford's cold nature now.

Cinema trips aside, the few times Crawford interacted with

his stepfather often exposed him to yet another lecture on hard work, respect, and discipline, although he often received backhanded compliments on the latter two.

"You're in a high society now, boy," Anthony recalled Crawford Senior saying. He rarely used his stepson's given name. *"Certain etiquette and hard work are required and I simply do not accept failure. Whilst you will never inherit the family business, I expect you to be a success in whatever career you pursue!"*

Having now reached the bottom of the wide staircase, the master and mistress made their way into the Great Hall, where they would always receive guests. Anthony made the decision to follow them in but waited to be invited to sit down. The codes of etiquette could be exhausting and frustrating.

Philip had already rung the bell which soon meant the arrival of the most senior and fearsome of the servants, Soames, the butler, who appeared in the doorway.

"You rang, Sir?" said the rather emotionless servant, who had only been in employment a few months, following the departure of Bracewell, who had served his master loyally for over twenty years and had retired due to ill health. Anthony had liked Bracewell.

"Yes, Soames, I did," said the master, who nodded to Crawford to take a seat. "See to the drinks. I'll have a whisky and soda."

"Very good, Sir" replied the servant, who to Anthony seemed anything but servile. Around forty-five, with black hair and mean, narrow eyes, Soames kept as tight a leash on those in service as possible. As tall as young Crawford, his slim build and pale complexion, coupled with his ability to seemingly glide rather than walk, reminded Anthony of a ghost. He had often heard the new butler provide a stern dressing down to various servants. Never raising his voice, he had an uncanny ability to be both intimidating and threatening and was not to be crossed. Ruthless in approach, he'd already exerted his authority in seeing off Morgan, the footman, citing standards not befitting to this household. Clearly having the ear of the master of the house, Soames had ensured the poor unfortunate soul from the Welsh

Valleys had closed the huge white front door belonging to one of the country's most influential businessmen for the last time a few weeks ago.

"Madam?"

"I'm fine, thank you, Soames," declined Jane when offered a drink.

"Oh, for Heaven's sake, woman, have a bloody drink!" Philip boomed. Anthony watched his mother quail and then meekly opt to have a gin and orange.

"Very good, Madam." said the butler, while placing a crystal glass nearly half full of expensive whisky and a splash of soda on the small, circular oak table next to where the master sat glowering at his wife from a leather armchair.

"Master Anthony?"

"He'll take what I'm having," interrupted Philip. "A man's drink for a young man."

Nodding, Soames attended to the mistress' refreshment, before busying himself by pouring a smaller measure of the master's whisky and was seemingly more liberal with the soda before handing the glass to Anthony.

"Do you require anything else, Sir?"

"That will be all, Soames. Is everything ready for our guests?"

"Yes, Sir, everything is ready for your evening, although dinner, I believe, will be served within the half hour."

"That's fine, Soames, we shall receive here and then move to the library to await dinner," replied the master.

"Very good, Sir." The servant gave a small incline of his head before walking backwards and turning to the entrance door to await the arrival of the guests. They had not yet replaced the footman.

Sitting straight in the rigidly uncomfortable sofa, Anthony surveyed the Great Hall. The huge fireplace was the focal point around which the sofas were arranged. The room, predominantly brilliant white with compliments of gold, played host to three huge, glittering chandeliers. Four white display cabinets stood, two on each side of a grand sweeping staircase in the centre of the room, which Anthony would often use as a prop when imaging himself at the premiere of his latest cinematic offering.

His ideas were in his head and ready, he simply needed his big break.

Anthony had been surprised by the bookcase, in the Great Hall, it was perhaps his favourite part of the room, perhaps the whole house. Covering half the wall on the far side of the huge fireplace, every type of literature you could hope for was present. Showing a natural aptitude and thirst for reading, Anthony, and his mother, had to beg his stepfather to let him enjoy the works of Dickens and Conan Doyle. Never allowed to take any book out of the Great Hall, Crawford would pick his moment, before devouring the tales of *Sherlock Holmes* and *Nicholas Nickleby* with the same passion he showed when watching his screen idols in their latest masterpiece.

The sound of the doorbell snapped Crawford out of his thoughts and back to this evening. He had never met Robert Ford, nor the new wife, to whom his stepfather's businessman friend had only married a few months ago. A man of great wealth and standing, his wedding was seen as a high point of the social calendar and those who did not receive an invite were clearly not deemed elite enough. Anthony hadn't been invited and was slightly piqued that he was not considered on equal terms with his stepfather. Watching his poor mother practically reduced to tears over what to wear and say, coupled with his stepfather running through the day like a business plan rather than a social occasion of enjoyment, had made young Crawford even more resentful of the fact he wasn't considered good enough, although to be fair, he also thought that could Philip Crawford have attended the wedding without his new wife, he would have. Anthony sipped his whisky and silently seethed with an anger he had to take pains to disguise. Turning his mind back to this evening's guests, he knew Ford was in the jewellery business and suspected that his stepfather saw an opportunity. Both members of the same club, their relationship was business first, friendship later, as far as Anthony could gather. Another fifty-something, he envisaged Ford's wife to be younger than her husband. In this society, image, convenience, and vanity were of far greater importance than love and finding your soulmate. Her name, Cecile, and the fact that she was now Robert Ford's wife, was all the Anthony knew of her. He felt like an extra in a film in which he hadn't quite read the script correctly.

Upon the sound of the doorbell, Anthony sprang to his feet, his father giving a cold, but somewhat approving nod to his stepson. His mother smiled sweetly, while stoically hiding her nerves on what was a huge night for her.

Anthony heard indistinct chatter. Soames had greeted the guests and was leading tonight's dinner guests into the Great Hall. Philip straightened his bow tie and took a healthy gulp from his drink as the door opened and his stepson gave him a quizzical look. His stepfather nervous? That was interesting.

Suddenly, Robert Ford and his younger and incredibly beautiful wife were approaching their hosts, and Anthony forgot everything except for the tantalising thought that he'd just found his future leading lady.

Chapter 2

"The thing is, old boy, you must always remember that all of it is just an act."

Harry Hewson-Greaves was always full of advice and encouragement, and Anthony now required every bit of it. His initial tactic had been to remain indifferent to his stepfather's guests, while using his acting ability to play the role of an engaging young man enthralled with every word uttered by the Fords.

He had not reckoned on what he would feel when he laid eyes on Cecile! A vision of unrivalled beauty, her blonde hair hung in finger curls reaching just above her shoulders and perfectly complemented her oval-shaped face. Her mesmerising blue eyes reminded Anthony of those starry, summer nights he was so entranced by when watching the sky from his bedroom window. Allowing her husband to remove her dark fur coat, she revealed her long, blue evening gown, which clung to her seductive curves, and perfectly matched her eyes. She moved with perfect grace, Anthony noticed, watching her extend a long, gloved arm to his mother as the two women greeted each other.

Anthony allowed himself a quick fantasy about what type of corset was underneath the dress as he felt his face burning up with a mixture of nerves and excitement. Removing her silk gloves, now that she had dispensed with Jane, she extended her arm to allow the older woman's husband to kiss her slender hand, before quickly turning attention back to his mother, who clearly felt uncomfortably out of her depth in the presence of someone who looked as though they had just stepped out of a cinema screen.

Robert Ford extended his hand to Anthony. Acutely aware that his stepfather was already thinking of something he'd got wrong, Anthony switched into character and firmly greeted the man who wore an impressive mop of thick, grey hair, neatly combed back. Impeccably dressed in what Anthony recognised as a Huntsman bespoke suit, Ford had already given Soames his scarf and overcoat and his piercing stare was now firmly studying the young man standing before him. He seemed to possess a similar knack to that of his host, in making young Crawford seem small and not worthy of his company.

The idle chat and small talk were of little interest to Anthony, who was already constructing the love story between himself and Cecile. Would Chaplin's vulnerable charm and humour win her heart, or would this require the swashbuckling Fairbanks to down his foe before getting the girl?

"So, this is the young man you and Jane were telling us so much about, Philip?" Cecile's words thrust Anthony out of his daydream and back to the evening that had taken an unexpected turn.

Extending her delicate right hand in a manner that suggested a kiss would be the correct etiquette, Anthony bent forward and gently brushed her warm skin with eager lips. As he straightened, he spotted the huge diamond engagement ring and the thickset gold band which glistened and sparkled on her other hand. They probably cost more than the combined wages of the entire staff in service to his stepfather, thought Anthony, with a sudden rush of antipathy towards the social set he found himself moving in.

"Delighted," uttered young Crawford, who, in his state of complete enthral, had kept hold of Cecile's hand for far longer than etiquette demanded. Realising his faux pas, he released her before forcing himself to avert his gaze and turn his attention to her much older husband. He gave Robert a brief smile.

"Good evening, Sir," said a confident-sounding Anthony, who was anything but in this situation. If he were to achieve his dream of acting, now would be as good a time as any to deliver a performance of supposed interest in Robert Ford, his jewellery empire, and his business interest with his stepfather. Forever playing a part, Anthony slipped into the role of supportive stepson and interested dinner guest. Without the part to play, he would just be himself and that would not be acceptable.

"Anthony," replied Robert, nodding briefly to the younger man, who at least knew how to address him.

Turning detective, Anthony reasoned, without any real evidence other than his own instincts, that this man didn't have friends, but rather acquaintances and possessions. Human or otherwise. With everyone now seated, Soames had already poured the guests' drinks. Ford was another whisky man, while his wife delicately sipped a martini, demurely sat next to her husband, who was deep in conversation with Crawford senior.

Jane, wearing an awkward smile, seemed to be picking her moment to engage Cecile in societal small talk. Anthony hated how his mother always had to make so much effort to fit in, but she was a dutiful wife and was determined to not let her husband down with a slip-up that showed he had married beneath himself.

"Soames, how long did you say before dinner is served?" asked Philip, who became even more irritable when hungry.

"Mrs. Blackshaw informed me that dinner would be served in thirty minutes, Sir," replied the butler, checking his old and worn pocket watch. "That was approximately twenty minutes ago, I shall be seating you in the dining room shortly, do please excuse me."

Gliding out the room to probably go and intimidate the family cook and anyone else that may incur his displeasure, Anthony caught Cecile's gaze. Taking a sip from the martini glass, her attention was grabbed by Jane, who was desperately racking her brains for a subject to discuss with the younger, beautiful woman whom she was forced by convention to converse with.

"I take it the honeymoon was a good one?" Jane asked, before realising that it had probably taken place months ago.

Anthony quickly gazed over at his stepfather, whom he knew would be keeping a mental note of what he deemed were his mother's errors of etiquette. Jane tried so hard and was easily the most genuine person in the room, but that wasn't a quality overly welcomed or wanted in this class structure, as he was quickly learning.

"Charming," replied Cecile, with a giggle in her voice as she gazed quite pointedly at her husband. Jane blushed, while

Anthony gave a knowing grin. "France was frightfully hot, but the beaches in the south were so delightful." Her well-spoken tone was so appealing to Anthony, who was fighting a losing battle in not keeping his eyes off her. Her ample bosom and striking features completely engrossed him and evoked a real desire of wanting this night to end quickly but remain with her forever.

"And what exactly is this strapping young man going to do with his life," Ford suddenly boomed at Anthony.

"He's not overly sure yet," Philip answered quickly. "You know children these days."

"Probably best speaking to Philip," Anthony began, "I don't seem to be a fit for the family business, so it is back to the proverbial drawing board."

A silence suddenly descended over the room. Anthony's polite stab at Philip had clearly irked his stepfather, who was now trying to give an impromptu performance of his own as someone trying to contain his anger in a dignified manner. Young Crawford's ambitions and employment status were clearly embarrassing issues for his stepfather, despite the fact that in a heartbeat, Anthony would have jumped at an opportunity to join Philip's company. Such an opportunity, however, had never been forthcoming and he could feel the searing resentment coursing through his body at the ignominy, which he doubted Philip had ever acknowledged and certainly never told Robert Ford, who broke the silence.

"Should give him a chance, Philip," he said as he turned his attention to the master of the house. Philip was uncomfortable and Anthony was enjoying the fact that this was his round; a scene where his character had triumphed. He imagined himself sporting Chaplin's trademark Bowler hat and tipping it towards the screen in victorious acknowledgement!

"Perhaps he's creative," Cecile pondered, giving Anthony a look that spoke far more than words ever could. He felt himself blushing again. "What do you think, Jane?"

Anthony seemed unsure as to whether the object of his affection was genuinely interested or simply mocking both he and his mother.

"Well, he does rather hope of becoming an actor one day," Jane replied, proudly, although quickly regretting her new-found confidence as she met the cold, disapproving gaze of her husband. She had listened for hours to her son as he would regale tales of conquering the film industry and how he and Chaplin would work together. *"And why shouldn't he?"* Jane thought, who was often dismayed at her husband, who had never even thought about a place for her son in his business.

"Acting? Really? How exciting," remarked Cecile.

Mocking or interested? Anthony remained unsure.

"Hardly a noble profession," Philip retorted, barely disguising a disgusted snort. "As I say, childhood dreams before reality dawns." His reply now had an air of pettiness that was reminiscent of child looking to say something nasty after being embarrassed by another. Anthony smiled contently.

"Oh, I don't know, it has done that fellow Chaplin no harm," Cecile answered. "Although I rather imagine that a more physical role would suit young Anthony." Again, she gave him that tantalising, or was it mocking, look.

Ford seemed more than happy with allowing his wife to dominate proceedings. He sipped his whisky contentedly, watching Cecile, who was more than just a pretty face; she exuded confidence as much as sex appeal and was proving quite an adversary to match Philip Crawford, a man not used to women being this opinionated. He gave Jane a rare smile of approval, which made her glow with pride. This situation was not something Anthony was used to, having been dominated by this man of tradition and old-fashioned values. He couldn't help but feel slightly amused when wondering how Philip would handle this.

"Hardly a man of real moral fibre. A dodger of the Great War, it certainly wouldn't surprise me if he was involved in other matters of immorality, as well as deviance." Philip said now, of Charlie Chaplin. His composure was returning, as well as his bombastic nature.

Anthony's stepfather often referred to acting as an

'effeminate pastime.' Despite enjoying the work of Fairbanks, whose films and performances were anything but, Crawford senior seemed fixated on lumping the acting profession together.

Keen to carry on the discussion, Cecile retorted, "A changing world is something that we simply must get used to, Philip. Wouldn't you agree, Jane?"

"Oh, I have no issue with change," answered Philip, on his wife's behalf. "But I am of the opinion that hard work and respect are what make Great Britain and her empire the envy of the world. Businessmen who show endeavour and provide opportunity for those without the acumen to succeed on their own, are the very fabric of this nation, and we are in pretty good shape," he concluded before taking a healthy gulp of his drink. "Acting is fine for entertainment purposes, but it is hardly real life. Merely a distraction or a pipe dream for those who have bosses to do their worrying for them."

Robert Ford nodded in agreement. A hugely successful businessman, he was perfectly content with watching how the evening may play out and getting the measure of those around him. Anthony's early impressions were that he enjoyed watching his strong-minded wife more than hold her own in a society that certainly wasn't ready for it.

"I do hope you enjoy the meal," exclaimed Jane, keen to get conversation back onto safe and sure ground where the chance of tension would hopefully be reduced. "Mrs. Blackshaw is such a fine cook and can perform all manner of miracles when at a stove."

"I'd forgo the miracle, I'd just like dinner to be bloody served!' Philip was becoming irritated at the delay and rang for Soames again.

"I would expect nothing less from such a well-run house," Robert commented to Jane. Anthony glowered. Was the pompous old goat criticising his mother for the cook delaying dinner? How he hated the upper classes, always taking an opportunity to put someone like his mother down.

"Couldn't agree more, darling" added Cecile, looking pointedly at a thin gold watch on her delicate wrist.

She sipped her martini and gave Anthony a long look. Seemingly enjoying the power she exuded over males, she gazed around the library.

"Such a wonderful house."

"How very nice of you to say," said Jane. "My husband's hard work and business mind has served us all well."

"And I imagine the view of the countryside in the summer is simply stunning," Cecile remarked, nodding towards the window at the far end of the vast room. Turning her attention to both her husband and Philip, she gave an odd smile and said: "Oh, they do look quite the pair, deep in their clandestine conversation."

The two businessmen, engaged in what looked like a mini conference, seemed suddenly irked in Cecile's last comment. Indeed, this was the first time Robert had looked anything but overtly confident and commanding, whilst Philip, attempting to hide his frustrations at what he saw was a challenge to him and a rather flippant way of getting under his skin, smiled coldly before finishing his glass of whisky. Anthony thought he looked rather nervous.

The atmosphere was growing a little uneasy and, for once, Anthony was relieved to see the reappearance of Soames, who calmly addressed the master. "Excuse me, Sir, dinner is served."

Chapter 3

Anthony only realised how hungry he was as he took his place at the dining table. Remembering to sit up straight and not slouch, something that had earned him regular scolding from Philip, he quickly recalled more wise words from Harry, whose awareness of etiquette was as natural to him as breathing. But then, of course, his friend had been born into wealth and socialising and the observance of the rules and etiquette had been imbibed along with his baby milk. He had not been suddenly thrust into it, an uncomfortable outsider whose every move was watched, commented on and ultimately, corrected. For a moment, his resentment bubbled to the surface. How he hated all this, he thought, forgetting how he had also hated being hungry all the time and not just because of the cook's mistiming. He stared down at the place setting of silver cutlery, gleaming crystal glassware and gold rimmed fine bone china as Harry's words resonated in his head.

"I'm sure your father will have been through this, old boy, but always start on the outside with your cutlery, keep your elbows off the table, and try not to eat as though it's your last meal."

"And for God's sake, never speak with your mouth full!"

Anthony never corrected Harry when he referred to Philip as his father. He knew that his friend meant nothing by it and was, Mother aside, the one individual in his life he could truly trust. Always generous with advice, the heir to the Hewson-Greaves empire was his only friend. The eldest of three children, Harry often referred to Anthony as his brother, particularly in the early days of their friendship when they re-created famous battles and assumed the roles of their heroes from both film and literature. Crawford often reminisced about those summer days playing in the garden with his friend before the inevitable chastising from Philip over another ripped shirt that had torn on a stray branch as he scaled one of the huge oak trees.

His stepfather's reprimands never stopped him; Anthony's

imagination and sense of adventure was too strong, although guilt now stung him regarding the tongue lashing several house servants received for *'failing to control the boy.'*

The presence of Dennehy, the under butler, serving the first course brought Anthony back to the present. He believed Philip had requested tomato soup simply as a test designed to allow him to scrutinise Anthony's table manners. Cecile, sat with her back to the huge window, which was now covered with thick white curtains, delicately sipped a glass of claret as Dennehy set down her starter. The two businessmen were deep in conversation, seemingly oblivious to anything else happening around them.

Reaching Anthony last, which he reasoned was another deliberate move from Philip, Anthony thanked Dennehy, who was a quiet, unassuming man and unlike Soames, human.

"Very good, Sir."

Usually addressed as Master Anthony, 'Sir' was a step up for Jane's son, and something which actually pleased him. Jane, looking more nervous than ever seated to the left of her husband, took the wise move to keep conversation on the safe topic of food.

"I do hope you like tomato soup," Jane said, her voice nervous as she addressed those around the table.

"Oh, it is delightful, Jane," Cecile answered immediately, her gaze settling on Anthony. "Rich in taste and very appetising."

Anthony was being seduced and struggling with how to handle the situation. He wanted her more than anything but was acutely aware he was sat in his stepfather's dining room during an evening of significant importance to the man married to his mother. It would be a terrible impropriety if Anthony were to make any sort of advance to Cecile, of course it would. With Jane eagerly discussing the culinary skills of Mrs. Blackshaw with Cecile, who conveyed interest whilst probably having none, Anthony had to content himself with listening to the ongoing discussion of Philip and Robert. This closed shop of conversation was not looking for another occupant, but Anthony reasoned that sitting in silence and listening was far safer than being powerless to Cecile's seductiveness.

"I see it as an absolute banker of success," said Robert. "Crawford's clothing is perhaps the finest in the land and the jewellery I produce boasts an unrivalled reputation. Pair the two together, and the most influential figures in the world will want to wear our collaborations."

Taking a sip of soup, Philp answered, "Clothes made with the jewellery to suit, or vice versa. Even Mrs. Baldwin would be in a Crawford/Ford creation." This caused both businessmen to laugh.

"We are not in competition and together our rivals would be considerably weaker. Women can simply not resist a beautiful bracelet which compliments what they are wearing." Robert smiled beatifically.

"Well, there is talk of Baldwin extending their right to vote to over twenty-one," Philp smirked. "So that will mean a host of husbands having to spend money on garments or gold in celebration!"

The two men laughed heartily. Robert, glass in hand, added, "Oh yes, they want the same rights as men, but I am more than happy for them to buy me a necklace which matches my dress."

Cecile and Jane had both heard Robert's latest comment, with the former clearly irked. Anthony was quite enjoying being the outside observer of two conversations and reasoned that this was safe ground. If the discussion was to get heated or awkward, he would not be the cause. Still laughing, Anthony noticed a look of affection on the face of Philip, who was clearly enjoying Robert's company and the fact that the two tycoons were about to team up and probably expand their empires. Noticing that Anthony was watching, Philip quickly re-assumed the role of cold-hearted patriarch.

"You're not hungry, Anthony?"

The young Crawford wondered if that was a question or an observation. Although ravenous, he hadn't touched his soup, a mixture of fear and conversation curiosity, but he knew that cleared dishes would make both his stepfather and mother happy.

"Oh yes," Anthony replied. "Just engrossed with the

conversation and the evening's company."

Jane looked proud, Philip surprised, while Anthony's last comment drew simultaneous smiles from the Fords.

"My, he is a fine young man," observed Cecile. "Such marvellous manners complimented by such delightful decorum."

"A damn fine young man," agreed her husband, who took a generous gulp from his glass as though his observation had left him with a raging thirst. Was the key to upper class acceptance simply a case of saying appropriate things in the right tone at the correct time? Anthony knew what his next topic of conversation would be the next time he was in Harry's company.

Taking a few healthy mouthfuls of soup, he felt an air of confidence and belief. This was simply just acting, something which was his chosen path, and this evening was perhaps showing that it would be a profession he would flourish in.

"We are all actors around this table," he thought. The only exception being his mother, who despite her genuine and kind-hearted nature, he could only place at the bottom of the pecking order, by some distance.

"Please excuse me, darling," Cecile suddenly directed to her husband. Placing her hand on his, she rose from the table. Her expression was serious, she did allow her face to give Anthony the briefest of smiles, before making her way to the door.

Presuming it was her intention to go to the lavatory, Jane said, "Soames or Dennehy will show you where the powder room is, Cecile." She earned a glower from Philip, who knew, of course, that his wife should not have drawn attention to Cecile's needs, but rather simply rang the bell to ask for a servant to attend their guest.

As if by magic, the tall, cold figure of the head of service emerged to open the door and offer advice as to where the nearest lavatory was in the Crawford residence. Perhaps he had timed the finishing of the starters as the reason he was at the door as soon as Cecile had ventured towards it? Anthony wouldn't have been surprised if Soames was the kind of man who would listen at the door.

Following confirmation from the head of the house that the

first course was complete, Dennehy collected the dishes in an efficient, professional manner. Anthony thanked him, as always.

"Very good, Sir." The reply was almost anticipated.

Anthony wondered how many times servants uttered those three words. The repetition would be like acting in the same scene over and over again. Although if Cecile was in that scene, then that might not be a bad thing.

Robert turned his attention back to Philip. Anthony was convinced that the two men seemed to be closer together since Cecile left the room, almost as though there were dealings and information she was not privy to. While the young Crawford had reasoned that women were told what their husbands felt they needed to know – certainly the case in the household he lived in – Cecile seemed different. Not only stunningly attractive, but her confidence to also verbally dual with Philip gave Anthony the distinct impression that this was a lady who cared little for the ideal that women should know their place.

Another thing he found mesmerising about her.

"I'm so proud of you, Anthony." His mother's delicate voice broke through his trail of thought. Her voice was quiet: "You're jolly well better than the lot of 'em."

He was taken aback by this. Jane rarely voiced her opinions, knowing that to do so would cause her husband immense displeasure, and she treasured the newfound security her marriage had given both her and her son. Anthony thought she had lost the old fight and determination that had kept the two of them together when his real father had died, but now he sensed she was perhaps also playing a part. Why hadn't he realised this before, he thought, giving his mother a loving smile.

Anthony wanted to reach out and hold his mother's hand but knew, of course, that public displays of affection were frowned upon and would be viewed dimly. To curb the urge he had to hug his mother, he glanced over at his stepfather, and was somewhat surprised by Philip's happy demeanour. Leaning close to Robert, the two tycoons were engaged in an intimately clandestine discussion, presumably about the business deal he'd heard snippets about. Philip's concentration was broken when he caught sight of his stepson's gaze. Staring coldly at his stepson, Anthony realised he was guilty of another faux pas and averted his eyes to the door just as Cecile re-emerged, followed almost immediately by Dennehy pushing the trolley with the evening's main course. Anthony felt Soames was nearby and probably even listening. He was very unsettled by the butler.

The filet mignon was beautifully cooked, and certainly worth the wait, Anthony thought, as he surveyed his dinner plate. He always felt most vegetables tasted the same, but he gamely ate the parmentier potatoes and seasonal vegetables, knowing that clearing his plate was a very English display of gratitude and good manners. Levels of conversation were brief and largely from either Robert or Philip, the latter somewhat bothered by Anthony catching his eye a few minutes previously. He wondered why his stepfather was so ruffled by the occasional look. It was a new thing to Anthony, and it gave him a slight feeling of power, knowing that he bothered Philip to the point where the older man grew nervous.

Cecile was taking the smallest mouthfuls Anthony had ever seen. Her full lips not even getting wet, nor her lipstick smudged, she delicately enjoyed her plate of food. Also high on her list of enjoyment was the fact that whenever she caught Anthony's attention, it would result in the young man blushing, before forcing himself to look away from her captivating beauty.

Turning to Jane, Cecile said, "I do so feel that young Anthony would make a fine actor, Jane." Sipping her drink, she continued, "The look, the personality, I believe both the camera and public would truly love him."

"Oh," began Jane, somewhat caught off guard by Cecile's comments. "Thank you. It is something he is very interested in."

"Did you see *A Woman of Paris?"* Cecile directed her conversation at Jane knowing that Anthony was listening.

"Err… no," Jane replied, blushing at what she perceived her lack of finesse because she didn't attend the cinema.

"Not a huge success for Chaplin," Anthony confidently chimed in. "But very brave for an actor predominantly known for slapstick to explore more serious material and a film I somewhat enjoyed, despite the lukewarm reviews."

"A very interesting observation, Anthony. You do know your cinema." Cecile was impressed and sensed Anthony knew exactly why that particular Chaplin film had been the topic of her conversation.

Made a few years previous, Anthony recalled the story of a kept woman who runs into her former fiancé and finds herself torn between love and comfort. But was it a rather bold and cruel observation of her perception of Jane's situation, or a reference to her own? Was Anthony being seduced through a shared knowledge of film and a passion for the work of Chaplin, who had only a small acting part in the picture but had taken up directorial responsibilities and the writing of the screenplay? Or was Cecile simply making small talk around the dinner table. Anthony didn't have the savoir faire to know.

"Back to film again, darling?" Robert addressed his wife for what seemed to be the first time this evening.

"Well, we all have to have our interests, Robert." Cecile retorted.

For a relatively newly married couple, there didn't appear to be much love, reasoned Anthony. The sudden thought of being Cecile's illicit love interest was overwhelming for him. Would she be *his* woman of Paris?

"And there is nothing wrong with interests." Philip suddenly joined the conversation. Draining his glass, he added, "But I repeat, it is hardly a substantial and secure career for the boy."

The last person around the table Anthony thought would reply would be Jane. But either Dutch courage or a sudden desire to vocally defend her son's dreams and ambitions gave her a confidence to publicly contradict her husband.

"Well, someone gets there, darling. Why not Anthony?"

"A fair point," agreed Robert. "There are those who enjoy that luck. But I have always been able to rely on acumen and good old-fashioned hard work."

Anthony was grudgingly impressed by Robert's comments. The ability to agree with both sides showed a political skill that had probably been one of the main reasons for his success. In the budding business partnership between the Ford and the Crawford empires, Anthony believed Robert was the dominant one.

"And what are your plans for Christmas, Jane?" Cecile's sudden question caught everyone off guard. Surely, she couldn't have known Philip disliked this season, or was it an educated guess? Or was Anthony overthinking as usual.

"Oh," Jane was struggling for words and Philip was silent. "I hadn't given it much thought. We haven't even put the decorations up yet." Jane's laughter was a mixture of awkwardness and embarrassment.

"I think we should have a party." Robert announced. "This has been a damn fine year and why not celebrate prosperity in the company of close friends." Cecile looked at Anthony, her gaze making him hot under the collar. He certainly wanted to be *very* close to her.

"We could hold it here." Jane instantly regretted her comment and looked apologetically at her husband, who was doing his level best to hide his anger.

"A splendid idea, Jane." Robert addressed Anthony's mother for what must have been the first time this evening.

"I agree," Philip lied. "Let's have a Christmas to remember, no expense spared. I trust the Fords will be in attendance?"

Anthony had to grudgingly admit that Philip had put on a very good performance. He'd been backed into a corner and Jane would probably be chastised later but he had been relatively convincing at playing the role of someone eager to celebrate Christmas with a grand soiree, although Anthony was not fooled.

"We wouldn't miss it for the world, Philip," Cecile answered sweetly before turning to Anthony. "I'm sure it will be unforgettable."

The dinner party continued along the expected lines. Philip seemed keen to conclude the evening, as though his business deal being struck and his disdain for not having control of the conversation plus being coerced into throwing a Christmas party in his house had strengthened his desire to bring this soiree to its end. When the courses were concluded, after dinner drinks were served in the drawing room. Philip and Robert enjoyed a cigar; the cabinet-sized Chesterfields were something saved for special occasions and Anthony was never offered one. Sipping his whisky, the young Chaplin fan suddenly felt tired and struggled to hold back a yawn, something else his stepfather took a dim view of.

Cecile had just finished her cigarette as Soames arrived with the coats, at the request of Robert. What followed were formal goodbyes, Anthony enjoyed a lingering grasp of her hand, something she seemed perfectly happy with, as her husband made his way to the double doors.

With his guests in their chauffeur-driven Rolls Royce, Philip made his way to the stairs.

"Will you require anything else, Sir?" asked Soames.

"No thank you, Soames," replied Philip, who turned to his wife,"Darling."

His call to Jane was more of a polite command than a gesture of affection. Quickly hugging her son, Jane made her way to her husband's side. Anthony wondered how she would be chastised for disagreeing with him earlier in the evening. Though he was not physically abusive toward her – Anthony would never allow that – Philip's psychological torment could be even crueller.

Anthony was suddenly overcome with a sharp feeling of guilt. She'd stood up for her boy and would be put back in line for that dissention. Jane was a protective cloak for Anthony, something which Philip truly resented.

"Begging your pardon, Master Anthony," Soames' voice brought Anthony out of his deep thought for the second time this evening. "Mrs. Ford was most insistent that you should have this before you retired." Anthony noticed how he had been relegated from the title of 'Sir' and couldn't resist a little smile.

Handing Anthony a small light-brown card, the butler enquired: "Will that be all, Master Anthony?"

"Yes, thank you Soames. Good night."

"Goodnight, Master Anthony."

Hurrying to his room, Anthony refused to look at the card that had been handed to him until his bedroom door was closed firmly behind him. Why did Cecile hand it to Soames to give to him? Why did she want to pass him a message in such a clandestine way?

And what did it say!

Now he was alone, in the sanctuary of his bedroom, he could now at least find out the answer to that question.

Chapter 4

"So, what exactly are you going to do, old chap?" Harry's blunt question was something Anthony had been pondering ever since he'd became aware of Cecile's message.

He took a long look at his best friend. Sitting there sipping whisky and soda in the huge drawing room, Harry never ever looked comfortable. A bi-product of upper-class society – along with the phrase 'old chap', seemingly – one could never look as though they were relaxing, particularly in other people's houses. Shoulders straight, he'd even declined Soames' offer of taking his jacket, which meant him moving ever so slightly to avoid the sun's rays and the inevitable sweating. Dressed in a full tweed suit with matching tie and crisp white shirt, Anthony envisaged Harry going clay-pigeon shooting once they had finished their conversation.

But they had much to talk about. Friends for years, Harry was always in awe of Anthony's creativity and what he perceived, his care-free nature. Anthony, however, was fascinated, and perhaps somewhat envious, by how a human being as genuine as the twenty-two-year-old heir to the Hewson-Greaves empire could mix and mingle with such shallow people and speak their language.

"Because it is my language and my people." Harry would often explain to Anthony. Not in any way want to sound conceited, Harry had to repeatedly tell his friend that he had been born into this life, while Anthony had inherited it through a marriage. Harry knew Anthony had difficulties with the whole transition; from guttersnipe to great wealth cannot have been easy and Harry was perhaps more sensitive to his friend's new station in life than most were. However, Harry had to admit, even if only to himself, as it was something he perhaps could not share with his best friend, Anthony did not make it easy for himself! His belligerent attitude to the man whose wealth he benefitted from was something that did not go unnoticed throughout the circles

in which Anthony now moved. Harry knew that his friend's condescending attitude to those he felt contemptuous of, simply because they had been born into wealth and he had had to acquire it by someone else's benevolence, did not sit well with the people whom Anthony tried to befriend. But, of course, his friend did not see it that way, Harry thought now, as he glanced at the curl of discontent on Anthony's lips. Talented and creative he might be, but he was also an altogether difficult person to know. Harry, through his own tenacity, had managed to at least break down some of Anthony's self-imposed barriers and he knew there was much to admire about the young Crawford. It could be said both were perhaps a bit envious of each other's situations, personalities, and lives, but their bond was a strong one, as was their respect for each other.

Although not an only child, Harry had often felt lonely growing up until he had met Anthony, who compensated for the fact that his only younger siblings were female and identical twins to boot. The girls had the strongest of bonds and were never stuck for company, which meant Harry had felt pushed out and isolated.

Perhaps the only advantage the poor had during these times, was family size and the fact that children seemed to always have company their own age, Harry reflected.

Anthony - an only child - had never felt lonely, at least not before Philip Crawford came on the scene. Harry recalled the one time his dear friend had spoken of his earlier childhood, being a young boy, a dirty, filthy, skinny urchin. He told Harry of Lincrusta lined walls, shiny with what Anthony had thought was a special paint effect until he reached out to touch it and his fingers had come away moist at the contact. It was damp, which seeped in through poorly constructed walls, riddled with cracks and holes. He spoke of cold that penetrated his very bones and made him cry as he pulled a thin, coarse wool blanket over himself during winter nights when you could see your breath forming in icy particles hung amidst the frost laden gloom of long, uncomfortable nights. Harry knew there were days when Anthony had not eaten but had thrown himself out onto the mean tenements and grubby side streets along with the other boys and girls of poverty; how he played whip and top or sat huddled together in doorways atop filthy steps. The surroundings may not have been as salubrious as the ones he enjoyed now, but the company - Harry aside - had been a richer and warmer than anything Philip Crawford could have offered. When the struggles of what had gone before were replaced with acres of wilderness, a home tutor and servants addressing him as 'Master' the culture shock was a huge one and something Anthony was still struggling with.

Now, as he watched him, Anthony glowed with warmth as he realised Harry was more than his best friend and spiritual brother, he was his saviour from madness and unhappiness Their mutually beneficial bond meant that problems and issues could be discussed, and advice provided, and that worked both ways.

It felt to Anthony like Harry had asked his question regarding Cecile, hours ago, and he turned his thoughts back to the present. He couldn't get the woman out of his mind, not that he wanted to. One thing he would happily eradicate from his thoughts would be Soames, but that was proving impossible. Had he read Cecile's message before handing it to Anthony? And what would he do if he had? Soames was, after all, a butler in one of the wealthiest and most prestigious houses in England. He would not give anything away. Anthony grudgingly admired that fact that the head of service could probably walk around with a bullet in his leg, and no one would notice the pain he was in.

Anthony began to answer Harry's question. "Well, my gut instinct is to g-," the door opening suddenly disturbed his rhythm and, right on cue, Soames was there. Both men had heard the knock, but the speed in which Soames appeared was both incredible and impressive.

"Begging your pardon, Sir, but will Master Anthony and his guest require anything else?"

"Err, no, thank you, Soames." Anthony's answer was a mixture of nerves and annoyance due to the sensitive nature of his conversation and the fact there was something, or someone, disrupting his discussion. He'd already had to get rid of Jane, who greeted Harry with warmth and delight. She knew how much his friendship meant to her son and was always pleased to see young Hewson-Greaves.

"We'll let you know if we need anything, Soames, so you can run along, old chap. That will be all." Harry took charge of the situation. A master in etiquette, he knew his place and that of the servants.

Now it was Soames' turn to look bit annoyed, although just for a second. Snapping himself back into a servile mode almost instantaneously, he replied, "Very good, Sir." Soames nodded towards Harry and then, almost as an afterthought, towards young Crawford. "Master Anthony," and retreated, closing the door firmly.

"I could swear he listens at the door," said a still irritated Anthony.

"Paranoia, old boy," replied Harry, sporting a smile. "He's the butler. It's his job to tend to your every need. He knows his place, but do you?"

Harry was one of the few to truly support Anthony in a way of lecturing him but showing support at the same time. Anthony always felt he was being talked *at* by his stepfather, but Harry talked *to* him.

"Like it or not, your status is far higher than those in service. They accept that. Trying to be friends with them and understand their struggles is not fair to either you or them. This is life, you may as well live it and enjoy it."

"Like you do?" Anthony answered back, a little ruffled.

"My situation is somewhat different to yours, old boy." Harry sounded forlorn.

"I know, my friend. I do apologise."

Harry's father had blazed a path into the automotive industry. His ability to both understand and perfect the mechanics of engineering made him a key component for the manufacturers, who were so desperately keen to turn their ideas into reality. By the time Harry had come along and was following in his father's technological footsteps, the industry was in a very healthy place, and owning a car was a rich man's expensive privilege. Marrying money, Harry's mother also came from a well-to-do family who'd made their fortune in cotton. Their marriage appeared to be very much agreed by several parties aside from the bride and groom, and Harry seemed destined for the same path.

His intended, Margaret, was the daughter of a wealthy landowner who had made a fortune from obtaining what appeared to be derelict land and turning it into profitable ventures. Her parents had also been born into wealth, simple as that. A family who seemed to be as used to money as they were dependent on fresh air. Harry and Margaret had known each other from before birth, if such a thing were possible, by the fact that their respective mothers were both giving birth to them at the same time in the same nursing home. Both women had eschewed home births, and both had had difficult pregnancies leading to the decision to have their first child in a nursing home with the best two obstetricians in the country (and that money could buy, of course). They became firm friends and Harry and Margaret spent a lot of time during their formative years together. It was only natural that they should marry. Whether Harry or Margaret felt the same way was never considered. Both came from influential and affluent families, the two eldest children, the heirs to the fortunes both had been born into. Their marriage was probably decided before their christening parties, held jointly in the Hewson-Greaves' magnificent country manor in East Anglia, and at huge inconvenience to everyone in London.

Anthony always disliked greed and always felt the richest were, of course, the greediest. He always felt that Chaplin's messages were subliminally inserted through his comedy and were poking fun at those ridiculously wealthy people. This made young Crawford smile although he often failed to realise the wealth and privilege he was now afforded and enjoyed, before being bitten by a hypocritical guilt, made him resentful of almost everything, including himself. Perhaps, as Harry suggested, he should simply enjoy the gravy train his mother's second marriage had given him the right to embark upon.

"I'm awfully sorry, old fellow, I must go," Anthony suddenly announced. He needed to break the tension in the room and knew that Harry much preferred providing advice to Anthony rather than the other way around. Perhaps Harry reasoned that Anthony had a bit more hope.

"Well, that address is not a hotel." Harry pointed out.

"I'd guessed that much," Anthony smiled.

"Well, exactly what is it she is hoping you are good at?" Harry asked the question, although he had idea enough!

Anthony looked at the small, beige card for what was probably the thousandth time.

110 South Pier Street
Southwark
London

11am, Wednesday

Let's see how good you really are.

Cecile x

"That's the question, old boy." Anthony had a glint in his eye as he sipped his whisky. One of the many things he did enjoy with his new life was the afternoon drinking of expensive spirits. Harry was well liked by Philip, so he knew that he could get away with taking some of his single malt, although Anthony did not have access to his stepfather's absolute finest offerings, which were under lock and key and only available on occasions such as the other evening when the Fords had graced their table.

It transpired that the address was once a warehouse used for storage of ammunition during the Great War. Harry believed it to be abandoned, while decisions were being made to do with the structure. Perhaps one advantage of being engaged to the daughter of a landowner, was the advanced knowledge of geographical plans, something Harry's father had utilised before opening another factory as his empire expanded.

"Just ensure that you aren't getting into anything illegal," Harry's cautious nature was in stark contrast to the wilful Anthony. But he knew his friend had a point. Cecile clearly wanted a meeting that her husband knew nothing about. That was obvious, but, as Harry pointed out, surely a hotel room would be far more suitable for an illicit liaison.

"She expressed some interest in film, perhaps it is a cinema that shows all the classics and frequented by enthusiasts and those in the know." Anthony wasn't sure if his latest statement was a suggestion or a whimsical fantasy he'd just dreamt up.

"There are perfectly good theatres a few miles away," Harry argued, "yet she is suggesting a meeting point that we don't even know is a cinema."

"Damn good story though!"

This caused both men to laugh. Their contrasting personalities complimented what they had in common. Harry knew full well Anthony would be at the meeting point in two days' time, whilst Anthony knew Harry would exercise his customary caution.

Another knock came at the door and hastened the appearance of Soames. The well-rehearsed rhetoric followed,

"Begging your pardon, Master Anthony. Will Mr Hewson-Greaves be staying for dinner?"

The etiquette always seemed to be addressing those that lived in the house, even if it was about a guest currently in the same room. To Anthony, this appeared ignorant, yet Harry showed no such qualms, and he shook his head.

"No, thank you, Soames," Anthony confidently answered. "Har- Mr Hewson-Greaves has a prior engagement this evening."

"Very good, Sir." Soames began to leave the room before Harry jumped up and called the servant back. "Actually, Soames, my coat, please." He examined the time on his gold pocket watch. "Time is creeping on, and I mustn't keep the lady waiting."

"Of course, Sir." Soames glided out the room to fetch Harry's belongings. This provided Anthony's best friend with the chance to provide one final bit of advice.

"Look after yourself, Anthony." His handshake firm and honest. Soames returned with Harry's overcoat and stood waiting whilst he threw it over his immaculate attire. "Let me know how you get on." he said to his friend.

"Will do." Anthony replied, "It may be Christmas come early for me." Harry turned and smiled at his friend, whose cheeky innuendo-filled humour always brought a smile to his face. Anthony watched Harry make his way to front door, led by Soames, who was doing first footman duties until the new man, whom Crawford was sure was named Stevens, took up his position next week. Once the door was firmly shut behind his friend, Anthony's familiar feeling of displacement and loneliness returned and he headed for the stairs to change before dinner, leaving Soames alone in the vast and brightly lit hall.

Chapter 5

"Like a young, more chiselled Don Chaney." Jane's words made Anthony smile as he journeyed towards East London, in the back of one of the family cars, driven by the chauffeur, Wright. He hadn't had the heart, that morning, to correct his mother with the actor's actual name, nor did he have the heart to point out that, whilst he admired Chaney's acting ability, he was not exactly going for that look.

He'd been awake for hours and had wrestled with the dilemma of what he should wear for whatever he was going to. All he knew was that he was going to a rendezvous instigated by Cecile and that he was desperate to impress her. With the latter in mind, he'd dressed similarly to the night they'd first met. The suit and shirt were the same colour, but the bow tie had been replaced by a dark-coloured tie that Jane had insisted on helping her son *'do properly'* as though he were still in short trousers.

His choice to wear a black trilby may well have given his mother the notion of making the Chaney comparison. But Anthony didn't care. Too wrapped up in a mixture of anticipation and excitement, he looked out as the world quickly changed from countryside to busy city streets, almost as though he was going back in time to when he was a boy in the dirty city, forced to make his own entertainment amidst the dirt, poverty and other hardships that faced the city's underclasses. The flashbacks hit him hard. Jane, working ridiculous hours to make ends meet, then crying endlessly at night due to the guilt she felt because her son was cold and hungry. Her pitiful sobs still haunted Anthony, who would still often wake at night convinced his mother was in tears next to Philip. Maybe she was? He recalled that not only did she cry for the hardships her son faced, but Jane had also wept for Anthony's father, overseas defending King and country. The fact that both his parents' sacrifices still meant that the family had to endure extreme cold and the worry as to whether they would eat today, concocted a potion of feelings that were a mixture of resentment, hate, guilt, and a sprinkle of thankfulness that the financial hardship and squalor was now behind both he and Jane. Anthony's childhood had been tough! There were some fun times; a natural climber, he recalled being chased by many a wife and mum for climbing on rooftops where he had no business being and quickly making his speedy escape, before getting his alibi in order with his accomplices before their own mothers were informed.

Now he was the one chasing the women, or specifically, one woman who was considerably younger and more beautiful than the females sporting wooden brooms and aggressive snarls of his childhood. This was far from Cecile's idyllic Oxford abode, and Anthony's mind was in overdrive at what she wanted with him. It must be something clandestine, in which she had a vested interest, but which her husband and social circle knew nothing about; or so Anthony thought.

His cover story was a simple one. He was going to Fleet Street to interview for a job at a regional newspaper. He liked the idea of being the *Fulham & Hammersmith Chronicle's* film correspondent but would also need to think of a good cover story for when he didn't get the job. Philip being away on business was also advantageous; the awkward questions and interference was not something his mother did, at least not in a controlling way.

A sudden announcement and his stepfather had departed for France. Often displaying a very jingoistic opinion when discussing foreign policy, Philip had grudgingly admitted that the French were leaders in fashion, usually following up with a statement that belittled their military ability before declaring Paris a city of loose morals that could well do with some 'English standards'. To Anthony's knowledge, Philip had only been a handful of times which, in his mind, hardly constituted an expert.

Jane had simply accepted her husband's trip like all good wives were expected to do.

Anthony sat up straight and looked at Wright. The man looked older than his years, his face hard and sporting a thick, black moustache that drooped down to his chin. His smile often reminded Anthony of a piano, due to the number of teeth missing. A car enthusiast, Wright was also an expert driver and struck Anthony as man willing to work hard for a quiet life, with driving an expensive Rolls Royce very much a bonus.

"You know this area well, Wright?" Anthony questioned his chauffer.

"I do, Sir," he replied, offering no more information than asked of him. A man of few words, he'd been in Philip's employment for as long as Anthony could remember. London born, he made no effort to conceal his Cockney accent but always remembered his Ps and Qs and carried out his duties efficiently. Anthony loved the family chauffeur's surname, often making up comedic scenarios that Chaplin himself would love. The young fan of film would often think of a production where Wright and going right would be the subject of much confusion. As film was a silent industry, there would be much finger pointing, first at the chauffeur then the direction set against some humorous music before the words came onto the screen. *"Turn right, Wright"* or *"Next left? That's right, Wright."* Anthony's sense of humour had served him well during the poverty-stricken times, as well as now. He often reasoned that one needs a sense of humour when living in the same address as Philip Crawford.

Wright turned the car around a left-hand corner, heading deeper and deeper into what looked to be a rough part of town with cheap housing and dirty streets being inhabited by tough people whose way of life was more a statement of survival in a society that looked to profit off their labour. Anthony had lived both sides of the coin, and the guilt of now being part of the ruling society was hitting quite hard as they drove through the mean little streets.

"How much longer?" he asked, with a sense of irritation in his voice.

"I'd say about five minutes, Sir. If memory serves, it's a big warehouse and not near any 'ouses."

Anthony smiled. He enjoyed hearing someone who was happy to speak with an accent and not worry about pronunciation and etiquette.

"Thanks, Wright." Anthony heard a bit of London creeping back into his own voice. He smiled happily.

The site of the River Thames came into view as the houses descended into the background. A more industrial feel took over as a series of factories and dockland area dominated the landscape. Wright pulled the car into what appeared to be abandoned wasteland. A huge, grey building that looked as though it hadn't been inhabited for some time stood before Anthony and his driver.

"This is it, there, Sir," Wright told him. "Want me to wait around… Sir?"

"Erm… yes… er… please. Thank you," answered a distracted Anthony.

"Very good, Sir." Despite using the same phrase, the chauffeur sounded nothing like Soames, something that always pleased the young Crawford.

Stepping out of the car, Anthony used the wing mirror to critique his appearance. The cold December air bit savagely and he was grateful for the hat, despite his mother's gangster comparison, and the expensive white scarf which hung around his neck was more of a fashion statement rather than protection against the cold. His new, black, Oxford brogues firmly struck uneven ground that was filled with holes and other obstacles that could easily sprain an ankle as he made his way towards a double iron door. What was on the other side? What was he walking into? Would Cecile even be here?

He was now directly in front of the huge iron doors. Glancing back at Wright, now engrossed in his newspaper, he turned to face the drab structure. Before being given a chance to knock, one half of the double doors swung open with a loud creak. Stood inside was a small, shifty looking man with beady eyes that peered from under his brown flat cap. Dressed in a brown waistcoat with matching trousers, his white shirt had seen better days and sported several creases. Slender in stature, his menacing gaze somewhat intimidated Anthony who, ever the actor, was doing an admirable job of not showing it.

"Good morning," Anthony began. "I'm looking for Cecile

Ford."

"Mrs. Ford's been expecting you," answered the man in a soft, Scottish accent. He stared speculatively at Anthony. "This way."

Anthony followed this man whom he'd never met before down a dark corridor, deliberately slowing up his walk so as not to overtake his guide's much smaller strides. Reaching a door, the man gave a quiet knock before stepping inside. Anthony saw Cecile sitting behind a wooden desk. Her eyes fixed on her guest as she allowed her jaw to rest on her hands before rising from behind the desk, her light green knee length dress looked beautiful on her, although all Anthony could think of was removing it from her.

"Anthony!" she exclaimed. "Delighted you came."

"I wouldn't have missed it for the world, Mrs Ford." Anthony's voice as well-spoken as it had ever been.

"That will be all, Benson." Cecile glanced over at the individual who'd escorted Anthony to her.

"Yes, Madam," came the reply as he swiftly left the room, closing the door behind him.

"Our right hand man. Chauffeur. Been with Robert for years and he sort of came as part of the package when I married my husband." Cecile gave a knowing smile, and to Anthony, that told him to whom Robert Ford's right hand man owed his loyalty now.

Anthony returned the smile rather nervously. He quickly thought about what Chaplin would do next. Often depicted as the scruffy, awkward little comedic figure, his pictures often saw him emerge with the girl at the end, something Anthony was very interested in right now. Though not scruffy, or even awkward, he always felt his working-class roots gave him the sense that he was a bit of underdog which, in his mind, gave him an affiliation to the man who was his acting hero.

Addressing Cecile's last comment, Anthony said, "He seems very capable, Mrs Ford."

"I don't know how you could possibly deduce that from your brief meeting?" Cecile smiled and seemed to enjoy the fact she made Anthony blush. "But yes, he is rather capable, Anthony." Again, she gave that smile which made him wonder exactly what the other man was capable of.

Motioning for her guest to sit down on what looked to be a quite uncomfortable wooden seat, she took her time to move back behind her desk, which afforded Anthony to admire her long, slim legs and shapely backside. Finally taking her place in her considerably more comfortable looking chair, she looked into his eyes.

"And please, do call me Cecile."

Anthony had removed his hat and scarf. Placing both on the small, rectangular brown desk, he suddenly exuded a new-found confidence. "Very well, Cecile, what exactly can I do for you?"

Cecile's smile widened. "Well, isn't that the question!" Her seductive tone was such an aphrodisiac for Anthony, who realised that even his finest acting performance wouldn't disguise his lust for her. Still determined to look relaxed and in control, he allowed himself a small chuckle at the sheer strangeness of the situation he was now in.

"Perhaps my question should be: 'what exactly is this all about?' or 'Seeing how good I am' at what, Cecile?' The questions came our rather more sharply than he had intended, and he noticed an angry look in Cecile's returned gaze. Anthony wasn't sure if the direct approach was the correct move, but if he was to succeed in the life he chose, then he'd have to risk ridicule.

Cecile had not taken her eyes off the young man that sat before her. This made Anthony strangely uncomfortable as he, rather hypocritically, would rather be eyeing her without her knowing. Christ, he thought, running a hand over his collar, that made him sound like some sort of pervert! He supposed it wasn't that he didn't want the blonde beauty to notice him, he was simply struggling with being the sole focal point of her attention.

With his mind and eyes full of Cecile, the British army could have opened fire on any of its enemies at this point and Anthony would have failed to hear it, so it came of little surprise that he hadn't noticed the re-emergence of Benson carrying a tray containing a bottle of champagne and two glasses. Leaving the room as quickly as he entered, it was now just Anthony and Cecile, with the former keen to break the silence.

"Celebrating something?" Anthony's efforts to sound confident and assured were failing him, he was certain, and no wonder! He didn't feel either of those things. If anyone had asked him at that precise moment, he would have said he was uncomfortable. Again, a smile was all Cecile offered as she poured two glasses of Bollinger, sliding one across to her guest.

"A bit early?" Anthony suggested, immediately regretting his comment for fear it made him sound somewhat boring.

"Early for who?" was Cecile's instant reply. "We both have chauffeurs and, it is my understanding that you don't work." Her tone was light but with an air of authority to it. "So, as I say, early for who?"

"Alright then, what exactly are we celebrating? Champagne is often an indication of such." Anthony was pleased on how he'd changed the subject and liked putting the onus of conversation back on Cecile. He craved to know more about her and felt that she may know a lot about him or could certainly deduce information. As intelligent as she was beautiful, he was certainly in Chaplin territory in terms of being the underdog, a role Anthony's screen hero excelled at playing on film.

Taking a delicate sip of her champagne, again not even getting her lips wet, she pondered the question thoughtfully. Placing the glass on the desk, she looked at Anthony. Her eyes as mesmerising as the sapphires that went such a long way to making her husband such a wealthy businessman, the young man's composure was fighting a losing battle against other emotions, as he gazed back at her.

"We live in a time of prosperity, for some," Cecile began. "A time where one can enjoy oneself if one is lucky enough. I believe that one makes their own luck. I see and hear your working-class beliefs but know that you crave the lifestyle and opportunities afforded by your situation."

Anthony was unsure if he was being complimented or ridiculed. And that was something Cecile realised and perhaps, even enjoyed. He felt cross, knowing, or at least thinking, that he was being made a fool of. His expression must have reflected some of his innermost thoughts because Cecile changed tack and became less predatory.

"Let me explain." Her tone now exuded more empathy. "Opportunity is not for everyone. And that is not my fault or yours. It is simply human nature. Natural selection. We possess privilege and opportunity. And in your case, lots of untapped potential."

Anthony was growing tired of the ambiguity. Taking a healthy gulp of his drink, which went totally against upper-class etiquette, he bluntly asked, "Are we talking about acting here?"

A small chuckle rose from her throat, yet her obvious amusement stung Anthony. Cecile sensed that the young Crawford possessed a very passionate, as well as fiery nature. Unbeknownst to him, this was something which aroused her. Anthony may well dress like a dandy, and live in a wealthy household, but the rough edges of his nature delighted her as much as his athletic physique did.

"We are talking about acting. And other things." Her response intrigued Anthony.

"Other things?"

"People like to enjoy themselves in several different ways," Cecile responded, by way of explanation. Then, seeing Anthony's stern look, she continued. "The building you sit in is one of several properties owned by my husband. I have many passions, money being one of them. I, and a select crew, are involved in our own brand of film making. Young actors looking to make names for themselves come to us and we make dreams come true... and we make money. This building helps me to facilitate my ambitions, although of course, Robert knows not what I do here."

Anthony was initially shocked. He knew Cecile didn't require employment to live well, so why did she do it? He glanced again at the self-assured woman before him. She was older than him, but not by many years, Anthony reckoned, yet she carried herself with an air of confidence that he knew he did not possess and never would. Perhaps it was only bestowed on those born into it.

So, what was this project? Probably little more than something to satisfy her interests and perhaps escape her boredom.

"I take it, then, that as your husband does not know of this, it is not a joint venture with Mr Ford?" Anthony questioned.

"Oh, good lord, no," laughed Cecile as she topped up both glasses. "Robert is effectively married to his business. I'm something he chooses to show off at social occasions. Even now, he is pursuing another business deal somewhere oversees."

"Europe?" Anthony was curious.

"I believe so," she replied. "Either way, let's not spoil what could be a wonderful day by chatting about my husband. The key to a successful marriage, Anthony, is to not be too dependent on one another. Have different interests."

"So, he knows nothing about this venture of yours?" Anthony had so many questions he wanted the answers to.

Taking another delicate sip of champagne, Cecile answered, "Well, I may have mentioned it to him, but he is always so frightfully busy."

Anthony laughed. He couldn't help it. Before him was a femme fatale who would prove a match for any of the silver screen's leading men. To have somehow acquired access to one of her husband's buildings, without his knowledge and set up some sort of business enabling actors and actresses the route to the silver screen, he had to hand it to her for sheer audacity. He tried to think for whom she would make an ideal leading lady. He likened her to Louise Brooks. She had been a dancer, he recalled, in the early twenties. She even did a season in London with the *Deninshaw* company, although Anthony had not seen her dance. Brooks had then made an appearance in the *Zeigfield Follies* and was currently rumoured to be having an affair with Charlie Chaplain. With his eyes still on Cecile, he could well imagine her capturing the eye, and possibly, the heart of Chaplain or maybe it would be an entirely different type of actor. Perhaps Rudolph Valentino? The *'Latin Lover'* was certainly a hit with the ladies with his sharp, good looks and screen presence already capturing the heart of screen star, Jean Acker, before moving on to Natacha Rambova, although it was being murmured by the press that this union was also an unhappy one. Neither lady was comparable to Cecile, but certainly the latter had that mesmeric presence and the kind of eyes that drew Anthony in as though he was looking into the gateway of her soul. And he felt the same way about the lady sat before him. Her eye-catching looks were just part of her appeal. Her deportment, the way she held herself and her ability to simply look at Anthony in a way that would have men young and old desperate to possess her. My God, Valentino and Cecile would be electric on the big screen! Young Crawford suddenly felt a wave of jealousy wash over him. He scolded himself for feeling envious of a scenario *he'd* created but wondered if the same feelings ever happened to Chaplin.

"So, are you recruiting for actors at the moment?" Anthony returned his mind to Cecile's business venture. He thought he was beginning to understand why he was here today. He was also aware that he was using the word 'so' an awful lot. This bothered him as one of his pet hates when reading literature was repetition.

"I want you on board," said Cecile. "You have desire, talent and the look to be a valuable addition to my projects."

"How could a gentleman refuse such a tempting offer from such a wonderful lady?" Anthony delivered possibly the most upper-class answer of his life so far.

"Then my choice of champagne was simply inspired." Cecile offered her glass for Anthony to touch with his own. He duly obliged.

"Well, please tell me more, Cecile." Anthony hadn't addressed her by name very often. He loved how it sounded and what it implied.

"All in good time, darling. Life is to be enjoyed. We can go into details later." Cecile rose from her chair.

Anthony looked up at her and smiled. "Please don't worry, I am the sole of discretion and know how to keep a secret."

"Another key to a successful marriage." Cecile's tone was incredibly seductive. She swirled the last bit of expensive liquid around her glass, her eyes never leaving Anthony. She rose, as did part of Anthony, who could feel his breathing getting faster.

Cecile stood before him. Standing inches away from him, she twirled around so her back was to him, her stance allowing Anthony maximum visually enjoyment. Putting her glass on the desk permitted Anthony to enjoy her rear, her attire complementing her shape to perfection. He noticed tiny, mother of pearl buttons running down to the small of her back, by now he wasn't thinking with anything other than his libido and he reached out and undid the garment as far as it would go. This was bold for Anthony, who, upon completion of unbuttoning Cecile's dress, stood hands by his side hoping and praying that the move he'd just made was the correct one as he admired her lightly coloured corset. He had never removed one before and was desperately hoping that this would be his first time. Her hips seductively swayed as she kept her back to him. She ran her fingers through her hair, the movement accentuating her curves to the young man's erotic delight. He wanted to ravish her but knew that everything with Cecile would be driven and controlled by her. This was the part of the film that no one would dare show, but the type of film romantics pieced together in their minds or was it simply Anthony, piecing it together in his mind and reaching a fantastic climax? Now he was in the scene, but he still didn't know his next line. His co-star, director, and his fantasy had control and both she and he knew it. Turning toward him, he took a slight, nervous step back. She allowed her now unbuttoned dress to slide to the floor where it lay as she stroked his erect nipples through his shirt. Anthony felt as though he would explode with excitement. Her corset perfectly complemented her shapely body, whilst the nude stockings provided another delight for Anthony, who felt like a young boy given free rein in his favourite sweet shop. She ran her hand down his body and eased him back into his seat. Placing both arms on the chair, he attempted to look every inch the suave male lead, like Valentino, but the performance levels were failing him. She had him exactly where she wanted him, this seductive, gorgeous, intelligent lady. Straddling Anthony, she placed his big hands on the top of her stockings, his fingers caressing her soft, smooth skin before settling on her backside; the pleasurable moans she made aroused him still further. Pressing against his growing manhood, he could feel her moistness as she held his face with both hands, her soft, full lips now in kissing distance of his.

"I knew I could count on you. Merry Christmas, darling," Cecile's final words before her ripe, red lips crushed down upon Anthony's and made him forget all about what season it was.

Chapter 6

Anthony knew he'd be facing a heap of questions as he journeyed back to the Oxfordshire residence. Jane would be keen to know if her son had got the job; when he would be starting and what were the people like. Strictly speaking he had got a job, but the interview process would not be something he'd be going into with his mother.

Cecile hadn't gone into details with what exactly it was he would be doing – at least not on the job front. Their afternoon had been one of sex and champagne. Anthony knew he would do anything she asked of him and was more than happy to combine his passion for film with his passion for her. Upon completion of their illicit tryst, she had said very little, seeming quite keen to get rid of her young lover. Anthony had been slightly annoyed by this, but she'd quickly won him round again with a promise of another meeting soon, as well as further details of the project he was now a part of.

"We'll be very close, both personally and professionally, darling. I trust you are more than happy with that?"

Anthony was ecstatic. This was a story no film studio or actor would dream of going near. He often thought of how Chaplin appeared in real life, envisioning him as a ladies' man. Despite his often-on-screen persona as that of an awkward, comedic underdog, he usually ended up with the girl in the end of the film, too.

Cecile dominated his thoughts. Her beautiful body next to his, her effortless ease in knowing how to please him sexually, she'd captured every inch of him, from the mind downwards. His pondered upon what seemed to be her vision of life. Was she right? Was it worth worrying about people he couldn't really help? It was not his fault he had inherited privilege, and wealth, so why shouldn't he enjoy it. Cecile had opened his eyes and he'd had the time of his life with her. He craved her. The danger of their tryst excited him almost as much as the woman herself.

Where would this lead? Was it an affair?

"Doesn't really matter," thought Anthony. He'd slept with the woman of his dreams and had perhaps taken a step towards his chosen path. Would Philip be impressed if he defied the odds of becoming a star of the screen? Obviously, his stepfather would be furious if he knew of his methods. Anthony thought of Philip as a tyrant and a bully, but never had him down as a womaniser who enjoyed the pleasures of multiple lovers. Business and power were his pleasures, and he would not approve of Anthony's.

He was quite relieved that Philip was still away on business. Whilst Jane would be somewhat irritating with her questioning, his stepfather's interrogation would be on a whole different level. Anthony was somewhat conflicted, so far as his stepfather was concerned, as he still harboured hopes of a place in the Crawford empire. It was something he didn't quite understand, perhaps it was a mixture of security and Philip's approval that were his driving force. Anthony was personable and knew he could work hard, why wouldn't Philip believe in him? He recalled many discussions that quickly escalated into arguments, often throwing the fact that Philip would not induct him into the family business as a defence against his stepfather's badgering to seek *'gainful employment'*.

"I don't want you anywhere near my business interests, but you will get a job that I deem worthy to the family name,"

Anthony suddenly became very bitter and vengeful against Philip, and his seeming rejection of Anthony's desire to join the family business allowed his mind to fill up with images once again of he and his leading lady, passionately cavorting on the desk unbeknownst to everyone. Cecile hadn't rejected him, far from it!

The huge mansion he called home suddenly appeared. Wright reduced his speed as he made the final stretch of the journey up the nearly half-mile drive. Going clockwise around the water fountain, the chauffeur pulled up outside the three steps that led to the enormous front doors. The Rolls Royce engine idled almost silently, but the noise on the gravel swept driveway had probably alerted Soames, who was waiting at the door. Anthony took a look at the sky; the December afternoon was a cold and dark one. The overcast clouds had made the day dull but had not yet produced the anticipated rain.. Smiling to himself, he knew his day had certainly been a lot brighter than the weather.

Wright, though a heavy man who did his best to hide his limp, was deceptively quick and had whizzed around the car to open it for the young master. Anthony did not thank his chauffeur but did remind him to clean the car ahead of Philip's return.

"I'll get onto it right away, Sir." Wright made his way back to the driver's seat and headed off towards the garage where he would complete the task set for him by Anthony.

"Did you have a pleasant afternoon, Sir?" asked Soames as Anthony strode up the steps. The question brought Anthony up short. It was unlike Soames to make such personal enquiries and the young Crawford, buoyed up by an afternoon of illicit sex and still slightly drunk from the champagne, quelled the servant's question with a stern glance and a curt reply.

"What I was doing, Soames, is no business of yours," he replied. Anthony felt as though there was a new air about him. One of importance and status. He was, after all, the man of the house at least until Philip's return. The servant inclined his head and made an apology, which Anthony grudgingly accepted.

"Where is my mother, Soames?"

"In the drawing room, Sir. May I take you to her?"

"No, I can find my own way."

"Would you care for anything else, Sir?"

"No thank you. That will be all."

"Very good, Sir."

Soames headed downstairs, not displaying an iota of emotion in relation to the rather unpleasant exchange between him and the young master, but inwardly seething. Anthony watched him and acknowledged the man's restraint. He had been short with Soames, feeling that the butler was always trying to glean bits of information to feed his employer, but if he had been spoken to in the manner in which he had just addressed the servant, he would have vented his displeasure. Soames, to give the man his due, had taken it well. Although Anthony did still feel as though his every move was being monitored.

"Paranoia, old boy."

Remembering Harry's words, Anthony stopped thinking about Soames, and headed into the drawing room. His mother was up quickly out of her chair to greet her son with a warm, welcoming hug.

"Well, how did it go?" Jane's question caught Anthony somewhat off guard. His day had gone exceedingly well but he wasn't about to go into detail. Then he remembered, he'd fed his mother a line about going for an interview! He relaxed his shoulders and gave her a huge grin.

"I got the job." That was the truth but was probably the last time he would be telling it in this conversation, Anthony thought.

"Oh, that's bloody good of you!" Jane's upper-class terminology and pronunciation always gave way to her former East end vernacular when she was talking to Anthony or when her husband wasn't around. "What a bloody Christmas present! I couldn't 'ave hoped fer better! Let's have a drink to celebrate."

"Why not?" replied her son, who was not only touched by his mother's sincere joy upon hearing his news, but also relieved that he was not going to have to deliver an overly taxing performance of deception. Lying was a form of acting, but it looked as though he wouldn't have to do too much of it at this moment in time, although he couldn't help but feel a twinge of guilt that a lie had brought out such honest adulation from his devoted mother.

Jane rang the bell to summon a servant, and Soames appeared in no time.

"A bottle of champagne, please Soames," the proud mother instructed.

"Very good, Madam." Soames disappeared to attend to his mistress's command. Luckily neither she nor her son saw the look of absolute loathing on their servant's face.

"I'm proud of you, Anthony. This has made what has already

been a good day even better." Jane sat down on the leather couch and motioned for Anthony to join her. He noticed her speech had become more refined and well enunciated again. He was maybe not the only person performing this afternoon, he thought.

"Thank you, Mum." Anthony loved getting the chance to use the shortened, familiar version of the word 'mother'. Although he was seeing things a bit differently, Jane had been the only person behind him every step of the way. He was a mother's boy.

Soames appeared with a bottle and two glasses balanced on a silver tray. He made his way over to Anthony and Jane, when the latter told her son, "And I spoke to Cecile Ford today."

The news seemed to take Soames unaware as much as Anthony, the butler nearly dropping the bottle of champagne when transferring it from tray to table. Showing exceedingly sharp reflexes in catching it, he apologised profusely and went to replace the bottle with a fresh one which had not been ruined through excessive shaking.

"Accidents will happen, Soames. No harm done." Jane told the servant upon his return with another bottle of Moet.

"Thank you, Madam," replied a relieved Soames. "Most kind and gracious of you. Will that be all?"

"Yes, thank you, Soames," said Jane.

Soames had poured the drinks, uncharacteristically allowing some the fizz to spill over the glass. Two errors, albeit small, were hugely uncharacteristic of the man who Anthony still had to often convince himself was human. He didn't spend too much time analysing the butler's mistakes, however, he too needed to compose himself after his mother's shock announcement. His mother, talking to Cecile? What was going on?

"Cecile Ford?" he said, lightly, although his feelings about the matter were anything but! He feigned confusion.

"Oh, come now, Anthony," laughed Jane. "I know you see a lot of beautiful women in the films you watch, but you are hardly likely to forget Cecile Ford so quickly."

If only she knew! Did she?

"What exactly did the two of you talk about?" Anthony's

tone was interrogative and rather like his stepfather. He didn't really like that.

"She telephoned to thank us for a wonderful evening. And to return the invite for next week."

Anthony was still reeling. When had Cecile spoken to his mother? Before they'd met? After their meeting had concluded? What on earth was she playing at!

Jane took a sip of champagne and continued, "An invite she was most insistent that you accepted. I take it you don't mind?"

Anthony would happily spend every waking hour in the company of Cecile but was not overly thrilled with the thought of spending it with his mother, stepfather, and Cecile's husband.

"Why was she so insistent I should be there?" Anthony's tone somewhat defensive.

Jane smiled. "I may be accused of bias, but I find your company delightful. I think Cecile does too, plus, I do think she enjoys teasing Philip about your love of acting."

Anthony pondered his mother's last comment. He'd enjoyed the verbal dual between his stepfather and his guest and the fact that Cecile had verbally bested Philip. Without warning, Anthony's resentment grew again as he thought about Philip's stance on the family business. It was hard enough for Anthony feeling rejected by his stepfather, but for Philip to then mock and cast aspersion on his stepson's interests was both infuriating and cruel.

"But let's not mention acting," Jane's tone turned serious as though she was reading her son's mind. "After all, Philip is doing business with Robert and our duty is to support."

"I won't let you down." Anthony's solemn response instantly conjured feelings of real guilt. If his activities of this afternoon were to come to light, he would certainly be letting his mother and the whole house down. Sipping his champagne, he composed himself. He was an actor, playing the part.

"I'm sure it will be a delightful evening; the Fords are charming people," he boomed, getting in character of the Young Master. "Plus, there is a Christmas party to organise and look forward to."

"As are you and I, my darling son. We too, are charming people!" Jane, like Harry, couldn't help but appreciate Anthony's dry wit which could often stray into sarcasm territory. "And you need not worry about organisation, the Lady of the house will ensure that the invitations are sent, the catering is mouth-watering, and the decoration is befitting of a home occupied by the Crawfords." She gave Anthony a wry smile, which he could have interpreted as either happy or sad; for once, he wasn't able to read his mother's thoughts. "Drink up, you and I are going to have a marvellous Christmas. Our best yet!" It was something Jane told him every year, and he had to smile as he felt a calmness rush over him. His mother had a way of making him feel safe and childlike. Whether the stately home, or the dirty, cobbled streets of London, her kind words and protective arms were always of great comfort.

The moment of tranquillity was soon shattered by Soames' re-emergence. "Begging your pardon, Madam, the master appears to have returned from his trip early."

Jane and Anthony quickly rose to their feet as Philip appeared in the doorway. His gaze firmly fixed on Anthony, he said ominously, "Is there something that you wish to tell me?"

Chapter 7

Time stood still for Anthony. He was an actor who'd forgotten his line. The star who'd not read the script and a victim to a cruel plot change. Gripping his glass, he stared blankly at Philip, who hadn't moved from his position in the doorway.

"What exactly do I want to tell him?" Anthony's thoughts were circling. Surely his stepfather couldn't have known of his afternoon delight. He'd been in France but had returned unexpectedly.

Why?

Jane broke the awkward silence as she walked towards her husband. "Darling, I wasn't expecting you back till at least tomorrow."

Philip gave a half smile, as his wife kissed his cheek. "I was hoping to surprise you." He offered no explanation in regard to his sudden and unexpected return, Anthony noticed. As though his mother wasn't worthy of such, he thought, sourly. "You certainly did that. And what a wonderful surprise it is. Isn't that right, Anthony?" Jane sounded genuinely happy.

Anthony was still in shock by both the appearance of his stepfather and his opening question. He had never been an individual that was often left speechless, but this was one of those times.

"Well, as the boy has clearly lost the power of speech, please Jane, do fill me in on why you are drinking my champagne. Are we celebrating something?" Philip was still holding Jane in an unusually affectionate way and seemed in a relaxed mood.

Anthony breathed a sigh of relief. His stepfather merely wanted an explanation of what Jane, and he were doing drinking! It was nothing to do with his act of deception with Cecile! Though hugely enjoyable and something he wanted to repeat often, his clandestine meeting with his stepfather's friend's wife had made him even more paranoid than usual. This was a secret that would blow several worlds apart if discovered, but the dangerous situation only added to the excitement for Anthony. He was an actor. He could play the part and be something different. Cecile had lots to lose and seemed adept at covering her tracks. He suddenly realised that he knew little about her as a person, despite their intimate liaison, simply assuming things about his lover and employer without knowing them.

"Anthony has secured employment," announced a proud Jane.

"Doing what, exactly?" Philip's demeanour remained cheerful. He was in as pleasant a mood as Anthony could ever remember seeing him since they had met. France, although a country Philip had little time for, had certainly put him in a good frame of mind. Or at least whatever he had been doing there had.

Anthony was about to answer the question when Soames appeared in the room. Addressing Philip, the butler said, "Begging your pardon, Sir, there is a telephone call for Master Anthony."

"Then he must take it, Soames." Philip conducted the conversation as though his stepson were not even in the room. "And bring me a glass. We are celebrating."

"At once, Sir."

Anthony was out of the room quicker than Soames and headed straight to the telephone. Finding the receiver off the hook on the round mahogany table in the Great Hall, he instantly felt the overpowering aroma of the flowers that had been picked fresh this morning. Philip was a lover of gardening and would spend considerable time lecturing Anthony as a child, after his boisterous games disturbed his geraniums. Picking up the receiver, he gazed at the tall vase containing what he thought were winter aconites. Philip's lecturing had at least had a positive impact on the younger Crawford, who now had a love of flora himself.

"Hello, Anthony Crawford speaking."

"How did it go, old boy?" The familiar, friendly voice of Harry brought a calmness over Anthony, who just realised how fast and hard his heart had been pounding. Harry's voice and the flowers served to remind him of breaking two vases whilst playing soldiers with his friend and how a raging Philip was far more of a scary foe than any fictional enemy they were battling. "A gentleman never tells," laughed Crawford, who couldn't wait to go into details with his best friend in the same way a child relishes sharing secrets with peers that make them seem so very interesting. Anthony pondered this. He was no longer a child and was embroiled in something both illicit and very adult. He knew the repercussions, should this be made public. The scandal would be huge.

But Harry was his best friend and could be trusted. They'd shared a strong bond for a number of years now. Different personalities that had very different beginnings in life but two individuals who had a mutual respect and affection for each other.

"A gentleman never tells?" Harry replied. Anthony noticed that his friend was sniffing quite regularly. "Well then, it's a good job it's you I'm speaking to." Both men laughed at the comment.

"Do you have a slight sniffle, Harry?"

"Just a cold, old boy. Usually get the sniffles in the run up till Christmas. Cross that I have to bear." Harry laughed again.

Anthony had known the Hewson-Greaves family for a number of years and had never recalled Harry having a cold before the festive period. Remembering the Spanish flu that had raged through Britain, and many other places across the globe, Anthony hastened to advise his friend to see a doctor. Harry was evasive.

"Anyway," Harry sniffed again, ignoring Anthony's impassioned pleas. "Don't change the subject. My best friend has a mysterious, clandestine meeting with a married beauty, whom he seemingly wooed over a dinner whilst her husband was also present... I do believe that jolly well entitles me to hear all of the details."

"I can't argue with that," agreed Anthony. "But I do believe that it's a conversation worth having face to face. What's say the polo club this week? That is if you are up to it with your sniffles?"

"I think I will just about make it," chuckled Harry, who blew his nose vigorously. "My apologies, old boy."

"Don't worry, just get well soon. We have a lot to talk about and it would be nice to speak somewhere I know that the walls don't have ears."

Harry chuckled again in between sniffles. "Soames paranoia, again?"

"Always there, always!"

"It's what butlers do, Anthony. Norris may be several years past his prime but that unerring knack of appearing out of nowhere is something he will never lose."

Norris' tenure as the Hewson-Greaves family butler even predated Harry. Anthony had always liked the small, balding man with the squarest jaw he'd ever seen and viewed him as friendly and helpful. He did not feel the same about the menacing Soames, whose presence in the corridor gave Anthony reason enough to be paranoid. Whether it was because Anthony had not been born into the privileged position of having servants was something he and Harry never spoke of. His friend knew already, even if he himself didn't, that Anthony was grossly insecure.

"Goodbye, Harry, speak soon."

"Cheerio, old boy. Watch your step with our lady friend, won't you?" were Harry's parting words. Replacing the receiver, before Anthony had time to ponder upon Harry's warming, he was greeted by the ever-present Soames.

"Is my mother still in the drawing room?" Anthony asked, curtly.

"She is, Master Anthony." Soames replied, seemingly unphased at the younger man's apparent terseness. "Both the master and the mistress are there. If you will excuse me, I must see about dinner."

Anthony watched as Soames seemed to glide along the well-lit corridor towards the kitchen, which was downstairs. The butler did not look round and moved at his usual, quick pace. Anthony's attention was quickly diverted by the sound of raised voices coming from the drawing room. Curious, he moved quickly towards the noise. It was unusual to hear Philip and Jane argue, usually his mother would often take a telling off from her husband in an obedient silence. This disagreement was two-way.

His hand on the doorknob, Anthony made the decision to do something he reasoned Soames was a past master at and although disliked the butler for doing it, Anthony pressed his ears to the door and strained to hear the conversation. Only some muffled words could be heard beyond the thick wooden doors.

"You want for nothing!" he heard Philip say.

"Yes," Jane shot back. "And I turn a blind eye to a lot, Philip. I have been a lot more understanding than most wives."

"I know, and you know I appreciate it." Philip sounded apologetic.

"Just don't make a fool of me and bring that sort of thing home. I ask you for very little."

"And you are provided for, as is your son." Philip seemed to be regaining his confidence and composure. "This is an arrangement that suits us all."

An arrangement? Anthony was confused. What was an arrangement? What had Philip done that Jane turned a blind eye to? The young Crawford never had his stepfather down as a womaniser but that seemed the only logical explanation. Sensing that his mother may appreciate his presence, he opened the door. Both Jane and Philip made feeble attempts to act as though nothing had happened, but Anthony was about to deliver a performance of blissful ignorance that even Chaplin would admire. Picking up his glass from the small, round glass table where he'd left it, he smiled and said, "So, what have I missed?"

Now it was the turn of Philip and Jane to be speechless.

"I must say, I'm famished," Anthony continued. "What is for dinner?"

"I think Mrs. B is cooking some fish delicacy," answered his mother.

"Jolly good," Anthony raised his glass. "To the Crawfords."

He was enjoying Philip's awkwardness and his brief taste of power. Today had been a good day for the young would be actor, but this argument between his mother and the man at whose hand he fed, had somewhat dampened Anthony's spirits. He felt suddenly deflated.

And he was determined to get to the bottom of what he'd overheard.

Chapter 8

Anthony lay on his luxurious bed and gazed at the ceiling. Dinner had been a quiet affair, with seemingly everyone concealing something. He had taken up the role of making small talk as the usual performer of that task, his mother Jane, was clearly elsewhere in her mind. Philip had made his usual grunts and comments about 'quality food' and 'excellent wine' but they had been more like statements rather than invitations to conversation.

Not that Anthony minded. He had a number of things on his mind. Cecile may have been at the front of those thoughts but hearing his mother argue back with Philip had invaded his head and was refusing to leave. It was not customary of Jane to argue, she had become so adept at taking verbal blows and directing conversation back to where Philip could feed his ego and stay true to his traditional views of how people of his class should live life.

What had his stepfather done to evoke such a reaction?

Anthony gazed down and decided to remove his shoes. His shirt was unbuttoned at the collar and his tie removed. This was something he felt comfortable doing in the safety of his bedroom. Philip's standards must be maintained, which meant dressing for dinner, even if the Crawfords weren't entertaining. In his room, though, he needn't worry. Citing a long day and desire for an early night, he had politely asked to be excused from the dinner table, kissed his mother goodnight, and acknowledged his stepfather before ascending the grand staircase and hastily making his way to his room at the end of the long corridor. He'd quickly brushed off Soames,' *"Will there be anything else, Master Anthony?"* and, closing the door behind him, he strode to the window and drew back the soft, off-white curtains to gaze out over the vast, open grounds that stretched as far as Anthony could see in the matt darkness of a stormy night. Troubled by thoughts of his mother, Cecile, his own future, Harry's cold, and the last conversation, which all ran amok in his head, he'd thrust the curtains shut again and threw himself on his bed, where he now lay, half undressed.

He fantasied about Cecile alongside him. It would surely be a risk she would not be prepared to take, but he hoped that their next encounter would be somewhere more comfortable than the pokey, drab office where they'd consummated their 'arrangement'.

Not that he was complaining. Her beauty was matched by her confidence. She knew what she wanted, and she was going to have it. Women like that excited Anthony and Cecile was a craving he wanted and needed to continually satisfy. He thought about her – how she'd felt, how she'd smelt, how her nails had raked against his back as she kissed his neck. A passionate lover, she was in charge and knew how to get pleasure in whatever she did. Anthony had been curious as to how much Benson could potentially hear, but it hadn't bothered Cecile as she devoured her new leading man.

Leading man! At least that is what he hoped. His mind drifted back to Fairbanks as Robin Hood. Though cinema was silent but for the music, the dashing American had an uncanny ability to say so much through facial expression and physical prowess. A different acting style to Chaplin, Anthony always felt he combined the best attributes of the two. Enid Bennett had been Fairbank's love interest as Maid Marian and was an attractive lady with a charming look of innocence, although Anthony reasoned that Cecile would never be as subservient, and winning her heart would probably be an even more formidable task than defeating the evil Sir Guy of Gisbourne. But, of course, he would do it with a sense of style, panache and humour that would even draw the praise of Hollywood's leading lights.

In the cold light of day, there was no way they could be together, and Anthony knew that this wouldn't have the fairy tale ending where the king would give the happy couple his blessing. Where would this lead? He didn't know, but he would take from it what he could, which hopefully included many stolen moments with the beautiful wife of Robert Ford. Cecile had assured

Anthony that she would explain more about the film projects upon their next meet. Not too interested in making conversation as they had hastily dressed after their encounter, it was as though she had overrun and was perhaps late for something else. Or maybe she had developed a sudden fear of being caught in the act and the eschewing scandal that would undoubtedly follow.

Kissing him softly while running her hand down his chest, she had whispered, "*Till we meet again,*" before motioning his departure by turning from him. Anthony walked away briskly and with purpose, barely able to hide the smile or spring in his step. This was a danger that appealed to his rebellious and creative nature and the sort of story Hollywood would crave but never admit it was ready for. Perhaps he, Anthony Crawford would be the revolutionary trailblazer to drag the film industry forward and free of inhibitions! He was on top of the world, and anything was now possible.

His good mood had been briefly halted by the sign of Benson. His creepy eyes followed Anthony out of the door, but the young Crawford had been polite enough to acknowledge Cecile's chauffeur. He had taken an instant dislike to the man but was unsure why. Perhaps he acted as a stark reminder that if what Cecile and Anthony were doing became known, it would create such a scandal amongst high society that two extremely important families, both great London households, would be gravely impacted – perhaps even destroyed – by the revelations.

Replaying the day's events had made his restless. He sprung up from his bed again and paced up and down. The thick carpet felt soft and comforting beneath his feet and he removed his socks to enjoy the sensation even more. This was something he enjoyed as a child and recalled how much his mum would chuckle as she watched her son enjoy stepping on the carpet as though he'd never stepped on anything like it before. Which was true. Jane often hid her guilt of not providing for her young son behind a smile; burying her thoughts and fears and carrying on with life for the benefit of others. Anthony tried so many times to say that she had no need to feel guilty, but it was not the kind of conversation Jane would entertain. He'd understood why she had worked long hours doing all manner of jobs. He had friends that were as hungry as he but, for a man who loved literature, he could never articulate to his mother that her love was enough to make him happy, despite those long, cold nights and endless days of deliberately avoiding the chip shop as the aroma of salt and vinegar were too much to endure on an empty stomach. His mother's marriage to Philip had guaranteed both her and son's future and provided opportunity. That was enough and she was willing to play whatever role was expected of her to ensure that future remained secure.

This brought Anthony's thoughts full circle. What had Philip done to cause his mother to argue with her husband? Business? Possible, but unlikely. Although Jane had been Philip's secretary and knew more about his business than she ever admitted, she was never consulted by Philip and was certainly not privy to any of her husband's business plans. Personal? This was more likely, Anthony surmised. Was it an affair? Anthony never saw Philip as a philanderer, more married to his work than anything, but of course, he was a man who had the opportunity and the wherewithal to conduct an affair. He never talked about where he'd been, or what he had done, so neither Jane nor Anthony would ever know if he was engaged in a clandestine relationship. But something about this scenario didn't sit right with Anthony. He was miscasting his stepfather into some villainous, straying husband and Philip was nothing of the sort.

Maybe he had been meddling in Anthony's life again? Philip did so like to interfere, always wanting to be in control and not accepting anyone was entitled to a private life. This could be a possibility. Jane always put her foot down where her son was concerned, and Anthony knew that his mother would go into battle for him and had done so on several occasions in the past. Had this been one of those times? Or had Philip simply caught Jane on a bad day?

The trouble with the upper classes, Anthony thought, was that they were so bloody straight-laced – or at least they gave that impression when, in actual fact, the air of respectability was often nothing more than a deceptive smoke screen for anything from marital rows, business troubles and even hedonism involving extra marital affairs.

Anthony's fears were now bordering on paranoia. He returned to the window again and opened his curtains before lifting the sashes and letting the night air into the room. The storm was still threatening but it remained dry. The night air was bitter, but Anthony welcomed the cold, fresh breeze on his face. He found that fresh air often cleared his head and provided oxygen for creativity. Still full of crazy thoughts, he could feel his mind beginning to ease, as though each and every topic was being carefully arranged in a filing cabinet for him to address when ready.

Feeling refreshed and calmer, Anthony remained by the open window, enjoying the cold night air. What was going on outside? Metaphorically transporting himself into the homes and lives of others was a usual escape for him during the numerous times Philip had scolded or belittled him over something he had or hadn't done. As the conversations had grown into various pitches for a place in the family business usually followed by a firm rebuke, Anthony continued to use this tactic of imagining life away from the Crawford residence. He would make up comedic, exciting tales about the scandalous goings on in the various addresses that he could barely make out over the horizon. Stories that would one day become cinematic classes that would be endorsed and celebrated by Chaplin and the elite.

But could Cecile help make this dream a reality? Could this illicit encounter provide a springboard for achieving his dreams of a career in film and would it enable him to no longer have to worry about wanting to be part of the Crawford empire? Anthony felt another bout of anger towards his stepfather boiling up before a twinge of guilt cut through him, reminding himself that he was using Cecile to gain revenge against his stepfather for not wanting him in the business. Anthony shook his head, the cold realisation that he was no better than the hypocritical elites he purported to despise! How had that happened? Taking a deep breath of cold night air, Anthony quickly reminded himself that Cecile was a grown woman who had approached him with offers of opportunity and passion, and all he had done was accept what was on offer. He was guilty of nothing, he thought, rather complacently, as he stepped away from the window, full of self-assurance that he was the victim, not Cecile!

Closing the sashes and swishing the curtains closed again, Anthony knew that sleep would not be his friend tonight. He sat at his desk and prepared to write to Cecile. He didn't dare communicate via telephone; the only other form of communication he could think of, short of a face-to-face encounter. He needed to know when they were to meet next, he wanted to tell her how he felt. Ten minutes in, and he was still struggling with the opening address.

Dear Cecile. My dearest Cecile. My Darling. Frantically crumpling pieces of paper, he was at a loss to know how to write his feelings down and reasoned that perhaps it would be a task better completed when not so emotionally charged. Deciding he needed a drink, he put on his shoes and socks and made for the door. Anthony would never venture out his room without shoes, years of etiquette training from Philip had made the very thought seem peculiar. His shirt was still unbuttoned at the collar which he reasoned was fine since he was only looking to quench his thirst and at this late hour, there would be no-one about.

Making his way down the stairs, Anthony should have known that Soames would appear, as if by magic. The butler greeted him as soon as he stepped into the hall.

"Master Anthony," Soames bowed his head, deferentially. "Is everything alright, Sir?"

"Fine, thank you, Soames. Just a bit thirsty."

"Allow me to assist, Master Anthony. What do you desire?"

She lived in another house with her husband about eight miles away. The thought made Anthony smile as he answered Soames.

"A glass of hot milk would be fine, thank you."

"I will get Rose to fetch you one, straight away. Should I instruct her to bring it to your room?"

Anthony knew that was code for 'get yourself to bed', but he agreed and made his way back to his bedroom. He was unsure if he would write to Cecile tonight but would make his decision after his drink, which he discovered he was looking forward to. The frothy milk, and a hint of cinnamon had become a firm favourite with the young Crawford and even now that he was a grown man, it still sustained and calmed him. Back in his room, he waited for the knock at the door, which followed almost immediately. Suddenly feeling a tinge of tiredness, he bade the servant 'Enter!' and thought about Rose. A maid, who been in service longer than Anthony had been alive, she was painfully thin with grey hair that was always pulled into an excruciatingly tight bun, which sat beneath her maid's cap. A popular figure in the household, Rose's pleasant demeanour and positive voice were always something that cheered him up.

That happy feeling was short lived as Soames entered his room with a glass of hot milk.

"Your milk, Master Anthony."

"I thought Rose was bringing it?"

"Apologies Sir, it slipped my mind but after you'd retired, a message addressed to you was delivered." Soames' eyes motioned to the platter, which had a small, brown envelope on it. 'I felt it more appropriate for me to deliver it, rather than entrust it to one of the maids.'

"Thank you, Soames." Anthony took the message with his free hand, almost spilling his milk due to his eagerness to obtain the envelope.

"Will that be all, Master Anthony?" Soames asked.

"Yes. You may retire." Anthony answered quickly and closed the door, his earlier paranoia returning. Soames never forgot anything, delivering the envelope the way he had was deliberate. But why? Setting aside his much-desired milk, he sat down at his desk and opened the envelope. There was no address on the front, simply his name. He didn't recognise the writing. Somehow, it made him feel uneasy. Unfolding the paper, a cold shiver came over him as he silently read the message.

History has taught us through the years,

Most situations will end in tears.
Your actions will cause you much remorse,
Playing with things that are not yours.
Think on your sins, I ask not that much,
Carry on your wicked ways, and I shall be in touch.
Bad things happen when people are scorned,
Think on your sins, you have been warned.

Chapter 9

"It has to be Soames; it can't be anyone else!"

"Can't? Or you won't allow it to be?" Cecile's observation struck Anthony unexpectedly. "He is your butler," she continued. "Paid to run the house, and someone, darling, whom you don't like."

Anthony lay on his back and gazed at the ceiling. He'd spent what seemed like an endless twenty-four hours negotiating a meeting with the object of his desires, only for her to make plans of her own, which, happily for young Crawford, included him.

Overlooking Brighton's world-famous seafront, The Grand Hotel was one of the city's more exclusive establishments and a venue Cecile seemed to know well. A favourite haunt for poets and other literary types, its Italian influenced Victorian architecture seemed to attract them. Indeed, it was a striking building, and Anthony had been delighted to ride in the 'Ascending Omnibus', a hydraulically powered lift – the first of its kind in this country – and befitting the tallest building in Britain at the time of being built in the mid eighteen hundreds. Its whitewashed fascia matched the interior décor of the rooms, which were predominantly white and complimented by daring glass and steel furniture and large, colourful artwork. The hardwood floor was a bad choice, Anthony felt, particularly the noise of the heels when striking the surface. That being said, it seemed to work well with the room, adding yet more texture and colour to the stark interior. Why was he sitting there, enjoying an illicit lunch with his married lover, thinking about the noise of heels on hardwood floors, he wondered, shaking his head. Their lunch had quickly turned into an afternoon of stolen passion where Anthony had forgotten his troubles thanks to his lover, whose creativity in the bedroom left little to the imagination.

Anthony had never finished his letter to Cecile. The night he had received the quite terrifying note, he had worried beyond himself, and eventually went to bed only to spend a restless night tossing and turning and achieving very little sleep. The lack of sleep made it quite easy for him to then feign illness and spend the following day in bed, being sent soup at regular intervals from the kitchen, was instructed by his mother that morning who seemed to think a bowl of chicken soup as a remedy to almost anything. It was while he was in bed with his imaginary illness that Soames delivered the telegram from Cecile instructing him to attend a 'meeting' on the South coast. By some stroke of divine intervention, Philip had, that same day, organised a trip away with Anthony's mother, and it was a godsend, although Anthony was convinced the gesture had been offered by Philip because of the previous night's argument with his mother that young Crawford had overheard. Taking off for Cornwall, Philip had felt the urge to clearly stress the importance of being the man of the house to his stepson.

"Your mother and I need a break away. It shan't be for too long, but you are responsible for the reputation of house while we are gone."

Anthony was unsure if it was threat or encouragement and, in truth, cared little for it, particularly upon receiving Cecile's notification. The urgency of the message being delivered by telegram and the clandestine nature of its contents only served to transport the young Crawford into idle fantasy, as he likened himself to William Hooker Gilette, who had played Sherlock Holmes many times on stage, as well as the eponymous hero in the 1916 big screen adaptation. Though much older than Anthony, young Crawford admired the American's screen presence and had been captivated by the picture, in which the sleuth takes on his arch nemesis Professor Moriarty amidst a potential scandal involving a young prince and the incriminating letters he penned to his lover during their affair. Anthony's current status was more akin to the prince rather than that of Holmes, but he was the hero of *his* movie and plots were often adapted in his head to suit him.

He'd arrived by train, the expense of which was covered by his lover, before making the short walk to the hotel. He'd pondered a horse-drawn taxi but decided to enjoy the cool, but fresh sea air, as he strolled along the pleasant esplanade towards his next liaison with Cecile. Not once did it cross his mind that he was being bought, that Cecile's interest in him was perhaps not all that it seemed. Anthony began believing he was in love with her, and her willingness to share his company and his body compounded his belief that their liaison was more than how it was viewed by his leading lady.

Seeing her at the table wearing a maroon chemise dress, her mesmerising gaze put paid to Anthony's issues, as he took his place across from the femme fatale for whom he would do anything. The afternoon tea consisted of dainty sandwiches, exquisite looking cakes, and pastries, expertly arranged on three tier serving trays and accompanied by the best tea the establishment could get its hands on. Anthony had shown his working-class roots by taking a delicious looking ham sandwich on soft white bread before the tea had been poured from the expensive silver teapot into the elegant fine bone china teacups. Remembering where he was and who he was with, he quickly replaced the item as Cecile softly giggled at her lover's obvious embarrassment before giving him that alluring smile that excited him so much. The sweet and savoury spread was befitting of a hotel with such a reputation, but all he could focus on was having Cecile for dessert. Her intentions were similar, and something she was only too happy to let him know of, as she told him about the room that awaited them.

"A most delightfully comfortable bed, darling," began Cecile, "the softest pillows and silkiest sheets." Anthony's attention was hers!

She went on, "The view is quite delightful, but I imagine we will be keeping the curtains shut for most of the duration." Cecile sipped her tea and enjoyed the fact that her lover was captivated by her description of room 162, which would be their temporary love nest. "There is a quite a bit of art scattered about the place, should you wish to look at anything."

"I think I already have plenty to admire without deciding if the Constable is a fake or not," Anthony seemed pleased with his witty remark which he also felt allowed her the knowledge of knowing he was a man of culture that went beyond the cinema.

She smiled at him sweetly.

"The rooms are all carpeted, too," Cecile said as though she was revealing something important, "much more comfortable for one walking around bare footed." Replacing her teacup on its saucer she leant in closer to Anthony and whispered, "And the bath is just about big enough for two."

Afternoon tea could not end quick enough for Anthony!

The young film lover was unsure how long this tryst with Mrs Ford would last. He'd noticed a small trunk in the corner of the spacious room. Why was she here, alone, he wondered. How long would she stay? He deliberately did not ask the question 'Who else would she be seeing?' but it did momentarily cross his mind that he might not be the only person to have engaged Cecile's attention and indeed, her ardour. Laying naked in the king-sized bed, he gazed at the portrait of Brighton Pier, which took pride of place on the wall opposite a large window that was already covered by silk curtains as they had entered the room. Cecile had already checked in, her clothes were hung up and a few accessories, a hairbrush and make up arranged neatly on the dressing table next to the bed. Anthony's mind kept filling with unwelcome thoughts. Had Benson transported her to this rendezvous? He surely knew what was going on. Anthony knew only too well that servants turned a blind eye to goings on, but where did his loyalties lie? He chauffeured and served her husband, as well as Cecile, so her activities would obviously divide loyalties. Normally this would not concern Anthony, but he was the leading man in this deception and knew that someone other than he and Cecile were aware of their activities. Still of the opinion that Soames was the poisonous poet, he thought it prudent to explore every option.

A small, pale gold sofa and matching armchair made the room that bit more homely, while the square wooden table had a bottle of champagne on ice sat in the middle. Anthony reasoned that this was one of the hotel's finest rooms, even enjoying a romantic notion that room 162 may even be one that was frequented by honeymooning couples. Their rabid, passionate activity a few minutes before, certainly was befitting of a honeymooning couple, or so he thought.

Cecile lay with her head on Anthony's chest. Her left leg sprawled across his thighs; she ran her hand across his bare torso. Kissing her head, he held her nude body tightly, enjoying her soft touch and big breasts against him. He could feel her heartbeat, slow and steady now, and would have been content lying next to her forever.

And yet the niggle of the note still refused to leave his mind. Like a foreign oppressor invading home shores, he knew that the problem wouldn't simply go away and could potentially destroy him. His paranoia was intensifying; someone was out to get him and, possibly, Cecile.

"Champagne?" Her request broke his trail of thought.

"Why not?" Anthony kissed her again before moving the silk sheets and chenille bedspread aside and climbing out of bed to retrieve the bottle. Popping the cork at the table, before pouring two glasses and making his way back to bed, he smiled lasciviously at Cecile, now sitting up, allowed the bedcovers to slip, exposing her bare breasts. Looking him up and down, she held out her hand to accept the glass as Anthony slipped into bed, beside her. Clinking glasses and enjoying a quick embrace, Cecile exclaimed, "To us."

Anthony loved the idea of *us* and reasoned he loved her too. He smiled at her and touched her cheek with his hand. Enjoying his touch, she arched her head towards his hand, her eyes shut, a look of contentment warmed her young lover's heart.

"Are you not worried? About what I received." Anthony sipped his champagne.

"It is a concern, darling," Cecile held his gaze. "But I am not one to labour on things. The kind of person doing this is not one I allow to bother me."

"The kind of person?" Anthony looked puzzled.

"Unless you have told someone, it can only be someone in service."

Anthony lied. "I haven't told anyone."

He instantly thought of his telephone conversation with Harry. Whilst he'd admitted nothing to him, he'd intimated everything. But he was Anthony's closest friend and wouldn't betray him. Their friendship was strong, and their differences of personality and ambitions meant that there was never any rivalry, rather mutual respect.

"Well," Cecile took another sip of champagne after she turned to face Anthony. "It can only be that man. That chauffeur of yours."

"Wright?" Anthony looked surprised as he reminded Cecile of his chauffeur's name. He'd not given him a second thought. He liked him. He didn't like Soames. Perhaps he wanted it to simply be the butler due to his disdain for him. In truth, Wright, and Benson were more likely suspects than Soames, and Anthony thought of Benson as a suspicious figure who would be suited to a career in blackmail. Not that this had become blackmail, yet, the note was more threatening and cerebral, which was more Soames' style. In truth, he liked Wright, the Crawfords' family chauffeur had driven him around since he'd joined the family and he didn't want to believe he was capable of something like this, but of course he could be.

"Why not your chauffeur, Benson?" Now it was Anthony's turn to sip champagne as he waited for Cecile's reply.

"Really?"

"Hardly a surprising deduction," Anthony tried to sound clinical and intelligent. "He showed me into the office and seemed very cautious of me."

Cecile was amused. "A Chaplin fan who speaks like Sherlock Holmes." She noticed her comment had hurt, or at least annoyed Anthony. She leant forward and kissed her lover. Her delicate hand stroked his face, his annoyance and embarrassment gone. She whispered, "We shall discover who it is. No one will get the better of us."

They kissed again. Anthony felt his troubles ebb away. He was in very good, and very skilful, hands. Passion and excitement pulsated through him like a strong electric charge powering an industrial generator. Chaplin always had a good record in films of getting the girl, so he was at least emulating his hero on that front. Anthony did often wonder what an actor's private life would be like. Chaplin was currently unmarried after his first marriage had ended, something young Crawford knew of through the copies of the New York Times he'd harangued Philip to buy for him under the pretence of being interested in journalism. His stepfather's fierce patriotism had always scoffed at the notion that anyone other than the English could truly speak the language, but a few copies had been secured, thanks to a combination of Jane's word and Anthony's annoying persistence.

Now here Anthony was, with his own leading lady. Ever the dreamer and, completely disregarding the fact that they had only met alone twice, he allowed himself a glimpse into the future, at least one he thought possible. It would be role reversal, but Crawford enjoyed the notion of Cecile in Marie Dressler's role in *Tillie's Punctured Romance.* Here it was Chaplin who was the city slicker that seduces Dressler, despite already having a lady friend, which would mean Anthony assuming the role as the one attached and in control of proceedings, which was far removed from the clandestine liaison that he hoped would be more than just physical. Would this be more than just sex? He didn't see how they could allow this to become public. Cecile seemed to have a life where everything she wanted, she had. A mixture of stunning beauty and a strong, forthright personality coupled with her husband's wealth and standing made that possible. But what of her before she married the wealthy and successful Philip Ford? He knew little of her emotionally, or personally, concentrating far more on her physical attributes, but Anthony was not a gigolo and had a romantic side about him. Chaplin was the king of comedy, but many a story portrayed by the genius who came from the same part of the world as the young Crawford, often saw a romantic angle feature heavily in the plot.

Cecile roused Anthony out of his daydream. "I haven't only brought you here to simply have my wicked way with you." She rose quickly out of bed and reached for a thin, white robe that hung over the antique chair by the side of the bed. Admiring her bare backside before she put on her robe, Anthony cheekily replied, "Really? Such a shame."

Turning to face him as he lay in bed, she tied her robe. "Pleasure is wonderful, darling. And even though you are irresistible, there is some business to this trip."

"Do go on." Anthony's curiosity was aroused.

"Brighton has always been a place that plays home to acting talent," answered Cecile. "Tonight, we will be having dinner before I take you to a charming little club that I'm sure you'll find, well… interesting."

"I didn't bring a change of clothes."

"I didn't imagine you would. I took the liberty of buying you a new dinner suit. One befitting of a gentleman such as yourself."

Anthony suddenly felt embarrassed. He was so smitten with Cecile but deep down knew that he was out of his depth in almost every way with her. But he didn't want to appear ungrateful. She had chosen to spend money on him, and Philip's allowance ensured he had some money on his person.

"How incredibly generous of you." Anthony worried he may have sounded sarcastic.

"I like you, Anthony. Physically, you are wonderful and unbelievably satisfying. But there is much more to you that young, virile body of yours."

"I'm pleased you have noticed," he replied, with a grin.

"Our reservation is at eight o'clock," Cecile informed him. "Which gives us enough time to finish up here then make ourselves look presentable."

"Finish up here?" Anthony was confused.

"Oh, come now, darling," Cecile smiled, before untying her robe and allowing it to slip to the floor. "One is not that naïve, surely?"

"I'm sure all will be revealed," grinned a lustful Anthony as he pulled back the covers for his leading lady.

Chapter 10

Anthony felt resplendent in his brand-new dinner suit, although the shirt, also new, hadn't been washed, which was something he preferred before wearing. He felt very sharp and worthy next to Cecile. Wearing a flowing, sleeveless gold dress with a black shawl, she was every inch the movie star and wouldn't have looked out of place as the guest of honour at one of Hollywood's latest premieres, which put Anthony into mind of Douglas Fairbanks, who had starred in the 1922 film, Robin Hood. It was the first film ever to have a premiere and one that had set a standard in the film making world.

Sherry's didn't look much from the outside. Pulling up, Benson's beady eyes scanned Cecile's young companion before he got out of the driver's seat and opened the rear door for his mistress. He moved around to Anthony's door and the chauffeur's eyes remained on Anthony as he got out of the car, his mind awash with thoughts and questions. Who was Benson's loyalty to? He couldn't be that unaware of what was going on and, whilst he wouldn't be in regular conversation with Robert, the atmosphere would be awkward should the master of the house question his wife's activities away from the family home. They had not been married long, but Anthony couldn't help but wonder if this was her first affair. Was it her only current affair? The sudden notion gave him a twinge of jealousy; he'd fallen for Cecile and even sharing her with her husband was a feeling he hated.

Cecile had gracefully stepped out of the car and was standing on the pavement waiting for Anthony, her shiny black clutch bag glistened in the moonlight, as did her expensive earrings that probably cost more than her chauffer would earn in ten years. The thought made Anthony scowl as a wave of anger and social conscience swept over him. Why should she be entitled to wear such earrings? Why were people starving, living in poor tenements, dripping with damp, not diamonds? The 'roaring' twenties only roared for those who could afford to make the noise, Anthony reflected bitterly Anger then became conflicted by guilt. No longer could he truly complain about such injustice when he was a beneficiary of all that society was affording to the rich and ruling class. He had to admit, he was part of the problem now. Of course, he made little, in fact, no effort to fight the perceived injustice. Prevarication was very much the young Crawford's style.

"Have a good evening, Madam," Benson said, bringing Anthony back to reality.

"Benson," Cecile barely acknowledged his comment. "Write this down for me: *Lowood Lodge, King Street.*"

Cecile's chauffeur and general dogsbody did as he was told. He handed the paper to Cecile, who made no attempt to take it. "Thank you. Now, put it in your pocket. We will be collected at midnight."

"Very good, Madam." Benson nodded, and completely ignored Anthony as he returned to the car and drove off to park it and settle down to wait as instructed.

"I don't think Benson is my biggest fan," Anthony smiled. 'I get the distinct impression he doesn't like me.'

"I like you." Cecile's reply, though simple, melted his heart.

Walking through the double doors, they passed two large, tough-looking, yet smartly dressed individuals stood either side. Expressions as dark as their suits, the menacing looking men simply nodded in the direction of Anthony and Cecile, the former still taking in these surroundings. The corridor became narrow as they entered the building. The stone walls were drab and gave a cold feeling, although Anthony's adrenaline would currently keep him warm in the Arctic, while Cecile showed no signs of shivering. Cecile hurried; her heels click clacking impatiently as Anthony quickened his step in an attempt to keep up. She stopped abruptly at a small window. Anthony peered into what was a tiny cloakroom filled with a number of winter coats and a round, grey-haired woman of about fifty. Cecile handed her shawl over and motioned towards Anthony, who took his time in realising that he should be removing his white scarf.

"Oh, I do apologise." His chuckle attempted to hide his embarrassment. He handed his scarf over to the woman, who was growing impatient with the young man. Cecile seemed to enjoy the situation, her expression was one of either affection or humorous ridicule, Anthony could not decide which.

"This way, darling." Cecile began walking again. The carpet was red and not covering the floor entirely, which reminded Anthony of an actor, at a premiere, walking into the auditorium on a narrow red carpet. His large strides allowed him to catch up with Cecile. Side by side, he longed to have the courage to put his arm through hers, or even hold her hand, but he was unsure of etiquette, despite the fact that by their very liaison, they had broken all the rules of etiquette, but in a public situation, on show, it mattered and he wasn't going to overstep the mark or do anything to cause neither she nor he any embarrassment. The jazz music grew louder. It was a sound Anthony enjoyed. And his mother did too. Anthony recalled the time when the wireless was alive with the sound he associated with America. Jane hadn't long been married to Philip, who didn't share the same taste in music and was, to say the least, unimpressed with the sound, nor was he impressed with his new wife dancing along to Jelly Roll Morton. Looking back, that was an early indication of Philip's dour and domineering personality. Anthony had endured many a lecture on why British was best and how foreign influence will ultimately corrupt the world and, more importantly, The Empire.

Anthony's thoughts were broken as he noticed that two narrow corridors seemed to appear from nowhere. The main ballroom was in sight, but his focus was on a sight he'd never seen before and was struggling to comprehend.

The sight of two men in a passionate embrace shocked Anthony to his very core. They made no attempt to hide the illegal act they were performing and seemed perfectly at ease to be kissing and caressing in public. He immediately bristled with embarrassment and his eyes darted around, not that he knew what he was looking for. Noticing his uncomfortable surprise, Cecile placed her hand on his, the warmth of which seemed to calm Anthony.

"I need a drink, darling."

Cecile led him into the main hall. A large, round stage stood to the right and was set up for what looked like a full orchestra, given the amounts of instruments on show. Anthony recognised the trumpet but would struggle to name most of the others. He was a fan of music but was by no means an expert, always preferring the details and rudiments of literature and film.

The dark-haired, moustached man's approach was a bit too quick for Anthony, who spun round in an aggressive manner and looked down at his foe, who seemed visibly shocked. Quickly defusing the situation, Cecile stroked Anthony's arm and said, "Thank you Alfonse, please show us to our table." She turned to her companion and smiled, amused.

'The Maître de, Anthony, darling. Do try not to make such a fuss.'

Anthony felt like a fool. He was still reeling from what he had seen and was now feeling completely out of his depth. He took the seat Alfonse had pulled out for him and thanked him without looking at the other man. Alfonse received a nod from Cecile and scurried away as fast as his skinny legs would carry him. He too was in some shock. Never before had he been treated in this way!

Cecile was her usual calm self, after her out of character reprimand. She eyed Anthony and waited patiently for his eyes to meet hers. Already smoking a cigarette, and using a cigarette holder, she let out a puff of smoke into the air above his head and moved the case in his direction. Anthony took one and lit it with a match from one of the tiny books of matches scattered around the central lamp on the table. He looked her straight in the eyes, his expression a mixture of surprise, confusion, and anger. Why had she brought him here, to this den of iniquity, where men kissed men, and the women obviously didn't seem to mind. He seethed quietly until Cecile spoke.

"You have some questions?" She raised her eyebrows.

"Where do I start?" Anthony noticed the nerves in his voice. He needed to regain his composure. Cecile said nothing and didn't avert her eyes from his. He flicked ash into the ashtray on the table and prepared himself to speak again, only to be interrupted by Alfonse hurrying to their table carrying a tray. Standing by Cecile and away from Anthony, he quickly placed the glasses and bottle of champagne on the table.

"That will be all, Alfonse." Cecile dismissed the slight figure, who was clearly unsettled by her companion.

"Thank you, Madam." Anthony detected a foreign accent, perhaps eastern Europe. Not that his knowledge of dialect was expert, but he knew the voice wasn't English. Anthony had a few questions for Cecile and started with the waiter t whom he had mistaken for a common thug.

"A friend of yours?" A healthy gulp of champagne seemed to settle his nerves, or at least his voice.

"Hardly, darling," smiled Cecile. "But when one frequents an establishment on numerous occasions, it pays to remember the Maître de. If you become one of the crowd and more importantly, one of his favourites, it guarantees you certain things.' She didn't elaborate on what things, and Anthony, not wishing to appear ill-informed and crass, didn't ask her to.

"And people seem to remember me." She concluded, as she enjoyed her cigarette and the fact that she'd angled the conversation to where she wanted it to go. Anthony was under her spell and took the bait.

"You are hard to forget."

"Thank you, darling." Cecile seemed sincere with her gratitude.

Anthony lost his trail of thought. So keen to pay his lover a compliment after her comment, his momentum was derailed. He finished his glass and poured himself another. Perhaps it was the alcohol, or his overdeveloped sense of curiosity, he decided to continue his questioning.

"I wouldn't have thought this was Robert's scene?"

Cecile sipped her champagne before placing her glass on the table. She eyed Anthony with interest before answering his question. "Never judge a book by its cover. People always surprise you. As you have seen this evening."

She'd done it again. Anthony felt thwarted, as if she had deflected any concerns of suspicions her younger lover might have, and he got the distinct impression he had been outmanoeuvred. She knew Anthony had weaknesses that she could exploit, his jealousy, his naivety, and she could use this knowledge against him if she so chose.

Or was this Anthony's paranoia constructing a scenario that played into that end?

"Well, let's address that first, darling," Anthony's tone was more serious. "Just what kind of club have you brought me to?"

Cecile laughed. "Oh, you sound exactly like your stepfather."

"No, I don't!" Anthony snapped. "I'm merely asking a question, Cecile. We do not know each other that well, but I am nothing like Philip."

"Anthony, I apologise." Cecile seemed amused. "It was insensitive and incorrect. As you say, I don't know you that well, but I know that you are nothing like Philip."

"Intelligent as well as incredibly stunning." Anthony now had control of proceedings. He poured Cecile another drink and waited for her response. This was a clever lady who took her time when she needed to, and he needed to respect that.

Cecile smiled and stroked his hand. With her other hand, she was fiddling with her hair, immaculately set in the latest 'Marcel' wave. She had no need to, which caused Anthony to wonder what it was that Cecile was nervous about?

Anthony exercised patience. His ego was massaged as his control on proceedings strengthened, while he had the visual pleasure at staring at the breath-taking lady who sat across from him. He made the bold decision to touch her hand, and as he did so, he was aware of how petite and delicate Cecile's hand felt in his. Her long, thin fingers with their brightly painted nails felt like filigree when crushed in his. She readied herself to speak.

"You know, of course, that the purchasing and consumption of alcohol is prohibited in America, Anthony?"

"I am aware," he answered. "They call it prohibition."

"And I'm sure it wouldn't surprise you to know that many an American is enjoying alcohol, despite the laws passed."

"It doesn't surprise me." Anthony was honest in his answer. Utilising the New York Times both he and Jane had persuaded Philip to acquire, he'd kept himself firmly abreast of the battles between police and bootleggers, as well as the many raids where thousands of dollars' worth of expensive spirits had been seized. Anthony felt that it would only be a matter of time before the cinema covered the topic, with stars like Edward G Robinson assuming roles of gangsters and bootleggers running illicit empires and staying ahead of the law and rival gangs. He'd suddenly turned into a director, something that also interested him greatly.

"So, you are not surprised, and drink yourself, yet you know that drinking alcohol is illegal in America?"

"I'm not in America." Anthony answered shortly.

"Quite true," Cecile smiled patiently. Anthony felt patronised. "But the act of owning and drinking alcohol is illegal in America."

"I know that." Feeling belittled made him curt.

"But do you know if the act of sex between two men is illegal in every country in the world?"

"I beg your pardon?" Cecile's question had caught Anthony completely unaware. He stared at his companion incredulously. This was something he'd given no thought to. To the young Crawford, it was a was a crime and not something that should or would enter his life. He'd been attracted to women at an early age, which was, in his opinion, entirely normal. Many a time he'd been told about finding a girl to marry and becoming a father. Not that marriage or fatherhood had interested him greatly, but the opposite sex always had. He simply could not comprehend how one man may be sexually attracted to another. To be honest, the idea repulsed him somewhat. His mind was transported back to Mr Mills, a tutor who'd had great influence on his thinking, both academically and personally. A man of literature, he'd introduced a younger Anthony to many an author, including Arthur Conan Doyle. Also a man of devout, Christian values, Anthony recalled how Mr Mills had bristled upon mention of Oscar Wilde, describing the playwright as a degenerate corruptive pervert who targeted young men to indulge in his own twisted, immoral thoughts. The act of homosexuality was dimly viewed by the public and often demonised in written media. Anthony had never questioned it and preferred to simply go along with the notion. He'd greatly admired his former tutor and appreciated the time and interest he had shown in him. Although paid for by Philip, Anthony always felt that he went above and beyond and had a steadfast belief in his talents, although God knows what he would think of his former pupil in a place like *Sherry's,* something along the lines of, *"God created Adam and Eve, Anthony, not Adam and Oscar!"*

"Mark my words, young man, the degenerative American culture will try and infest Britain and her empire with its deviance and debauchery."

The Roaring Twenties had seen homosexuals establish a presence in places like Harlem and Greenwich Village, as well as Times Square, Anthony had known this through access to copies of the New York Times and had never questioned the negative angle in which it was documented. And why should he? The papers were printing the facts and the act was illegal.

Cecile was patient during Anthony's thought time. It was almost as though she enjoyed schooling him, like he was a project of hers. Anthony was keen to learn more about her philosophy, thoughts, life; he was infatuated with her, and she knew that.

"My point is," Cecile finished her cigarette and let a puff of smoke that Anthony thought gave her even more of an air of movie star. "You enjoy a drink, as do I, but it is illegal in another country. And yet you continue to do so."

Anthony looked at his glass. A group of musicians were setting up ready for a performance. The quintet was an all-male troupe and deep in conversation, presumably about the performance ahead.

"I'm sorry, Cecile, perhaps I am missing the point here. The consumption of alcohol in England is legal and homosexuality isn't. I don't make the rules, and I have never given it that much thought."

Cecile digested his comments. "Of course, Anthony." She

allowed him to light another cigarette for her. "But do you believe that the law will stop illegal acts from happening."

"I believe that laws protect decent people and act as a deterrent to those out to break them." Anthony felt like Philip with his comment. He didn't like that, even though he thought he believed it. Cecile seemed to be reading his mind.

"I can't help but think that is you echoing someone else's thoughts," she said.

"We don't know each other that well. Can you truly be qualified to make that assumption?" Anthony was impressed with his return. He often thought of Chaplin using his humour to deal with argument and conflict, he would use his brain. Cecile was an intelligent lady; Anthony was not used to women expressing themselves the way she did. He was intimidated, intrigued, and excited. He was also acutely aware of how correct she was that Anthony was indeed echoing the thoughts of another.

"Life isn't fair, and I'm not really concerned about that, as my situation is a very comfortable one." Cecile explained. "You are like me, darling. You see the hypocrisy of society; we just deal with it in different ways. You can either see injustice or see opportunity."

"And just what opportunities does societal hypocrisy bring? Or homosexuality, for that matter." Anthony hid his confusion. He wanted to know more and wasn't going to let Cecile lead the conversation into yet another tangent.

"Our first meeting was held in a drab, derelict building in an area away from prying eyes. Did you ever wonder why I have a place of business, there?"

"I did. But when we *sealed* our deal, I wasn't too interested as to where we were." Anthony's flirtations drew a smile from Cecile.

"Film is your great interest, correct?"

"Among other things." Anthony continued to employ a flirtatious tone.

"Combine those two together." Cecile's comment caught him off guard, but it didn't stop her following up with.

"Assuming the *other* thing is fucking me?"

Anthony had never heard a lady swear. He'd often been present around bad language on the streets of London, he and his friends frequently in awe of the men coming home from work or the public house with their rough demeanours and colourful speech. He'd assumed that taboo words were something that existed only within the languages of the working classes. But he needed to stay on track and not daydream.

"It was," he answered.

"Chaplin often intimates romance, through the medium of comedy. Many of his films involve him pursuing his interests, which are often females." Cecile was a fan or had at least a good knowledge.

"Agreed." Anthony was impressed.

"Essentially, if the camera was to remain rolling, we may just see the kind of thing you and I were engaged in earlier today?" Cecile wasn't being naughty or flippant, this was a serious question.

"I'm not overly sure the film studios and law would allow that. I read enough in the papers that paint a dim view of Chaplin, they'd crucify both him and his career if his films veered into that territory."

"But what if there was a market for that sort of thing?" Another serious question from Cecile.

"An opportunity. I see." Anthony felt he was being cryptically spoon fed the business that Cecile wanted him to be a part of. "And there is a big market for this sort of thing?"

"You'd be surprised, darling." Cecile sipped her champagne.

"So, you have a big building, away from prying eyes where you show films of a *certain* nature to those wanting to indulge their fantasies?"

"Not just a handsome face," Cecile's compliment pleased Anthony. "I knew you were the right man to recruit."

"What exactly am I being recruited for? Anthony was curious.

"I always need men of talent and experience. It is my intention to make films in the mainstream. You recognise a good actor, can recognise a good plot." She let a silence develop whilst looking intently at Anthony.

"And I enjoy your company." Cecile surreptitiously touched Anthony's leg, her look becoming seductive.

Anthony caressed her hand, but he had a question for her. "You are a woman with means, Cecile. Why not just make mainstream films? It could be something special and give opportunity to aspiring actors looking for a big break."

Cecile laughed. "The army provides opportunity, working in service is opportunity. This is a pleasurable and profitable pastime. I like to watch, as well as do, and you can never have too much money."

"So where do you find your recruits," Anthony asked. "Not something that you can simply drop into conversation."

"What do you think of this place?" Cecile answered his question with one of her own.

"It has its charms." Anthony was non-committal.

"What you saw in the corridor; *Sherry's* is a safe haven, as it were, a place where we don't judge. Criminals, police, those in society with tastes that are perhaps frowned upon in today's world."

"Illegal?" Anthony pressed Cecile.

"Quite." She replied. "But for our business, it is a happy hunting ground for both talent and customers."

Anthony was about to reply when the band suddenly came to life with a dance that encouraged patrons to move to the dance floor. The noise was a perfect excuse for Anthony to get close to Cecile.

"Our business?" He questioned.

"You are in, darling, but right now our business is dance." Cecile rose to her feet.

"Erm… I don't dance. Not m…"

"You wouldn't want to disappoint me, would you?"

Anthony was unsure if her rather pointed question was a threat or not. Right now, he didn't care.

Chapter 11

Cecile was as natural to the Charleston as she was to pleasure in the bedroom. Her effortless rhythm and sensuality meant that all eyes were on her. Anthony did his best to keep up, but his athleticism was not naturally transferable to the dance floor. He wondered how a married woman was so brazen, as to dance with another man. Even though the Charleston was not an intimate dance, Anthony was close enough to have people watching. He found his mind awash with questions. Had she been here with Robert? How many people knew her? Alfonse did for a start, but how? The clientele all had their stories to tell, but did they all have secrets to keep? "*The scandalous tales that could be told.*" Anthony was deep in thought. He quite enjoyed the notion of being part of a den of iniquity and the sight of Cecile dominating the dance floor with her mesmerising moves ensured his thoughts were lustful. With an alluring smile, her gaze seemed to evade every other person on the dancefloor, except Anthony. Males were transfixed, whilst the other women vying for attention were either insanely jealous creatures or begrudging admirers of the blonde beauty. Anthony afforded himself a moment to feel like a star. Perhaps she could get him to that next level? He had the humour of Chaplin, the athleticism of Fairbanks and could be the romantic like Valentino that made many a lady week at the knees. Anthony Crawford could be that breakthrough star that had it all and his lover would help him get there! He and Cecile would probably never be officially together, but their stolen moments and her determination and desire to have him onboard and a part in her ventures meant he was going to spend a lot of time with her. Scrumptiously, this made him the envy of many, even if those on the outside of their illicit liaison didn't realise that it was he they were jealous of.

Anthony's thoughts then turned again to what would happen if their affair were to be exposed. The social scandal, the dishonour, how would Philip react, how would Robert react?

Cecile and her husband had not long been wed. Anthony doubted if Robert would be in the mood to share his wife. This thought led Anthony to wonder about Cecile. He knew very little about her. Had she been married before? Who were her family? Would they suffer for her dishonour? Maybe they already had, and that was why Cecile mentioned them not. Perhaps she had had other affairs? Anthony's jealousy began to rise.

The music ended and Anthony chose that moment to visit the lavatory. Cecile's effortless glamour saw her remain the focal point of everyone's attention as she made her way back to her seat. He made no effort to hide his admiration as he blew her a kiss before exiting the dancefloor. He felt like a man, the lover who was on the verge of breaking free from the clutches and wishes of his stepfather, yet Philip often plagued his mind like an unwanted visitor that refused to leave. Having availed himself of the facilities, he splashed water on his face and tried to make sense of his thoughts. He stared at his reflection and flattened a rogue hair that was protruding in the wrong direction. His mother often used to say how much he reminded her of his father, in looks, traits and mannerisms. This was something she stopped once she married Philip. Anthony never asked Jane about his father, also named Anthony, but thought about him often. A factory worker, Anthony had memories of him as a large man with dark hair and a strong London accent. Also, a fan of film, Anthony's father had taken his son to the cinema, where they had enjoyed moments they both treasured. He often would chuckle when he recalled how his father reminded him of what his mother would say about sugary sweets, which Anthony knew was a clever ploy to distract him from the fact that his wage simply couldn't afford such luxuries. *"Too much sugar will rot your teeth."* His father's terrible impression of his mother would make young Anthony laugh uncontrollably and he believed it was his father from whom he had inherited his sense of humour. The lack of money for sweets aside, his teeth weren't in decent shape, something Philip had targeted when he'd insisted that Anthony visit the dentist, an experience which he'd hated, because he'd initially required a lot of treatment, but which now Anthony realised were absolutely the right thing to do. He doubted he would have attracted someone like Cecile with a smile full of broken or missing teeth.

So entrenched in his thoughts and his determination to ensure that his hair was perfectly presented, he'd not realised that one of the cloakrooms behind him was occupied. Drying his hands with a thick, rough towel, he turned round to see Alfonse in front of him. Anthony was immediately defensive in his stance, despite having at least four inches in height on the waiter. Alfonse's dark gaze stared blankly at Anthony, who wondered what he wanted. Thinking back to what he'd seen in the corridor upon his arrival at the club, his mind wandered into the realms of worry. He didn't physically fear Alfonse, but he didn't want to become embroiled in a fight of any sort. He sidestepped out of the way of the sink and proceeded to leave.

"She will eventually destroy you." Alfonse declared in an accent which Anthony believed was European.

"Excuse me?" Anthony tried to emphasise masculine depth in his voice, but his irritable surprise meant the question had come out a little higher pitched than he wanted.

"She's so beautiful, but the only thing that matches her beauty is how dangerous she really is." Alfonse moved to the sink to wash his hands.

"I think you should realise your place," Anthony turned to face Alfonse, who now had his back to him. "It is not customary for a waiter to speak to a guest in this way. But if you have something to say then please, get it off your chest."

Alfonse remained emotionless. He dried his hands and turned to leave. "Don't say I did not warn you."

"I haven't got the time to play cryptic games with you," Anthony remembered his status and for once, was grateful to the class structure he was now part of which meant in terms of the conversation Alfonse had instigated, Anthony had every right to be insulted and take whatever course his hurt feelings demanded. Blocking the waiter's path to the door, he said, "You dare to accost me in this way then leave. I don't think so."

"Sir, let me pass."

"Not till you tell me why you dare to speak to me in this way, and why you should cast aspersions as to the good character of my companion! Mrs Ford is a business colleague, and we are out for the evening. Not that it is any of your business." Anthony's voice was now more of a growl. "Now, tell me what you mean."

Alfonse laughed nervously. "She has a number of *colleagues*." His tone was sarcastic. Anthony failed to understand the import or chose not to.

In response, he struck Alfonse square on the jaw with his right hand. A boxing fan, he was sure that heavyweight champion Jack Dempsey would have been proud of that punch. Alfonse crumpled into the corner. Standing over the waiter's dazed form, Anthony weighed up the merits of continuing his questions once Alfonse came to. There was a sudden sound of clapping, which caused him to swirl around. Standing at the door was a man sporting a huge moustache, peak cap, and long overcoat. "Very impressive," said the man in a strong, Midland accent. "You a fighter?"

"Only when I have to be," replied Anthony, still high on adrenaline. He knew that he didn't have to be on this occasion but his temper and desire to defend Cecile's honour have got the better of him.

The man laughed heartily. "Well, have a good evening. I'd get moving though, those two gentlemen on the door don't seem to be the friendliest, as you'd expect."

"Thank you. Enjoy your evening also." Anthony looked over at Alfonse, who was still on the floor but moving.

"He'll be fine," the man said as he adjusted his cap. "Not sure if he'll remember much though." His laugh rang out as Anthony left the toilet quickly.

Anthony's mind was racing. He was trying, in vain, to make sense of what happened. The second and third knuckles were smarting from where he struck Alfonse. He had so many questions that needed answering and only one person could do that. He purposefully marched across to the table where the alluring Cecile was enjoying the music and another cigarette. Her smile when she saw him was quickly replaced by surprise when she noticed the look on his face.

"Anthony?"

"Alfonse!" Anthony said bluntly without sitting down. "The full story, now."

Cecile's surprise turned to sorrow. Her eyes filled with tears as she averted his gaze. "Can we leave, Anthony? Please!"

Chapter 12

Anthony stood in the foyer of The Grand Hotel and looked at Cecile. As she had asked him, he had left the nightclub, *Sherry's* and been dropped off at the Lowood Lodge, a more inferior hotel to the one in which he now stood, but necessary to not cause any suspicion about their relationship. Once he'd arrived at Lowood, he waited until Cecile and her driver were out of sight, before beginning a brisk walk to the Grand, and hence where he stood now, sweating profusely and slightly out of breath. And it had worked, to a certain extent.

The journey back from *Sherry's* had been quiet, awkward, and somewhat surreal. Cecile had been silent, speaking only to bat away Benson enquiring if his employer was alright. She'd been abrupt and brief, staring straight ahead with a glazed look in her eyes. Anthony felt guilty. He'd come on too strong and made her feel like the accused when something was clearly amiss with the situation. Alfonse's comments had cut to the bone, he'd demanded answers from her and had not considered her feelings or reaction. She'd not looked at Anthony once. Her hurt feelings were palpable, but for once, despite his guilty conscience, Anthony didn't care – he wanted answers.

Anthony had watched Benson speed off with Cecile in the rear of the car. She did not look back and the beady little man hadn't had the grace or the manners to ensure Anthony was inside the hotel safely before departing.

The Lowood Lodge was more like a big house than a hotel. Clean and tidy on the outside, with a simple front door, as opposed to the huge, well-lit entrance complete with footman welcoming guests which was what awaited him at The Grand, where he hoped to be spending the rest of the night and early morning. Turning away from the modest building and the small sign that let people know of its existence, Anthony began his walk back to where he hoped Cecile would be waiting.

Without a coat, the scarf was little more than decoration. He utilised it as best he could, wrapping it around his neck to stave off the biting night air. His strides were long and purposeful, his feet making crunching sounds on the gravel pathway as he ate up the ground like he devoured Mrs. Blackshaw's apple crumble and wondered if the evening would end as sweetly as the culinary delight tasted.

Anthony kept his head down as he walked. Part of this strategy was preservation against the cold, although he wasn't completely sure he wouldn't be recognised by someone, albeit the chances being slim. And why would he want to make eye contact with anyone on the streets? There was a lot on his mind, as it tossed and turned about how he would confront Cecile. Alfonse had touched a nerve and he needed to know what the exact story was between the two. He knew he needed to keep his temper and jealousy under control, his traditional approach and aggressive demands had only succeeded in upsetting Cecile, and that was the last thing he wanted to do. He was smitten, and she knew it, as much as she knew she was in control. Like a skilful detective or diligent actor, she knew or at least deduced a lot about Anthony and held all the cards. This was something that didn't overly bother Anthony's masculinity, but it did mean he was always chasing the conversation whilst she dictated. He pondered humour; Chaplin's slapstick worked well onscreen. Many a picture saw the actor amble his was through a number of awkward situations against his protagonists and love interests. Could Cecile be both? Was this a game to her? Was Anthony a mere instrument of pleasure and amusement whom she could manipulate and toy with whenever she pleased?

Anthony scolded himself. His emotions were usually extreme, but this night had been as such a mixture of pleasure, intrigue, curiosity, rage, and now fear. He needed to take control of himself, and he allowed the frigidly frosty night air to act as a cleanser to all his thoughts. The Grand was in sight, and, although Anthony suspected that his evening's taxi driver would already believe his employer's new business associate had less than honourable intentions, equally, Anthony didn't believe

Benson would rock the boat where Cecile was concerned. Formidable, as well as possessing looks that would melt even the toughest of the silver screen's directors, Anthony reasoned that most who got on the wrong side of his lover probably lived to regret it.

Once inside the huge double doors and being greeted by the hotel footman, he thought about how busy the evening was still, despite the lateness of the hour. He was unsure of the exact time but thought it around midnight. The area was affluent, filled with enormous houses with imposing facades and the streets, as Anthony had made his way to the hotel, were still alive with conversations held by mainly well-dressed couples who had enjoyed various entertainment throughout the evening. Now, he pondered his next move. An incredibly well-dressed man in a dinner suit that screamed Saville Row rushed past him, accompanied by a slender beauty who was at least twenty years his junior. He was tempted to enquire the time as the man took out his gold pocket watch, but instead had a chuckle to himself, knowing the man was using it as trinket to impress what looked like his mistress. Watching the duo hurry past the door attendant, the same one who had been on duty when Cecile and Anthony had left for *Sherry's*, Crawford thought about how people would perceive both he and the beautiful Mrs Ford's liaison. It was far more acceptable in society that a rich, older man would pursue younger love interests whilst the wife sat at home and ran the house. Cecile was different, though. A woman ahead of her time who didn't consider herself equal to men, rather superior to them. The conventions and etiquette of the society she inhabited were merely obstacles to be overcome, she had her own vision of the life she wanted.

A woman ahead of her time, thought Anthony.

He reached the door and noticed that the attendant was looking the other way. Anthony's paranoia kicked in. Was his working-class background showing through despite his obviously expensive clothes, and that fact that he could afford to frequent such an establishment as the Grand? Crawford had yet to learn that money didn't make the man. Either way he didn't care, conversation with a doorman was not high on Anthony's priority list. Looking around the reception area, Anthony's eyes drank in the scene before him whilst he admired the huge, crystal chandelier that shone a shimmering myriad of light below it. The red carpet, the extravagant and extremely expensive gold flocked wallpaper that adorned three of the walls whilst the wall which housed the largest and most ornate marble fireplace that Anthony had ever seen, was painted a fiery red to match the carpet. Huge pillars held up the foundations and the décor on the ceiling put Anthony in mind of the *Sistine Chapel*, though Michelangelo's masterpiece was something he'd not seen.

The couple who'd hurried past him on the steps had just collected their room key and were heading to the stairs. The lady linked the man's arm, as he made brief small talk that Anthony couldn't hear. Long sofas and elegant armchairs were scattered around the foyer, each creating a little trio on either side of a glass and gold effect coffee table. One of the long sofas contained Cecile, who had already noticed Anthony and was suddenly on her feet, rising with a calculated finesse that try as he might, Anthony would never possess. She had her place within the upper echelons of society, he was a mere intruder. She still looked as fresh as she had when she emerged from the bathroom ahead of their evening. If she'd been crying, her makeup didn't show it. She made her way through the doors which led to several flights of stairs. Anthony followed his lover. Her room was on the first floor, the corridors and stairwells were well lit, the red carpet of the reception gave way to a more muted, thick maroon carpet which felt comforting underneath their feet. Anthony's gaze never left Cecile; he admired her figure and felt his lust rise but knew he needed answers to his questions. He was still unsure as to how she would greet him when they were in private, but he would soon find out. She glanced back at him at the top of the stairs, before turning right and making her way to her bedroom. The lock made a loud click as it was turned, Cecile walked in leaving the door ajar for Anthony, who pondered Chaplin's funny walk as he approached, but decided against it. Humour wasn't the tonic needed for this, but he was an actor at heart and film was his happy place that relaxed him. And he needed to be relaxed if he were to get the answers he wanted.

Pushing the door and entering with a confidence he didn't have, he stared at Cecile, who was standing by the window but looking at him, her liquid eyes returning his gaze. Anthony took a deep breath, noting the room was lit only by a bedside lamp which he thought created a mysterious, romantic ambience. But this story needed answers. He needed answers. Removing his scarf and throwing it across the armchair to his left, Anthony said only one word to his lover.

"Alfonse?"

Cecile's expressionless look changed as she moved toward Anthony. Having taken off her shoes, she moved far more quickly than Anthony had surmised and the initial slap to his face took him unaware. Regaining his composure quickly, he blocked the next blow and managed to grip her wrists.

"Cecile, what is this!" Anthony's confusion was met with silence. Her eyes were wide, her expression troubled, bewildered almost. He'd never seen Cecile like this. She continued to struggle but his physical strength was too much for her. He pushed her towards the bed, her slim body fell onto it, and she made no effort to get up, whilst he made no movement towards her. His heart was pounding, and he was in shock. So, the mention of Alfonse touched a raw nerve; he knew she was feisty but didn't see her as a physically violent woman. Why had the name caused such a reaction from her? What was going on between her and Alfonse? Anthony stroked his face and wondered if a mark would show. The blow was well placed, and his cheek stung beneath his fingers. Cecile sat up but did not get off the bed. For one crazy moment, Anthony's thoughts went to the Wild West, as though they were two gunfighters scared to blink first, although to his knowledge, Cecile was not armed.

Anthony chose to break the silence. "I'm not going to hurt you; I simply want answers. Which is hardly unreasonable given what has occurred this evening."

Cecile rose from the bed and grabbed Anthony's shirt. He was ready this time and took hold of her wrists again. "Cecile, please!" She didn't speak, nor struggle, just lay her head against his chest. "Cecile," Anthony started. "We need to talk."

Silent, Cecile began kissing his neck. He let her wrists go and noticed the bright red marks his big hands had made. She began to unbutton his shirt. He got hold of her hands and stopped what she was doing. "I need to know about Alfonse!" He could hear the desperation in his own voice.

Breaking her silence, Cecile grabbed his crotch, replying, "And I need to know about Anthony, again."

They embraced passionately, frantically undressing each other, and exploring each other's bodies. If this was another of Cecile's ploys to stop Anthony's questions, it had worked, at least for now. Her look, her seductiveness, her intelligence, Anthony was ultimately powerless to resist.

Chapter 13

"Alfonse is a very jealous, vindictive individual."

Cecile's sudden statement smashed through Anthony's train of thought as he lay flat on his back next to his lover. He'd just been enjoying replaying the moments of their lovemaking; Cecile had been very attentive and held him tight. Their earlier trysts had been very much on her command, the older, more experienced woman leading proceedings and ensuring that her pleasure was very much, first, and foremost. The Cecile that Anthony had experienced now seemed to take comfort from his body, almost as though she wanted protection just as much as pleasure. He turned his head and looked at her. She was smoking a cigarette and gazing up at the ceiling above.

"Of me?" Anthony replied. Cecile looked puzzled; Anthony rephrased his question. "What is it Alfonse is jealous of? Is it me?"

"He is jealous of much, Anthony," came the enigmatic reply.

"We need to begin at the beginning. How well do you know him? My thoughts are you know him a little better than simply waiter to customer. As beautiful as you are, Cecile, that kind of relationship hardly warrants Alfonse confronting the man you are accompanying in the bathroom of the establishment of which he is employed!"

Cecile let out a long sigh, exhaling a cloud of smoke. Her hand stroked Anthony's arm and an awkward smile crossed her face.

"Did you and he have a.... thing?" Anthony didn't quite know to word his question but would not stop until he had answers.

"No, darling," Cecile turned to him, with a beseeching look. "But that did not stop him from wanting it."

"Did he hurt you?" Anthony struggled to keep the anger out of his voice. He found it strange that he believed her so readily.

"No." Cecile stroked Anthony's arm again and kept her gaze

firmly on him. He let his fingers wander through the tangle of her hair and returned her look, his eyes softer, although his face was emotionless. He imagined himself cast in a role for a film that required an emotionless actor. So many questions and scenarios invaded his mind like a plague of locusts, but Cecile was talking, and he sensed he was about to learn more.

She looked away from him as she spoke, almost as though she were ashamed of what she was about to tell him. "You see, I was a dancer at *Sherry's*. Dancing the Charleston brought back so many memories. I felt so free, so happy knowing that people would watch me and admire my work. Alfonse was a merchant seaman who, like so many, arrived on our shores looking for a job." Cecile paused to take a long puff on her cigarette.

"Go on." Anthony's tone was assertive but not impatient.

"He spoke reasonably competent English and was an industrious worker. He was happy doing any job, so he was quickly in permanent employment. I was always nice to him as he was nice to me." She turned back to Anthony. "We were only friends. At least that is what I believed."

"And he wanted more?"

"In more ways than one," Cecile answered. "Alfonse was, is, an extremely ambitious man who is not the most patient of people, nor the greatest respecter of all that is legal. You've seen what goes on in *Sherry's;* people come to be themselves. It is almost a door to a world where law, moral fibre, and societal protocol cease to exist. And with that, Alfonse spotted an opportunity."

Anthony leaned forward and kissed Cecile's cheek. "I'm listening."

"Many a patron in that place is a *happily* married someone who goes there to get away from the strains of said married life."

Anthony nodded.

"Alfonse had a plan where he would use me to entice men into compromising positions and use that leverage to illicit money or he'd tell the poor, unsuspecting spouse just exactly what her beloved husband was up to." Another puff on the cigarette. She continued, "The plan was idiotic; he stole some sort of contraption which he believed was a camera but didn't know how to use it. I was not interested in his plan, but he insisted I was the only one he trusted. Every day, he'd have some new idea or fresh information about how his plan would work and how he could use the camera. But by then I was making plans for leaving *Sherry's*."

"Robert?"

Cecile nodded and smiled. As if she knew the next question that was coming.

"Did you meet Robert there, whilst you were dancing?"

"What can I say, my husband clearly loves the Charleston." Her confidence and old self seemed to be returning.

"I did not envisage that place as Robert's idea of entertainment." Anthony was genuinely surprised.

"What can you actually glean from someone after one dinner party?" Cecile questioned him. "From what I remember he was the person whom you spoke to the least. And he does love the Charleston."

"You are correct," admitted Anthony, recalling the dinner party at the Crawford household where he had first encountered Cecile. How long ago it seemed! "So, I take it Alfonse was not too keen on your plans?"

"He'd seen Robert and I together. He was more crushed than angry. I told him of my plans, and he refused to speak to me. Robert knew something was wrong and a conversation was had which resulted in some thugs beating Alfonse quite badly. Robert knew that an immigrant would not report it, who would believe him anyway."

"And Alfonse reasoned that it was you that had orchestrated the attack?"

"Yes, Anthony. What he never knew, though, was I stopped Robert from going further and ruining his life completely. I am a little stupid, I think. I kept going to *Sherry's,* even after Robert had forbidden it. I find the lifestyle, the freedom, extraordinary. There, people can be themselves instead of what society expects of them."

"Why, Cecile? Why keep going back to somewhere a

potentially dangerous man, at least dangerous to you, would be working, knowing full well you would come into contact with him?" Anthony again tried to keep anger from his voice. This time, he was not as successful. He did not know it at the time, but there was something that didn't quite ring true, although he would never admit to Cecile, or even to himself, that he thought she was lying.

"I don't know, Anthony." Cecile's eyes filled up. "I wanted to show him, rub his nose in it, show him how well I'd done!" Her hand went round the back of Anthony's head as she ran her fingers through his hair. A tear rolled down her soft cheek. Anthony delicately wiped away the drop of water with all the tenderness of a man who was as devoted to his lover's features and feelings as Picasso was to his art. He reasoned that it would be a suitable time to interject some humour into proceedings.

"I'm flattered you view me as a sign of doing well." Chaplin himself would have been proud of that line, he thought.

Cecile laughed through her tears. She rested her head against his chest. "I am sorry, darling. It wasn't my intention to use you as a way of getting back at him."

"No harm done," whispered Anthony. "And nothing permanent to Alfonse, either." His sudden sting on two of his right knuckles reminded him of his earlier altercation. Cecile laughed again. Anthony's comedic performance was right on point. His expression suddenly turned more serious. "You don't think he would try anything? I mean, try to damage your reputation and life?"

"Alfonse is not a man of violence. More a coward in the shadows looking to use leverage to get what he wants. I'm astounded he confronted you if I'm honest." She positioned herself so that she was now lying on her front. "And I am exceedingly flattered that you defended my honour." Her smile grew seductive.

Now it was Anthony's turn to laugh. He got out of bed and proceeded to the ensuite bathroom. Turning his head back to Cecile, he said: "Shan't be a minute."

In the bathroom, he laid his head against the coolness of the mirror above the sink. He needed to think. He knew he was into something that was probably going to prove too much to handle, but his sense of danger and desire to escape his boring existence, coupled with his uncontrollable lust and passion for his lover was far too strong for him to simply call it a day. And making love to a beautiful woman was beyond the wildest dreams of a former working-class boy who was destined for factory life until Philip Crawford had married his mother. But she was not free. His mother had struggled all her life to make ends meet. And when she finally did, she surrendered her freedom and opinions to satisfy and placate a man whose views were so set in stone, the God Philip himself professed to follow, wouldn't change his mind. Perhaps this affair and business venture with Cecile – though still getting to grips the latter and not comfortable with the legalities of her proposal – would give him the freedom to get away from the financial and emotional clutches of Philip. Though he often complained, Anthony's stepfather provided an allowance which was more than enough for the young man to enjoy himself. But Anthony wanted independence. The overwhelming sense of confliction frequently consumed his thoughts, he wanted to be free of them by being his own, independent man. Cecile seemed to embody everything he ever wanted. He couldn't just give that, or her, up.

And would she even allow that? Anthony was of the opinion that Cecile had a habit of getting what she wanted when she wanted. The more he saw and experienced her, the stronger that thought grew. He'd seen a more vulnerable side this evening, but he understood she was a beautiful force to be reckoned with and he would much rather be on her side. And in her bed. He was looking forward to chatting with Harry as soon as possible. He knew his best friend would provide insightful opinions as well as wise words and, whilst he didn't agree with everything he may say, he knew that Harry genuinely cared for him as a sibling would. Plus, he knew that the young Mr. Hewson-Greaves would be keen to share in his adventures, and tonight had certainly been one of those.

Anthony could hear Cecile moving around in the bed. He

turned away from the mirror, completing his toilette before returning to the bedroom. Pondering many thoughts, his mother was the most prominent. How had Jane fared being away with Philip? Had they settled their differences during their break away? Anthony was unsure if it would make any difference. His depiction of married life had derived from his mother's union to her second husband. With few memories of her marriage to his father, all young Crawford knew of marriage was what Jane and Philip had, and he wanted no part of it. This liaison with Cecile would probably have no long-term future, but Anthony would most certainly enjoy the present. He wanted to live life, and she was an enabler. She was smart, there was no way she would allow this to ruin her life or reputation, and with that, he would be safe too. He seemed to be making her happy and she was showing him what real life was like and the opportunities that went with it. Getting to truly know her would be a long, drawn-out pleasure, and he had all the time in the world.

His positive thoughts still floating around his head, he found Cecile sitting upright, breasts bare, smoking again. He made his way back to bed and climbed in beside her. Lighting a cigarette of his own, his next topic of conversation would be trying to discover the identity of the poet whose cryptic and unsettling message had been sent to him a few days ago.

"Any more thoughts on the author of my poem?" Anthony decided to get straight to the point, refusing to be detracted by Cecile's buoyant, delicious breasts.

"Well, it isn't Benson." Cecile was adamant, but didn't look at Anthony, who kept his gaze on her.

"How can you be so sure?"

Cecile smiled. Anthony admired her sharp cheekbones, her delightful, sculptured face which lit up when she allowed it to. "I asked him to note down *your* hotel. As well as that being a ruse to make him think that you were staying there." Anthony looked perplexed. Cecile's smile grew wider. "It was also a rather useful way of comparing handwriting."

"And I can say with all assuredness that Benson is not your author. I imagine that signing his own name would be a struggle."

"Could he have an accomplice?" Anthony was not quite ready to simply eliminate the creepy little man from his inquiries. The question caused Cecile to break out in laughter.

"Oh, darling, just because you don't like someone doesn't mean they are guilty of what you believe. Why would my driver do it? And his accomplice is whom?" Cecile looked at Anthony incredulously but gave him little time to answer.

"Benson is a useful driver and efficient servant, who does what my husband and I tell him. He is wise enough to not rock the boat and knows his place, and class."

The last part of her sentence made Anthony feel stupid, patronised, and crass. How was it that she knew what buttons to press to stop him in his stride? She certainly had brought him down to reality and now he felt like a fool, as well as a fraud. He didn't stop to think which of them had been the dancer in *Sherry's*. Who was he kidding? He was no more one of the upper-class elite that he was Charlie Chaplin playing the lead with a stunning supporting actress. Feelings of inferiority coursed through him, and no amount of acting ability could hide what he was feeling. Cecile had a hold over him and knew what buttons to press and when. The only time her guard had seemingly split was when they had just arrived in the hotel room. Anthony didn't want to upset her, he was infatuated and wanted to know so much more about her; good and bad. He knew that it was he who would have to learn to conceal his emotions rather than evoking her most raw feelings.

Cecile could see Anthony's embarrassment, watching him literally seeming to swallow his pride. She placed a hand on his knee and moved her face closer to his before whispering, "For what it's worth, I don't particularly like Benson either. But he is useful to me."

Anthony quailed inwardly. The apology he had expected had not materialised and Cecile proved herself to be as cold and brutal as her words implied. She was not in the least interested in his feelings but insofar as Benson was concerned, Cecile was right. Benson was her employee, not her friend. Anthony had blurred the lines of friendship and those in service. Probably his working-class roots coming to the surface, he thought, ruefully. Now he realised that he could like and dislike whomever he chose, but if they were in the service of the house and did their job well, then what did it matter? He didn't have to speak to them and would never socialise with them. If he were to succeed the way he wanted, if he were to fit into the echelons of society in which circumstances had placed him, he needed to be a more clinical thinker, like Cecile. It was not his fault that he had not belonged to the ruling class from birth. His humble origins had made him so set against the society that had actually afforded him the opportunity of bettering himself, so, why not truly join it! Decision made; he was prepared to be magnanimous, despite the voice in the recesses of his mind that told him Cecile had not been born into society either. So how did she fit into it better than he?

"I will get to the bottom of this, Cecile." His tone was placatory, at last, and she knew she had won.

"I sincerely hope that you do, Anthony." Cecile had finished her cigarette and was now lying down. Anthony was leaning on his elbow, admiring his lover's curves.

"I understand that we will be joining you for dinner in the coming days?" he changed the subject.

"It is customary to return an invitation, particularly after such a delightful evening spent with you."

"Just to be clear, are we talking about the dinner party at the Crawford residence or the private evening you and I have just enjoyed?" Anthony gave Cecile a cheeky wink. Cecile laughed heartily. Anthony's humour and quick wit was another thing of his that she clearly enjoyed.

"Oh both, my darling!" Cecile continued to laugh. Anthony felt a wave of affection and lust come over him. Was he falling in love with her? Had that already happened?

"You fascinate and thrill me, Mrs. Ford. Getting to you know is an absolute pleasure I'm experiencing on a level I never considered possible." They embraced and kissed passionately. It was the early hours, but sleep was the last thing on their minds.

They would both be returning to their lives soon and wanted to enjoy these stolen moments as much as possible. Anthony kissed Cecile's neck, as she shuddered with pleasure beneath him.

"Getting to truly know someone should be a slow, drawn-out, but ultimately pleasurable experience," Cecile's seductive whisper drove Anthony's passion wild. "There is much to discover on both sides, take your time."

"I will." Anthony panted whilst in the throes of extreme passion.

"I mean," Cecile continued in her sensual whispering voice. "It has not escaped my attention how good you are at pleasing me."

"I aim to please." Anthony's answers were short as his hands explored Cecile's naked body.

"I can only assume that I am not your first." The comment brought Anthony to an immediate halt. Sweat dripped from his forehead and he looked straight at Cecile and struggled to find anything to say.

"My point is, there is no need to rush the act. I enjoy being seduced and I am willing to take my time in getting to know you, I'd appreciate the same courtesy, my darling. Slow down and enjoy me." Cecile was calm and collected, but not angry. She'd, yet again, drew in Anthony and subtly conveyed her point of view in a way that was not chastising, but rather words of wisdom. Her deductive reasoning was as good as *Sherlock Holmes,* she was a beautiful force to be reckoned with.

"I suppose this is where I apologise for being a bit too hasty and insensitive?" Anthony was contrite and feeling bad. He didn't want to upset or disappoint her.

"Nothing to apologise for, darling. Merely my opinion and advice." Her comments drew a smile to Anthony's face, which was still flushed from the enthusiastic exertion that he had desperately wanted to finish.

"But if you do want to make it up to me, I can think of far better ways than simple words."

"Are you suggesting something I could purchase you for Christmas? I'm not sure how well that would be received in either home." Anthony's humour again caused Cecile to laugh.

"Oh darling, I have already unwrapped the best present and look forward to doing so on many more occasions." She pulled Anthony back towards her, the young man duly obliged his gorgeous, intelligent, and very seductive lover.

Chapter 14

Anthony looked at the barn that was once so enormous to him when he was younger. Situated at the bottom of the garden, it had once been home to several horses, although he had never really taken that much notice of them. Horsemanship was again an elitist thing, something that Anthony did not understand, and he had no desire to be thrust into a saddle, dressed in what he considered fancy dress and go jump fences and hunt foxes in the country. However, the barn had been a haven for him when life had gotten hard; many times, he'd run and hidden from Philip's temper, but it had also been a great den for both he and Harry to talk about adventures and tease the ideas of what would make a good film. Though not young children, they had enjoyed many hours in their fantasy world within the barn. Anthony found sanctuary here, as though this wooden, dilapidated building acted as a bridge between the world he and Jane left behind, and the one he now inhabited. Often reading books and penning stories, the young Crawford loved the barn and hoped it would stay here forever. He tried the huge door, which made a tired-sounding, loud creak as he opened it. The overpowering smell of old wood invaded his nostrils, and he allowed the memories to continue flooding in.

He'd arrived home a few hours ago. Wright had collected him from the station and the journey back to the Crawford house had been reasonably quick. Soames had engaged in the customary pleasantries a butler should, but Anthony had shown little interest, instead requesting to bathe and eat. A long, hot bath and one of Mrs. Blackshaw's delicious cheese and pickle sandwiches later, he was dressed in a comfortable white shirt and trousers, strolling down the garden towards the barn. Soames had busied himself with offering Anthony a jacket or coat, but the acting man of the house had politely rebuffed his offer. Soames had looked quite surprised, as the weather was still sharp and cold, but Anthony assured the butler that he simply wanted to enjoy the brisk air.

The barn now seemed out of place. Rundown and in a corner of a huge, two-acre field at the back of the formal gardens, Philip had wanted to tear it down. Still in the honeymoon period with Jane, he had been persuaded by to keep it, knowing Anthony had a deep affinity for it. Perhaps Philip reasoned that the dilapidated wooden eyesore would keep the young man suitably occupied and out of his way. Over the years, a huge oak's continued growth had covered more and more of it, which meant seeing it from the house itself was more difficult. If Anthony were honest, perhaps the foliage from the tree was the only thing keeping the barn intact.

As always, there was much on Anthony's mind, which was something that rarely rested. Cecile's comment about her not being the first person Anthony had bedded, was playing on his memory, and he couldn't get her words out of there. The female Sherlock, as he was now calling her, had yet again made an accurate deduction. She hadn't been the first he'd gone to bed with and now he was facing the very place where he'd lost his virginity. Sarah had been a chambermaid ever since both he and Jane arrived, later going on to be his mother's ladies' maid. The young Crawford's hormones were already raging as he moved toward the age of majority, which meant that the pretty servant, herself only a few years older, was the equivalent of nectar to a particularly hungry honeybee. The pubescent Anthony was developing a passion for women. Sarah reminded him of screen siren, Agnes Ayres. In truth, there was little similarity, but Sarah's piercing eyes and beaming smile always stirred something in Anthony. Always professional, she'd been polite and attentive to her mistresses' son and ensured that their time alone together was minimal. That was until Anthony turned eighteen and growing into a man. She began to notice him and his transition towards manhood. Having always gotten along, their chemistry grew as Anthony was not backward at coming forward. With Sarah in the most awkward of positions – not wanting to upset or hurt Anthony versus an inappropriate relationship with her employer's stepson – she eventually succumbed to his charms.

Their physical union was first sealed in this very barn. It had been a bright summer's day and Anthony devised some trumped-up notion of showing the maid his acting ability. He knew she also liked Chaplin; Anthony had often made her laugh with his accurate impressions of his screen hero. Soames' predecessor was losing his grip on discipline within the house, and Philp and Jane were busy enjoying drinks in the conservatory with Anthony out of sight and out of mind.

Sarah and Anthony were alone. When it became apparent to the young maid that the excuse Anthony had given her to be there was nothing more than a ruse, Sarah had tried to talk him out of acting on his desires, but in truth, she wanted him, too. Their first time together had been a passionate, but messy affair. Anthony recalled how big Sarah's breasts were and how the uniforms the maid wore certainly didn't do her figure justice. After the event, both had felt awkward, with Sarah desperately fixing her uniform and appearance before attempting to get back into the house before she was missed.

But the danger of being caught was something Anthony enjoyed almost as much as the sex itself. He'd even been so emboldened as to sneak Sarah up to his room one night. They'd made love in Anthony's bed and talked for hours afterwards in each other's arms. The next day he remembered Sarah scolding him for almost getting her caught. Anthony had done a great job of distracting the meek and placid Morgan, as his lover had frantically sneaked back to her quarters. Sarah had left not long after that encounter. It saddened Anthony, but only from the perspective that he no longer had anyone to share his sexual needs with. He had never stopped to wonder about the reason why Sarah had left. It never crossed his mind that maids left service suddenly because they had been dismissed after their master learnt of a pregnancy. Shrugging now, Anthony turned and looked at the colossal mansion, he knew that there would be no way that he and Sarah would get away with behaviour like that with Soames. Morgan had been kind, but his grip on things had loosened and Anthony had seen an opportunity to exploit the weakness, often blaming himself for the butler's retirement, which was partly true.

He definitely did have a hand in Sarah's departure. He recalled arriving back home following a game of tennis with Harry. Sarah and Jane were in the drawing room deep in conversation. Philip arrived later from a business trip, and by the evening, Sarah was gone. The only reason given was another offer of employment nearer to where she had grown up. Anthony had wanted to confront Philip about it only to be confronted himself by his mother. He recalled her words: *"The problem is taken care of. Sarah has moved on."*

"And whatever you do, do not mention this to Philip, or to anyone. Is that clear, Anthony?"

It was perhaps the only time Anthony had felt resentment towards Jane. Sarah was not a *problem,* rather someone he cared about but now, he realised he had only cared for her for his own selfish reasons. He had probably ruined her life, he thought morosely remembering he had waited for months for a letter, an explanation, but none came. It was many months before he realised that Sarah had not written to him because she had been forbidden to do so and in time he grew to believe that Jane was only trying to protect him, but the self-loathing was harder to shake. Sarah was part of the same class he'd been part of and now, simply because of his mother's marital status, he was able to mess with people's lives and get away with it. He had never wanted to make trouble for her, Anthony had simply thought with one part of his anatomy and not considered the consequences with the other.

As always, Harry had been his sympathetic ear, his voice of reason. Anthony needed to tell someone and who better than his closest friend, who possessed wisdom that far exceeded his years.

"Well, you are only human, old boy." Harry's reasoning and outlook always cheered Anthony. *"And you aren't the first, and I don't imagine the last, to have been in this situation. At least there was no husband and wife involved. Scandals of that nature bring down the most powerful of families. Might not seem like it now, my friend, but you'll get over it."*

And Anthony did, in time, or at least learned to live with it.

His involvement with Cecile was a clear indication of that, but the overriding feeling of being a flawed, two-faced individual had remained. The injustice was something he always felt he would have to battle with, in relation to how Sarah had been 'dealt with'. He knew he was the one to blame, but it had been Sarah who was punished. Sighing at the memories and the whole class thing, which had decreed how Anthony's life had not been interrupted at all by his indiscretion, but Sarah's had been ruined or at least, her career curtailed. And all because she was working class and Anthony was not, or at least was not on the outside. You can't make a silk purse out of a pig's ear, he thought. Despite the fact that Anthony's new lover was opening his eyes to a different point of view – one that she told him meant he was lucky enough to be part of a ruling, elite class now, so he might as well enjoy it – Anthony was haunted by the injustice of it all.

He took a sharp intake of the crisp, early evening air. It was dark and the lights from the house were aiding his vision. He remained in thought until a hand touched his cold back. Spinning round in shock with his fists clenched, he was both relieved and surprised to see his mother staring back at him. Jane's face was frozen in fear and Anthony was unsure if it was shock or cold that was causing her slender frame to shake.

"You frightened the life out of me, Anthony."

"Likewise, Mother. Please don't sneak up on me. A simple *hello* would have been fine."

"You were deep in thought," Jane's voice was slowly returning to normal as she continued to shiver. "Otherwise, you'd 'ave heard me say *hello* at least twice."

"My apologies. How was your weekend away? You and Philip… all well?"

"'Course we are, son. Chip off the old block, is Phillip," Jane's voice always seemed to revert to working-class type when speaking to him, which he loved. "Falling out wiv each other, it's part of being hitched, something you will learn one day."

Anthony smiled. His mother seemed in a good mood and was relaxed. Clearly, the argument he'd heard before their trip had been settled. Anthony doubted he would ever get to learn of the details but was more than content with Jane's happiness.

"And what have you bin up to while we were away?" Jane questioned her son and pulled her thick, long coat tightly around her.

"Working. I am learning a lot about the rudiments of filmmaking, editing, and other behind-the-scenes jobs. Obviously, I want to be in front of the camera, but this is a good learning curve." The lies simply rolled off Anthony's tongue. He knew his answer would mean little to Jane, who had no interest in film but would be very happy that her son appeared to be doing well.

"Excellent. I'm proud of you, son."

She wouldn't be if she knew what he was really up to and with whom, Anthony reasoned, before Jane said, "Now why don't we go inside?"

"Good idea, it is rather cold and dark." Anthony allowed Jane to take his arm as they strolled through the garden, their feet making scrunching sounds on the gravel pathways that snaked in and out of the lush green lawns. "Where is Philip?"

"Already gone to bed. It has been a long day for him." His mother's voice, he noticed, was reverting to a well-modulated upper-class drawl. He preferred her East end accent. Jane held Anthony's arm tightly. "A quick brandy and he was ready for sleep. Would you care for a nightcap before bed?"

"No thank you, Mother, I'm a bit tired myself. I think I shall follow Philip's lead and retire," Anthony did suddenly feel fatigued.

"Some other time, then."

"Definitely."

Dennehy, the under butler, was waiting at the side door of the house, but Soames lurked nearby. The former opened the door for Jane and Anthony, but it was the head of service who offered them drinks. Jane accepted a gin and tonic to be taken in the lounge, whilst Anthony politely declined and made his way to his room. Once inside the privacy of his sanctuary, he began to unbutton his shirt when he had a sudden urge to smoke. Looking for his cigarettes, he remembered that his manual striker lighter and a packet of Player's Navy Cut were still in his overcoat that was hung on the coat rack downstairs. The house was settled, apart from Jane enjoying her drink and Soames, who probably never slept anyway. Anthony slipped out of his room and crept silently towards the stairs. Despite his size, he could be quiet when walking, which was beneficial as he didn't want to wake, or at this moment, talk to anyone. Entering the reception hall, he enjoyed the feel of the carpet underneath his feet, which were shoeless. He reached his coat and found both cigarettes and lighter in the inside pocket. He was about to go back to his room but was distracted by what sounded like giggling. All the lights were out except for the lounge. Anthony had to pass by that room on his way back to his bedroom. The laughter belonged to Jane. What would she be laughing at? Anthony enjoyed that sound. His mum was relaxed and happy, the very least of what she deserved. His sense of curiosity got the better of him and he decided to peer in and check on her. Perhaps he would have that drink and share in her pleasant, happy mood. Silently pushing the door, which was already ajar, his own happiness turned to a range of emotions, including confusion, rage, and disgust, at what he saw.

His own mother and Soames in a passionate embrace. Their arms were around each other as they kissed passionately without a care in the world on a sofa he would never sit on again for as long as he lived. Anthony couldn't and didn't want to believe his eyes. He felt sick. His mother, acting like a common whore with the hired help. His own indiscretion with Sarah and his affair with Cecile briefly forgotten in his rage and disappointment, yes, disappointment! His mother was, after all, the person he loved and respected most in the world and now, now, he knew she was merely human. A fraud. And Soames! What of him? Why him? Anthony's legs were like lead but he moved as quickly and silently as he could back to his room, his mind ablaze with the scene that he would not forget for a long time.

Why would his mother do this? With Soames of all people!

Chapter 15

Harry pressed his foot down on the accelerator. He was unsure as to where he and his passenger was going but knew damn well that his best friend needed a change of scenery if he were to open up about exactly what was bothering him. Anthony had turned up at Harry's family home in a forlorn state. Polite as always, the normally loquacious Anthony had been very quiet, confining his answers to one word only, if possible. Harry had suggested a drive, convincing his father that a test drive in the Rolls Royce Silver Ghost Open Tourer would be hugely beneficial if they were to get ahead of the competition in terms of perfection and performance. Anthony had always marvelled how Harry had almost a sixth sense in knowing how to perfect an engine and spot the flaws and subtle differences between rival models. He didn't understand it in the slightest but admired his friend's gift.

He had not shaken the cold that had been so evident to Anthony when they had last spoken on the telephone. Though not an overly cold December day, the wind was biting and both men were beginning to think that a soft top vehicle, though a showy and decadent vehicle, was not the most sensible of choices for the time of year.

"You still have that cold, Harry." Anthony stared straight ahead, his mind on many things.

"Time of year, old boy," Harry's reply was nonchalant. "And I'm not sure that my wellbeing is the biggest concern at this moment in time." He made a left turn and didn't force the issue. Anthony glanced over at his friend but didn't speak.

"Where exactly are we heading?" Harry's change of subject sparked Anthony into life.

"I'm not quite sure yet, but I suppose we will find out when we get there."

"At last," sniffled Harry. "My old friend is back with us. Missed you, old boy."

Harry could always make Anthony smile. He was his go-to when times were tough, or he felt lost, and the feeling of the latter was strong.

"Is it Cecile?" Harry was blunt in his question.

"No," came the equally blunt reply. "But that situation is playing a part in my thoughts."

"I'm sorry, old fellow, you have lost me." Harry was confused and Anthony was speaking in riddles. The young Hewson-Greaves knew very well that his best friend was sleeping with the wife of Robert Ford but was unaware as to what exactly it was that was bothering Anthony.

"Do you think I'm a hypocrite, Harry?" Anthony's question caught Harry unaware. He wiped his nose with a handkerchief from his top pocket, and sniffed again, making Anthony frown.

"What has brought this on?"

"Do you?" Anthony persisted.

"No more than anyone else." Harry looked at Anthony and was unsure if that answer had provided any comfort at all. Especially to himself.

"Every man is a hypocrite at some point in life," Harry stated. "I realise that it is difficult for you; you have been thrown into a class you weren't born into, and I know that every time you enjoy something due to your new surroundings, a twinge of guilt stings your soul." He paused before adding, "But I think there is more to this. Has your fath- "

"My mother and Soames, they were together, and I saw them. The night before last." Anthony felt a sense of relief in releasing that sentence but still felt the rise of anger and disgust upon laying his eyes on his mother and Soames in the throes of passion. Harry took the revelation with his usual, unshakeable demeanour. He'd slowed the car right down till it was crawling no faster than ten miles per hour.

"When you say *together*, you mean?" Harry nodded. Anthony understood the gesture. The two were on a wavelength that they both understood.

"Yes."

Harry was deep in thought, wondering exactly what to say

next. Anthony knew his friend was mulling over everything he had just learned. Gazing up at the dusky afternoon sky, there were few clouds, but it would soon be dark. Thinking of how he had not wished to burden Harry with his newfound knowledge, but also knowing he didn't have anyone else to turn to, Anthony sighed heavily. Cecile was not someone he knew well enough and besides, how could he tell her? In what capacity would he have done so? To everyone else, they were mere acquaintances, two people who had met at a dinner party. That aside, he didn't want Cecile to think less of his mother. Harry's long association with the Crawford family and his understanding persona qualified the young engineer as the perfect confidante, much to Harry's chagrin. He knew Anthony would always be there for him, but it often felt it was he was called upon far too often by his friend for advice on etiquette and how to deal with situations that Harry frankly thought Anthony would do well to avoid.

Harry sniffled. His cold showed no signs of easing, and he looked pale. Anthony's problems took a backseat and concern for his friend was his immediate priority. "You don't look well, Harry." The car began to move a little quicker as though Anthony's solicitousness had touched a nerve.

"Just a cold, old boy." The reply was typical Harry. An embodiment of the stiff-upper lip mentality that was renowned and respected throughout the world, according to Philip.

Harry changed the subject. "How long do you suppose this *thing* with your mother and Soames has been going on for? "And what do you propose to do about it?"

Anthony carefully pondered Harry's questions. They were heading towards the city. Rural landscape was slowly being replaced with the hustle and bustle of an urban setting. This got Anthony pondering his past, a place he had no desire to revisit and what he knew could destroy. His answer to Harry's second question suggested as much.

"I don't know, and I don't know." His reply was honest but useless.

"Have you spoken to your mother?"

"Not since it happened." That was the truth. He'd remained

in his room, feigning illness, with no one able to get even the briefest of conversation out of him. This morning had seen Anthony shower, dress, refuse breakfast and any other offers, before ordering Wright to take him to the Hewson-Greaves residence where he had, fortuitously, found Harry at home.

"Your mother is an intelligent woman," Harry began. "She knows something is up with you, you are her son. Whatever you decide to do, it needs to be decided quickly."

"Would you mind taking me to Southwark, South Pier Street?" Anthony suddenly felt an urge to go to the hub of Cecile's operation.

"Not at all, old boy. What exactly is there?"

"It was where I had my *interview* with Cecile." Anthony and Harry both smiled.

"Oh, I see. And is she at work today?"

"That is what we are going to find out," Anthony told Harry. "Unless you have other plans?"

"No, not at all," Harry answered. "I'm having dinner with Margaret tonight at her parents' residence, but I have a good few hours before I am required. I think we'll be in Southwark in about fifteen to twenty minutes."

"Thanks, Harry."

Anthony looked over at his friend. He still thought Harry looked ill and drawn, but he realised his friend was deflecting him from making further enquiries by focussing on Anthony's affairs. He gave himself a mental shrug and decided to keep on the subject of Harry's fiancée. "Things with you and Margaret going well?"

"They are." Harry's reply was abrupt and suggested the end of the conversation.

"Good."

Anthony could think of nothing more appropriate or insightful to reply with. They drove for a few minutes in silence, both taking in the change of scenery as hordes of children were walking down the dirty, cobbled streets, avoiding the filthy water that contained urine and faeces that were simply discarded into the gutter to become someone else's problem. He gazed at the women with their hair up in scarves, as they swept the pavements in vain, as though making the effort to keep them clean would act as a distraction to the broken windows and dilapidated outer layers of homes that were barely fit for purpose. Anthony wouldn't let a dog live in any of them now, he thought, forgetting how humble his own beginnings had been. He shuddered a little. There but for the grace of God I travel, he thought. It wasn't that long ago he had been one of the grimy cluster of ragged looking children dispiritedly chasing the fine, fancy car. He had once lived the way they had, in a mean little room in an even meaner street. A room where his mother had fought a losing battle with the damp and the dirt and her ability to care for Anthony and keep him clean had been hampered by the restraints which social and economic conditions had thrust upon her and her family.

"Cecile has not embroiled you in anything illegal, has she?" Harry had been mulling this question over and carefully considering its delivery.

"No, Harry, do you think I would be so stupid?" Anthony returned.

"I don't believe for one minute you are stupid, old boy. But this is a lady you are clearly taken with, and one that has opened your eyes to many things. I do worry that she will manipulate you for her own ends."

"You don't know her, Harry." Anthony was defensive.

"Correct. But she is a married woman offering another man some form of employment in regard to film, as well as mixing business with pleasure. Part of what she is doing with you is probably why you are so irate with your mother." Harry's comments stung Anthony and had touched a nerve. 'You're feeling guilty.'

"That's different," he snapped. "And I am not feeling guilty about what Cecile, and I are doing."

"How is it different?" Harry's question wasn't an easy one for Anthony to answer, so he didn't.

Anthony felt completely childish and embarrassed by his friend's question. He knew Harry was right, but his belligerence was preventing him from agreeing.

"And have you considered your mother in what you are doing? Your father is doing business with a man whose wife you are sleeping with. How exactly do you think that is going to end when it comes to light, which it will."

"We are careful." Anthony's response was paltry.

"Really? You have already told me and a man in her service has already been present when you met at the very place we are heading to now. Though in service and probably uneducated, he is not blind and most likely not stupid. You are not being as careful as you seem to think!" Harry's truth continued to sting but Anthony knew, deep down, that he was right.

"Well, you aren't going to say anything, and I highly doubt if a man employed by the Fords is going to damage their reputation." Anthony retorted angrily.

"And you are probably correct." Harry was as calm as ever. "But don't you see that your actions and the actions of your mother are not so different? Perhaps there is a touch of hypocrisy in your views regarding this?"

Anthony felt defeated. His friend had perfectly highlighted the selfish dangers of Anthony's actions as well as his hypocritical view of his mother, whom he clearly held to a greater standard than he did himself. Harry sensed that his friend was doing some internal wrestling and pulled the car over. Switching off the engine, he wiped his runny nose and let out a sigh. He looked over at Anthony, who kept his gaze firmly averted.

"Look, old boy, you are my friend. Things in life are not always how you would expect or want. I want you to be happy, I want everyone to be happy, but that is not always possible."

Anthony remained silent.

"This is the day of prosperity and hedonism for people like us, and you are now part of that elite society. But you have to realise that it is a world of hypocrisy and image. Many secrets and scandals are taking place, it is something you have to accept or run the risk of blowing many lives apart. Believe me, I speak from experience."

Anthony stared at Harry. "You do?"

Harry smiled. "Let's just say my idyllic family existence is not what it always appears to be. Though only a child, I was old enough to remember that former employee of my father who came to the door one night brandishing a baby. The clandestine chats between my parents and the chilly atmosphere that went on for what seemed like forever."

"I'm sorry, Harry." Anthony was sincere but felt useless.

"Hardly your fault," Harry's acceptance was typically Harry. "My point is, you have a choice: either raise merry hell and run the risk of ruining everyone's lives all in the sake of honesty or learn to live with things as best you can, whilst enjoying it as much as possible. You don't want to be turning a secret into a scandal now, do you? Either yours or your mothers."

Harry's impassioned speech had given Anthony a moment of clarity. He would never accept his mother and Soames, whatever that relationship was, but he needed to find a way of dealing with it before he could not hold back any longer and he let the secret out. Secrets were only secrets if no-one told and Anthony knew, eventually, that he would be the one to do the telling. That made him think of Cecile, and his own clandestine affair. He felt his heart beat a little faster at the thought of anyone discovering their liaison and how it would destroy his mother. Harry was right. His heart rate was returning to normal, and clarity was descending over him. His life was comfortable, and as long as no secrets surfaced, it would continue to be. Philip discovering what his mum and Soames were doing would be a worry, but surely, they would be careful, as they both had lots to lose.

"Do you still wish to go to Southwark?" Harry's question interrupted Anthony's thoughts.

"Would that be alright?" Anthony asked politely.

"Of course, we are not far now. I hope this discussion helped?" Harry started the car, listening to the satisfying purr of the engine before moving off slowly.

"It always does, you have a real ability to rationalise life and bring reason to situations," Anthony admitted.

"Well, we can't all be the creative types, can we?" Harry

chuckled as he delivered his compliment to his friend.

The remainder of the journey passed uneventfully. Anthony enjoyed the refreshing wind, made all the more exhilarating due to being in a car with no roof. His vanity ensured that a comb was always about his person, and he wanted to look his best for Cecile. Harry pulled up to the large, drab building and Anthony took the opportunity to restyle his hair. Thanking Harry for the lift, he was about to get out when Harry placed a hand on his shoulder.

"Be careful, old boy." Harry was solemn.

"I will, my friend," Anthony assured him.

"I know you will, Anthony. As I said, life is not all about …" Harry stopped speaking and his pale face grew even paler.

"What's the matter, Harry?" Anthony asked, as he stepped out of the car and swung the door closed. His concern for his friend had returned and it was a troubled look he gave Harry.

"Oh, er… nothing." There was none of Harry's upper-class composure as he stuttered a reply. It was as if he'd seen a ghost. "I need to go, Anthony." Spinning the car round, he sped off leaving a bemused and concerned Anthony alone. What had happened to change Harry's mood? Anthony turned around and noticed Benson staring back at him. How long had he been standing there?

Chapter 16

The temperature grew even cooler. Anthony stood and glared at Benson, who stared back insolently. His worn, brown cap obscured some of his face, but those beady eyes unsettled and annoyed Anthony in equal measures. He knew that the Ford's chauffeur would be around if he was to maintain his liaison with his lover, but he didn't like nor trust the slender little man who always seemed to be loitering in the background. Personal prejudice aside, the sight of Benson had completely unnerved Harry and Anthony was going to find out why. Taking long, purposeful steps towards the doorway where Benson stood, the heels of his expensive, shiny black shoes made a click click sound as they hit the solid paving stone beneath them. Drawing level with Benson, Anthony noticed that he was shivering, but that could be more to do with the company he now found himself in, than the weather.

"Good afternoon, Sir." Benson's thin moustache twitched at the sides as he spoke. "Is Mrs Ford expecting you, today?"

"Do I require an appointment, Benson?" Anthony's reply was curt.

"Oh no, Sir, it's just that Mrs Ford is a busy woman."

"Probably why she recruited me to her business." Anthony was trying to disguise his aggression with thinly veiled humour.

Benson chuckled humourlessly. He was blocking the doorway and Anthony was unsure if it was intentional. He moved closer to Benson, detecting a strong smell of tobacco that clung to his worn, brown jacket and matching trousers. Usually decked out in a smart uniform provided by his employers, his appearance today was far more shabby than normal.

"Not driving today, Benson?"

"Oh yes, sir," he replied. "May I enquire why you ask?"

"You are usually in your chauffeur's uniform when driving for Cec - I mean Mrs. Ford. But not today?" Anthony enjoyed playing Sherlock Holmes. He would often use the word 'elementary' shortly after reading another Conan Doyle classic, or torment Jane with his 'pure deductive reasoning'. He thought of Harry, who could be his Dr Watson, but at the moment his investigation very much centred around him.

"Oh, I see, Sir. Mrs Ford required me to move some things around inside the warehouse. I didn't want to dirty my uniform." Benson's reply was plausible but not convincing. "Shall I let Mrs Ford know you are here?"

Anthony ignored Benson's question and fired one of his own at the driver. "How exactly do you know my friend?"

Benson became obviously flustered. He looked at Anthony as the words struggled to formulate sentences. After what seemed like a long time, he said, "I'm sorry, Sir, I don't understand."

"The gentleman who dropped me off. His demeanour changed completely, and I turned around to see you looking over. Just gave me the impression that you two were familiar. Not sure how, though."

"I couldn't tell you, Sir," Benson was still flustered. "My eyesight isn't what it should be, and I couldn't really see the gentleman you were travelling with."

That sounded plausible. Benson was at least in his early fifties, but both he and Harry had seen each other before. Anthony knew this and he also sensed that Harry would be the one to speak to if he were to get to the bottom of this. What was his best friend mixed up in? He'd always been the one far more likely to air on the side of recklessness, his current behaviour was testament to that, but scandal and secrets were something he never thought Harry would be susceptible to.

"I only came outside when I heard the car." Benson was still flustered.

"Oh, don't concern yourself, Benson," Anthony told the other man, who was clearly ruffled. "I'm sure there is a perfectly innocent explanation for my friend's behaviour." He didn't believe that for a second.

"Now, please take me to Mrs Ford." Anthony was assertively friendly.

"There's no need, Benson." Cecile's voice cut right through

the atmosphere, startling both men. Anthony turned to look at his lover. Her business suit was navy blue and simple, yet she still exuded glamour and class.

"Forgive the intrusion, Mrs Ford," Anthony's tone now far gentler. "There is something I needed to discuss with you. Benson was explaining how busy you are and -"

"Oh, I'm never too busy for you, Anthony, follow me." She turned her head towards her chauffeur. "Thank you, Benson."

"Madam." Benson nodded and bowed his head slightly before taking his leave.

Anthony followed Cecile to the office where they had held their first meeting. The large, open space which formed the warehouse element of the building, was filled with at least ten people and much camera equipment. He enjoyed taking it all in. By no means MGM, the space still felt like a film set and, as a fan of the cinema, this excited him. The crowd was oblivious to him, engaged as they were in a multitude of conversations. Smoke filled the air as almost everyone seemed to be indulging. Anthony gazed over as a scruffy, black-haired man wrestled with a camera problem while a cigarette dangled from his mouth. He didn't look like a director, although Anthony was unsure what a director would look like. He noticed that Cecile had gone into the office but had left the wooden door ajar. He followed her and closed the door behind him. Moving around to her desk. she handed him a drink and invited him to sit down. Anthony didn't think this was going to end up like their last meeting in this office had. Even Cecile wasn't that brazen.

"What brings you here?" Cecile's question was brusque. He sensed that she was the person who demanded meetings, not the other way around. Well, things were just about to change!

"A compulsion to see you," Anthony replied as he sat and made himself comfortable, crossing his legs and taking a sip of the excellent malt from a crystal glass. For once, he felt in control and the power made him ebullient. "We are in business together; I want to pull my weight."

"Charming." Cecile lit up a cigarette. Anthony noticed that she had a new holder which was incredibly shiny.

"I do hope that it is not inconvenient."

Cecile laughed. "Of course not, darling. I just didn't envisage seeing you until we had dinner together in a few days."

"And as much as I am looking forward to that, it will be somewhat spoiled by the presence of your husband, my mother and stepfather also being present." Anthony's tone was jovial, and Cecile was enjoying it.

"A cross we simply have to bear," Cecile laughed softly. "Was everything alright between you and Benson? I sensed perhaps not."

"Absolutely fine," Anthony answered quickly. "Absolutely nothing for you to concern yourself with. I was making conversation – trying to make more of an effort. If being around him means spending more time with you, then that is a sacrifice I am willing to make."

"Ever the charmer," Cecile said again. "So, are you ready to see the operation for yourself?" She let out a deep puff of smoke.

"Now that would be a good idea," Anthony placed his glass on the table. "Be good to see exactly what I am getting into."

"I thought I had made that all crystal clear," Cecile's tone was seductive and aroused Anthony's passion. He got up and leaned forward towards her for a kiss but was stopped by his lover. She moved her head towards his ear and whispered softly, "Business, darling."

He laughed heartily. He was more confident in himself, but he sensed the balance of power had shifted again. She was now in command of what went on between them. This did make him want her a lot, he couldn't deny that. He opened the door for her, and she made her way into the open space. The area was vast and drab, a make-shift set was set up near the far wall, with additional lighting positioned for greater vision, which helped to relieve some of the gloominess of the whole building, which had no windows, Anthony noticed.

The colour of the walls reminded Anthony of his old Scout hut. He recalled he and Harry were sporadic members of the Scout Movement, a decision influenced by Anthony viewing a re-run of the 1911 comedy short, Charley Smiler Joins the Boy

Scouts. The titular character's overcoming of the obstacles he had faced upon joining the movement had interested Anthony, although he found the reality somewhat different. A fan of the great outdoors he most definitely was not, and the serious, regimented style of the Boy Scouts was not something that ever sat well with Anthony, whereas Harry had taken to the movement like a duck to water.

"Has the problem with the camera been fixed, Forster?" Cecile addressed the scruffy black-haired man.

"Yes, Mrs. Ford." He answered in a thick, London accent. Anthony noticed a fresh cigarette had replaced the one he had been working his way through when Anthony had entered the room.

"Positions, everyone."

Cecile's command saw the conversation stop and everyone scrambled to where they needed to be. Anthony moved towards the set to get a better look. The scene was a bedroom, the bed was placed in the middle of the set, with the usual paraphernalia set against the 'walls' – two bedside cabinets, a wardrobe, a ladder-back chair, and a chest of drawers. A young woman who was just a little bit older than Anthony pulled a set of black curtains over the painted window. Her hair was a light brown bob and she had soft features with wide eyes, painted garishly because of the studio lights. She undid her robe and removed it to reveal her undergarments, the stockings and suspenders reminded Anthony of Cecile. The girl's big, round breasts were disproportionate compared to her slender frame, but something Anthony was struggling to take his eyes off. Her legs were long and shapely. She lay on the bed as her co-star appeared. He was older with slicked-back blonde hair. He was dressed in a white shirt and grey slacks that were held up by matching grey braces. They both looked over at Forster.

"Are we ready?" asked an impatient Cecile, glancing over at Anthony, who was unsure if she was jealously watching him admire the actress or simply weighing up how he was handling proceedings.

"We are ready," replied Forster who never looked up or away

from the camera, which was large and bulky. Ever the enthusiast, Anthony thought it could be a Mitchell Standard and with the wealth he reasoned Cecile had access to, it wouldn't have surprised him if it was the real deal. Forster turned on the projector as a head in the crowd of the now dark room barked "Action!" The two stars began fornicating, she unbuttoned his shirt as he fondled her breasts and kissed her head. Anthony suddenly felt a hand explore the small of his back. Thankful it was Cecile, he smiled back at her and whispered, "I see. This is the business."

"You will see a lot more," came her cheeky, whispered reply. "I trust you are broadminded enough to appreciate what we are doing and why?"

"We all want something, why shouldn't we make money out of what other people want." As he spoke. Anthony felt like a different person. It was part of the sacrifice, he realised, suddenly. He could either join them, or be defeated by them, as he wouldn't beat them. In a swift moment of clarity, he understood that the society he was part of was laden with hypocrisy and ran by those who had, who controlled those that didn't. It was the way of the world; the balance of power would never topple over into the gutter. The glitz and glamour of the heady excesses which he had come to despise only served to emphasise the wide class chasm that existed between the haves and have nots of society. Anthony's difficulty in coming to terms with this insight came from the fact that he had once been a have not and he understood what it was like to be part of the lower echelons of the very unequal society into which he was born. The ruling classes ruled and that was all there was to it. Cecile and her ilk were making money from those who didn't have it, by inviting them to partake of the more earthy elements of the cinema, where life was very far away from that depicted upon a silver screen. Now Anthony had to decide whether to be one of those who did the telling or one of those who obeyed. He reasoned that if he was to achieve his ambition of emulating his acting hero, he would have to do and take part in things he would never speak about or be proud of. Plus, his passion and lust for Cecile were massive driving forces in his current decision-making.

The show on the makeshift set was intensifying. The actor and actress were now both naked and having sexual intercourse. The room was quiet, all you could hear was the camera and projector in motion as well as the moans from the actress as she ran her nails down her co-star's back. Anthony glanced at Cecile, who had an emotionless look on her exquisite face. He enjoyed the aroma of her fragrance, which he was close enough to catch scent of and he remained as close to her as was possible without indulging in what was being filmed.

"May we speak, alone?" Anthony whispered to her.

"Of course, darling. When this is over." Her tiny hand squeezed his as her eyes remained fixated on the show. A new actor entered proceedings as the blonde-haired man dived out of bed so he couldn't be seen. Anthony let out a confused chuckle which drew a few looks of disapproval. The new actor was older than the naked lady he was remonstrating with and was fully clothed. The acting was both hammy and over theatrical, as the woman desperately tried to conceal her lover whilst the older man continued his tirade with his co-star, questioning her as to why she was in bed and in a state of undress.

"Always good to have a bit of humour, even in the most adult of productions," Cecile whispered, her mouth close to Anthony's ear. "As I am sure you have guessed, it is a case of the husband arriving home that little bit too early and catching his wife doing something other than making dinner."

Anthony smiled and kept watching. Cecile continued, "A scenario I'm sure you appreciate." That made Anthony laugh, which earned him another round of disapproving looks.

"That's a wrap!" The words came from the same voice that had called action a few minutes before. The lights went up and the noise levels rose. A thick-set gentleman in a white shirt matted with sweat, and dark trousers, got up from a chair. His bushy moustache drooped down his round, red face and his dark eyes and several frown lines made it hard to know if he was annoyed or just permanently looked disgruntled.

"He with you, Mrs. Ford?" He nodded towards Anthony and didn't seem overly pleased to see him.

"New to the team, Mr. Pallister. Not that I have to consult you every time I recruit, of course." Cecile's answer caused a change in tone for Anthony's latest detractor.

"Oh, no, Mrs. Ford, begging your pardon, I just wondered…"

"Well, don't. Simply carry on directing. That is what you are paid for." Cecile turned and headed to the office, motioning for Anthony to follow. Pallister was busy shouting at someone else, whilst Forster continued to occupy himself with the camera.

"When can you have all that together and ready?" Cecile was standing in the doorway and directed her question at the cameraman.

"Shouldn't be too long. Couple of days." Forster was not a fan of eye contact, his devotion to his equipment was his true love.

"Shall we say tomorrow morning? Complete with the written words added in?"

"We shall." Forster seemed completely fine with the deadline his employer had just set.

Cecile walked into the office and sat on the desk. Anthony followed and took his time admiring her. Her legs crossed, she looked back at her latest employee and lover, and smiled.

"So, when am I making my debut in production?" Anthony's humour was one of a few things she admired about him.

"Darling, I am the jealous type," she laughed back. "I know your dream is to be an actor, but it is your creativity I crave, professionally."

"I'm listening, Cecile."

"The films we make, make money. This is true. But I do feel that it is the same old thing and I need an injection of fresh thinking into what we do." She poured two drinks, handing one to Anthony. "This is where I need you."

"Righty-oh," Anthony nodded. "Do tell me, Cecile, where is our market for our productions? I have always viewed England as a rather stuffy place bound by laws and censorship, with people more than happy to enforce it."

"It is all about contacts. *Sherry's* was a great place for finding someone who knows someone. If you know what I mean."

"I think I can figure it out."

"Plus, we have contacts abroad and the means to get it there," Cecile announced confidently. "My husband's business takes him around the world, and he uses means of exporting his goods abroad. Many of our films often follow him around on his travels."

She sipped her drink, which prompted Anthony to take a healthy gulp of his. Surely Robert did not know of Cecile's films?

"The French seem to be not so uptight as the stuffy English we are surrounded by. And Germany's Weimar Republic has a thriving industry with many looking to enjoy a little extra."

"Does he know?" Anthony was intrigued as to how much Robert was involved, if at all.

"Let's say he turns a blind eye to a number of things, as I do for him."

"Really. I always imagined a man like Robert Ford would be driven by uncontrollable jealousy and insist on no secrets between husband and wife." Anthony's assumption was bait for more information.

"You do not know my husband, Anthony. There is much about him that would surprise you." Cecile was almost taunting her younger lover as she got up from the desk and edged closer to him.

"Such as?"

"Oh darling, always so impatient, and impetuous in your thirst for knowledge. Don't you enjoy a bit of secrecy?"

"It all depends on who it is with," Anthony faced Cecile. He was desperate to kiss and make love to her, but it wasn't going to happen today. He knew that much.

"Life is a game, Anthony.You and your parents are dining with us this week. Outwardly, it is two very well-to-do, happily married couples, and you, enjoying each other's company with some excellent wine and food. You know that it is all a façade, as do I." She leaned in closer. "And I know that you enjoy the danger, that feeling of power that you physically possess another man's wife when his back is turned, whilst all the time politely pretending to enjoy his company like the gifted actor you are."

"I love you!" Anthony blurted out along with a deep breath he'd been holding for what seemed like an eternity.

Cecile, completely unfazed by Anthony's revelation, kissed his cheek. "Silly boy. Love is such an overrated, pointless emotion."

Chapter 17

Anthony marched through the door and was greeted by Soames. He could barely look at the man he now had even more reason to hate, and he ignored the butler's customary pleasantries together with information about where his mother and Philip would be. The journey home had been one of wrestling with how he would act when seeing his mother. He would have to speak, as he had hardly been in her company since seeing what he so desperately wanted to unsee. Benson had been instructed to drop him home. They had not spoken, although Anthony had considered grilling the chauffeur on Harry again but feared Benson's evasiveness and protestations of ignorant innocence would only incense him. Harry would have to wait, as his mother and Soames were a more immediate problem and one that he would soon be facing.

He'd broken his silence when instructing Benson to stop the Rolls Royce before entering the drive. He wanted to walk the quarter-or-so mile and didn't want the suspicious little driver to drop him at the entrance door. For some reason, Anthony wanted to keep Benson away from his home, his personal space. Stupid, he acknowledged, because the chauffeur had obviously driven his employers right up the gravel swept driveway to the magnificent entrance portico when his employer and his wife had attended dinner with the Crawfords a few weeks ago. But Anthony had long since stopped trying to analyse himself and his feelings. Or rather, he didn't want to, because if he did, he might discover things about himself that he did not want to.

The night, when the Fords had come to dinner, had changed everything for Anthony.

He found his mother in the drawing room. Dressed in a pale blue, flowing dress, she rose from her chair and enthusiastically hugged her son. He held her tightly. Anthony loved his mother, nothing was going to change that, but he was still disgusted by what he'd seen. It wasn't so much the act, but rather her choice of co-star. Harry's words had stung him, but he was quite correct. Both the actions of he and his mother could potentially destroy marriages and lives; nevertheless, he did need to know how long this thing with Soames and Jane had been going on, and why it had started. This would be information his mother would not want to discuss, but Anthony's nature and his desire to understand were going to be too much to resist.

"I have been worried about you Anthony," Jane commented, in a slightly raised tone . "You have hardly said a word to me the past day or so, where have you been today?"

"Harry's," Anthony was partly truthful. "I've had a few things on my mind and have not been feeling well, though I do feel better now. Drink?"

"I have one, son." Jane motioned to a delicate crystal sherry glass. "I'm glad you are feeling better. Are there still things on your mind?"

Anthony was sure that Jane was fishing for information as mothers often do regarding their children.

"Where's Philip?" Anthony ignored Jane's question by asking one of his own.

"In the lavatory. Is everything alright, Anthony?"

"Fine, Mother." He rarely used the word, *mother*, and Jane knew that. "I just wanted to speak with you alone."

"Oh, sweetheart, you can speak to me and Philip. He's a decent man and he's trying."

"I appreciate that, but I do think, or rather know, that this would be better discussed alone." Anthony had poured himself a large whisky and was looking directly at his mother whilst hearing the clipped tone of his own voice.

Jane began to speak but was interrupted by Philip returning to the room. His suit was buttoned, and his tie impeccably knotted, as always. This was a man who was alien to relaxation.

"Anthony, my boy," he was unusually cheerful and friendly. "Feels like it has been a while since I have seen you. I trust you are feeling better?"

"Much better, thank you. How are you?"

"I'm very well," he answered cheerfully. "A break away with

your wonderful mother was the perfect tonic. Back to it now, though." He sipped his drink, also what looked like a sherry. "How are your prospects on the work front?"

"Positive. I am part of a company that makes lower-budget films. It is more behind the camera work, but I am learning a lot." Anthony's answer mixed truth and deceit with the same flair Mrs. Blackshaw would mix the ingredients for one of her delicious cakes. The analogy suddenly made the young man hungry. "What is for dinner?"

"Beef," answered Jane. "A fine fillet that I trust you will enjoy."

Anthony smiled at his mother, whilst Philip was still interested in Anthony's employment prospects.

"Is there much in the way of a future in this?"

"Oh, Philip darling, Anthony is doing something that he enjoys and is learning." Jane squeezed her husband's hand.

"I believe there is, Philip," Anthony replied to his stepfather's comment with confidence. "It is a growth industry that is expanding rapidly. Who knows, there will probably be a day in the near future where we see a film with sound other than the music that plays over the visuals."

Jane looked impressed whilst Philip was displaying a look of scepticism. "Well, if it is a steady job with prospects then good luck to you. Now I wonder how long dinner will be, I'm starving." Philip's mood always worsened as hunger took control. Jane commented on it.

"Let me get you another drink. Dinner shan't be too much longer, and it is always worth the wait."

"Of course, my love." Philip watched his wife pour him a sherry. An odd smile adorned his face. Smiling was something, like relaxation, he was also a stranger too. Anthony felt that the two of them were putting on a show, almost forcing this happiness.

"I wonder what we'll get tomorrow?" Philip's question was about food, Anthony assumed.

"Tomorrow?" Anthony looked at both Philip and his mother, the latter handing the former his drink.

"The Fords have invited us to dinner," Philip reminded him. "All of us. I trust you have no plans, or is your new job requiring you in the evenings?"

Anthony was unsure if Philip thought he was being humorous. As it happened, he didn't have any plans but had genuinely forgotten about the invitation. Whilst he longed to see Cecile as much as possible, an evening of watching her play the role of the dutiful wife was not something he wished to see. He would have to attend; he was resigned to that. He would simply think of the awkward situations that Chaplin turned into comedy gold, as well as the next stolen moment with Cecile.

"As it happens, I have no plans and that sounds delightful." A mixture of truth and lies were in Anthony's answer, again.

"Well, that is settled, then." Philip finished his drink just as Soames appeared. Anthony gave the butler a sour look, as he addressed the master of the house.

"Excuse me, Sir, dinner is served."

"Excellent! Thank you, Soames. Mrs. Blackshaw is a marvel, but she does take her time."

"Apologies, Sir." Soames' replies were so well rehearsed.

Anthony alternated furtive glances between Soames and his mother. Neither seemed to be making eye contact with the other. The weight of knowing what he knew was a pressure Anthony was not used to. He gulped down his drink, which drew a comment from Philip.

"Thirsty, boy?"

"I am, Philip, and hungry." Anthony's reply was matter of fact.

"Great minds! I am looking forward to dinner." Philip stood up and headed to the dining room. Soames held the door and waited for Jane and Anthony.

"That's quite all right, Soames." Anthony took the door, letting Soames know that he could move away.

"Oh, I…" Soames was flustered for the first time Anthony had seen.

"Thank you, Soames," he said, bluntly. "I am quite capable of holding a door."

"Very good, Master Anthony." Soames moved off, rather quicker than usual. As Jane walked past Anthony and out of the door, her son got hold of her arm. His grip was light, but it made her stop.

"Anthony?" Jane looked puzzled.

"I know, Mother."

Jane stood silently as though she had heard something so shocking it had rendered her speechless. Anthony let go of her arm, but his gaze was firmly locked on her. He patiently waited for her response.

"I do not know what you think you know, Anthony, but I am growing tired of these moods and cryptic games. Maybe you don't know as much as you think you do."

Now it was Anthony's turn to look puzzled. Was Jane double-bluffing her son or talking about something completely different? Was she aware of what Anthony had seen or blissfully ignorant?

"We live a good life. You have wanted for nothing since Philip came into our lives. And I have always protected you and tried to encourage your interests. I don't appreciate being accosted by anyone, least of all my son," Jane looked hurt but determined. "Maybe you need to do some growing up."

Anthony was boiling up. He'd decided that Jane had no idea Anthony knew about her and Soames. If only she did, would she be lecturing him as though he were a five-year-old child? He suddenly had an urge to blurt out everything and see the reaction but thought of Harry's advice and elected to keep his counsel. Anthony had handled the situation wrongly, and he knew it. He didn't want to hurt his mother, the only person who had always been there for him.

"I'm sorry, Mum," he said, solemnly. Jane noticed she had become 'Mum' again but did not pass comment. Internally, she was just grateful for Anthony's volte face.

"And I forgive you, my beautiful boy." Jane reached up to give her much taller son a kiss on the cheek. "Now let's go and enjoy a nice dinner. I remember you as a small child, I'd often worry if we'd eat at all, let alone have our evening meal cooked for us."

Anthony smiled at his mum. "You never let me down," he said.

"And I never will." Jane turned and made her way to the dining room. Anthony stood alone with his thoughts. The thing was, whatever was going on with his mother and the vile butler meant that Jane *was* letting him down but just didn't know of her son's knowledge of the situation. Anthony slowly proceeded to the dining room. He could hear Dennehy pushing the trolley and could smell the wonderful aroma of that fillet.

Sitting himself down in his usual position at the table, he thanked Dennehy for pouring the expensive claret into his glass and for the food on his plate. He didn't want to give this up, why should he? He knew that the situation between Jane and Soames was something he could not simply ignore.

There was only one thing for it: he had to get rid of the head of service!

Chapter 18

Despite having cleaned the car to a high standard for as long as Anthony could remember, Philip had insisted on checking Wright's work ahead of the evening's trip to the Ford residence. Anthony's stepfather was a mixture of excitement and nerves, and it was manifesting itself into an inability to sit still in the Rolls Royce and a continual asking of Jane if she was all right. His wife was her usual quiet self, customary of her when she was joining company. Jane was favouring dark colours this evening and looked elegant in her long-sleeved gown and fur coat. Her hair was neat and tidy, and she sat with her legs crossed by her husband, who was fighting a losing battle at keeping still. The look in her eye suggested that, no matter what she wore, her younger, more glamorous hostess would upstage her. The only time Anthony had seen Cecile and his mother together, he'd had the impression that Cecile perhaps intimidated her with her beauty and confidence. Coupled with her husband and his often-overbearing demeanour, these nights were often difficult for Jane.

Dressed in his usual dinner suit attire, Philip fiddled with his bow tie repeatedly, which prompted Jane to reassure her husband that the bow tie was fine and that he looked like a *'perfect gentleman.'* With the business deal seemingly in the bag, Anthony was unsure if Philip was actually nervous about these soirees himself, or if he was just embarrassed by his wife and stepson. Image was so important to Philip Crawford, and whilst he certainly had some form of affection for Jane and enough reason to marry her, Anthony always felt that the working-class world he'd plucked her from was always lurking in the background.

Anthony, seated opposite Jane and Philip, felt every inch the gentleman in his attire, a dinner suit similar to Philip's. Men's fashion was much more straightforward than women's, Jane had agonised over what to wear, whereas Anthony and Philip had a much more limited choice for this type of engagement. Anthony was ready early and envisaged his mother repeatedly asking the opinion of both her husband and ladies' maid; these evenings always raised her levels of anxiety.

He tried to make eye contact with Jane, but she was not reciprocating. It had been less than twenty-four hours since the two had argued and the tension was still there. Fortunately, Philip was not someone who was an expert at picking up on an atmosphere, so he hadn't asked questions. Anthony was annoyed with himself about how he handled things with his mother and had resolved to put things right by dealing with Soames. Despite that predicament, he was quite calm about the evening ahead, a chance to deliver a performance of a young man impressed by the older male company and keen to learn from their success and knowledge. He suddenly realised how ludicrously hypocritical all this was. His mother was involved with the butler, Philip and Jane were clearly hiding an argument and putting on a front, whilst he was sleeping with the wife of his stepfather's business associate, whose house he was about to have dinner in. And then there was the business his wife, Anthony's lover was involved in, something Anthony was now a part of. The scandal, the secrets contained within the confines of this car were enormous. Anthony wondered what Robert was hiding: surely, he couldn't be the only one without a skeleton in the closet. The thought drew a smile to Anthony's face.

"Something amusing you, Anthony?" Philip asked somewhat irritably.

"Oh, no, Philip. Just wondering how much longer before we arrive." Anthony's reply was weak and made little sense to the question.

"Not much longer now, I shouldn't wonder. Wright, how much longer!"

"I'd say about five minutes, Sir." Wright accelerated the car as Anthony grinned again at the London drawl of the chauffeur's voice and thought about his childish jokes of asking the chauffer if he was going left or right, Wright. Was Chaplin someone who entertained early? Anthony figured that he was and often pictured a young boy with a gift of captivating many a raucous crowd in a dingy London theatre before finally realising his dreams of conquering the film world.

"Thank you, Wright." He remembered his manners on his stepfather's behalf, Philip's faux pas preventing him from slipping into a reverie about his childhood, again, the London accent setting a trail of memories alight.

The Fords lived in the outskirts of Banbury, quite close by country standards to the impressive Upton House, owned by the Viscount Bearsted, whose father Philip said vaguely was 'something to do with oil.' The second Viscount was currently in the process of remodelling the house and Philip knew his friends had dined at Upton House, just prior to the renovation work commencing. Things like that mattered to Philip and he hoped an introduction to the lord of the manor might be forthcoming from Robert one day. This was an affluent part of Banbury and very befitting of a couple like the Fords. Anthony wondered if Robert and Cecile's house would be bigger, perhaps more grand and have more servants than Crawford Park. And, if it did, how would Philip react? There was a competitive edge to Philip, which Anthony admired. Somewhat lazy, considered a fop and a dandy by Philip, Anthony didn't possess an ounce of competitiveness. Things happened to Anthony; he didn't make them happen. His creativity was limited to an overactive imagination and a love of performance, whether onstage or off. He was a natural showman, however, and liked nothing more than displaying his physical capabilities and his acting prowess (such as he thought of it). Perhaps it was Anthony's lack of competitiveness which helped the friendship with Harry, also lacking in the competitive spirit, although he did admire Anthony's creative brain and his acting ability, such as he had seen.

"How is Harry?" Anthony thought about his best friend with concern. He had not heard from him since his sudden departure upon sight of Benson. That was another thing for Anthony to consider and solve. Why would Harry react in such a way? What were they both hiding? And then there was the letter that Cecile had assured Anthony was not the work of Benson. But someone

was responsible, and Anthony would find out, one way or another.

The thoughts whirled around Anthony's head as Wright pulled onto the gravel drive. The evening was pitch black, but the huge house was well-lit. A colossal water feature stood in front of the house where Wright circled and pulled up just outside the front door, before leaping out of the car, straightening his cap, and opening the doors for his passengers. Anthony followed his mother and stepfather, halting at the foot of the impressive stone steps which led up to a covered portico and a pair of solid looking wooden panelled doors painted as black as the night itself. All three stood and admired the vast mansion. Jane shivered slightly, the night air was cold and despite her attire, she felt poorly insulated against the biting wind which swept across the north facing entrance.

"The kitchens are that way." Philp addressed his chauffer without looking at him. "There is some food and refreshment available for you."

"Yes, Sir. Thank you very much, Sir. Please convey my thanks to the hosts." Wright started towards his dining area for the evening.

Anthony could see at least four balconies and three floors. In excess typical of those who could afford it, light blazed from every room at the front of the house. A stocky man, of average height and with slicked back ginger hair was waiting at the door as the three guests made their way up the steps. His attire told Anthony he was the butler, although this individual had a much more endearing personality and carried himself with far more class than Soames. It struck Anthony suddenly that this was what was wrong with the Crawford's' butler. He had no class.

"Good evening," the butler's voice had a hint of a Scottish accent. "My name is Rawlings. Mr and Mrs Ford are waiting in the drawing room. Please follow me. Thank you, Clark."

Anthony then noticed a young, painfully thin gentleman emerge from behind the door. Obviously, the footman, he closed the door behind their guests and avoided eye contact. He was only a year or two older than Anthony and probably quite new to the role.

Philip, Jane, and Anthony surveyed the house. A huge chandelier hung from the ceiling and the foyer was tall and wide. Gold was prominent in colour, Cecile's influence, was Anthony's guess. The gold curtains and trim on the carpet made the room even brighter, while mahogany panelled walls contrasted sharply with the gold and white décor. Rawlings led the way through the vast foyer to the drawing room, knocking before entering and announcing the arrival of the guests.

"Mr. and Mrs. Crawford and Master Crawford have arrived, Sir, Madam."

The butler stepped aside allowing the trio to enter as Robert and Cecile stood to receive them. Immediately, Anthony's eyes were drawn to Cecile, who looked striking in a long black, glittering evening gown which hugged her womanly curves and displayed a daringly low-cut neckline. Her blonde hair was styled in its customary neat, sharp bob but was arranged around a black headband covered in tiny glittery sequins. The effect was chic and very stark together with her pale make-up, dramatically dark eyes, and her deep, luscious red lips. How Anthony longed to kiss her, but of course, he could not. She stood proudly next to her husband whilst Jane seemed to cower behind hers. Anthony suddenly felt a sharp twinge of injustice. What gave Cecile the right to be treated as an equal to Robert, whilst Philip Crawford demanded subservience from his wife, whose eyes were downcast and her outfit, carefully chosen, seemed to pale into insignificance.

Had Anthony cared to evaluate his feelings, he would have understood what irked him about the situation. Class. The Fords and Philip Crawford reeked of it, Anthony had been dusted with it and his mother, his poor, dear mother, was still, metaphorically, in the gutter. Jane Crawford would never shine and sparkle like Cecile Ford and his relationship with the latter meant that he had grown further away from the former. He now believed himself to be equal in terms of status and class, whilst Jane would always be, in her mind, Philip Crawford's secretary.

He and Cecile had both made eye contact with each other,

but both were actors. Anthony felt the tension like a sudden electrical charge, and this was a strangely empowering feeling. Had deceit seduced him as well as Cecile?

"Delighted to have you, old boy." Robert and Philip's handshake was full of warmth and mutual admiration. By contrast, the pleasantries exchanged with Cecile and Jane were polite, lacklustre, at best. Anthony was then greeted by Robert's firm handshake. "Looking very well, young Anthony. I hear congratulations are in order?"

"I'm sorry?" Anthony looked confused as he reclaimed his hand from his host's powerful grip.

"I hear that you are in gainful employment."

"Oh, yes, my apologies," Anthony composed himself. "Yes, that's correct but I don't want to bore you good people with that."

"Nonsense darling," Cecile cut in and planted a delicate peck on Anthony's cheek. "We want to hear all about it."

She acted impeccably, as though he were not her lover, and this was only the second time they had both met. Anthony grudgingly admitted to himself that Cecile was a better thespian than he'd ever be. Whilst he had not imagined she would embrace him passionately, no one else would be any the wiser of their passionate affair. Nor did she seem in the least bit awkward to the fact that she was entertaining her lover and his parents in the family home she shared with her husband.

"Rawlings, champagne!" Robert was in a jovial mood. "Business is booming, and Christmas is coming. Two perfectly good reasons to celebrate."

"And wait till you taste the pheasant, Jane." Cecile attempted conversation but it was Philip who answered.

"I'm sure it will be delightful, Cecile," Jane commented politely, after listening to her husband's declarations of gratitude for their invitation tonight. "And that dress is positively exquisite."

"Thank you, Jane." Cecile made no attempt to return the compliment. "Just a little number we picked up in Paris. Isn't that right, darling?"

"Worth every penny. But for God's sake don't remind me how much it was!"

Robert's joke drew laughter, but it was he who was most amused. They had taken seats in the drawing room, and Anthony took time to admire the high-backed couches, upholstered in a dark green chenille which matched the floor to ceiling curtains. The furniture was dark wood, and featured low coffee tables, a green baize covered card table and a large and ornate pedestal desk. The room was obviously Robert's styling, there was little imprint of Cecile here. The furnishings matched a circular green table that sat in the corner which looked as though it had seen many a high-stakes card game. Again, the setup was very similar to Philip's. This was Robert's room, most definitely.

Turning his attention back to the company, Anthony could see that the two businessmen were deep in conversation and felt as though his presence wouldn't be a welcome contribution. Cecile was sipping her champagne with an amused expression on her perfect features and Jane sat demurely, her fingers clutching the delicate stem of the gold rimmed champagne glass. She looked unhappy and Anthony felt a pang of sympathy and guilt at the way he had been treating her since his discovery. Forgetting for a moment where he was and, in whose company, he leant towards her and asked, quietly,

"All fine with you, Mum?"

"Fine, thank you, Anthony." Jane's reply was brief and rather curt. Anthony couldn't blame her, though, he reflected ruefully. He was in two minds as to whether her attitude was one of nerves or her still being upset with him.

"He's such a fine young man, Jane." Cecile eyed Anthony with an expression of such wide-eyed innocence that Anthony almost choked on his champagne. She recrossed her legs, her eyes never leaving his. She was enjoying this.

"He is, Cecile." Jane thawed slightly. "Have you ever wanted children?"

Cecile was taken aback by the question, as was Anthony.

"Not something I ever really considered and something that is not really on my horizon. My husband nurtures his business, I think that is his baby."

"I see." Jane sipped her champagne and smiled at Anthony. Was she simply making conversation or was she biting back? Philip and Robert both seemed oblivious to anyone else in the room. Rawlings re-entered and announced, "Dinner is served, ladies and gentlemen."

"Ah, thank you, Rawlings. Time is getting on. Dear old Mrs Primrose," Robert was now addressing the room.

"Not quite as quick as she once was but what she doesn't know about cooking really isn't worth knowing."

"She can't go on forever darling," Cecile declared. "I imagine she is passing the tricks of the trade on to one or two of her under cooks right now. I always thought young Ruby would make a suitable replacement."

"I think her bread-and-butter pudding alone makes her irreplaceable." Robert chuckled away. He'd clearly had a few drinks before his guests had arrived, which was contributing to his jovial mood.

Still laughing away to himself, the quintet rose to their feet. Jane and Cecile both taking the arms of their husbands, leaving Anthony to walk behind. Cecile couldn't resist stroking her young lover's hand with her little finger as she brushed past him. Danger was clearly thrilling to her, as it was to Anthony. He followed the two couples, his eyes fixed on Cecile's delicious figure when he noticed some paper on the floor by Robert's desk. He quickly dashed across and picked it up to place it back on the desk when something caught his eye. He didn't read the contents of what appeared to be a letter, but the writing was familiar.

"Is everything alright, Sir?" Rawlings startled Anthony, who quickly placed the paper on the table.

"Erm, yes, Rawlings. I was just retrieving this piece of paper from the floor."

"Most kind, Sir. Are you ready for dinner or will you require to do anything else?" Rawlings was ever so politely asking Anthony to leave with him.

"No, nothing except dinner, Rawlings, lead the way, old

chap." Anthony headed towards the door.

"Very good, Sir," replied the butler, who escorted Anthony to the dining room.

Chapter 19

Souffle was certainly not Anthony's first choice of cuisine, but it was delicious. Mrs. Primrose had a flair that more than matched Mrs. Blackshaw, but the young Crawford would always be loyal to that big-hearted lady who was persistently cheerful and pleasant to everyone other that the kitchen staff below her. He recounted tales of him as a younger boy being scolded for messing around in the kitchen, but always getting a few sweets sneaked to him by the house cook before she roasted one of the poor girls for not cleaning up her mess. She had been there forever and had never changed. A short, well-made woman who had a warm smile and kind eyes. Another feature of her character was that she refused to be intimidated by Soames, as was proven at one of their first meetings. Anthony had heard raised voices; Mrs. Blackshaw stood her ground and reminded the butler that the kitchen was 'her space to look after the family that also employ you.' Anthony had been thrilled by this; he knew Soames was a bully and also the sight of Jane smoothing over the 'misunderstanding' after Philip had attempted to settle the situation had made Anthony laugh even more. Philip could be a tyrant, he was master of the house and the head of a successful business, but man-management was something in which Jane excelled and was not part of his skillset. Philip would have final say on who was employed, but Jane handled the day-to-day running of the house.

How long had Soames and his mother been having an affair? The butler's grip on the household was even tighter now, and Anthony was unsure whether this was an ebullience displayed by Soames because of his entanglement with the lady of the house, or whether it was just because he was a natural bully. Either way, Anthony was determined to break it. He would plan Soames' demise in a way that would allow his mother to come away unscathed. The finer details of his plan were not yet finalised, he'd thought of recruiting Harry but quickly dismissed the idea as stupid. Harry was too honest for his own good and, after their last meeting, he was clearly having troubles he wasn't prepared to share with his best friend. This was another thing on Anthony's mind and something he would get to the bottom of.

Sipping his claret after digesting the delicious meal, Anthony observed the huge dining room. Black curtains with a gold trim covered the only window in the room and a round table that would have comfortably fitted ten people around it was covered by a soft gold tablecloth and black placemats took pride of place in the middle. Robert had explained that a round table gave a more intimate feel for a dinner party, something that Jane seemed to champion but Philip's look said he wasn't sure. A huge portrait of both Cecile and Robert looking resplendent and very serious was in the middle of the far wall and behind a rose-gold sofa that gave Anthony a fantasy involving Cecile. The comfy-looking sofa blended perfectly with the wallpaper, which had a black trim running at the bottom. The colour scheme reminded Anthony of a movie premiere, and he wondered if Cecile pictured herself as the leading lady posing for pictures from pressmen before going to enjoy the production of which she was the star. Of course, the films that Cecile, and now Anthony, were helping to churn out would never be the subject of mainstream cinema, more likely to appear in the crime reports towards the back of the publications that acted as the main source of news for many as well as very good fish and chip paper that was used in abundance on Friday nights throughout London. Anthony loved expensive wine, whisky, and fine cuts of meat, but he did often pine for the intoxicating smell of salt and vinegar as it decorated the crispy batter and fried potatoes.

The conversation had been minimal during the meal. Cecile and Jane were making an effort to discuss Christmas preparation and the very English topic of the weather. Cecile had said very little, even less than Jane, and was perhaps a little annoyed by her guest's interest in whether she wanted children. In truth, Cecile dominated Anthony's thoughts. His mind whirred with images of him frantically tearing off her dress and undergarments before making mad, passionate love to her. Philip and Robert were engrossed in business, or so Anthony thought. He needed to try and take his mind off his improper thoughts of his lover, so he endeavoured to intertwine himself in man's talk, but came in at the wrong time.

"It's always nice to be around a man's man." Philip's chuckle following Robert's comment had a hint of a childish giggle that caused Anthony to almost choke on his wine, the noise of which caused both Jane and Cecile to look in his direction.

Both men were also staring straight at Anthony, Robert spoke first, "Everything alright, Anthony." His comment was more accusing than that of concern, as was Philip's expression.

"Of course," Anthony started. "Just took a bit too much of this excellent wine." He then turned to Jane. "I do think we should advise Mrs. Blackshaw on this souffle, Mother."

"I can safely assure you that recipes that Mrs. Blackshaw has not thought of herself will be met with some resistance," Jane's answer was matter of fact. She was not in a good mood and was now appearing somewhat prickly, which was most unlike her, particularly in public. This couldn't be solely due to her confrontation with her son, whom she had no interest in rescuing from his embarrassment.

"Fearful of change, Jane?" Cecile questioned Anthony's mother, who looked surprised. "Mrs. Blackshaw, I mean."

"Let's just say, set in her ways. She has served the house well for a long time and food is her domain." Jane sipped her wine delicately. "And I often feel that change can spell trouble."

"Oh, I don't know, Jane. A bit of variety can often add that little bit of spice that keeps life interesting." Cecile too sipped her wine and offered a cursory glance at Anthony, who was beginning to suspect that the topic of food was a cover for the two women to verbally dual. Both Philip and Robert remained silent, the former's gaze firmly fixed on his stepson.

"Well, I think it is all absolutely delicious." Anthony's attempt to offer some friendliness drew looks ranging from pitiful humour to almost scorn. It was all he could do to laugh awkwardly and look toward Philip and Robert for some refuge.

And his stepfather would, surprisingly, be the one to provide it.

"Do listen, Anthony, I think it is a splendid idea and we would be happy to host it." Philip always got louder the more he drank.

"And what might this *splendid idea* be, Philip?" Cecile was interested and Jane looked on.

"A Christmas soiree," Robert explained. "You remember, darling? We discussed it whilst dining with our guests the previous week. It has been a wonderful year for both our businesses and our families, so why not hold the social event of this past twelve months to celebrate both it and the festive period. I think Philip was initially a bit reticent in regard to hosting a Christmas party, but our discussions have been favourable." He smiled at his business partner as though the venue of Christmas soiree was a big deal that had just been finalised.

"And it will be an honour for us to hold it. I'm sure Mrs. Blackshaw will relish the challenge," Philip stated confidently.

"I shall insist that Mrs. Primrose write down the souffle recipe that Anthony enjoys so much." Cecile's offer-cum-thinly-veiled-insult was met with a smile by Jane, who continued speaking to her husband.

"We will have to hire some added help for Mrs. Blackshaw. I'm not sure how she will react to that."

"Whatever she needs," Philip drained his goblet and waved his hands about ostentatiously. "I'm sure once you have had a chat with her, she will be absolutely fine. That can be your little project, give you something to do." He had regained his composure and was returning to his old self.

Jane was visibly irritated by her husband's patronising, pompous nature. Normally so accepting and immune to his demeanour, tonight saw a different Jane and one that unsettled her son. There had to be more than a simple verbal altercation. What had Philip done? Had she fallen in love with Soames? Was she aware of Anthony and Cecile? Questions shot through Anthony's mind at such a rate, his head began to hurt.

"You alright, boy?" Philip now turned his attention to his

stepson.

"Fine, thank you, Sir." Anthony would always use his Christian name and this sudden bout of respect shocked Philip, but also impressed.

"Such wonderful manners," purred Cecile, irritatingly. "You have done a wonderful job, Jane." She glanced over at Philip. "And you too, of course."

"Thank you." Jane was proud of her son.

"Yes, he's not a bad young man." Philip boomed in, cutting across his wife who sat looking at her husband and ignoring the fact that Anthony was present, he continued to deliver his opinion of his stepson for the benefit of everyone around the table.

"And will a strapping young man such as yourself be bringing a lady friend to the party?" Robert's question drew a look from Cecile. Perhaps a hint of jealousy.

"There is no one special," Anthony lied. "I'm sure it will happen soon."

"Of course, it will," agreed Robert. "Say, I have a close friend who has the most charming daughter. Good stock, lovely young girl and…"

"Oh darling," Cecile cut in. "I do believe young Anthony is more than capable of finding his own lucky lady."

Anthony was unsure if Cecile was irritated or simply trying to change what could become an awkward conversation for her, unbeknownst to her husband.

"It's different these days, young people all seem to enter into marriage much later than in our day." Philip's statement was somewhat ludicrous given Anthony's age, but he chose to simply smile through it. Jane did comment. "He is twenty-one, darling. He's just found a job and is making his way in the world. Give him time."

"Absolutely, Jane." Cecile raised her glass as the two women finally found something that they could both agree on this evening. In true butler fashion, Rawlings had appeared and sought permission to clear their dinner plates before serving the final course. Jane had eaten little, and this was noticed by Philip.

"Not feeling well, Jane?"

"I'm fine, just not very hungry. I do believe I'm coming down with something."

Anthony suspected that Jane invented being under the weather to avoid appearing impolite to her hosts. Whatever was bothering her, it wasn't illness. His mind then drifted to his lover. An exceptional actress, so passionate when alone with him yet played the doting wife and hostess effortlessly while seemingly treating him as nothing more than the son of an acquaintance.

"*Who was the real Cecile?*" The thought-provoking question burned into Anthony's brain.

"Oh, that is a shame, Jane?" Cecile enquired. "I do hope you will be better in time for the gathering." Her tone always made it difficult to know if her comments were genuine or patronising.

"I'm sure I will be fine," Jane replied. "Rawlings, please send my apologies to Mrs Primrose."

"Nonsense," said Robert. "We all feel a bit under the weather from time to time. Rawlings, get the cheese board and perhaps a medicinal brandy for Mrs. Crawford."

"Very good, Sir," Rawlings answered in that deferential tone all butlers seemed to possess.

"Thank you, Robert. Most kind of you." Jane said gratefully.

"Best medicine you can buy." Robert chuckled at his comment.

"So how is business, Philip?" Cecile suddenly decided to change the subject as she waited for Rawlings to return with the cheeseboard. A sly smile upon her lips, she knew she was goading him; Philip had never been a fan of discussing his work with women in general and he wasn't going to start now.

"Oh, you ladies don't want to hear about business, that's a man's conversation to be discussed at a more appropriate time. Anthony, fill us in on what you do. I'm sure we would all be delighted to hear." His deflective tactics were impressive, but they had put Anthony firmly on the spot. Cecile's smile became wry, as she was keen to see how good a storyteller her lover truly was.

"Well, I make tea and do a lot of running around," Anthony

began confidently. "They have permitted me to write about a few films and do a bit of research on actors and genres."

"Sounds wonderfully exciting, Anthony." Cecile enjoyed this. "Any published articles yet?"

"Not as of yet, but that is my ambition. Along with getting in front of the camera, of course."

"Well done, darling." Jane smiled at him with real affection for the first time this evening. It was a bittersweet moment for Anthony, as that affection was founded upon complete fabrication. He knew full well his mother, and Philip, would be horrified if they knew what he was really doing.

"I do enjoy the cinema," Cecile piped up, slightly irritated by Jane's admiration of Anthony. "But I do find that it doesn't go far enough?" Cecile's question intrigued the room. Anthony was about to answer as Rawlings appeared with a large brandy and a substantial-looking cheeseboard.

"Well, I imagine there is only so much that filmmakers and actors are permitted to do." Anthony smiled at his lover.

"Seems such a shame. We English are terribly repressed romantics with all that pent-up animal magnetism waiting to get out." Something which certainly happened with her productions.

"Perhaps one day censorship may relax, somewhat," Anthony suggested. "But we still have the genius of Chapman to keep us enthralled and entertained.

"I for one am glad we have a bit of censorship," Philip chimed in. "Far too much in lowering the standards that Great Britain's empire was built on."

"Do you not feel the world is changing, Philip? People starting to enjoy themselves after enduring war." Cecile's comments were challenging.

"I will always believe that standards must be maintained. We have enjoyed ourselves this evening, without resorting to debauchery," Philip's tone had a hint of belligerence. Anthony chose to be the voice of reason.

"Film is a bit of escapism, a chance to settle down and be entertained whilst forgetting the troubles of life. From the working classes upwards, it can be a great leveller."

"An excellent point, young man. You do have a good brain in that head of yours," Robert sounded almost surprised.

"Thank you, Sir." Anthony was playing this perfectly. His performance seemed to restore a calm, which was ably assisted by some excellent port. Conversation returned to Christmas and life in general. Jane appeared to thaw as she enjoyed her brandy, but she was ready to leave, although she did not deny herself another medicinal nightcap in the drawing room. Brandy and whisky were poured and enjoyed. Anthony had requested a whisky and had finished his malt quickly before declaring he needed the lavatory and excusing himself. It was a ploy he hoped Cecile would realise and sure enough the woman of his dreams was waiting outside the bathroom for her lover. Still as resplendent as she was at the start of the evening, Anthony had to seriously resist the urge to kiss her.

"We are doing a bit more filming tomorrow; will you be there?" she asked, idly although Anthony knew full well there was no innocent or accident about the enquiry.

"Try and stop me," Anthony enthused. "I was hoping to get some alone time with you."

"My, my, you do have some appetite," Cecile laughed which made Anthony laugh.

"I actually need your help and advice." Her lover turned serious.

"Intriguing. Of course, darling. I look forward to tomorrow." She turned away and made her way down the wide staircase, stopping to turn and blow a kiss to Anthony. He waited until it was safe and made his way back to the drawing room. Philip and Jane had their coats on and had said their goodbyes. The former was leaning heavily on his wife, the alcohol finally taking its toll, although he'd never admit it. "Come along, boy, let's leave these good people at a decent hour." His words weren't slurred, although he was smiling inanely.

"A fabulous evening, Anthony," Cecile kissed him on the cheek before excusing herself into the drawing room. Clark had the door open for Jane and Philip, whilst Rawlings had retrieved Anthony's coat. The young man extended a hand to Robert, who took it firmly.

"Very impressive, young man," Robert told him. "Cecile is very interested in film and clearly appreciates your knowledge."

"One does one's best," Anthony answered, politely, as he tried to retrieve the hand that Robert was not quite ready to let go of.

"Always remember to whom she belongs." Robert looked Anthony straight in the face. Anthony felt a cold sweat all over him, just as Robert released his hand and laughed heartily. "Goodnight, young man."

"Good night, er, Mr. Ford." Anthony felt like a child. He allowed Rawlings to help him with his coat and took his hat before making swiftly for the door and to the car to head home.

Was what had just happened Robert's sense of humour or a warning? Anthony couldn't be sure.

Chapter 20

It was only just past eight o'clock in the morning and Anthony, Jane and Philip were still struggling to digest the news. Soames and the rest of those in service had rushed around picking clothes, making tea, and ensuring those other tasks were completed without the usual extra minutes the weekend often afforded. Detective Inspector Frank Naden, a very matter-of-fact gentleman with ideas of grandeur had broken the news: Charles Edward Benson had been found dead. Murdered to be precise. Found by one of those in service at Mr and Mrs Ford's Oxfordshire residence, her deafening screams could have, *"woken half of the county,"* according to Naden. The cause of death was something the Inspector had not yet revealed.

Philip had, at first, looked bewildered upon hearing the name. It was only when the officer explained it was the Ford's family chauffeur that the penny finally dropped. A snob, who looked as though he was trying so hard to shed his humble beginnings, so Anthony thought, Naden seemed far more interested in his wealthy hosts rather than the investigation itself. Apologising profusely for calling so early, as well as repeatedly expressing concern for their friends in regard to this terrible tragedy rather than the victim himself, Naden's questions were relatively routine. The Crawford's did all have a cast iron alibi, not that he even considered any one of them a suspect, preferring to focus on Benson's other interests and activities.

"It appears that he was found at the entrance of the property. Young girl – a maid – found him by a tree in the early hours," Naden reported. His attempts at hiding the Midland twang in his accent were failing miserably. "Around half past two, some two hours or more after you left."

"What on earth was she doing out at such an hour?" Philip questioned the detective.

"She claims to have gone outside for a cigarette. Apparently doesn't like smoking in the house." Naden was making a real effort with his elocution. "It turns out she was meeting a man, boyfriend. She found the body and raised the alarm."

"She shouldn't have been out meeting men." Philip's comment was censorious and met with an approving nod from the inspector. "Philip and Cecile are impeccable people and those in service to them, much like those in service to us, should have respect and understand that they represent their masters."

"The poor girl," said Jane, who shot a disapproving look by Philip.

"Is she a suspect, Inspector?" Anthony asked as he thought of both Cecile and Sarah. Perhaps respect was a two-way thing, he thought, brusquely.

"We haven't ruled her out, Master Crawford, but it seems unlikely. Turns out she knew Benson quite well, socially I mean. He had a few interests that his employers knew nothing of. Spot of blackmailing. These are lines of inquiry that we will be following up on. My primary purpose for the intrusion was to check if you had seen or heard anything whilst having dinner?"

"No, Inspector." Philip replied bluntly. "We barely knew the man, he was a servant of a friend, no more."

"Of course, Sir," Naden was almost apologetic. "Just establishing a full picture." An overweight man in his forties, he was large in stature with hands like Jack Dempsey. Anthony wondered if Naden had ever boxed when he was younger. The inspector's thinning hair was greasy with sweat from his hat, which he'd removed upon entry, and his grey waistcoat looked to be fighting a losing battle in keeping his burgeoning stomach encased inside it.

"Poor Robert and Cecile," began Philip. "How are they bearing up?"

"A bit shocked, Sir, but determined to help us as much as they can," answered Naden.

"Damned inconvenience," Philip shook his head. "Good chauffeurs are as rare as hen's teeth." Naden nodded in agreement, although he had no idea whether this statement was true or false.

Anthony felt a twinge of disgust, as did Jane. The former

didn't like Benson, but he was still a human being who'd had his life taken from him, yet all his stepfather and the investigating officer really cared about was the inconvenience a man's death had caused to his well-to-do employers. Did the chauffeur have a wife, a family? Who would truly miss the man?

And who had killed him? Anthony's mind began to race. He had been troubled by Robert's comment to him as he left the house last night. *Just remember to whom she belongs*, his stepfather's business associate had said. Cecile was a woman who will have many admirers. Was Robert the jealous type? The violent type? Did he know about his wife and Anthony or was it just his idea of humour or a friendly warning to not get too close? The questions tumbled around his mind. Could there be a link to Benson? The detective had mentioned blackmail, who was he blackmailing? If Naden knew the full story, then Anthony would be on his list of suspects as the policeman could certainly argue motive. Cecile had disproved that Benson had been behind the note Anthony received, but was she right?

And could she be capable of murder?

He suddenly remembered that he would be seeing her today. Would that still be happening? Anthony was unsure if Cecile would feel anything for her now-former employee, but she may want to give that impression to the outside world.

Naden was just about finished. He drank the rest of his tea and made a very conscious effort to not slurp, before rising with a grace that belied his size and shaking hands with Philip. As he was about to leave, Jane asked, "How was he killed, Inspector?"

"Shot, Madam," replied Naden, without emotion. Anthony supposed he saw enough violent crime in his line of work to not be affected by it. His bowler hat under his arm, Naden was shown out by Soames, leaving Jane, Anthony, and Philip alone.

"I have a lot to contend with today, Jane. Perhaps a telephone call to Cecile would be appropriate more than asking how the bloody man had died?" He seemed somewhat troubled with Jane asking how Benson has died. Anthony wondered why.

"Of course, darling," Jane replied, unperturbed by her husband's tone and the recrimination "A terrible shock. That poor man."

"Life goes on, Jane, it is our friends who need our support and there are things to be done." Philip was quite matter of fact, as if they were discussing arranging an afternoon out.

Anthony felt his disgust and anger rising and Philip could sense it. Addressing his stepson, he continued, "It is a tragedy, Anthony, but it seems as though that man was involved in things which, quite frankly, he shouldn't have been involved in. He who lives by the sword, dies by it."

Jane and Anthony's gaze followed Philip as he left the room. He was talking to Soames outside, but Anthony could not hear what was being said.

"Will you call Cecile?" Anthony asked his mother, then realised he had called her 'Cecile' and not Mrs Ford, but luckily, his mother was distracted enough not to notice.

"I suppose I will," replied Jane, who did not seem overly enthusiastic about it.

"Are you not a fan of Robert's wife?"

"I have not given it much thought. But for our husbands being in business together, we do not seem to share much in common." Jane took a drink of her tea. "I shall call after breakfast. Do my wifely duties." The remark on the surface seemed perfectly innocent, but Anthony sensed something he couldn't quite put his finger on.

He looked at his mother but said nothing. There was tension last night from Jane. She had not been her normal, easy-going, and rather demure self and was prepared to verbally fire back. Anthony wondered if what he had seen between his mother and Soames was the cause of this, or if the argument that both she and Philip no longer seem to acknowledge, was behind her sudden change of mood. He pondered this, as well as what to have for breakfast, when Jane added out of the blue, "Looks are not everything, Anthony."

"Excuse me?" Anthony was taken off guard.

"You are young, enjoy the attention of a very attractive lady, far more mature than you, who supposedly has your best interests at heart, but she may not be all she seems."

"Where is this coming from? And what on earth do you mean, Mother?" Anthony felt both irritated and patronised and also a little afraid. Did his mother know? Had she suspected he was involved with Cecile in more intimate ways than that of employer and employee?

"All I am saying is that something doesn't sit quite right with me about Cecile Ford."

Neither mother nor son had noticed Soames enter the room but upon hearing Cecile's name, the butler showed some real emotion, as though he was irritated. Anthony targeted the man he was desperate to rid the house of. "Is something the matter, Soames?" he asked, rather irritable himself.

"No, Sir. I was simply informing you and Mrs. Crawford that breakfast is served."

"You seemed in pain, Soames." Anthony watched the butler trying to rid himself of the grimace which the young Master had noticed.

"Oh, that is just a touch of arthritis. Thank you, Master Anthony, for your concern."

"I have never noticed before and can't recall you mentioning it." Anthony's continued questioning was unsettling both Jane and Soames, but the latter had regained composure.

"I wouldn't trouble you with my ailments, Master Anthony, you have enough things to be concerned with, I'm sure. Again, thank you for your concern."

"Well, I hope the pain subsides, Soames," began Jane, who glared at Anthony. "Breakfast is ready, you say?"

"Yes, Madam. The Master has informed me that he won't be joining you." The sound of the telephone gave Soames the perfect excuse to make his exit and attend to it. Anthony and Jane watched him go.

"What has gotten into you, Anthony?" Jane seemed more shocked than angry.

"I might ask you the same question," came Anthony's barbed reply.

"Anthony!"

"Don't, Mother!" He got up and left the room. His appetite

had disappeared, and he needed to get out of the house. He thought of going to see Harry but wanted to get word to Cecile. Perhaps Harry may fancy another spin? This led him to think about the last time he'd been out with his friend. How Harry had looked as though he'd seen a ghost upon sight of Benson, who was now deceased. Anthony's mind was suddenly consumed with dark thoughts. He needed to see Harry; he needed answers. He turned to go up the stairs to his room when Soames confronted him.

"Excuse me, Master Anthony. Mr. Hewson-Greaves is on the telephone."

"Thank you, Soames," replied Anthony. "I do hope you feel better. Arthritis is quite painful, I believe."

"Yes, Master Anthony, and thank you for your concern." Jane had since passed and made her way into the dining room, where she would dine alone. Soames headed in that direction, watched all the way by Anthony, who then remembered that Harry was on the telephone. He rushed to the mahogany cabinet where the phone rested and picked up the receiver.

"Harry, I was hoping you'd call I really need to see you, today…"

"This is not Harry, Anthony. It is his father. It is regarding Harry." Harry's father sounded a lot like Harry. But for the deeper voice and even more well-spoken tone, you could easily mistake the two.

"Oh, erm, apologies, Sir. What is the matter?" Anthony's disquiet deepened. Something must be wrong for Harry's father to have telephoned before breakfast.

"Harry has been injured and is in hospital. He's been asking for you. Would you come and see him?"

"Hospital! What happened?" Anthony's voice was pitching higher than normal due to panic.

"It appears he was in an automobile accident last night. Thankfully his injuries are not life-threatening." Mr. Hewson-Greaves had little to no emotion, almost as though he was reading a script and doing it rather badly. One of the many things Anthony could not fathom about those born into the ruling classes was their distinct lack of emotion in public when faced with the most dire situations. "Would you come down please, Anthony? He is asking for you."

"That is a relief, Sir. And of course, I will be down as soon as I can. Which hospital?'

"Brompton Hospital on Sydney Street in Chelsea. We have a private room where we aren't disturbed. His mother is with him."

"And how is she bearing up? And you?" Anthony could feel himself becoming more common, but that didn't matter at this moment in time.

"We are doing as well as can be expected. Thank you for asking." The first twinge of emotion crept into Harry's father's voice.

"Take care, Mr. Hewson-Greaves. I am on my way."

Anthony replaced the receiver noisily and almost ran into Jane.

"Anthony, what is the matter?"

"It's Harry, he's been hurt in a car accident." Anthony was moving as he was speaking. "Soames, notify Wright that I require the car."

"Begging your pardon, Master Anthony, sir, but Wright has driven your father to his office." Soames said almost smugly.

"Well get me a taxi, then! Brompton Hospital. Chelsea."

"Very good, Sir," Soames was unflappable, as usual.

"Anthony," Jane began.

"Not now, Mother!"

Chapter 21

Brompton Hospital struck Anthony as a cross between boarding school and stately home. It was a facility for those who could afford the best possible medical care. The young Crawford paid off the taxi and was now staring at the rather grand building. Its two floors paid host to hundreds of windows which made Anthony wonder how many people were being treated and how many were doing the treating. And what were they being treated for? Anthony had been born at home, as was common for the working class, and had never visited a hospital in his young life. He remembered an 'auntie', who was just a friendly neighbour taking care of him as Jane had gone to a hospital for some reason or another when he was younger. He'd often suspected that his father had made it back to England and was in such an institution when he succumbed to his war injuries, though he chose never to ask his mother due to not wanting to upset her further. It was not long after Jane's 'visit to hospital', that he received the devastating news of his father's death and little did he realise how much his life would actually change in the coming years.

It was a cold day, and thick, battleship grey clouds scudding across a low sky made it seem dark and depressing. Had Anthony been of a different frame of mind, he would have stopped to admire the magnificence of the red brick building, nestling along a tree lined avenue. He imagined that in spring and summer, the effect would be quite stunning, with greenery and flora for the patients to admire out of the tall, majestic looking windows. It was a testimony to Anthony's concern for his friend, which attributed to his state of mind and the fact that he was unable to even think of what actor he would be today, what part he would play in a medical drama film. Today, for once, Anthony thought little of himself and more about his friend.

The reception area, which he walked into from some incredibly heavy, wooden swing doors, was vast and he looked around for someone to assist him with directions. He had no idea where he was going and could hear groans of pain and muffled conversations down a long corridor that branched off ahead of him. There didn't appear to be anyone around, so he decided to follow the noise and see where it led. His thoughts were full of his best friend. How badly hurt was *not life-threatening?* And what had exactly happened? Harry was an accomplished motorist who was not one for taking risks whilst behind the wheel. But his best friend had shown behaviour that Anthony was not used to. And the man whom he believed was the cause of that behavioural change was now dead. The sight of Benson had scared Harry that day, and Anthony could not help but wonder if this hospitalisation was somehow connected to the chauffeur's demise. It would be something he would never want to believe, but there was enough evidence for Anthony to be at least suspicious. Wrapped up in his thoughts, the sound of a familiar voice shocked him.

"Anthony!"

The sound came from behind, but he already knew who it was. Spinning around quickly, Mr Hewson-Greaves was approaching. Walking briskly, his hand was extended and his face emotionless. His dark, expensive tweed suit made Anthony feel rather underdressed, as though they were attending some sort of important social event and not meeting each other in a hospital where their friend and son lay, with his not life-threatening injuries, but injured nevertheless and injured enough for Harry to ask for Anthony. Hewson-Greaves' features made Anthony realise what Harry would look like when he was older, despite being an inch or so taller than his father and having slightly darker hair. Their physical mannerisms were similar, too. Momentarily, Anthony felt as though he had been placed in a time machine and fast forwarded to Harry's middle age. If he reached middle age, Anthony thought, suddenly.

"Thank you for coming, Anthony. A difficult time, to say the least."

"Think nothing of it, Sir."

Anthony shook hands with Mr. Hewson-Greaves', recalling

that he had never been invited to call his friend's father anything else, other than 'Sir'. Also called Harry, the older Mr Hewson-Greaves was a dour and formidable man, which prevented anything akin to affection for him from anyone, let alone Anthony. To his knowledge, Harry's father had never hugged his son, never encouraged, or enthused with him, only brought him up rigidly to show respect for his elders and criticised and chastised Harry into the quiet, sometimes serious, young man that he was. Anthony suddenly wondered how he himself would have been brought up, had his own father survived the war.

Shaking himself out of his reverie, Anthony asked after his friend. "How is he?"

"Let's walk and talk."

Mr. Hewson-Greaves led the way, his walk somewhat slower than when he had approached Anthony. He was clearly trying to decide what to say to Anthony and how to say it. Image and a stiff upper lip were of paramount importance to Harry's father, who definitely saw emotion as a sign of weakness, no matter what the circumstance. Anthony was impatient and decided to continue his line of questioning.

"Was anyone else hurt?" The question clearly caught Mr. Hewson-Greaves off-guard, and he was struggling to formulate an answer.

Eventually, he said, "It appears that Harry was travelling alone." He kept his gaze straight ahead. "He lost control and collided with a wall somewhere near Holland Park. This was late last night."

"Had he been anywhere?" Anthony felt like a policeman with his comment and wondered how Inspector Naden would handle this matter.

"He had attended a dinner at the Duncan residence." Mr. Hewson-Greaves didn't elaborate further. Anthony knew Duncan was Margaret's surname, and he was also well aware that Holland Park was not too far from the London home of Robert and Cecile Ford. Tension swelled inside him; his mind was racing.

"Has Margaret been informed, Sir?"

"Harry's mother did that earlier," replied Hewson-Greaves. "Naturally she is both upset yet relieved his injuries are not life threatening."

Anthony was about to speak when Harry's father said, "It is important that not too many people know."

"Why?" Anthony was genuinely confused.

"A scandal is never a good thing, particularly for families of such standing."

"I'm confused, Harry crashed his car. Am I missing something about a scandal? He is in hospital, hopefully recovering and no one else was hurt, which is surely the main thing." Anthony's tone was tinged with impatience and anger.

"Anthony, I'm not sure that Harry is recovering. I certainly think he has not been himself for some time and both his mother and I are concerned," Hewson-Greaves gave a sigh of irritation. "His nuptials will be the social event of next year and he is a young man with a lot of responsibility. He will eventually inherit the family business, the Hewson-Greaves empire. If anyone needs to be himself, it's Harry!"

"I expect so," said Anthony, wondering where all this was leading.

"You have been friends with him for a long time, Anthony," Hewson-Greaves replied. "If he shall not talk to you, I fear that he will talk to no one."

They turned a corner. The long corridors were narrow, and cold, or was the chill Anthony felt emanating from the man walking beside him? Harry's mother came into view, sitting ramrod straight on an uncomfortable looking bench a few hundred yards away. She stared blankly at the door of a room opposite, that Anthony reasoned was Harry's. Her dark, wavy hair was covered by a black, wide brimmed hat with a veil, which was hung over her face and her fur collar was pressed up against her chin. She was a handsome woman, but she hardly ever wore clothes to accentuate her figure and today, she looked dressed for a funeral. The thought made Anthony shiver.

Hewson-Greaves stopped short of his wife and turned to Anthony. "I need you to find out what is going on. He will talk to you, Anthony."

The hidden request must have cost Harry's father a lot, young Crawford thought. He was not a man given to asking anything of anyone.

"I shall do my best, Sir," said a solemn Anthony. "I assume he is in the room opposite where Mrs. Hewson-Greaves is sitting?"

Her husband nodded. Anthony squared his shoulders and approached Harry's mother.

"My condolences."

Anthony froze in horror, as realised it was a crass and stupid thing that was to say. He felt himself blush. She was a woman who had made him feel uneasy as a child and that feeling carried on into adulthood. With a cursory glance at her son's best friend, she ignored Anthony and resumed looking blankly at the door. Deciding he was not going to get an answer, he gave a small knock before entering.

Inside, the room was plain, rather small and dominated by an uncomfortable-looking bed, next to which was a small wooden cabinet where a jug and small glass sat. The only other furniture was an ugly armchair, where Anthony now sat, on the edge of the seat and looked at his sleeping best friend.

"How long would he be staying in?" Anthony thought as he looked at Harry's injuries. There were cuts and bruises that looked superficial, as well as a large swelling above the right eye. It was hard to tell if there was any permanent damage. Had he suffered an injury to the brain? Was that what troubled the Hewson-Greaves'? That their son would awaken and somehow be different? Anthony despised himself for thinking the same thing, imagining a life where Harry came out of hospital, reduced to the mental capacity of a small child, or worse, with the loss of all his faculties.

Benson's face suddenly appeared in Anthony's mind. Harry had been unnerved by the sight of him and now Benson was dead. He did not want to think of his friend as a killer, but he would be lying if he denied that thought had crossed his mind. But what could Harry's motive possibly be, if indeed, he was involved in the demise of the Fords' chauffeur? Anthony needed answers and pondered waking Harry before deciding against it. He turned around and looked at the closed door, unexpectedly moving his seat, which made an unpleasant scratching sound on the cold, linoleum covered floor. It was silent, outside. No muffled speech, Anthony noted, and realised that was what he expected his friends' parents to do - sit there together in silence. He knew Harry's father would struggle sitting and doing nothing. A workaholic, Anthony had always remembered a man who could never settle and simply relax.

The noise of Anthony's chair had woken Harry. Anthony waited for his friend to gather his wits and noticed that this was the first time he'd seen any kind of stubble on his face. Harry was always incredibly neat and tidy, not due to interest in his appearance so much, like Anthony, but more that the environment he was raised in demanded it. The family was almost mechanical in their day-to-day life, and standards were everything, which was probably why Harry enjoyed Anthony's company as it was a chance to be a natural human being.

A smile crossed Harry's battered face upon sight of his friend. "Anthony, old boy." His grimace suggested a lot of pain, but he was no doubt pleased to see young Crawford.

"Hello, Harry," Anthony said softly. "You've looked better."

This caused Harry to laugh, something he regretted instantly as he began to cough loudly.

"Don't make me laugh, old boy," he choked out before coughing again.

Anthony moved around the bed to the cabinet and poured some water from the jug into the cup. Harry sipped it gingerly before handing it back. Anthony remained standing and asked bluntly, "What's going on, Harry?"

Harry stared at his friend before putting his head back and closing his eyes. "I was in a car crash, Anthony, these things happen." His eyes were still closed, and Anthony had a feeling it was because Harry didn't want to look at him in case he saw his own lies.

"Your father seems to think that there is something more to

it," Anthony replied, his hands behind his back like a policeman, and there he was, thinking he could not, or should not, step into character. Once an actor, he grinned ruefully to himself.

"I'm tired, old boy, let me sleep."

"How do you know the Ford's chauffeur?" Anthony was direct and was losing patience. The question acted like a bolt of electricity through Harry's body. His colour drained and his eyes were wide awake suddenly.

"I don't." Harry lied.

"You dropped me off that day and your attitude completely changed totally out of the blue," Anthony leaned forward. "You noticed the man by the door, and then you left, rather too suddenly for my liking. That man is, or rather was, called Benson. He was the chauffeur of Robert and Cecile Ford. He claimed that he didn't know you." Anthony stood up straight. "I believe you are both lying."

Harry's eyes filled with tears. He looked like a man at the end of his tether. His pain was not only physical; Anthony realised his friend was in some sort of mental turmoil. Returning to his chair, Anthony did not take his eyes off his friend. Was Harry ready to tell all?

"You are sleeping with Cecile, correct?" Now it was Harry who was the questioner.

"Yes." Anthony was blunt and quite enjoyed being honest for a change.

"Other than the physical, do you know much about her?"

"Harry, where is this going?" Anthony was growing irritable.

"It is difficult living up to the expectations of others," Harry said, in response. "Mother, father, fiancée," he let out a sigh and wiped away tears. "I always envied your spirit, your freedom."

"Harry, I'm not free, believe me."

"You are in yourself; I've always wanted to be like you." Tears streamed down Harry's face. "I needed something that allowed me to escape my life. Escape Harry Hewson-Greaves."

"I'm not following," Anthony said with empathy. "From what I can see, your life is pretty top notch. Money, career, future wife, you have it all, Harry. There are many that would envy you;

the person I was before my mother married Philip Crawford, for instance.'

"Perhaps you aren't the only one who can act," Harry smiled. "Come on, Crawford, I can see right through you sometimes, you know. Oh, you might sit there telling me your former self would envy me and feeling all sorry for yourself because of the person you used to be, but admit it, Anthony, you enjoy the wealth and the position. You enjoy your status now and the future you are headed for. Who wouldn't? Although I must say, I don't particularly enjoy my wealth and my so-called privilege and as I say, maybe you aren't the only one who can act." Harry coughed; the effort of his small, sad speech had left him spent.

Anthony was taken aback and felt that if he wasn't sitting on his chair, he would have fell down in shock at Harry's admission. Yet his friend's unhappiness at his position in life was something Anthony found hard to understand. Maybe it was because he had actually experienced both sides of the social spectrum, whereas Harry only knew what he had been born into. Anthony had endured extreme poverty and now he enjoyed great wealth and knew which he preferred.

Yet in many ways, he could perhaps understand what Harry meant. Anthony had long since come to the conclusion that the elite, the wealthy, those who mixed in the highest circles were bound in a mire of hypocrisy and duty. Duty to uphold their rank-and-file lives together for the sake of appearance; trapped by the boundaries of etiquette and social standing, many of Harry's friends who had all been born into the upper classes were simply playing their part to the best of their ability. Perhaps Harry was right, they were all acting.

His sympathy for his friend was overwhelming him, he'd always seen Harry as someone who was so in control. A man who he would seek out for advice on etiquette and how to handle situations.

Both men were thinking about what to say next, but it was Anthony who spoke first.

"How do you escape Harry Hewson-Greaves?"

Harry laughed again before the pain took over. Breathing

heavily, he began.

"My father has a colleague, a business associate. He has a son, about our age, who uses cocaine. I accompanied him to a business meeting. He discussed how he handles life; it seemed like a good idea."

"You took it?" Anthony tried not to sound shocked.

"And I have every time I felt pressure. Dinner with Margaret, pressures of work. I don't think my sniffles are solely to do with a cold." Harry sounded relieved with his admittance.

"Did you take it last night?" Anthony was thinking about Benson's murder.

"Yes," admitted Harry, but elaborated no further.

"That is why you crashed," Anthony stated. "I imagine you will blame the alcohol."

"No, old boy. Margaret and I had words. We didn't make a scene, but I was glad to get out. A few drinks and, hmm, some cocaine, and I was not in an ideal state to drive."

"And how much does Margaret know? And your parents?" Anthony was curious.

"Nothing," he snapped. "They never listen, anyway."

"Were you heading home from Margaret's, Harry? When you left last night."

"Yes," Harry answered in a confused tone. "Why?"

"Benson was murdered last night. The man you claim not to know," Anthony said.

"I didn't kill him," Harry protested, after a long silence. "I'll admit, I know him, but this is the first I've heard about him being dead. Please believe me."

"How do you know him?" Anthony was determined to get to the truth.

"Cecile!" Harry's comment was more of an announcement.

"Cecile?" Anthony was unsure if Harry was baiting him due to his association with the blonde temptress.

"*Sherry's*. You know it, don't you?" Harry already knew the answer to his question.

"Yes. I've been there with Cecile."

"That is where I first took it. A quick toot to blow away the cobwebs," Harry fought back tears. "She was there, with Robert Ford. He knows my father."

"And?" Anthony encouraged Harry to keep talking.

"One night, I had taken cocaine and felt a presence, as though I was being watched," Harry was breathing heavily. "Next, that man was asking me to do things on behalf of his employer. Things I didn't want to do."

"What things? What man?" Anthony was genuinely upset to see Harry suffering. "Are you talking about Benson?"

Harry nodded. He was now crying hard. Anthony felt a rage inside and knew he needed to calm down. There were still questions he needed answering and all this gave Harry even more motive to murder. "What did he want you to do? You can tell me." Anthony put his hand on Harry's arm.

"I hated that man," Harry wiped away tears. "But I didn't kill him."

"I believe you, Harry," Although Anthony had his doubts. "But I don't think the police would."

"You won't tell them," Harry pleaded.

"No, of course not. But there is a chance that they may find a trail that ends up at your door."

"Too many important people have too much to lose," Harry sounded suddenly confident in his comment. "One of the many benefits of being upper class."

The remark rankled with Anthony. Of course, even if the police did question Harry, his family money and social status would answer. How unfair life was, Anthony thought, suddenly. He imagined one of his old friends from the gutter, grown up, involved in the same scenario as Harry, having the same suspicions cast upon him as those the police would undoubtably direct at Harry. Anthony knew which of them would walk away unscathed. It simply wasn't fair that money was able to buy you innocence when any one of his old friends would be instantly guilty. Turning back to Harry, who was snivelling again, Anthony said,

"When did you figure out that Benson was in the employment of Cecile? I mean, aside from him being the Fords' chauffeur?"

"I guessed," came Harry's reply. "I was giving you a lift and he was there. I knew that you were going to see her. Two and two, and all that."

"Very perceptive," Anthony admitted. "So, Cecile was blackmailing you through Benson. Why?"

"That I don't know. She hardly needs the money. Perhaps she enjoys the power, likes the game." Harry noticed the hurt on Anthony's face. "Are you all right, old boy?"

"That's the Harry I know," Anthony smiled. "Always concerned about others." Although his remark didn't perhaps have the sincerity that once would have been there. Anthony continued, "Seriously, who could have killed Benson if you didn't? You have to admit, you are an obvious suspect."

"Agreed. But I am not the murderer."

"Did you see anyone, anything, that could help you? Your blackmailer is dead, that doesn't look good," Anthony didn't hold back in his assessment.

"My blackmailer… and my dealer," Harry revealed.

"He was the one who supplied you?" Anthony digested the revelation and continued his questions. "Did Cecile know?"

"That I can't be sure," Harry replied. "He only mentioned his employer when he asked me to…" Harry welled up again.

"Do what, Harry?" Anthony was desperate to know but tried to show empathy to his friend.

"Please, Anthony."

"Alright," Anthony held Harry's arm. "How did Benson approach you? Was it through the man who introduced you to cocaine?"

"Yes," Harry was beginning to calm down. "Someone who worked in the club was also involved. Sounded foreign. I can't remember his name."

"Funnily enough," began Anthony, "I think I know exactly who you mean."

Harry yawned. He didn't acknowledge Anthony's last comment, instead shutting his eyes. The emotional outburst had taken it out of him. Armed with information, the young

Crawford rose with the purpose of finding Alfonse. A trip to *Sherry's* was in order and this time, it wouldn't be for pleasure. He laid a hand on Harry's arm, who was now snoring, before leaving the room hastily. He gave the Hewson-Greaves' little to no chance to ask him of the conversation, they may already know if they were listening at the door, and right now, Anthony would put nothing past the upper classes. Needing air, Anthony made for the exit. Where would he go next? He had money but needed something to do for a few hours before he paid Alfonse a visit. His mind drifted to Cecile. He was infatuated with her, but this had moved away from a charming Chaplin comedy to something a lot more sinister. Just what game was she playing and who exactly was involved?

The rain was coming down hard as Anthony left the hospital. He was grateful for his coat and hat and was busy fastening the former when an umbrella came out of nowhere and covered his head. Jerking away, he spun around and saw that the rain protector was attached to a slim, middle-aged man. His loose-fitting suit blew vigorously in the wind as rain soaked his worn face.

"This way, Sir." His voice was low, and Anthony couldn't detect an accent.

"Excuse me?" Anthony glared at the man, his heart beating rapidly, his senses on full alert as he wondered who this man was and what he wanted.. The man's eyes were dark and fixed on Anthony, who noticed decaying teeth when he spoke.

"Over there, Sir." The man motioned his head in the direction of the Ford's family car. Anthony approached quickly, a mixture of curiosity and wanting to get out of the rain. The man hurried past him and opened the back passenger door. The sight of Cecile sat in the back excited and surprised Anthony, who climbed in beside his lover. A loud thud of the door closing stopped him from speaking straight away. Cecile was wearing a black dress, as though she was in mourning, he thought and then remembered Benson. But her face was emotionless as she eyed her passenger.

"Well, this is a surprise," Anthony attempted a light-hearted, humorous approach. "My condolences on Benson."

Cecile smiled. "And mine with your friend."

"Thank you. How did you know?"

The car was being driven off rather swiftly. Anthony idly wondered where they were going.

"Not important now, darling," Cecile's response was dismissive. "I was somewhat worried about you, Anthony."

"New driver, I see." Anthony ignored her last comment.

"Life goes on and all that."

Not for Benson, thought Anthony, who had so many questions racing around his mind. How did Cecile know he was at the hospital, and why was she here?

"Thank you for the lift," Anthony started. "Not the most pleasant of days; weather or circumstance."

"Quite," said Cecile.

"Where exactly are we heading?" Anthony was hiding his confusion well. His literary thoughts had switched to Holmes rather than Chaplin. This was a mystery he was determined to solve. The only problem being that there always seemed to be more questions every time he looked for answers, particularly when the object of his desire was around.

"Are we talking metaphorically, Anthony?"

"I don't think so," Anthony tried to remain cool. "I just want to know where we are going. And we need to talk."

Cecile looked at Anthony. A dazzling gold necklace hung in front of her ample bosom as she let out a sigh. Her expression turned serious as she reached into her handbag. Anthony caught the driver's gaze and, thinking of Benson's sudden demise, a wave of paranoia and genuine fear swept over him.

"Wait!" he yelled.

The driver slowed the car dramatically. Cecile looked confused. She handed Anthony a small card before saying, "What's wrong?"

He'd completely misread the situation. His mind had taken him to a place he'd rather not go. He'd suddenly happened upon the notion that Cecile would be pulling out a gun from her expensive bag. He now felt completely stupid. His hands still shaking, he took the card.

"It's a thank you note for your mother," Cecile informed him. "I thought it would be rather nice, as Robert and I have been invited to a Christmas gathering at your address."

Anthony took a deep breath. "I'm sorry, I thought…" he had no idea how to finish that sentence.

"You seem incredibly tense, darling, you need to relax."

"I don't know where you can get a drink at this time?" Anthony could have certainly done with one about now.

"Oh, we can always get a drink," Cecile replied. "But alcohol was not exactly what I had in mind." He hand was now on his thigh.

"Cecile," Anthony's resolve was weakening, although he managed to say, "I need to talk to you. I need your help."

"My needs first, darling, always!" Her hand travelled upwards as she looked him up and down. "Think of this as an early Christmas present."

"Well, I do love unwrapping a gift," his reply as stared into her alluring eyes.

Chapter 22

Anthony rolled onto his back and felt in need of a cigarette. Cecile was caressing his chest, her soft hand tantalising her lover. Anthony had expected a hotel, but Cecile wanted him on set, and the thought had instantly made him hard. The bed wasn't the most comfortable, but they weren't using it to sleep. The young film enthusiast recalled the two actors in the throes of passion when he was last here, watching the proceedings. All those other people watching. Did they enjoy it? Were they attracted to each other? Anthony felt like an actor but did not think his acting ability stretched to pretending to make love with someone in front of others. Plus, when he was with Cecile, his feelings and passion were truly genuine, albeit slightly tarnished now. He loved her, but feared her, yet was utterly captivated by her – and he knew that she knew it. He saw himself the hero of this story, when in theory he was out of his emotional depth with her and felt himself becoming immersed in the more unsavoury elements of the upper classes. It was no wonder he despised them, he thought, completely unaware of his own hypocrisy at that moment. He gave Cecile a delicate peck on the lips, before asking, "Do you ever worry that Robert will find out?"

"No," Cecile said, shortly. She didn't elaborate.

"The hospital," Anthony said, suddenly. "Good guess that I'd be there or are you stalking my every move?"

Cecile went rigid and said nothing for a while. Anthony watched her with interest. Was she stalling? Trying to think of something to say? Then, she piped up, "Robert and Philip spoke on the telephone. Business. Your friend was mentioned in passing. My husband conveyed his sympathy and enquired what hospital he was in. Then he left for work, whilst I wanted some fun." Cecile stroked Anthony's face. He didn't want to be placated, but also didn't want to upset his lover, after all, he had no proof that she was involved in any of the scenarios that were running through his head right now.

"I know he's your friend and that you would be there for him. It's also not been an easy few days for me." Cecile's voice penetrated Anthony's whirling thoughts.

"Harry said Benson was blackmailing him," he said, bluntly.

Cecile moved onto her back. Her erect nipples mesmerised Anthony. She wore only her pendant and wedding band, one leg protruding out of the bedcovers. He lusted after her sumptuous form, but he knew he had to keep his mind focused. Anthony kissed her cheek; deciding that he wanted her to know he was genuine and simply wanted the truth.

"I don't control and can't control what our employees do in their spare time. Benson was clearly mixed up in a lot, but he was a capable driver and never let Robert or me down." Cecile gazed at the ceiling. Anthony wondered if she was deliberately avoiding his eye.

"Who do you think killed him?" Anthony thought of Inspector Naden when he was speaking with himself, Philip, and Jane earlier. He likened himself now to the dour, cut and dried policeman as he questioned Cecile, trying to catch her off guard without quite knowing why. Did he suspect Cecile was involved in Benson's murder or Harry's accident? Or both?

Cecile turned to her lover. "I've no idea. I leave that to the police force."

"You have met Naden?" Anthony asked.

"Yes. Unfortunately."

Anthony laughed. "My sentiments, entirely."

Cecile turned on her side and pressed her backside against Anthony, who fondled her breasts and nibbled her ear before kissing her neck. Her sudden movements of pleasure let him know that she was enjoying this. He could only play along so far, he decided before declaring,

"I just want the truth."

He resumed kissing her neck, his hands clasping hers tightly.

"Be careful what you wish for," she told him, in a tone that Anthony found disturbing. He decided to make light of it.

"I know what I am wishing for right now," he told her, smoothly As he tipped her onto her back and climbed over her.

They made love again. It was a fast, passionate exchange. He enjoyed her nails up and down his back, while she appreciated every inch of his young, virile body. Finally, sated bodies and tired minds, they lay in silence, listening to the rain thudding against the window in a manner befitting of how Jack Dempsey would pummel those who dared to step into the squared circle with *The Manassa Mauler* to try and take his heavyweight crown. Anthony smiled to himself at his analogy.

Both lovers appeared contented and tranquil, but Anthony was in the mood to talk. His feelings were conflicted. He thought he loved Cecile, but doubt had crept in since he had learnt of Benson's death and Harry's accident. He enjoyed sex with her, finding her voracious and desirable, but he resented her control in the relationship. The male ego was hard to compress. Anthony always felt that Cecile used her beauty and her body as a method of keeping him in his place. And it had so far been successful.

He was nothing if not persistent, though, and broke the contended satisfaction that particularly good lovemaking had engendered.

"Harry has a dependency on cocaine," he announced, almost matter of fact in his tone.

"That is on him," Cecile responded. "No one forced him to take it. I know he is your friend, but he is a grown man who has freedom of choice."

"I believe Alfonse is involved, I think possibly Benson was involved and that is why he is dead, and I don't yet know about you, my lovely Cecile. Are you involved?"

Cecile turned to face Anthony. Placing both hands either side of his face, she looked into his eyes, her face furious.

"What exactly is it that you are getting at? You fuck me and then interrogate me!"

The foul language shocked Anthony, although he still pursued his endeavours to obtain the truth from this woman, who he thought he loved.

"I didn't mean to upset you." It was the nearest to an apology Anthony was prepared to make. "I just want the truth. A man is dead, my friend is in hospital as a result of taking drugs, and I'm not sure what I'm mixed-up in."

"It's called life., Anthony," Cecile snapped. "You have a childish innocence about you and life is not like that."

He felt patronised. "Do excuse me, I hadn't realised that wanting the truth was such a childish undertaking."

"The truth is that this is all an act," Cecile replied, somewhat wearily. "Nothing is what it seems, and weak people pay the price. I am not weak."

Anthony stared at her. She scared him as much as she aroused him. He sat up and ran his hands through his hair. "I'm not accusing you of anything. Look at the facts; your chauffeur is dead, a hospitalised man with a drug dependency claims that said dead chauffeur was blackmailing him. That man was your employee."

"Such an adult, masculine body yet a childish outlook," Cecile crooned, looking coquettish. However, the expression on Anthony's face did not waver and then she became belligerent. "Darling, you have so much potential, let's enjoy life."

"I fully intend to. But I desire the truth almost as much as I desire you," Anthony hoped the compliment would be found flattering by her. "I'm going to *Sherry's* tonight and will be speaking to Alfonse. I will get to the truth."

"And what exactly makes you think you can trust Harry?" Cecile said, suddenly. "A man with a dependency on cocaine."

"He's my friend," replied a defensive Anthony.

"How exactly was Benson blackmailing him? Did Harry tell you?"

"He didn't, actually," confessed Anthony.

"Why?" Cecile was almost triumphant. "You are his friend, his confidante. Surely, he would trust you with this information, if indeed it were true."

"Shame, embarrassment, perhaps," Anthony was beginning to have doubts about his friend. "Or maybe he just didn't want me to be involved any more than I already am!"

"Just be careful about who you can trust."

He was unsure if Cecile had just offered advice or giving him a warning.

"Does that include you?" Anthony asked.

Cecile smiled but said nothing, staring at him in a cool and unflustered fashion. The truth was, Anthony didn't trust her but was not thinking with his mind when it came to his married lover. Her seductiveness had overpowered his rational thoughts from the moment they'd met.

"You will be attending the Christmas party?"

He thought a change of subject was probably best.

"We shall," Cecile replied, curtly. "My husband and I."

"I'm sure it will be a delightful occasion," lied Anthony, who was not looking forward to it in the slightest. "I only hope that I will have gotten rid of Soames by then."

The comment took Cecile unaware. "Excuse me?" The cool and unflustered look was replaced by one of surprise and uncertainty.

Anthony was unsure why he had said what he did, but now he had, he felt obliged to continue. "He's trouble and he's a bit too close to my mother."

Cecile continued to look uneasy. She averted her gaze from Anthony and began looking for her clothes.

"What is it, Cecile?" Anthony asked, surprised.

"Nothing, nothing at all," Cecile replied. "You must do what you need to do. Please get dressed and go." She got up and began collecting her garments. A still naked Anthony got hold of his lover and forced her to look at him.

"What is it? I mentioned my mother and Soames and your demeanour has changed completely."

Caught in his grasp and sensing his mood, Cecile buried her head into Anthony's chest and began to cry. "It has nothing to do with that. Please be careful."

"I will," said a bemused Anthony. "Why are you so upset?"

Cecile took a deep breath. "I think I may be with child."

Anthony felt like a Jack Dempsey opponent. His head was ringing, and the room was whirling. He got dressed as fast as he could, without saying a word to Cecile. Getting outside the door, he felt an unbearable feeling of disgust rise in his stomach like bile. Was Cecile implying the child she may be carrying was his?

Or was she telling him that her husband had impregnated her, thus giving them both a way out of their relationship? He didn't stop to consider there was a third option – was she even telling him the truth.

He needed a drink! A trip to *Sherry's* this evening and hopefully a meeting with Alfonse would take courage, and he was not feeling in the least bit courageous. The waiter whom he'd last left in a mess on a lavatory floor was about to become part of his plan to rid the Crawford household of Soames. Cecile's potential bombshell would have to wait.

Chapter 23

Arriving at *Sherry's*, Anthony was feeling worse for wear. He'd not drunk a lot, but a lack of food and a plethora of problems and information was proving hard to both process and deal with. Cecile, Harry, his mother, Soames; all those in his life causing him issues that he needed to resolve. He allowed himself a brief smile when he thought of Philip – so often the protagonist in Anthony's story – who was at this moment in time not an issue. He could never feel sympathy for his stepfather, but knew his mother's behaviour was wrong and dangerous, although he hardly had the moral high ground where illicit extra-marital relationships were concerned.

The club seemed darker than last time. Anthony was seated in a booth and had ordered whisky. He was unsure what the etiquette was with regard to drinks but felt it inappropriate and pompous to order champagne when he was alone. The young man was also loathed to admit that he felt more comfortable in these surroundings than in his last two haunts. Needing sanctuary and alcohol, he'd swiftly left the potentially pregnant Cecile alone and proceeded about half a mile before finding a tavern that was popular with seafarers. Dressed in an expensive suit, he stuck out like a sore thumb and had felt decidedly uncomfortable and out of place with a number of bearded faces eyeing him cautiously. One or two had commented, but the governor had come to his rescue, offering him a quieter spot away from the main bar. Whilst Anthony was sure the landlord's motives weren't due to his kind nature and more to do with Anthony's look of wealth, he'd appreciated the intervention. He'd paid over the odds for the brown ale which he hadn't liked and had spent what seemed like an eternity staring into the abyss, whilst listening to predominantly London accents discuss football, politics, and a dislike of foreigners, a group that Anthony empathised greatly with after his time in this watering hole.

He'd been careful when checking his pocket watch as he was sure there may be a boozed-up opportunist who would make a pretty penny by robbing the rich man in the tavern. But he knew these streets fairly well and had planned his route, as well as assessing the right time to make his exit. Philip's allowance was coming in handy today, as that feeling of hypocrisy swept over him. Like it or not, he was part of that world, the streets of London and its people saw him as a stranger, an enemy, with little knowledge or interest of the fact that up until a few years ago he had been one of them and would have called this place home. Now part of the elite, he was a dandy, a film-loving lothario who had been seduced by a beautiful socialite who was the wife of a successful and powerful businessman. And this was all made possible due to the wealth and personal choice of Philip.

Anthony felt like someone trapped between two worlds, and he never truly belonged in either. Sitting alone in his booth, waiting for his whisky, he thought of Harry who, aside from Jane, was perhaps the only person to truly recognise how conflicted Anthony was. The Hewson-Greaves family were every inch the embodiment of what high society looked like to the outside world, rich, glamourous, and privileged, but Harry had an empathy that he balanced with a pragmatism he tried to bestow on his best friend, whilst all the time battling his own demons. Anthony was racked with guilt. Harry had always been the one advising, schooling, and helping, whilst he himself always had a gripe and a moan. Something had to change. Anthony either needed to accept what he was and embrace it or walk away from it all, including the handouts and other perks that being a Crawford afforded. And he knew that he didn't have the strength, or wherewithal to walk away. Besides, he reasoned; he loved certain aspects of this life far too much to give it all up for the sake of his conscience.

The waitress brought over his drink. Anthony's flirtatious nature appealed to the pretty, young black-haired girl, who couldn't have been much older than he. Her hair, reasonably short and teased around her face, complimented her rather pretty features and her piercing blue eyes gave Anthony the notion that she had Irish roots. With a petite figure perfectly suited to her short, figure-hugging dress, Anthony fancied that she was more suited to the role of dancer than server. She was a popular figure in the club but had given the young stranger more than a few passing glances as she went about her business.

Anthony lit a cigarette and surveyed the room. Despite being somewhat taken by the dark-haired, attractive server, the member of staff he was really interested in hadn't so far made an appearance. A rather bohemian group sat near the stage and could have been tonight's acts were it not for the amount of alcohol they were consuming. They had a literary feel about them, slightly effeminate, Anthony thought, as he recalled the first time he'd set foot in this establishment. Their clothing looked to be velvet, at least the jackets were, and two of the men wore capes. All in bow ties that were large and loosely tied, he was sure that one of the men was sporting eye make-up. His hair was long and flowing and he was clearly the obsession of the oldest member of the group. He was about Philip's age and thinning on top and couldn't keep his eyes off his companion, who was telling a story as much with his hands as he was with his mouth. Flamboyantly pointing and gesturing, he was the centre of attention and was clearly loving every minute of it. *"Was this how Oscar Wilde dressed?"* Anthony's thought immediately took him to Mr Mills as he recalled his former tutor's anger and disgust upon mention of the nineteenth century poet and playwright. He could make out some of the conversation, which seemed to be largely about music and the décor of *Sherry's*; they were extremely well-spoken and were complimenting the waitress' Marcel Wave, which Anthony presumed was a hairstyle. Their interest in her appearance differed from his. He thought of Cecile's attitude when discussing the two men passionately kissing. Anthony had referred to it as an illegal practice, whilst Cecile had barely batted an eyelid. Of course, homosexuality wasn't the only illegal practice going on at this club.

The mood changed from a dark, smoky relaxed atmosphere to something far more tense as a group of men wearing peak caps and long overcoats made their way to the bar. The band that was occupying the stage suddenly halted preparations as the clientele made their way through the club. Conversations and laughter largely ended as a hushed silence seemed to fall over *Sherry's*. Anthony detected a Birmingham dialect and thought of the gentleman who seemed so impressed with his knockout of Alfonse. A quintet in total, they all wore peak caps, overcoats, and serious expressions. Two of the five were clearly larger than the other three and Anthony suspected that these were the gang's muscle. The strong, silent types who said little but spoke the language of violence and terror perfectly. The other three may have been brothers. All similar in height, Anthony was sure that one of them was the man who had spoken to him after his altercation with Alfonse. But it was another who seemed to be the gang's leader. Emotionless eyes, the removal of his cap to scratch his head revealed a military style haircut that was short back and sides, with the top neatly combed over. He surveyed the room and its clientele and looked as though he was incapable of relaxation or even smiling. Anthony knew that America, and particularly Chicago, was being controlled by gangs and mobsters looking to make a killing on prohibition and other nefarious activities. Was this the English equivalent of the American gangster? A smartly dressed man behind the bar showed the group a door that Anthony thought may lead to a private function room. These men wanted to talk business that he was fairly sure wasn't legal. Criminal gangs assuming control were becoming regular features in newspapers, who revelled in sensationalised stories of evil figures battling for the streets whilst taking command of various venues to sell drugs or run prostitution. Where this group responsible for cocaine in *Sherry's*? Was Harry mixed up with them? He had only spoken of Benson and another whom Anthony believed was Alfonse, as those involved in supplying him.

He finished his whisky and took a long drag on his cigarette. Anthony's thoughts were now on Cecile. Like it or not, she was mixed up in all this, although she was steadfast in her denial. Her narrative that Benson was a lone wolf involved in criminal elements without the knowledge of his employers was becoming more dubious with everything Anthony discovered. Harry had offered a different story, one that implicated Cecile. Both had something to hide, and the truth was hidden somewhere. Whom did he believe? His best friend or the woman he loved. The woman who may very well be carrying his child. There was a possibility that it may be her husband's, whilst Anthony let the thought cross his mind that she may not be pregnant at all. He didn't stop to examine the implication of her lies, or the fact that he no longer believed everything Cecile said as the truth. In any event, he reasoned, Cecile had only thought she was with child, and Anthony hoped she was wrong. An unwanted pregnancy would yield so many complications, as if his life wasn't complicated enough. Thinking of the future, young Crawford never saw he and Cecile together. He loved her or thought he did, but he was even beginning to have doubts about his feelings and the scandal that a public revelation of their affair would cause would not be something Cecile would welcome. She enjoyed her current lifestyle and of course, should their affair be made public, Anthony would not be able to keep her in the luxury to which she was accustomed. In light of the merest whiff of scandal and disgrace, Philip Crawford would certainly withdraw Anthony's generous allowance and the life he enjoyed now, he would not be able to enjoy in a future which included the destruction of the marriage of one of Philip's dearest friends, and a business associate to boot. Anthony knew without a shadow of a doubt that the doors of Philip's London home, and the Oxfordshire mansion would be firmly closed to him. This led Anthony to wonder what he was to Cecile. Fun? A distraction? A useful tool in her own endeavours? Did she love him? Could Cecile love anyone?

The sight of the pretty waitress broke his thoughts. She seductively sauntered over to him; her eyes firmly fixed on the patron she'd been flirting with. Anthony's ego certainly enjoyed the attention of the pretty young thing, but his mind was on something else.

"Same again?" she asked softly, her smile lighting up the darkened main room.

"What is your name?" Anthony answered her question with one of his own as he repeatedly turned over his cigarette case on the circular table.

"Mary," she smiled, her gaze alternating between his and his nervous flicking of the diamond encrusted, silver case. She knew money when it introduced itself.

"Such a pretty name," his reply making her blush. "Oh, where are my manners, would you like one?" He held out the cigarette case.

"Oh, no thank you, Sir. We aren't permitted to smoke whilst serving." Mary seemed flustered by Anthony's offer.

"Such a pompous rule, considering what goes on in here," he commented. "Well, as you are serving, I shall have another, and I wondered if you could help me?"

"With what, Sir?"

"Anthony, please." He was enjoying this exchange and her attention. "I wondered if Alfonse is working tonight."

"Oh, he is in the cellar. Would you like me to get him?" There was definitely a hint of Irish in her voice.

"If it is not too much trouble? I certainly wouldn't want to put you out as I can see you are busy." Anthony's flattery was in overdrive.

"Not at all," Mary's voice went to a higher pitch. "I'll get you your whisky, Anthony."

"Good girl," Anthony placed another cigarette in his mouth, whilst Mary's eyes never left the little silver case. "Is it permitted for you to have a drink?"

Mary giggled. "I'm afraid not. At least not while I'm working."

She disappeared behind the bar. The group of actors were in full animated conversation, whilst a man and his much younger female companion sat gazing into each other's eyes. The stunningly attractive redhead seemed well versed in over-exaggerated laughs and feigned interest, as the man was in full conversational flow. Anthony loved to make up stories about people he observed; he envisaged a successful, married tycoon, looking for an ego boost in the shape of this much younger siren, who may or not have been paid to keep him company. *Sherry's* gave the impression of an exclusive venue, and was certainly too expensive for the working classes, but the underbelly of criminality, moral ambiguity and scandalous hypocrisy seemed at home here, and Anthony was right in the thick of it.

Mary re-emerged with Anthony's large whisky. Her walk was brisker this time, she was keen to get back to the table and carry on the flirtations. She placed his drink on the table, her mesmerising eyes not leaving his. Anthony slowly leant forward and whispered: "Alfonse?"

"Oh, of course, Sir," Mary said, startled. "Who shall I say is asking for him?"

"Say it is a representative of Mrs Ford," Anthony told her. "He will know what you mean." Anthony reached into his pocket; Mary stood holding the tray. He pulled out a crisp pound note, which caused her big blue eyes to open even wider. "Is it permitted for you to accept a gratuity? You have taken such good care of me."

"Oh yes, Sir." Mary's hands were as fast as lightning as she accepted the gift. She had also noticed the diamond clip holding a wad of notes together. He wore a gold signet ring on his little finger. "I shall go and get Alfonse. Representative of Mrs. Ford, was it?"

"That is correct, Mary," Anthony said. "Thank you for all of your help."

"Of course," Mary turned away and headed towards the bar. She turned back and said: "I finish at ten."

Anthony smiled and sipped his drink. It was Macallan, one of his favourites. "I see. Thank you, Mary."

She pretended not to hear a customer and disappeared into a room in the back. Anthony thought about how Alfonse would react upon sight of him. He expected a defensive individual but reasoned he wouldn't make a scene for fear of a complaint being received by his employers. Anthony's standing meant he could make trouble for Alfonse, which would probably result in his dismissal. For all young Crawford knew, Cecile's former associate may be running a little side business that his bosses knew nothing of and if his thoughts on the gentlemen from Birmingham were correct, they wouldn't take too kindly to competition, or private enterprise which didn't involve them.

So wrapped up was Anthony in his musings, he hadn't noticed Alfonse standing behind him. The waiter attracted his attention with the words, "Mrs. Ford's representative, I take it?"

Anthony slowly turned around upon hearing that mild, Eastern European accent. Alfonse stood, his bruised eye still shining from his last altercation with his adversary. His white shirt was faded, and his trousers worn. The bow tie, which seemed to be a new part of the uniform, was causing him as much discomfort as the sight of who was before him.

"Please sit," Anthony motioned to the empty chair. Alfonse slowly made his way to where he was prompted and took a seat opposite.

"It is not normal for staff to sit with guests." Alfonse's tone was a mixture of anger, nerves, and confusion.

"Yes," Anthony agreed. "I did get a full breakdown of club etiquette from Mary. Charming girl."

"What is it you want?" Alfonse was in no mood for small talk.

"We have a mutual acquaintance. One that is now hospitalised." Anthony cleared his throat.

"I know nothing about it," Alfonse shot back immediately.

"I am not accusing you of anything," Anthony was not aiming to reassure him. "The reason I am here is that he was able to acquire something other than your finest champagne. If you know what I mean?"

"I have no idea," Alfonse sounded nervous.

Anthony leant forward and brandished the wad of notes that had impressed Mary. "Can you help me, Alfonse? I can make it worth your while."

If he could get what he needed from Alfonse, Anthony had his plan in place to get rid of Soames. A butler found in possession of cocaine wouldn't remain in employment for very long.

Chapter 24

Alfonse had been gone a while and Anthony was beginning to get an uneasy feeling, although he did his best to exude an image of a powerful, confident man sitting and enjoying a drink and the attentions of a pretty waitress. Mary had passed by his table on three separate occasions to enquire if 'everything was to his satisfaction' and to ask if he had 'everything' he 'needed', each time lingering just a little longer than before. On the third occasion, he'd relented and requested another drink, but he knew he had to keep his wits about him if his plan was to succeed and pay off. Anthony didn't trust Alfonse and had made himself vulnerable to the murky, mysterious waiter who had his fingers in more pies than Anthony cared to count. Cecile's story – and it was a story, that much Anthony had worked out for himself - had told him probably as much as she wanted her younger lover to know, but Anthony wasn't convinced there was any truth to the tale, so now he was left with a feeling that whatever Alfonse was connected with, Cecile may well be implicated too. Young Crawford reasoned that the drugs didn't come from the *Sherry's* employee, he was clearly a middleman assigned to putting people together and making connections. Who gave him his orders was something Anthony mulled over as he waited for the other man's return. He could no longer be certain that the someone giving the orders was not Cecile, and where did that leave his relationship with her? He was convinced Alfonse was merely a 'runner', a fetcher and carrier, a go-between with illusions of grandeur and someone who would not let something such as legality get in the way.

A group of dancers were lining up at the dark-blue curtain, ready to perform. Anthony was admiring the group, dressed in 'flapper' dresses, the 'a la mode' of the twenties, he reflected, although he did wonder if any of the women who dressed and acted like 'flappers' actually knew the term's early use actually meant 'prostitute'. He supposed there was a very general connection, in some ways. Flapper girls were considered 'racy', wearing excessive makeup, drinking alcohol, smoking cigarettes in public, driving their own cars themselves, and enjoying a sexual freedom that was considered a flouting of modern convention and acceptable behaviour. Anthony wasn't sure he approved of some of the flapper girl's behaviour, his attitude displaying the hypocrisy he so despised in the upper classes. In fact, flappers were becoming the icons of the 'Roaring Twenties' – a term Anthony was beginning to hear more of, used to describe the social and political turbulence of the time, which was nurturing closer transatlantic cultural exchanges following the end of the war. Slipping out of his reverie, Anthony couldn't help but admire the flapper dress code, he enjoyed their short, gold dresses, bobbed hair, and matching gold headbands. They waited patiently for a band who were setting up with brass instruments.

This was very much a smaller show compared to the weekend offering he'd enjoyed with Cecile and there probably wouldn't be much dancing, although with the colourful group of thespians, who were getting more drunk by the hour, Anthony couldn't be sure. His mind then drifted to Cecile. Her body was every bit as athletic as the beautiful dancers about to entertain; he thought of that night where she stole the show, dancing the Charleston before they'd performed a much more intimate dance in their hotel room. Things were less complicated then; she'd been a fiery, desirable woman whom he wanted to ravish over and over again. Though no less beautiful or attractive to Anthony, her announcement regarding her potential pregnancy had given her a vulnerability, which had frightened Anthony and which he didn't like. Or maybe the whole story of the baby was simply calculated guile on Cecile's part, to get her off the hook of Anthony's awkward questions. He wasn't sure which of the two options frightened him most.

His thoughts were interrupted by the sound of a glass hitting the table. Looking round to make some witty remark towards Mary, he was shocked by the sight of Alfonse, who sat down uninvited, something Anthony couldn't resist sarcastically commenting on.

"Have a seat, please," he smiled, whilst Alfonse looked at him stonily, unimpressed by Anthony's humour, but undeterred. "Mary will be so disappointed she was not able to serve me with my drink," he reached for the glass and held it aloft. "Nevertheless, thank you, and cheers!"

"I can get what you need." Alfonse told him, without preamble.

"That simple?" Anthony questioned. "Are there any more details for this transaction?"

"I need money first," Alfonse told him. "What you need will be in the restroom, behind the lavatory basin."

"And exactly how muc…" Anthony stopped as the ever-eager Mary walked by, clearly disgruntled by Alfonse pulling rank to serve a drink to a man whose company she hoped to enjoy. Alfonse didn't even glance at her, preferring to keep his gaze firmly fixed on the man whom he hoped to make money from. Anthony let a smile cross his face. "Before we talk about money, I'm simply supposed to trust the fact that what I want is where you say it is?"

Alfonse was irritated but kept his cool. "Do you want it, or not?"

"I wouldn't be here, speaking to you now if I didn't, would I?" Anthony's voice had an almost belligerent sarcasm. "Please don't take offence, but why exactly should I trust you?"

"Because I am the one you came to when you wanted something." Alfonse's reply was almost triumphant. "You, rich people, always come to people like me when you want something you know you shouldn't have."

"You sound as though you know a friend of mine," Anthony took out a cigarette and placed it in his mouth as he thought about Harry.

"Perhaps I do," rasped Alfonse. "But what is one nice suit and posh voice compared to another?

"Now there I must concur, Alfonse," Anthony replied. "However, the group of men in peak caps, who came in a few minutes ago and disappeared to what I presume is a private area,

I wouldn't imagine they have posh voices, or nice suits, although they all seem to be treated with suspicious reverence here." He raised his eyebrows at Alfonse, who grunted irritably. "It may interest you to know that one very similarly dressed man praised my handiwork the night you and I had – a discussion – in the lavatory. Not that you will remember."

Alfonse was exasperated by this verbal jousting, which he had no chance of winning. His face red and his fists clenched, he said as calmly as he possibly could, "This is business. I feel nothing for you and don't let revenge come into to it. You want it or not?"

"I want it, Alfonse," Anthony said, calmly. "I would also like to enjoy the performance of these charming ladies and wouldn't mind another drink. And, if possible, could Mary bring it to me?"

Alfonse glared at Anthony, who motioned at the waiter to leave the table. Alfonse got up and couldn't resist with an addendum, "You think you are high and mighty, but Cecile destroys what she likes and will do it to you."

"Your advice is appreciated," Anthony told him. "Now, I wish you to carry out my instructions whilst I enjoy tonight's performance. After that, I will check the lavatories and, if you are telling the truth, I will pay you." Anthony lit his cigarette. "But, for now, please go away."

Alfonse moved briskly towards the bar just as the jazz music started. The quintet of dancers made their way on the stage and began their recital. Above the noise of the music, conversation hummed, and glasses chinked.

Anthony pondered his next move. His arrogant demeanour towards Alfonse was a potentially dangerous strategy. He was alone in Alfonse's place of work, negotiating illegal activity that would bring him closer to a world he'd always been happy watching at the cinema and reading about in novels. For all he knew, the waiter could at this very moment, be arranging Anthony's demise upon entering the public facilities. He could deny it all he wanted, but Alfonse had many reasons to harbour a grudge against Cecile's love interest, given what Cecile had told Anthony. But was any of it true? Whilst he had every reason to doubt Alfonse's character, certain events were conspiring to cast doubt on Cecile's and Anthony felt as though he could trust neither waiter nor lover. Fed up with his thoughts, and the flappers' mediocre performance of the Charleston, Anthony decided it was as good a time as any to visit the lavatory and check out Alfonse's story. Slipping out of his chair, he made his way to where he hoped he would find what he was looking for. Fortunately, the table he'd chosen was closer to the lavatories than where he and Cecile had sat. He felt nervous and wanted to get this part of the evening over with. Upon entering the restroom, his sigh of relief distracted another patron who was washing his hands.

"Good evening," said a flustered Anthony.

The man, who was about sixty and impeccably dressed in a full dinner suit, complete with bow tie, simply nodded back before leaving. Anthony recalled he'd seen several men who were enjoying the evening with much younger ladies and the thought calmed Anthony as the gentleman would have other things on his mind than the flustered young man who had just entered the lavatory.

Now the coast was clear, Anthony surveyed the landscape; there were two private cubicles, had Alfonse specified which one the cocaine would be in? Neither was occupied so Anthony elected to look in the one nearest him. He gently pushed the door, and slipped inside, making sure to lock the white door behind him. It wouldn't do for someone to walk in whilst he was examining the tiling behind the basin. Anthony sat on the basin and stared straight ahead. He was unsure what he was waiting for, so he reached down behind the toilet to look for something he wasn't sure even existed. The cold ceramic on his hands didn't cool his temperature, which was rising due to nerves he couldn't control. He didn't want to get on his knees for fear of dirtying his suit, so he let his hand explore without the benefit of sight. It seemed like an eternity of searching when his index finger felt what appeared to be paper. Reaching further, he clasped what was a small package that had been loosely taped to the back of the toilet. Seconds later it was in Anthony's hand. No bigger than a small diary, it was light in weight and heavily taped. He questioned if he should open the package when he heard footsteps outside and chose to remain in the cubicle. The sound of zips, muffled whistling and running water was soon replaced by a cacophony of screams, breaking glass, and scuffling. The unknown man dashed out of the toilet as deafening whistles assaulted Anthony's eardrums. Without thinking, he placed the package into his pocket and unlocking the door, peered outside. The lavatory was empty, but all hell had seemingly broke loose back in the club area. Fists were flying and the uniforms were unmistakable; the police had arrived on the premises and weren't here for the entertainment! Anthony froze. He hadn't a clue what to do. His initial thought was of his mother and Philip, should he become mixed up in whatever was going on outside, the shame would be unbearable for both and the consequences dire for him. He knew he needed to do something and figured that an escape may be the only real option. Without the power of rational thought, he slipped into the dark, chaos filled room and beat a hasty retreat to the exit, only for a hand to go on his shoulder and a familiar voice call out, "Not so fast, Sir."

Spinning round, it was a question of who was more shocked, Anthony or Inspector Naden? Both men stared at each other as the former suddenly remembered that he was in possession of illegal drugs whilst no more than two feet from a serving police officer and surrounded by many more of his colleagues. If Anthony were to escape this, he would need a huge amount of luck and a performance worthy of praise from Chaplin himself.

"Inspector?" Anthony assumed his most well-spoken tones, even and well-modulated, every inch the upper-class gentleman passing the time of day and thinking there was nothing unusual about the circumstances under which he had bumped into the other man.

"Master Crawford," answered Naden. "Do forgive me. May I ask what you are doing here?"

"Having a drink, Inspector." Anthony's look was implacable.

"Of course, Mr. Crawford."

"May I ask what exactly is going on?" Anthony was playing

the bewildered, upper-class gent to a tee.

"Anonymous tip-off," Naden told him. "Is this a regular haunt of yours, Sir?"

"Good God, no! I was meeting a friend after I concluded some business not too far from here. He had to leave, and I was just about to do the same," Anthony lied. "There does seem to be some less than salubrious characters in residence."

"Quite an unsavoury team from the Birmingham area, Master Crawford. Well overdue a warning, shall we say."

"Well, you are the expert, Inspector," Anthony switched to flattery. "I shall feel safer knowing that you and your team are doing such a wonderful job."

"Thank you, Sir," Naden's snobbery and ambitions of bettering himself were evident. "A policeman's work is never done, and we are often overworked and underpaid. If you get my drift."

Anthony sensed where this was going. "Quite, Inspector. And with Christmas approaching, I imagine that you and your hardworking colleagues are mightily stretched?"

"You could say that Sir." Naden admired Anthony's suit.

"I hope you won't too offended if I were to show my appreciation for the wonderful job you do?" Anthony slipped a wad of notes into Naden's hand and, judging by the fluency the Inspector placed them into his pocket, this wasn't the first time he'd accepted someone's gratitude.

"Thank you, Sir." Naden in appreciation.

"I hate to ask, Inspector, but is there any chance I could perhaps be allowed to leave?" Anthony eyed his opportunity.

"Constable Healy!" Naden bellowed.

Anthony was momentarily afraid. Had Naden double bluffed him and was now going to arrest him? He remained calm and in character, just an upper-class gentleman who had been having a drink with a friend and who was about to go home. A man of similar height to Anthony in a full police uniform approached. His black moustache looked sharp enough to cut glass and his small eyes gave him the look of someone permanently disgruntled.

"Sir."

Healy could well have been ex-military. The tone, the way he held himself; this man was the very essence of a disciplined service.

"It is imperative that we get young Master Crawford out of here. Escort him outside and find him a taxi. Understand?"

"Yes, Sir," Healy replied instantly before turning to Anthony. "This way, Master Crawford."

Healy kept his hand behind Anthony's back. He was escorting him without touching him. Anthony collected his coat and was heading briskly for the exit when he noticed Alfonse lying face-down on the floor. His bruised face caught sight of Anthony as he was about to leave. Anthony was unsure if Alfonse knew he was in possession of the cocaine but was not sticking around to find out. The waiter began to struggle and was desperate to speak but was struck by the officer. Anthony was sure he spotted two teeth fly out of Alfonse's mouth as he left *Sherry's* for what he was certain was the last time. His would-be-supplier had made the call, he was sure. He'd hoped to get Anthony caught in possession, but a corrupt police officer keen on improving his social standing had put paid to Alfonse's plan.

"Taxi rank is just over there, Sir," Healy stated. "Take care."

"Thank you, Constable."

Anthony dashed to line of waiting black cabs, jumped inside the nearest and instructed the driver to take him home. He needed familiar surroundings and his own bed. A plan to get rid of Soames was moving on to the next phase but could have so easily ended with his incarceration. His breathing heavy, he wound down a window and gulped the freezing December night air. Reaching inside his pocket, he pulled out the package. He thought of what this stuff had done to Harry and what trouble he'd almost found himself in. He'd been lucky, he knew that. He was nowhere near as clever or as worldly wise as he believed, he was a film enthusiast that was caught up in his own big-screen epic. Complete with a beguiling femme fatale, pornographic films, and now illegal substances. Meanwhile, the malignant butler had become involved with his dear mother which threatened to ruin everything. What Anthony was doing was wrong, but he believed it to be for the right reasons. He eyed the package and decided that he should open it. The driver was concentrating on the roads on this dark night and probably wouldn't care anyway as long as he was getting paid.

Anthony carefully opened the package. It was well-taped but, after a brief struggle, he was able to get it open. He'd never seen cocaine before and didn't know what to expect. Peaking inside, he noticed more paper. Four more layers to be precise.

And then, Anthony found nothing!

It appeared he had escaped *Sherry's* and not paid Alfonse for something he was not even in possession of. The waiter had worked his own sting on Anthony, who was feeling a mixture of rage and hopelessness. Alfonse may have been struck with force by an over-zealous policeman, but he'd landed the last laugh on Anthony.

His plan up in smoke, he put his head back and let out a sigh. He couldn't give up, Chaplin always found a way to come good in the end, one way or another, and so would he.

Chapter 25

"Know your enemy, boy!" A phrase Philip used so often in one of his many lectures. Whether discussing military service or business, the latter being a far more common topic, he would quote those four words. Anthony's stepfather often viewed everything as a competition, with every other person in the conversation an enemy, who must be either defeated or brought in line. It was a rhetoric that made his stepson roll his eyes and switch off as Philip went into his most vitriolic of selves, but today it was advice he was willing to pay attention to.

With his attempt to plant illegal drugs on Soames now null and void, he needed a new tactic if he was to rid the Crawford household of the butler he disliked so much and who was too close to his mother for comfort. He'd spent the night pondering the irony of using a substance that had ruined and almost ended Harry's life to help preserve the one he was trying to become accustomed to. Soames' behaviour with his mother threatened all of that, he needed to go. Once out of the way, Anthony could confront Jane and remind her of exactly what both of them stood to lose because of her actions.

Then there was Cecile. The woman of his dreams who was another man's reality. The irony of it was not lost on Anthony and plagued his waking moments. He loved this woman yet didn't fully trust her and knew that the romance was always going to be a short, passionate one that had to come to an end. But she was an addiction that would be hard to break; she was Anthony's fix in the same way cocaine had become Harry's. With the Crawford's Christmas get together a day away, the evening with both Cecile and her husband present, would surely test his habit and indeed, his acting ability. He planned to act as though nothing was wrong and play the dutiful, charming son in front of all of Philip's friends and associates. Cecile had too much to lose to rock the boat; Robert was a man of infinite wealth, influence and power, Cecile craved all three. Although a woman of some means in her own right, being married to a tycoon was befitting to her style and gave her access to limitless funds enabling her to keep her own. If Anthony had ever listened to Philip Crawford, he would have known Cecile was simply obeying the first rule of good business – always take risks with someone else's money, never your own.

The house was a hive of activity although Philip had gone into the factory as usual. The preparation for dinners and parties was the domain of the woman of the house. Jane had been going through the seating plan and having endless chats with Mrs. Blackshaw in regard to catering. The family cook had reluctantly agreed to have more help due to the size and importance of the occasion but was assured that sole charge of the menu was hers. Servants were busy putting up the Christmas tree which was to go in the main hall so guests could admire upon arrival, while tinsel and other festive decorations were everywhere. Soames stalked through the house, watching the servants perform their duties much in a way that was reminiscent of a cane-happy teacher desperate to dish out corporal punishment to any poor, unfortunate pupil who spoke when they weren't asked or stopped working for even a moment. The butler was revelling in his role as house schoolmaster. It was a job he did well, Anthony couldn't deny that. Personality aside, Soames ran a good house and was attentive to what his employers required, although a little too attentive to Jane's needs, which meant he needed to be removed from employment sooner rather than later.

Watching Soames, Anthony knew that as an adversary, the butler was quick thinking and meticulous to detail, something that would be hard to combat. However, as he watched Soames perform his duties with an air of supreme confidence and efficiency, Anthony realised he knew very little about the butler, aside from the man's totally unacceptable passion for his employer's wife. He needed to get to know Soames, understand what made him tick, gauge his interests and beliefs if he was to take Soames down., It was something he needed to do whilst protecting his mother and preserving her reputation. Anthony did feel uneasy about what he had said to Cecile about Soames and Jane. Though only alluding to an affair, he'd let slip his disdain for the family butler and his intentions of getting rid of him, citing his mother as a reason. Whilst still believing himself in love with Cecile, Anthony found he no longer trusted her, and the information about Soames and his mother was something she could use against him, and them, to her own advantage. Would she be a threat to his plan? Anthony didn't know, but perhaps the fact that she was carrying Anthony's child might deter her from anything that would detriment him and his family. If it were the truth, of course, and Anthony sensed the truth was something Cecile had very little time for.

The day was a surprisingly bright but bitterly cold one. A brisk blue December sky played host to no clouds, but a strong wind put an added chill in the air. Anthony stood on his balcony, his shirt blowing in the cold air, as he pondered life and the difficult choices he was faced with. Some were his own doing, whilst some had been foisted upon him. Harry had been discharged from hospital, but the Hewson Greaves' would be attending tomorrow's soiree without their eldest son. Harry's life would become increasingly unpleasant over the next few weeks; his parents were not the sort to offer sympathy and preserving their family name would always take precedence over recovery. There was an element of scandal about what had happened to Harry, and his parents did not want anyone else to find out about it.

Anthony took one look at the landscape, the winter garden bathed in the cold, December sunlight which dappled through the semi naked trees, huddled together as though sheltering from the winter weather, and then he sighed and went back into his bedroom. He looked at his brand-new dinner suit that was hanging on his double-doored wardrobe. It was a resplendent, bespoke Saville Row specialty that Philip and Jane had insisted on. Anthony had protested bitterly, mainly because he needed to be in London for the tailor to measure him, and for fittings, although he was secretly delighted with the end product. Anthony couldn't deny it, he loved the expensive clothes, fancy food, and the nightlife, all of which were afforded to him by his belonging to the decade's high society, albeit through his mother's second marriage. Then again, it was just another suit not too dissimilar to the many he already owned, and, in his more working-class moments, he often questioned why so few people needed so much. Jane would have a new dress, whilst Philip had also bought a new dinner suit. It was a pure show, a fallacy. The happy family were not happy because of their great wealth, in actual fact, the family consisted of no more than an emotionally redundant patriarch, an unhappy adulterous mother, and a son who was as reckless as he was hypocritical. Too socialist to fully embrace the life of a socialite without being dogged with guilt and a general dislike of the majority of people in his circles, yet far too comfortable and cowardly to step away from it, Anthony despised himself.

But there was no conflict regarding his agenda to get rid of Soames. If Anthony was to leave the life that he'd grown accustomed to, it would be by his choice rather than the reckless behaviour of his mother and the head of service. He knew Soames would be busier than usual today, and an unusually friendly Anthony wanting to make conversation may be enough for Soames to drop his guard enough to give young Crawford something he could use against him.

Making his way downstairs, he ventured towards the kitchens, where Jane would be today, without it infuriating Philip. Old habits die hard, and Jane often went to the kitchen to discuss menus with her cook, instead of summoning the cook to her own private sitting room, which was what was considered 'acceptable' and 'etiquette'. Today the lady of the house would have a legitimate excuse to discuss timings and schedule with Mrs. Blackshaw in the kitchen, due to the additional staff that had been hired and the fact the cook would be rushed off her feet and would probably decline to come out of the kitchen at all on this very special day. Anthony also knew, however, that the times in the kitchen with the servants were something Jane enjoyed, it was somewhere she felt comfortable. The mantle of lady of the house may have fallen on her shoulders, but that didn't mean she felt easy wearing it.

The sound of Soames' voice attracted his attention and Anthony saw an opportunity to engage him in conversation. Stevens, the Crawford's new footman, was the latest victim of one of the butler's scathing lectures. The young man, who had been in the post less than a week, looked shellshocked in his ill-fitting uniform, cowering in front of the butler as he tore a strip off his unfortunate underling. Anthony approached slowly, taking in all the Christmas decorations that were tastefully arranged around the room. Each room's Christmas dressings had been matched to the décor; the colour scheme picked particularly to compliment the room in which they had been placed. In the magnificent reception hall, the theme was winter white. Glittering white tinsel, white twinkling lights adorned the huge tree, which reached almost to the ceiling. White baubles and paper chains hung from the picture rails, the only colour coming from the resplendent tree itself, and holly and mistletoe bunches which were tied to all the doorframes. Anthony recalled Christmases of the past, when he and Jane had enjoyed a far more humble celebration. She hadn't been able to afford a tree, but she had always taken Anthony to the local park and broken off some branches from the abundant fir trees, which they took home and decorated with tiny baubles and candles. Jane had spent what little money she had on filling Anthony's Christmas stocking. Sometimes the toys she had placed inside were second-hand, but there was always at least one shiny, new car, or a book and precious tangerines and a bar of chocolate, but since residing in Crawford manor, the magic of Christmas had faded and a far more formal, albeit visually spectacular affair, was the order of the festivities. Sometimes, Anthony thought he preferred the broken branches and second-hand toys to the excesses of Christmas at the Crawford residence. He always believed that Christmas was another thing Philip found got in the way of his business and recalled the time he'd read *A Christmas Carol* and visualised his stepfather as the main character.

"How are you finding things, Stevens?" Anthony enquired of the footman, whose wide-eyed expression made him look even younger than he actually was.

"Master Anthony," Soames said, startled. "Yes, things are coming together and running smoothly."

"Thank you, Soames," Anthony replied politely. "I'm sure Stevens is capable of speaking for himself."

A brief but awkward silence was broken by Soames, who ordered the newest employee of the house to answer. Anthony enjoyed not only putting Soames in his place, but also sticking up for those who felt they couldn't. The young Crawford knew full well that, but for a marriage, he may well be in the place of the man who was now opening doors for him.

"Master Anthony is speaking to you, Stevens." Soames couldn't resist trying to reclaim control.

"I'm very much enjoying my job, Sir," Stevens' voice was soft and had a hint of Devon in it. Dark in complexion, his short haircut suggested that he'd been in the military services and looked young enough for Anthony to wonder if he'd ever had to worry about shaving.

"Excellent to hear, old chap," Anthony was beginning to sound more like a lord of the manor than he cared to think. "Well, if you have any difficulties, you have the guidance of Soames here, or you can indeed ask me."

"Thank you, Master Anthony," Stevens bowed his head as though he was addressing a man of the cloth.

"Very kind, Sir, but I am sure you have far more important things to do with your time," suggested an awkward Soames, who seemed put out by Anthony's intrusion.

"Actually, Soames, I was wondering if I may beg a moment of your time," Anthony asked, "I know you are busy."

"Of course, Sir," the butler replied, giving Stevens a superior look.

"Perhaps we could speak in the drawing room."

"Certainly, Master Anthony," Soames turned to the footman. "That will be all, Stevens."

"Yes, Mister Soames," Stevens scurried off, remembering to acknowledge Anthony first.

The two men walked to the drawing room. Anthony keen to continue making small talk. "You follow Woolwich Arsenal, yes?"

"Yes, Sir. Although if I may correct Master Anthony, they are simply known as Arsenal these days." Soames pretended to be sorry for correcting Anthony, but secretly enjoyed it.

"My apologies, Soames," Anthony wasn't in the least sorry. "I'm more of a fan of the squared circle. Eagerly anticipating Dempsey's next defence, July seems so long ago now. Are you a boxing fan, Soames?"

"I was a fairly keen pugilist in my younger days, Sir."

"I did not know that Soames," Anthony was genuinely interested. "Was that in the army?"

"It was Sir." Soames answered.

"What regiment were you in, if you don't mind me asking?"

"Not at all, Sir," Soames assured Anthony. "I was in Hertfordshire Regiment for four years."

"Good with weapons as well as fists." Anthony was probing the family butler.

"Quite, Sir." Soames seemed keen to end the conversation as they entered the drawing room.

"Apologies for all of the questions, I am a keen enthusiast of military history, and you seem like a man of knowledge." Anthony's flattery worked.

"Very kind of you, Master Anthony," Soames told the young Crawford. "Always happy to help. I was considered a decent shot during my service."

"I see," Anthony was pleasantly surprised that Soames had shared some information he hadn't been asked to. "Anyway, apologies again for talking, I know this is a busy day for you."

"Not at all, Sir. What is it you wish to discuss with me?"

"I'm worried about my mother," announced Anthony. Soames was flustered and somewhat bemused by his revelation.

"I'm sorry to hear that, Sir, but I can't see where I can be of any help on this. May I ask, have you spoken to the master of the house?"

"He has so much on, Soames," Anthony informed him as though Soames wouldn't know how busy his master was. "I just thought as the head of service… you would be able to notice something."

"I'm afraid this is not something I can help with, Sir," Soames was uneasy. "I'm very sorry."

"Not your fault, Soames," Anthony wondered where this was heading. "Perhaps it is just nerves, ahead of tomorrow night."

"I'm sure that everyone will enjoy an evening they truly deserve, Sir." Soames' comment sounded vaguely threatening.

Anthony stood up straight. "Thank you, Soames."

The conversation ended as Jane entered the room, her look was a mixture of anger, curiosity, and concern. "And what exactly is going on here?"

"Just me keeping Soames from his work," Anthony offered, as Soames stood in silence.

"That will be all, Soames." Jane dismissed the butler, who looked at Anthony and received a nod that signified agreement with his mother.

Jane kept her eyes firmly on her son as Soames quickly departed, closing the door quietly behind him. The room was seldom used on a day-to-day basis, most of the family meals were taken in the morning room; the drawing room only in use when the family and their guests retired after dinner, and the large, open fire was employed. Today, the room felt cold and sterile. Two sofas sat opposite each other, separated by a thick red rug and a small, light-brown coffee table. Neither Jane nor Anthony sat down, the former was the first to speak.

"Lots to be done today, Anthony. Soames is a busy man."

"I'm sure he will make time for you, Mother," Anthony was flippant.

"What exactly is that meant to mean, young man," Jane began to raise her voice and didn't wait for an answer. "Tomorrow's party is important to Philip. I thought I'd raised you better than to be acting like a selfish, spoilt brat."

"I was merely making conversation with our butler," Anthony protested calmly. "You seemed to have deduced a lot from very little."

"Your behaviour has concerned me for a long time, my son. A mother knows."

"And the children aren't as clueless as you may think," Anthony fired back. "I know, Mother!"

"Know what, Anthony?" Jane was exasperated.

"I saw you and him together," Anthony retorted and glared at his mother.

Jane was shocked. She sunk into one of the sofas and stared straight ahead. Anthony watched in silence, as his mother struggled to comprehend what her son had just told her.

"It really isn't what you think, Anthony."

"What *I* think?" Now Anthony was exasperated. He walked around the room, stopping to stare out of the window at the view of the estate, which was vast. It was almost as though the rest of the world couldn't get in. "I think that what you are doing will see us returned to the streets that frightened you so much before Philip came along."

Jane rose from her seating position and moved towards her son, who was still staring out of the window. Her small hand reached out, but he shook her off.

"Anthony," Jane whispered softly. "I want you to not worry and promise me to forget what you have seen and what you think is going on."

Anthony's fists pounded the windowsill which caused the glass to shake violently. Turning to his mother, he saw the fear in her eyes upon sight of his red, irate face. "Forget!" Anthony rasped. "And how do I do that, Mother?"

Jane cupped her hands on Anthony's fists and in the back of his mind, Anthony noticed how tiny she was, how her hands barely stretched across his. "Believe me, my son, there are things going on that you wouldn't understand," she implored, her face looking old and serious.

"Don't underestimate my understanding," Anthony was sharp, but made no effort to remove his hand from Jane's grasp. She let out a long sigh, leaned down and planted a kiss on Anthony's wrist. "What if I told you that Philip was well aware of what was going on?"

Anthony was stunned, struggling to comprehend what he had just been told. He struggled for the words to continue. Jane hugged her son before stepping back and inhaling a sharp intake of breath.

"Philip knows? You and Soames?" Anthony's confusion was sprinkled with disgust.

"Things aren't always what they seem," Jane looked sad. "I have always tried to protect you from Philip and the life we lead, whilst always trying to secure you every opportunity I could."

"Mum…" Anthony was still confused and had slipped back into the old, former East End vernacular. A knock at the door with a voice beckoning for his mother afforded Jane the perfect excuse to escape this incredibly awkward moment of confession and revelation that left Anthony more perplexed than ever before.

Chapter 26

Anthony tossed and turned but sleep was not his friend. The cold December wind howled outside his window like the multitude of unanswered questions and problems plaguing his every waking thought. His conversation with Jane had turned up yet more confusion and anguish for him. What was his mother protecting him from? What kind of life did Philip and Jane lead that meant the need for the former to protect her son, and where did Soames fit into it? A butler of only recent employment who had not only the rest of the household's servants on tenterhooks, but who had seemingly become intimate with the lady of the house, his mother! His mother, who was suggesting that her husband may be fully aware of this bizarre set-up. For once, his domestic arrangements took precedence over the tumult of worry and anguish he felt about Cecile. That made him smile briefly. Maybe he was getting over her?

Anthony knew Philip was a night owl; he'd heard his mum retire to the master bedroom and ignored her goodnight call. As Jane was in bed and presumably asleep, this would be the perfect opportunity to confront his stepfather. Anthony needed answers for the sake of his own sanity. Jane would not be giving anything else away, so targeting Philip seemed his only option, albeit a risky one.

Anthony's feet hit the carpeted floor and he luxuriated in the feel of the warmth of the thick wool pile. He never failed to appreciate the little touches of wealth, more so than living in a huge mansion, or having a limitless supply of money. Anthony valued the touch of wool on cold feet, a warming pan being slipped into the bed on a winter's night, or the kind smile of the cook, agreeing to make him a hot milk with cinnamon at odd hours of the day or night when she sensed he needed comfort. The other trappings of wealth he almost took for granted. The little things were the big things to Anthony, who would never forget the frigid coldness of bare floorboards, the dampness that permeated the bedclothes each night and how he and his mother had eked out a hot drink, using tea leaves again and again until they had little or no taste.

Clad in slippers and robe over his warm, brushed cotton pyjamas, he took a deep breath and made for his bedroom door. The muffled sound of servants still at work drifted upstairs from the kitchens, and the ferocious wind lashed at the huge window above the staircase as he strode purposely along the corridor. Once downstairs, he noticed Philip's study door had a chink of light underneath, indicating his stepfather was still up, and still working. As he reached the door, having the intention of giving it a sharp rap before entering, he almost collided with Soames, who had just opened the door and was making his way out. They both looked at each other in surprise.

"Master Anthony," Soames recovered first. "Is everything alright?"

"Absolutely fine, Soames," Anthony replied calmly. "I just require a minute with my stepfather."

"Very good, Sir." Soames stepped aside as though he'd just granted permission, a mistake not lost on Anthony. Or maybe the butler was trying to tell him something?

"Please ask cook to make me a strong cup of tea, Soames. Milk and two lumps of sugar," instructed young Crawford. "There's a good man."

"Of course, Sir."

Soames dashed off to the kitchen area to carry out Anthony's request. Philip had been silently listening to the exchange between his stepson and butler and was waiting at his desk as Anthony walked in. He wondered what the hell the boy wanted, although he admired the way the young Crawford had handled the butler's enquiry. Perhaps he, Philip, had made a silk purse out of a sow's ear, after all.

The head of the house looked tired but was still smartly dressed and not even loosened his tie. Not for Philip Crawford the preferred fashion of changing into more casual attire, or a housecoat after dinner, which was still a formal affair in the Crawford household, even when it was only Anthony and his mother and stepfather dining. As usual, this evening he had gone upstairs to change out of his office suit, to refreshen up and return downstairs for dinner wearing another suit and tie. Anthony sometimes wondered how on earth the suits were laundered so quickly, and that the careless discarding of garments was just another example of how those with money paid scant attention to something the working class would worry about. Memories of his mother, scrubbing at the tide marks on one of Anthony's shirts assailed him. Philip Crawford wouldn't even give his laundry maids a second thought.

Anthony looked at Philip now, at his thick, black glasses sitting on the end of his nose as he read a piece of headed paper whilst running his finger left to right as he digested whatever was on it. A large stack of paperwork was to his left and the ink pot into which the nib of his expensive black and gold fountain pen was dipped, was to his right. A steady chain of smoke rose up from the cigarette in his ashtray as Philip fixed his eyes firmly on his stepson. He motioned for Anthony to sit opposite him and waited while the boy duly obliged. Anthony would always wait to be asked to be seated, having been scolded many a time when casually sitting down without invitation. Philip had always been consistent; high standards at all times were to be maintained.

"Will you have any Christmas decorations in here this year, Philip?" Anthony tried to kick proceedings off with satire, but his stepfather simply stared through the young man and ignored his attempt at humour.

"What exactly brings you down at this hour?" Philip asked, bluntly.

Anthony had noticed the grandfather clock in the main hall, it was only just past half past eleven, though the cold, dark December night made it seem somewhat later.

Before answering, Anthony surveyed the room, noticing its austerity and that it lacked any vestige of Christmas finery. It was almost as though this was the domain to which Philip could escape, when avoiding the festive period. Anthony's mind drifted to Charles Dickens and wondered how his stepfather would handle the visit of four ghosts; *Jacob Marley* being the first, the one who had returned to haunt his business partner with warnings and advice about avoiding the same fate as he.

Sensing Philip's growing impatience, Anthony returned his mind to the present and forgot about Christmas past.

"Working late tonight, Philip," It was the first thing that sprung to mind, although his stepfather was in no mood for small talk.

"Anthony," he began. "I have much to get through, so please state whatever it is that has brought you down here. I'm not in the mood for idle chat and you know very well that I work late most evenings."

"I'm worried about my mother."

Philip removed his glasses and returned the piece of paper to the large pile. Now it was his turn to think about a response, which was interrupted by a knock on the door. Soames entered carrying a cup and saucer.

"Your tea, Master Anthony," he turned to Philip. "Do you require anything, Sir?"

"No, Soames. Please leave us." Philip's tone was serious.

"Very good, Sir," Soames seemed unfazed by the way he was spoken to. Turning quickly, he left the study and closed the door firmly behind him, leaving Philip and Anthony alone.

"Anthony," Philip seemed set to lecture. "You have always fascinated me. Your personality, I mean."

Anthony stared at Philip, who went on, "A young man plucked from tough streets, who has a better brain than he realises and possesses such an athletic physique ideal for the military or sport yet has this incredibly sensitive nature. This is not a film, boy. You are not some degenerate with a moustache and little hat meddling in the affairs of others and who considers himself funny, because believe me, Anthony, I find nothing funny in your appearance here tonight to lecture me about your concerns for your mother."

Anthony was shocked, although he didn't really know why. He had always known Philip looked down upon his love of the silver screen. He knew his stepfather had little patience for his creative and sometimes sensitive nature. So, why was he shocked when Philip had articulated it? Maybe it was the bit about Anthony possessing a better brain than he realised.

"Thank you for your character assassination of me, Philip,' Anthony began, carefully. "However, I fail to see what your opinion of me has to do with my concerns about my mother?"

"Just why are you worried about her, Anthony?" Philip questioned but didn't wait for a reply. "She, like you, wants for nothing and is part of the ruling class in a country that is at the forefront of growth."

"There is more to life than money." Anthony snapped.

"And yet you seem to enjoy it so much," sneered Philip. "Tell me, Anthony, when your mother and I were wed, were you not relieved to drastically move up the social ladder? Good food, education, a monthly allowance, and no need to worry again."

Anthony flared with anger, but only because the emotionally redundant man sat opposite was right; Philip had highlighted a lot of what Anthony enjoyed about the life Philip afforded him. The hypocritical feelings began to rise again and engulfed him as he struggled to contain his emotion.

"I'm a winner, Anthony," Philip announced. "In business, in life. The reason? I don't let emotion come between me and my objectives. But what are your objectives? You amble along with no real ambition or drive, wasting my time, my money, and your own talents."

Anthony felt like he was about to cry. It had been a long time since he'd been made to feel like a child and Philip's dissection of his life had certainly done that. His stepfather was not smiling. Philip finished his cigarette and said, "You say you are worried about your mother; do you know how worried she is about you?"

"I beg your pardon?" Anthony was startled.

"My wife and I do communicate," Philip enlightened him. "Your erratic behaviour is concerning her, and me. Tomorrow is a social event of huge importance. Very important people, men of high standing in business and society will grace our home. Nothing, and I mean nothing, must overshadow this event, understand?"

"I won't let anyone down," answered Anthony as he sipped

his tea and tried to regain his composure.

"You're letting yourself down," Philip countered, an expression of immense distaste on his face. "Maybe I should pay some more attention to you, and not allow you so much liberty. Perhaps I will have a word with some people to get you placed into a good career, find you a suitable young woman. A good job, a courtship, it could be the making of you. You are making very little of yourself as it stands."

Anthony put down his teacup and placed both hands on Philip's expensive wooden desk, looking Philip straight in the eye. "Then give me a place in your organisation, Philip Crawford. Pay me the sort of attention you know that I would welcome! Remember how, when I was younger, I used to ask you, beg you, to let me go to work with you? Yet always, I was refused and even now, you prefer to find me a job working for one of your contacts rather than admit me into your precious business! It seems I may share your name and live in your house, but you will never let into your business. Aren't I good enough?"

"Frankly, Anthony, no, you're not," Philip did not hold back on his version of the truth. "You cavort as one of these bright, young things – or whatever the degenerate youth of today are called, drinking champagne, socialising till all hours, with no income to call your own, no respect for your position in society. You particularly, of all the young men I know, you waste yourself on your idolisation of actors on the silver screen, seeing yourself as the next hero, so, no, Anthony, you are not good enough."

Anthony's rage settled itself into a cold fury, as he delivered some home truths of his own. "I may not be good enough, Philip Crawford, but at least I don't worship money as though it is my God! I don't waste my life and my relationship by putting my work above all else. I don't look down on other people as if they are some sort of dirt that has attached itself to my shoe. Well, at least if I am not good enough, I won't be beholden to you for my career, another thing I would have to thank you for! Maybe I don't want to be part of your business, anyway, because if I did work for you, then you would own me, and you will never own me, Philip Crawford!"

Philip began to laugh, "Oh I already do, boy."

He reached for his fountain pen but found Anthony's hand placed upon his wrist in an impressively fierce grasp. He found it impossible to move as his stepson's physical strength was much greater than his own.

"Don't push me too far," Anthony said coldly. He released Philip's hand and observed a flicker of fear in his eyes.

"I could speak to your mother about this," Philip's threat was weak.

"Why don't you?" Anthony was now in control and calling him out.

"I won't worry her," Philip replied, slightly regaining his composure. "You are her son, and you are the apple of her eye. I wouldn't want to disillusion my wife by pointing out what a wastrel her son is. Just don't make trouble tomorrow."

Anthony smiled at his stepfather. "You need not worry about me; you have others to concern yourself about."

He got up to leave, realising that if what his mother had told him about Philip knowing what was going on between Soames and his wife, then the stupid man didn't deserve any sympathy. To think, he'd felt sorry for his stepfather, after witnessing his mother and Soames in a passionate clinch. Image was everything to Philip and ignorance was bliss.

Anthony's final comment had touched a nerve for Philip, who had risen from his seat.

"Anthony, what…"

The sound of a thunderous knock at the front door interrupted his train of thought. Both men spun round and hurried into the main hall. Soames was standing in the open doorway, holding a package, as a drenched and out of breath Stevens rushed into the hall, shaking his head at the butler, who nodded. Philip and Anthony rushed to both servants.

"I didn't see him, Mister Soames." Stevens gasped. Soames was about to speak but was interrupted by Philip.

"Just what is going on?"

"Begging your pardon, Sir," Soames began. "I was completing my duties ahead of tomorrow when I heard a rather loud knock at the door. Unfortunately, someone was a bit late in answering and when he did all that was there was this brown envelope."

"Pardon me, Mister Soames, Sir," Stevens protested with a genuine fear of dismissal in his tone. "I went as fast as I could, but he was gone. I went after him..."

"Don't worry, Stevens," Anthony took charge and glared at Soames. "Go and get yourself out of those wet clothes and cleaned up. If cook is still up, get her to make you something hot to drink."

"Thank you, Master Anthony," replied the wet but extremely grateful footman, who scurried off in the direction of the kitchen downstairs. Anthony continued to look at Soames whilst Philp couldn't take his eyes off his stepson.

It was the head of the house who broke the silence. "Well, what is this envelope, Soames?"

"Begging your pardon, Sir, it is addressed to Master Anthony."

Anthony felt a cold chill run down his spine. He took the package from the butler. "Thank you, Soames."

"That will be all, Soames, you may retire." Philp dismissed his head of service, who bolted the door and headed below stairs. Philip looked at the envelope in Anthony's hand.

"Goodnight, Philip," Anthony tried to move fast but was stopped by his stepfather.

"What exactly is going on?" Philip's tone was full of accusation.

"I have no idea, and that is the truth."

"Anthony, I will not have any scandal at my door," Philip's voice began to rise.

"It may already be inside the house," Anthony retorted, attempting to make his way to the stairs, but Philip blocked his path.

"I am in no mood for your cryptic comments."

"Do you want to wake my mother?" Anthony turned to look at Philip, who glanced up at the second floor. His stepfather shook his head.

"Goodnight," Anthony said, curtly, and now, Philip stood aside to let him pass.

Leaving his stepfather standing by the entrance door with an unfathomable look on his face, Anthony set off up the stairs with all the fervour of a runner determined to break a record in speed. He was done with this life. Philip, Jane, Cecile! Their levels of hypocrisy were too much for him. Chaplin had gone on his travels and made his fortune, why couldn't he? He would attend tomorrow's soiree and stay for Christmas and then he was out. He was determined to be his own man, even if it meant the loss of all the privilege that came with living in this huge mansion. His mind made up; he felt an incredible rush of exhilaration.

His decision was made. He could be his own self again! The problem was, unbeknownst to Anthony, he didn't really know what his own self was capable of, or how such a decision to eschew the wealth and privilege granted to him by his mother's marriage to Philip would affect him in future. He had no true perception of realism anymore, although he did not realise it at that moment. He had been softened by a life of money, status, security, and he enjoyed the benefits of the expensive lifestyle Philip provided. He no longer had to worry about food in his belly, a warm bed to sleep in and a roof over his head. The privilege of wealth had made him forgetful of a life without money, a life where there was no certainty of where the next meal would come from or whether the rent was up to date. Out on his own would mean having to find a *proper* job, a place to live and a reintegration into a working-class background he had left behind. It never entered his head that he would not be wanted there; that his life now of abundance and excess prohibited him from ever being accepted by those who had once served him. With no real need to work, Anthony had been able to indulge his pleasures with no real fear or worry about what he was doing with his life. He didn't realise if he turned his back on what he had now, that what was waiting for him was something he was no longer equipped to deal with.

He reached his room and once inside, sat at his desk. Thoughts of his future plans would have to be on hold for a minute, as he looked at the envelope with the words: *Anthony Crawford* written on it. He pondered the contents; what was so urgent that required a personal, late-night delivery? There was only one way to find out. Carefully opening the brown envelope, he pulled out three photographs. The colour drained from his face upon examination of the images. A trio of graphic stills of both he and Cecile making love. His heart began to beat so fast it felt like it would explode from his chest. He placed the photographs on the desk, before noticing a small piece of white paper still inside the discarded envelope. Taking out the folded paper, his hand was shaking as he read the words:

This is what she does, and people die because of it.

Anthony struggled to remain calm. He rushed onto his balcony, despite the heavy wind and rain, and allowed the elements to wash over him. Somehow, it helped. The note still tightly clenched in his fist, Anthony wondered was this a threat or a warning. And who would send it together with three photographs that would cause a scandal from which neither the Fords nor Crawfords would recover?

Looking at the writing again, Anthony could only be sure of one thing: this was the work of the same person who'd sent the cryptic message he had shown to Cecile. She had been adamant that it couldn't be the work of Benson. And she was right.

This changed everything. His world was being threatened by a malevolent force and he was a target. Someone or something was threatening to destroy him and all around him. They knew of him and Cecile and could prove it. The implications of their knowledge made Anthony afraid.

Walking away was no longer an option. Anthony had to find out who or what was out to destroy him before he destroyed himself.

Chapter 27

Philip was desperate to know the contents of the envelope that had been personally dropped off last night, but Anthony had skilfully avoided being alone with his stepfather, who was still concerned about Anthony's cryptic comments regarding threats within the house. This prevented him from questioning his stepson further, for which Anthony was abundantly grateful. On the day of the Crawford's Christmas dinner party, Anthony had remained in his room till late morning, not wishing for the society of anyone. He had then opted to take a long walk around the estate and the outlying grounds.

The Crawford acreage extended to a boundary with one of the largest and most magnificent houses in the vicinity, Stonor Park. The fact that it had been in the ownership of one family for around eight hundred years fascinated Anthony. How had they acquired the wealth to build such a magnificent edifice? How had that wealth survived centuries, whilst lesser people like himself and his mother and his late father, had struggled to survive, eking out a meagre existence of the scraps from the tables of those who could afford to discard it. Just looking at Stonor caused Anthony some severe misgivings about his position within the higher ranks of society. How could one family own so much? How come he was entitled to be part of it? Once again, his love of the high life was at variance with his humble beginnings.

On his way out, he'd seen his mother, who had busied herself with last-minute jobs ahead of tonight's soiree. Anthony had been heading out of the door when his eyes met with Jane's. Their conversation was brief but sincere, as Anthony recalled.

"Just be happy, Mum," he told her, as he held her tight.

"You too, son," she'd replied. *"There are some things in life you cannot fight."*

He'd pondered those words for what seemed like an eternity whilst taking in another cold day. At least it wasn't raining, Anthony thought. He needed to get out of the house for a few hours but was happy he didn't have brave the torrential storms that seemed to have dominated the forecast these past few days. And the storms weren't restricted to the sky alone. Philip and he were more uneasy than ever, Jane's non-committal revelation had not really seen her admit anything, yet it had added to Anthony's angst and confusion. And to top it all off, the woman of his dreams was contributing to a literal nightmare, not that he could decide if that were her deliberate intention or not.

The tone of the note he'd received certainly suggested that Cecile had targeted Anthony deliberately and that far from falling in love with him, she had set out to harm him. He wondered how he would feel upon sight of her. They had not spoken since she revealed her news of a potential pregnancy and even that, now, Anthony believed was untrue, just a ruse to entrap him further. Into what, he didn't know, but he did know that whilst he was still a little besotted with Cecile, he had stopped believing himself in love with her. He also had to acknowledge that she was attending the Crawfords' party with her husband and that would limit any intercourse, social and sexual, that may take place between the two lovers.

What tired Anthony most, was that all this was being negotiated without Harry's words of wisdom. Anthony had called to enquire of his friend's welfare but had been met with messages ranging from his best friend either being asleep or otherwise engaged. The communicators had not been his parents, but rather the family butler, Rawlings, whose delicate Scottish tone had an uncanny effect of hypnotising you into becoming complicit with whatever he was saying.

"Perhaps all butlers attend some unique school that moulds them into certain types of human beings," thought Anthony as he took in the splendid greenery his surroundings had to offer.

Nothing having been settled in Anthony's mind, upon return, he'd enjoyed lunching alone, Mrs. Blackshaw's cold cuts and sandwiches were a work of wonder, and he felt sustained. Not wishing to converse with anyone, least of all his stepfather or his mother, he spent the rest of the afternoon in solitary pursuits before choosing to bathe, and dress, well ahead of the first arrivals, whose invitations had specified eight for eight thirty Yet another new dinner suit, this time a superb tuxedo. The long tails made Anthony feel very upper class. However, his decision to wear a Christmas-themed handkerchief in his breast pocket had drawn a smile from Jane and ire from Philip, the latter choosing to give a calm, yet irritable lecture on appropriate humour and maintaining the standards befitting of a Crawford. Anthony had not intended to upset Philip, merely wanting to add a bit of Christmas cheer. Philip had complimented his stepson on his appearance, once a plain handkerchief had replaced the festive offering Anthony preferred.

Anthony, Philip, and Jane were all on hand to meet and greet their guests, who enjoyed champagne on arrival. By nine, the Great Hall was awash with the social elite. What was before him was a who's who of the great and powerful of today's world, as well as key figures in an industry that was his obsession. Anthony's head ached as his eyes were ready to become detached from their sockets! Nancy Mitford and her sister Pamela! Was that one of the Astors and Emerald Cunard talking by the tree? And why on earth hadn't Philip told him that George Bernard Shaw would be here? He was a Nobel prize winner, for Christ's sake! There he was, in the Great Hall of Anthony's home, talking to Greta Garbo and her director, Maurice Stiller and Anthony didn't even know they were both in the country! He was livid with Philip, who obviously had connections within the world in which Anthony wanted to move and not once had Philip made any attempt to introduce his stepson to anyone who would have influence on his future acting career. At that moment, had there not been over a hundred guests present in the reception hall, Anthony would have wrung Philip's neck and not stopped until he was dead. Seemingly only His Majesty, George the fifth, and Prime Minister, Stanley Baldwin, were the noticeable absentees.

Robert and Cecile had been amongst the last to arrive. Cecile was always one to make an entrance and being one of the final guests to enter the Crawford residence was typically her. She looked incredible; her dark, sequinned evening gown formed a sparkling column around her slender frame. Around her shoulders she wore a mink stole, secured with a diamond clasp that glittered in the light from the chandeliers. Anthony watched her extend her gloved hand to the Duchess of Argyll with all the grace and confidence of someone born to wealth and not someone who had merely acquired it. She lapped up attention like a film star would work the press at a premiere. Anthony couldn't help it; he was in complete awe of this woman who had captured his heart, despite his suspicions. He was learning that he couldn't turn his emotions off like a tap. How easy that would be if he could temper the flow of his desire! He remained where he was, watching the woman he knew he still loved. She could hold a room like no one else he knew. She had opened his eyes to love and adventure he thought only existed in movies, whilst also keeping Anthony in his place and putting Philip in his! A man Anthony always felt he'd come up short against, yet Cecile was more than a match for him both intellectually and within society. The Fords approached their hosts, and Anthony knew they would all exchange the usual greetings as etiquette demanded. When she offered him her hand, her demeanour was cold; she did not offer him her cheek to kiss. Her younger lover felt like a love-sick puppy who wanted attention but would not really know what to do with it.

Jane stood close to her husband as they performed their hosting duties, a fact that probably annoyed Philip, who would have wanted her to mingle, to entertain the women whilst he guffawed and held court with the men of influence who graced his reception hall. His mother displayed an eloquent beauty in her ice blue evening gown which, like Cecile's, sparkled with tiny diamond like sequins although her constant desire to adjust the garment made her look uncomfortable. Anthony felt the same, uncomfortable, and out of place, although he was a better actor than Jane, and he also knew that the dinner suit he was wearing showed off his athletic young frame excellently, something Lady Smythe was only too happy to point out.

Lord and Lady Smythe almost made the Hewson-Greaves' seem common. He was around twentieth in line for the throne and was the very embodiment of upper-class aristocracy.

Anthony had only met the couple twice, once at a function where they were fundraising for a charity that he could not recall, and again at a birthday party for Philip two years ago. Lord Smythe sported a huge moustache and was the biggest advocate for colonialism and the British Empire as could possibly be. Lady Smythe had a pretty, round face, complete with fiery red hair and a flirtatious nature that aired on just about the right side of decency. On each meeting, her hands had wandered about Anthony's person, with tonight being no exception.

"I imagine you are a force to be reckoned with on a rugger field," Lord Smythe remarked, glass of champagne in hand, moustache bristling.

"I rather imagine a force to be reckoned with, anywhere," added Lady Smythe, lustfully, as she jiggled her bust in her splendid green evening gown that hugged her curvaceous figure and left little to the imagination. Had she not been who she was, the wife of a man in line for the throne, albeit distantly, she would be considered 'common' and again, Anthony was reminded of the hypocrisy and double standards by which the upper classes lived.

"One does one's best," Anthony said, turning on the charm offensive, before making his excuses and politely integrating himself into other company. For someone who loathed what the upper classes stood for, he was exceptionally good at playing the part. He looked at the magnificence of the main hall filled with the haves of society, while the servants slaved away downstairs preparing food and handing out glasses of champagne that would cost more than a month's earnings. But for a proposal of marriage, Anthony would belong downstairs, as would Jane. He allowed that to sink in as he sipped his own glass of champagne and enjoyed the compliments a number of guests had afforded him on his striking looks and his attire. *"The hero of this story is a two-faced one,"* he thought.

Pondering whether to approach Cecile, he wondered what he would say to her. They had not spoken since their moment of passion at her work premises had turned cold following her announcement of a potential pregnancy. They had exchanged brief pleasantries this evening, but the greeting was cold from both sides. She was to play the dutiful, glamorous wife of the rich and powerful Robert Ford, whilst Anthony played the charming and dutiful son whose parents were hosting a soiree that had nothing to do with Christmas, despite the decorations and the tree, and everything to do with appearance and position within the society in which they moved.

Draining his glass, Anthony noticed Soames, wandering the room carrying a tray laden with glasses full of champagne. He made his way through the throng of guests and, taking a fresh drink, he viewed the various groups that were developing as they always do at parties. Ladies discussing Christmas, men talking business. Anthony had noticed the Hewson-Greaves', minus Harry, were very much keeping their own company. The twins looked pretty in their matching sequins, the bright colours and looser fitting garments making them look younger than they actually were. A product of their upbringing, Ava, who was the eldest by ten minutes, was heard correcting Georgina on a number of occasions regarding her stance and pronunciation of certain words. Harry had often joked about marrying one of them off to Anthony, who could think of few things worse than joining that family in matrimony. Harry was his best friend, and his family was more interested in preserving an image rather than helping him through his troubles.

"I'm bored," a familiar seductive voice whispered into Antony's ear. Whether he wanted to confront Cecile or not was now incidental. As always, she'd made the first move.

"Good evening, Cecile," Anthony said politely. "Your husband not entertaining you?"

"Look around, darling. I can't see him anywhere."

"That is a shame, how are you?" Anthony continued with polite interest, the superficial enquiry everyone made, but no-one listened to the response.

"Since you last ran out on me?" Cecile questioned. "I've been fine, thank you."

"Cecile," Anthony began, but was silenced when she placed her slender index finger to her lips.

"I don't bear grudges, darling. And you can make it up to me, anyway."

Anthony felt that strong desire which excited him, and he wanted her. The thought of the photographs suddenly dominated his brain and gave him an idea. He was unsure if Cecile knew of the pictures and her reaction would be an interesting one, if he could show her the incriminating evidence. This could well be the perfect opportunity to find out if she knew more than she was telling.

"I could show you my room," smiled Anthony. "There may be a few things of interest in there."

"That does sound like a spiffing idea," Cecile said, with a naughty look. "Shall I go and powder my nose before following you? Hate to rouse gossip and suspicion, darling."

"A very good idea," agreed Anthony. "First floor, fifth room on the right. I'll be waiting."

Anthony had to tear his gaze away from the vision of beauty as she made her way across the room. And he was not the only one, as a number of conversations stopped as Cecile crossed the hall, she had such presence, such confidence that radiated from her. For someone who was about to embark on a clandestine tryst, she was extremely noticeable. The distraction allowed Anthony to hurry to his room and find the envelope that had caused him so much worry and confusion. Closing the door behind him, he made his way to his bed and lifted the mattress. Rose would make his bed every morning, tucking his sheets under the mattress. A lady of advancing years, she was no longer strong enough to lift the mattress but was still too proud to ask for help. Anthony knew this and knew that the envelope would be quite safe in the middle of the frame underneath the heavy mattress.

Reaching beneath the mattress, patting the springs of the bedframe, he gasped in horrified surprise upon discovering that the envelope was gone! Who could have done this? He'd been out for a long while today, but no one inside the house knew of the late-night drop-off, apart from three people. Quickly ruling out Stevens, he remembered how Philip had acted when

Anthony received the envelope. Desperate to see the contents, his stepfather was not beyond searching his stepson's room to get what he wanted. The rage grew. Philip's crime would not be unpunished! Anthony charged out of the bedroom, almost knocking Cecile off her feet.

"Anthony!" she cried, in complete shock.

Her lover didn't even acknowledge her as he marched towards the room Philip and Jane shared. With everyone other than he and the rather shocked Cecile downstairs, Anthony flung open the door, with every intention of finding what he believed was in this very room.

What he did find, was the most unexpected thing. The room was not empty. The lamplight cast a dim, orange glow across the rumpled bedcovers, as the two men who had just been passionately enjoying each other's company sprang apart. Their flushed faces and state of undress an indication of their illicit activity.

Anthony was unsure who was more horrified and surprised; Philip, Robert, or him!

Chapter 28

The silence was deafening as the three men stared at each other in stunned horror. By now, Cecile was alongside Anthony. Her face was emotionless, not something Anthony had expected. Still glaring at the two men, both of whom were now scrambling around the bedroom, finding discarded clothes, dressing quickly, Anthony felt sick. It was disgusting, immoral and more to the point, it was also illegal. No-one spoke for what seemed like an age, before Cecile placed a hand on Anthony's arm and said, quietly, "So, now you know, Anthony."

Anthony's mind reeled. Cecile knew? Cecile knew that her husband was engaged in an illegal, clandestine relationship with his stepfather? He gasped in horror and shook off the hand she had placed on his arm. Suddenly, it all made sense. No wonder she and her husband had separate lives. This was the reason why she was able to indulge herself in her film studio. This was the reason for her boundless extravagance, and this was the reason she had embarked on her own extra marital affairs. Was it revenge? Was she using Anthony to get her own back on her husband, who Anthony now understood was a homosexual. The bile in his throat rose and he thought he might gag.

Philip was now standing by the bed, fully clothed, looking slightly unsure of himself. He glanced towards the ground, shoulders slumped, breathing heavily. He looked as though he could collapse at any minute. Anthony immediately thought of his mother, where was she and what would she make of this?

"What if I told you that Philip was well aware of what was going on?" Jane's confusing question was another thing that suddenly made more sense to Anthony. Did Jane know of Philip's situation? Was this marriage one of convenience for both parties? Just another indictment of the hypocrisy of the upper classes. Cecile had sat down in an armchair, her eyes firmly on her husband and Philip. And it was the former who spoke first as he turned to Anthony's stepfather.

"I thought that you had locked the door?" Robert's voice was angry and accusing.

"I did." Philip continued to stare at the floor. His voice was weak and defeated. This was the most vulnerable Anthony had ever seen him and he felt a sharp pang of sudden sympathy for his stepfather. "Or at least, I thought I had."

Anthony rounded on Robert. "Is that your main concern at this time? Is all you can think about, protecting yourself and maintaining your image? You disgust me. Not for your – actions - with my stepfather, but for the fact that all you can think about is yourself."

Robert and Cecile turned incredulously towards him.

"Now look here -" Robert was belligerent, mulish.

"No, you look here, Robert!" Anthony's voice grew loud as his anger reached boiling point. "How long has this being going on? Whatever this is!"

"What made you barge in here without knocking, anyway?" Philip answered Anthony's question with one of his own. His stepson noticed he had regained some of his condescending attitude and was going to point out that his stepfather was in no position to castigate him for his actions, given what Anthony had just witnessed, when he noticed the way Philip was now looking at Cecile, and suddenly, another dreadful thought lodged itself in Anthony's battered brain. He spun around to face Cecile, who was gripping the sides of her armchair as though she feared falling off.

"You knew about this?" Anthony accused his lover, who refused to meet his gaze. "You knew that your husband and my stepfather were engaged in an illicit, homosexual relationship and all the time we were working together, you never saw fit to mention it?"

"Oh, spare me!" Robert suddenly came to life and shot Anthony a venomous look. "You think I don't know what you have been doing with my wife, you working-class parasite!"

Anthony charged at Robert and clasped the older man around the throat. Despite the years on his rival, Robert put up a fight as Anthony pushed him against the wall.

"I can now see what she saw in you," sneered Robert. "My *wife* does love her little bit of rough!"

His flippant comment earned him a broken nose, courtesy of Anthony's head. He crumpled into the ground, blood pouring from his face. Grabbing his blood-speckled shirt, Anthony rasped, "Maybe, but then again, she's not exactly out of the top drawer herself is she, your so-called *wife*? And although, given your sexual preferences, you probably don't know this, she's not too respectable and well-mannered in between the sheets herself!"

He heard Cecile gasp, and suddenly, she rose from the chair and picked up a pewter candlestick, rushing at Anthony with a look of sheer hatred on her face. She made as though to strike him, but Philip blocked her efforts and earned himself a heavy blow on the head.

"Philip!" Anthony screamed, rushing towards his stepfather, who had collapsed backward. Cecile dropped the candlestick and rushed to attend Robert, who was gasping for breath.

"Anthony," Philip's voice was weak as blood seeped from a thick, deep cut to his forehead. "I always tried. You can only be who you are, even if the law or the people do not understand."

"Philip, hold on, I'll get help. Soames! Soames!" Anthony charged out of the room and towards the staircase, meeting the butler, who had just appeared on the landing. From downstairs, the faint tinkling of glassware could be held, mingling in with the sound of the band Philip had commissioned for the evening.

"Master Anthony," Soames enquired, staring at Anthony's shirt with a look of alarmed surprise. "Is everything alright, Sir?"

"No, Soames," Anthony snapped. "I need an ambulance and for everyone to leave. Where's my mother?"

"I do believe she went outside, Sir. I shall telephone an ambulance and try to find the mistress."

Anthony pushed past Soames and flung himself down the stairs, shouting to Soames that he would find his mother, and instructing the servant to call an ambulance and, with hindsight, "The police, Soames." Cecile had struck Philip with a candlestick, a heavy pewter candlestick, and he was wounded. He suddenly realised that he could get his own revenge, by having her arrested and charged with wounding or worse, he thought, darkly. Suddenly, he felt a pain in his face. His fingers probing his cheek, he discovered a small, slight cut that he must have suffered in his scuffle with Robert. His adrenaline levels had possibly masked the pain which was now setting in. Anthony's appearance in the Great Hall was drawing attention, conversations petered out and were being replaced by whispers and finger-pointing. He quickly made his way through the stunned crowd and opened the door. A swift glance across the huge swathe of land that was the Crawford estate, and he noticed a flickering light in the direction of the barn that had played host to his many childhood adventures, as well as one or two adult ones. Why was Jane out here? Not that he cared, he simply needed to find his mother and explain the craziness and severity of the situation that was developing inside.

As the figure came into light, it was very clear that it was not Jane but another familiar face who had been a noticeable absentee from tonight's party.

"Harry?" Anthony was shocked at both the sight of his friend and his dishevelled appearance. He was carrying a small oil lamp that was encased in glass. He was not wearing a coat, and he was shivering in his tweed suit but without a tie, whilst his face had not seen a shaving knife in days.

"Hello, Anthony." Harry said, as if it was the most ordinary thing in the world to be found dishevelled and inappropriately dressed, carrying a lamp across the grounds of a family friends' home.

"Philip has been injured," Anthony began quickly. "Robert Ford is involved. I don't quite know how to explain."

"Is it concerning some compromising photographs of you and his wife, by any chance?"

Anthony went cold. The kind of cold that made tonight's climate seem tropical. He looked at his best friend, who remained expressionless.

"How do you know about those?" Nerves and anger invaded his voice.

"A late-night delivery," Harry ran his fingers through his hair. "Were you not curious as to who the courier was? Benson is dead, so it couldn't be him, could it?"

"You?" Anthony was incredulous. "Why?"

"That woman is poison. She was aware of my problem and used her band of not so merry men to ensure she gets what she wants, off me, and then, off you and anyone else whose life she wants to destroy."

"I don't understand, Harry. But I can't have this conversation with you now, with my mother missing and my stepfather badly wounded! Don't go!" he cried, as Harry turned on him to disappear again into the blackness of the night, but Harry did not acknowledge him, leaving Anthony alone in the darkness.

He raced back into the house, where scenes of surprised indignation were unfolding as Stevens, the footman, and Soames, were quietly approaching guests, explaining that an unforeseen medical emergency had taken place and the ambulance had been called for. Guests were being politely asked to leave. Some groups did as bid, put down their drinks, called for their coats as maids ran back and forth to the library, which was doubling as a cloakroom for the evening. Others were adamant they weren't going anywhere until they had an explanation from the master or the mistress of the house. The band was championed by several guests to continue playing, regardless of the scene unfolding before them. Some couples danced.

Anthony thought he'd be surprised, shocked at the actions of the guests, but in fact, he wasn't. It was what they did. Appearances were everything. Social standing was everything. Enjoying themselves was all that mattered. The shallowness and the hypocrisy were part and parcel of who they were. Anthony would never again be shocked at any aspect of upper-class life. This was what they did, he thought, shaking his head. He threw himself up the stairs and burst into the bedroom. Not surprisingly, Cecile had gone. Robert Ford was now sitting up, with his back resting against the wall, his broken face bloody and swollen, but it appeared that he was going to be alright, which could not be said of Philip.

Anthony knelt down by his stepfather's side, slid his hand under Philip's head which was sticky and slick with blood. He looked waxen and his breath was coming in short rasps. He was in a bad way, Anthony knew, as he bent forward towards Philip's blue lips. He was trying to say something.

"Jane. Fetch Jane," he said, weakly as Anthony nodded, wondering where the hell his mother had got to. He gently placed Philip's head back onto the floor and was alarmed to see it flop to one side. Was he dead? Unconscious? Anthony didn't have time to find out. He flew out of the bedroom like a man possessed. His stepfather had asked for his mother, and he was going to bloody well find her.

He headed outdoors again, reasoning that if his mother had been inside the house, she would have heard the commotion, and would have found out what was happening in the bedroom.

It was frigidly cold outside; the temperature having dropped considerably since he had been indoors. Every so often, he caught a sparkle of ice, glistening in the moonlight. He noticed there was a thin carpet of frost forming on the lawns and the branches of the trees. An owl hooted forlornly.

"I know how you feel," Anthony muttered, as he set off in the direction where he'd last seen Harry. He would feel better and safer if the two were together, besides which, Harry hadn't looked well, and Anthony was concerned for him also. His footsteps scrunched over the icy lawns and his smart, expensive shoes slipped occasionally, threatening to cast him to the ground in a broken pile. Carefully slowing down a little, he thought he heard a noise to his left. Spinning around, was that a splash of icy blue, glimmering in the darkness? His mother was wearing pale blue. He headed towards the flash of colour, gathering speed again when suddenly, he slipped, and fell over a heap on the ground.

There was a groan and the heap moved.

"Harry! Are you alright, what are you doing?"

"Spot of sightseeing, old chap," Harry told him, giving him a weak grin. "Fell over, Anthony. Help me up, will you?"

Anthony hoisted his friend onto unsteady feet. Harry patted his shoulder.

"I need to find my mother. Come on, you can help me." In truth, Harry would probably be more of a hindrance, but Anthony did not want to risk him disappearing again, particularly given the fact his friend didn't look at all well. "We can talk as we look around the garden. My mother can't have gone far."

"Why on earth would she have gone out, with your grand party going on?" Harry asked, walking painfully beside Anthony, almost bent double, as if he were an old man.

"Why would Cecile have you take pictures of us in flagrante, Harry. What's going on? And why did she have you send me that cryptic message?" Anthony retorted. He had a few questions of his own for his friend, as he struggled to piece things together. "What would she get out of that?"

"The pictures weren't her doing. They were the work of that degenerate, Benson. He wanted to go into business for himself. Came to me with the idea of blackmailing her and needed a partner to help him do his dirty work. I wasn't interested. I'd had enough." Harry took a deep breath. "Cecile and I had an affair, too, Anthony. It was her who got me into that addictive filth, and the jazz ciggies. She's poison. She goes after anyone who she thinks can further her ambitions – she likes us young, naïve, and totally besotted by her. It feeds her ego. And of course, it keeps her amused because she's frankly very bored being the token wife of a homosexual husband."

Anthony's jaw dropped. "You know about Robert – and…" He found he could not say his stepfather's name.

"Robert and Philip?" Harry asked. "Yes, of course I did. I could hardly not when she was at such pains to tell me." His face was as diaphanous as the moon, round and pale, as he looked his friend squarely in the eyes. "That was what she had over me, Anthony. If I didn't do what she asked, she was going to tell you about her – and me, and she was going to tell you that I knew about Robert and Philip. So, I did what she wanted. I didn't want you to think badly of me, I didn't want to lose your friendship, Anthony." Sighing sadly, he added, "Although I suppose I should have stopped to think what you'd do if you found out I was trying to put the frighteners on you, whilst keeping so many things secret. I'm sorry."

There was a long silence. Anthony felt as though he had been in the ring with Jack Dempsey. Battered, punched to a pulp, and hurting all over. His best friend. How could Harry have done this to him?

"So, then Benson found out about Cecile and me, and by then, he knew that she was beginning to make advances to you. He told me that she wanted to confuse and worry you, make you dependent on her. She would turn detective so you would believe she was helping you. That's what she does, Anthony, she makes you want her so much, so you think she can do no wrong, and then, she casts you aside in the cruellest way. She told me she was going to tell Margaret, so I basically paid her off, gave her money to keep quiet and in the meantime, I'd become addicted to cocaine, I was a mess. The night I crashed the car – I was hoping it would finish me off." Tears filled Harry's eyes. "I never wanted to do this to you."

Anthony had to sit down on the cold grass for a moment. Cecile was having an affair with Harry? And was seeing his best friend, and sleeping with his best friend at the same time as she was sleeping with him! So, the baby, if indeed there was one, could well be Harry's. Then a thought struck him. That child could be anybody's. Cecile may not have stopped with just he and Harry. How many others had she slept with, how many others had paid her off following an ugly threat to tell all? Anthony felt sick again. Then another thought struck his shell-shocked brain.

"Did you really have to kill Benson?" Anthony had no sympathy and regard for the Fords' former chauffeur, but he wanted to know why.

"As I told you in the hospital, I didn't," Harry replied. "He came to Margaret's address; I spotted him out of the window. We argued about Cecile, about me not wanting to work with him to blackmail people. Then he told me he knew about my 'habits' he called them and told me to watch my back, and yours.

Margaret saw us, and he left, mumbling threats. Margaret and I quarrelled, and I left. I'd been drinking heavily but got into the car anyway, then next thing I remember was the hospital bed and seeing you."

Shocked and disappointed though he was, Anthony believed him. Harry was his closest companion in the world, and it must have taken him some guts to confess all this. Now, Harry was at rock bottom and seeking redemption. The shame, the lack of family support, coupled with a society that regarded sympathy and empathy as weaknesses, had left a lonely, broken figure whom Anthony felt he needed to help. However, he still had something to ask his friend, who was blowing his nose into a fine linen handkerchief.

"If you didn't kill Benson, then who did?" Anthony was hoping Harry could provide an answer and also hoped it wasn't the answer that he was expecting.

"Of that, I do not know. All I know is that blackmail and manipulation is her game. Not that I would put murder past her."

"She certainly would have motive," Anthony thought out loud. Cecile had set out to damage Anthony, who had seen her aggressive side before and whilst she would probably not soil herself with the act of premeditated murder, it wasn't beyond the realms of comprehensibility that she could have ordered the killing of the backstabbing Benson.

"Are you safe, Harry?" Anthony enquired, suddenly. Harry knew too much. Was his friend going to be next? Was he?

"No one is safe, old boy," Harry's reply was ominous. "Look, why don't we split up? I know we might be safer together, but we're not covering much ground, are we? And we need to find your mother."

Anthony suddenly remembered Soames and Jane. Of course, he had told Cecile about their affair. He had given her the leverage for blackmailing him, but he had also put his mother in grave danger, given Cecile's attack of Philip. He needed to get back into the house. "Harry, I have to go, where are you going now?"

"I don't know, Anthony," Harry sounded directionless and sorrowful. "I'll probably head that way, towards the summer house. Please be careful. Cecile Ford does not act alone; you do not know who is mixed up in this."

"Do you, Harry?" Anthony was accusing. "If you know anything, please just tell me!"

The sound of a loud gunshot and a cacophony of screaming prevented him from providing an answer. Dozens of terrified guests spilled out of the house, shouting for their drivers, car engines were hastily cranked, as the great and the good tried to escape whatever was happening inside the huge mansion. Anthony began to run back to the house when he heard another shot ring out. He hit the ground, grateful for the cover the dark night afforded him. The grass was ice cold, he could feel the moisture seeping into his clothing. He looked around to see Harry, who seemed to have frozen with fright.

"Harry!" screamed Anthony, his voice piercing through the pandemonium around them. "Drop the light, they can see you!" He was a sitting target to whoever was holding, and firing, the gun.

And the next shot didn't miss. Anthony watched as his best friend was thrown to the ground. He crawled his way over to Harry, who had a wound in his right arm. He was alive, but for how long? He needed medical attention, and this weather would not be kind to Harry's already weakened state. Swiftly standing up, oblivious of the danger, he removed his dinner jacket, and wrapped it around his friend.

"Poor shot," joked Harry, whose humour and bravery forced a laugh out of Anthony. "They can't hit us both if we are apart. Run that way!"

Anthony looked confused by Harry's comments, but the latter had no time to explain. "Anthony, go!" He pointed towards the barn as he tried to stand up and set off in the other direction. Another shot rang out, and both men scurried apart. Harry limped as fast as he could towards the trees, whilst his best friend headed towards his safe space, picking up the lamp which Harry had forgotten. He headed for a place where he would go when his bedroom no longer sufficed, a venue where he'd re-enact the stories and films he loved as a child, as well as indulge his more adult fantasies with a chambermaid he considered his first love. Lamp held aloft, he prised open the wooden door and went inside the barn. The ground was slippery and caused Anthony to lose his footing and drop the oil lamp. Lying on his back, he considered himself safe, but for how long? Someone had fired shots, one injuring his best friend, whilst his mother was nowhere to be seen. And how was Philip? Was he still alive? He'd looked rotten. And where was Cecile? What was Robert doing?

These thoughts made Anthony's head pulsate with pain as he pulled himself to a sitting position. His back against the wall, he discovered a new problem; the oil from the smashed lamp was already devouring the barn he was using as sanctuary, and it would not take long for him to be burnt to a crisp or choked by smoke.

Chapter 29

So here he was! The lover, the film buff, the dandy, the hypocrite, the flawed hero! Back to where it all began for him. He recalled his first day as a scared boy when he saw his new home. He recalled how huge and grand it was. No bigger than today, but the small boy from the city had never seen so much greenery and reasoned that the mansion probably hosted more windows than the entire row of two up and two downs on the street where he'd spent his early years. Anthony had reasoned that it would take him about an hour to get to his room and from the front door and a further twelve months to explore every part of the estate, both inside and out. He'd remembered feeling dirty as the décor looked so clean and was fearful of not wanting to touch anything lest he broke an ornament or a vase. His reflexes had come in very handy when he backed into an expensive and very detailed vase that he nearly knocked to the floor only to recover it in time before it shattered into a thousand pieces. His actions had drawn a smile from Dennehy, who seemed ready to play the hero and catch the vase, thus sparing Anthony from one of Philip's lectures.

His thoughts then drifted to downstairs, thinking about the hive of activity as house staff worked and lived their lives all to please the family they served. How wrong it all was, he thought now, fleeting memories of tired looking servants and his own nervous arrogance, once the money had worked his magic on him and he became aware of the power it bought him. He shook his head, recalling how he had used the barn in which he was sitting as an escape route, when his conscience occasionally prickled him or when he had to retreat following a lecture from his stepfather. He had used this place as his den, his film set, and, latterly, his love nest. The barn was the place that would give him hope and inspiration to be himself and live his life.

And now it could well be the place of his death! The heat was stifling, and smoke choked him in a way that Philip's hypocritical rhetoric never could. He needed to get out. He needed to find his mother, he had to survive at least that long and his chances of living if he remained here, were nil. Anthony Crawford mustered all his strength and bravery and made it out into the night, just managing to leap out of the door as the flames were about to engulf him. The barn was well ablaze and would soon be no more.

Anthony threw himself on the ground, his energy spent in trying to escape what he knew had surely been his funeral pyre. He looked towards the house, chest heaving, mind working. Every window was lit, all the lights having been switched on before the party as a show of sheer ostentatious indulgence. No sound came from below, where the house nestled within the protection of the low, sloping valley. It was eerily quiet. He glanced towards the huge oak trees in the direction Harry had taken and thought of his best friend. Where was he and was he even alive? Anthony hadn't heard any more gunshots, but a gunman was still out there with intentions of murder. That much he knew.

"Harry!" He called out into the emptiness; his only reply was the howling wind that was rising. His best friend may well still be on the grounds or on his way home, either way, he wasn't answering, which gave Anthony a choice of leaving the estate to safety or going back into the very house that could spell his doom. His mother had always been the one loving constant in his life. A wall of protection, a metaphorical firefighter who had always fanned the flames away from him, she was in danger, and it may only be her son that could save her. Added to that, his stepfather had been gravely wounded, and could possibly be dead.

The choice was a very simple one: He was going back to the house.

The darkness was now Anthony's ally. He needed to stay out of the light as he had no idea as to where his trigger-happy nemesis may be lurking, whoever they were. He avoided the gravelled driveway and successfully made it to the low stone wall that surrounded the house and led to the stone steps that he now took two at a time. The front door was open, which added to his disquiet. Where was Soames? What on earth were the staff doing? Again, the quietness struck him, it was as though the house was deserted yet wide open for anyone to walk in. He was ready to accept that invitation, he needed to move quickly but carefully. Jane was vulnerable, he needed to see his mother. Could she be dead? The thought chilled Anthony to his bones, as he pushed the dreadful possibility from his mind. He focused on what he knew, injuries to Philip, Harry, and Robert. Cecile was missing, and Soames had gone off, ostensibly to find Anthony's mother, but in reality, Anthony didn't really know where he was or what the butler was doing. Walking into the grandeur of the reception hall, an air of lingering melancholy greeted him, that brought a lump to his throat. He thought to the tense, anticipatory build up to what was going to be the social event of the year – a grand party and dinner at the Crawfords! Well, it had certainly been the event of the year, but unfortunately for quite the wrong reasons. Anthony thought of the house servants as he stood in the middle of deserted room. The only noise in the main hall was the huge grandfather clock. Where were all the servants? Anthony spotted the telephone, had the police or fire brigade been contacted? An instinct made him head towards the mahogany table and he picked up the telephone receiver. Another cold shudder ran down his spine upon realisation that the line was dead. Outside, it was bitterly cold, and the wind had really picked up, and was howling bad temperedly around the house, but Anthony doubted that this had caused the line to be disconnected. The line had been purposely cut. Young Crawford leant his back against the wall as though that offered him some extra protection. His gaze settled on the drawing room; he could see a dim slash of light escaping beneath the closed door. His movements were quiet but urgent as he headed to the room where he had first laid eyes on Cecile. Her image flashed across his mind, feelings of lust when visualising her naked body, the revulsion when thinking about what she had done to – and with – Harry, and to him. Anthony was by no means an innocent party, but he had been seduced by a serpent who had struck him with a forked tongue, and he had no chance of fighting her poisonous ardour. His hand rested on the door handle; he was to open this door in a far more cautious manner than he had his parents' bedroom.

Carefully easing the door open, relief and horror flooded through him upon sight of his mother sat by her now dead husband. Jane was sobbing, her makeup running down her thin face, her evening attire saturated in blood as she clung to the man who had earlier this evening been found in an illegal tryst with the husband of Anthony's lover.

Not that it mattered to Philip now. Turning towards his body, Anthony retched and had to look away. The previous head wound, caused by Cecile striking him with a candlestick had obviously not killed him. There was now a gaping hole courtesy of a gun shot from close range, which had blown Philip's face apart and almost beyond recognition. Blood, loose skin, sinew, and bits Anthony could only assume were pieces of his stepfather's brain were splattered over the sofa and the walls. Philip must have staggered downstairs from the bedroom, perhaps he had felt dizzy and gone to rest momentarily in the drawing room for he was sitting, ramrod straight, as usual, on the sofa with his head blown backwards and what was left of his eyes, closed. Anthony couldn't see a murder weapon, but could he see a suspect? Jane's red hand was still holding her now dead husband's, could this sorrow be guilt as well as grief.

"Mum," said Anthony in a gentle voice, forgetting etiquette, not caring to be formal and address Jane as 'Mother'. Placing his hands on her shoulders, he eased her away from Philip's body. At first, he felt her resistance, but eventually, she turned and fell into her son's arms, holding him tighter than she ever had before. She buried her face in his chest as Anthony looked around the room, his eyes settling on his dead stepfather. The only question now was who had killed him?

"Mum," Anthony said again. "What happened, here?" Jane continued to cry, her whole body shaking in her sorrow.

"Did you do this?" Anthony continued in his gentle tone.

"No," she sobbed. "They…" Jane was hysterical. Anthony

knew he had to be more forceful.

"Mum, who?" he demanded.

"I do believe she means us." Cecile and Robert entered the room. Robert's eyes had already begun to bruise, whilst she still exuded glamour and calmness despite the evening's events. Robert was holding a revolver just as tightly as he was holding Anthony's gaze. An act of vengeance was the primary motive for him striking Anthony with it, the blow and weight of the weapon knocking the young man onto the same sofa where his dead stepfather sat. Jane was man-handled roughly and pushed down next to him. She clung to her son, and in turn, Anthony moved closer and put a protective arm around her.

Robert remained standing, gun in hand, whilst Cecile sat herself down. She had found a glass and had poured herself a brandy. Anthony had to reluctantly admire her bravado, her absolute detachment from everything. Looking Robert in the eye, still with his arm around his mother, he set about piecing together the night's events.

"Why?" Anthony looked at Robert and nodded towards his dead stepfather. "You seemed very close earlier."

Robert sneered at Anthony's comment, but it was Cecile who chose to speak.

"You know, you did cause this, darling," she said, before taking a sip of brandy. "You and that irritating little friend of yours. So determined to confront Philip about the missing pictures. So funny, considering he didn't even know about them." she laughed.

"My husband's only crime was to love another man," Jane fought back tears.

"A crime he couldn't handle, especially the consequences of people finding out.," Cecile answered, matter-of-factly.

Anthony looked at his mother, who swivelled around to look at her dead husband sorrowfully. "It's true." Jane began to cry again. "Philip ended his own life rather than face who he really was."

"And what you are." Anthony hissed at Robert, his contempt for the man stalking the room.

"Oh, don't be so naïve, darling," snapped Cecile. "America bans alcohol, yet people of all classes are inebriated in all states. You have been to *Sherry's*; you have seen what goes on there. This world is all about image, whether it is a true reflection of who you are." She rose to her feet and stood by her husband. "Just like your mother, I knew full well what my husband preferred. It worked to my advantage, just as it did to his. But you and your lower-class morals have ultimately contributed to the death of you, your dear mother and Philip."

"So that is the plan. Kill us all." Anthony said whilst successfully hiding his sheer terror.

"Unfortunate," said Robert. "My wife did truly enjoy you."

"Gave her something you couldn't," retorted Anthony.

"Not really my type," said Robert. "Although I can appreciate her seductive charms."

"Thank you, darling." Cecile planted a delicate kiss on his cheek, before turning to Anthony. "I was looking forward to having you again. But you had to let that heart of yours rule your head and interrupt Robert and Philip. What exactly was your plan? What did you think I was going to do when I saw the pictures?"

"How did you know of the pictures?" Anthony asked curiously. "I never told you. Or did you arrange for us to be photographed, so you could use the pictures to blackmail me, like you blackmailed Harry? And what about Benson? Did you kill him because he was going to become a supplier of cocaine, play you at your own game and reduce your margins?"

Cecile and Robert laughed heartily. Anthony's fury was palpable whilst Jane simply looked confused, knowing nothing of what had gone on between her son and this cold-hearted woman who was married to her dead husband's lover.

"People like Cecile and I, do not soil our hands with scum like Benson."

"You had motive," Anthony pointed out.

"So did you and your friend. So did many, regarding him."

"You ordered the killing," accused Anthony. "You may not have pulled the trigger, but you knew what was going to happen to Benson."

"And I always follow instructions, Master Anthony," Soames chose this moment to make his entrance. Jane gasped and almost collapsed with shock. Anthony stared at the butler disbelievingly. He didn't like Soames, indeed he never had, and that feeling intensified when Anthony had discovered the man in a passionate clinch with his mother, but he had never thought Soames was anything other than a loyal and dutiful servant, certainly not a murderer.

"Uncle," purred Cecile as she kissed his cheek. Now it was Anthony's turn to be shocked. It was not often he was rendered speechless, but this was one of those times.

"A damn fine recommendation I made to Philip," laughed Robert. "Didn't take him long to discover his weaknesses and gain the leverage needed for us to get what we wanted."

"Which was?"

"Power, money, what else is there?" Cecile almost sounded maniacal. "We knew his preferences made him vulnerable, therefore his business was, shall we say, there for the eventual taking. You, of course, you spoilt it all by wanting to inherit Philip's business and up until recently, Philip had resisted all your pleading to join him in the company, but of late, he had discussed with Robert his intention to name you as his heir and admit you into the business. That was when we knew we had to act, we had to do something that would discredit you, something that we could use against you to force you not to accept Philip's offer." Cecile held out her hands as she twirled around, a smug smile on her perfectly constructed face. "Ta-dah! That, my darling, is why you were able to have me. Don't you think it was a perfect plot? It was all going so well, too."

Anthony struggled to comprehend all that she had revealed. Philip had wanted him in the business? He was his stepfather's heir? Oh, God, he thought now, as he stared sorrowfully at Philip's body. Then, a thought struck him.

"And what of my mother, Soames," Anthony addressed the butler. "Was she part of your plan or is it something deeper?" Young Crawford was playing a dangerous game but causing a divide between the trio may be the only chance his mother and he had of surviving. Soames averted his gaze, something Cecile had noticed and seemed unsettled by.

"A mere perk," she spoke on his behalf. "A bit like you, shall we say. A lot going on down below but not much up top."

"Does she always answer on your behalf, Soames?" Anthony sensed the butler's uncertainty and was keen to exploit it. Cecile had the same look in her eyes as she had when she had attacked Anthony in her hotel room. He was thankful that she wasn't holding a gun, or he may well be dead by now. Jane gripped his hand tightly.

Robert cut in, "We need to hurry. You cut the phone line, but the police will probably be en route. We need to get our stories straight and having live witnesses that won't corroborate our story is hardly helpful."

"I couldn't agree more, Sir," said Soames as he pulled the trigger.

Chapter 30

Anthony had been told that your life flashes before you just before you draw your final breath. Everything that you have done, seen, felt, is right there as you go into the abyss. Robert was about to discover if that were true as he fell to the ground following Soames' point-blank shot. Jane looked like she was about to have a heart attack as Anthony shielded her with his own body.

"Why!!" Cecile shrieked at Soames.

"Three is a crowd," her uncle told her in a tone which belied his just having taken someone's life. "I dealt with the problematic chauffeur of yours, and Robert was a weak link, a deviant, and it was a matter of time before his tendencies made us weaker." Soames gripped his niece with one hand, gun in the other. "We have taken many a rich man down, we don't need anyone else."

"This is 1925, you fool," Cecile was livid. "A single woman, a widow, will not have the same power in this hypocritical society as the wife of a wealthy businessman. Albeit a homosexual."

"All this will be yours," Soames reassured. "We can get both businesses, everything."

He pointed at Anthony. "He kills both in a fit rage upon making his discovery of their illicit affair, before murdering his own mother upon finding out she knew of her husband's secret."

Cecile seemed unconvinced. This was another man who had gone into business for himself and contradicted her plans. Teeth bared, she dug her nails into the face of Soames, who cried out in pain as he tried to fend off his niece's attack, dropping his revolver in the process. Anthony saw his moment, and charged the pair, swatting away Cecile with the back of his hand. She crashed into the wall and screamed out in frustration and anger. He turned to Soames, whose well-placed kick to the groin felled his younger opponent already nursing a bruised jaw from the butt of the gun that was still in Robert's hand. Soames grabbed Anthony by the throat. His eyes were wild as he choked the young master he despised so vehemently.

"A keen pugilist, Master Anthony," he said through gritted teeth. "But I always did find the Marquis of Queensbury's rules somewhat restricting." Anthony gripped Soames' hands and began prising them away with every bit of strength he had left. Soames was a wily veteran in the art of combat and drove a well-placed knee into Anthony's solar plexus.

"A lot of spirit for a hypocritical mother's boy," snarled Soames. "The only difference between you and I, is luck. Well, your luck has just run out."

Anthony spotted the shine of the blade drawn from Soames jacket at the same time he heard the gunshot. The butler's eyes looked wide enough to burst out of his head as he staggered forwards. Anthony moved out of the way and saw the smoking revolver pointed at him, with Jane's hand on the trigger. She was stony-faced and shaking as she watched the butler hit the ground. She had given Anthony life and now preserved it by executing the man who had also been her lover. Anthony got up as fast as he could, pain wrenched through his body as he approached Jane, who didn't put the gun down, instead turning it toward her next target. Anthony glanced over his right shoulder; Cecile was frozen with fear as she looked in horror at Jane holding the still smoking revolver. It was the most vulnerable she had ever been. She was ready to plead for her life.

"Jane, please," she cried. "I never wanted any of this. Everything I said just then was part of the plot my uncle had hatched to gain control of both our husbands' businesses! I had to go along with it, otherwise he would have killed me, too. I am not blame, I'm in love with your son. I am carrying his child."

Jane shot a glance at her son, before quickly turning back to the terrified woman in front of her.

"Is this true, Anthony?"

"Mother, I'm not sure," Anthony answered honestly.

"It is, Anthony. I'm pregnant and the baby is yours. We could be a family." Cecile begged.

Anthony's head pounded. Cecile was certainly desperate enough to fake a pregnancy in order to save her own skin, but the suggestion of normal family life with her after this evening's events and the plans of her husband and uncle made him sick to his stomach. For the first time he looked at her with unbridled hatred. Something that was shared by his mother who pulled the trigger for the second time tonight.

The loud click made everyone jump. Cecile took a moment to realise that she was still alive, whilst Jane and Anthony looked at the firearm, the latter also pondering the fact that his own mother was about to kill the woman who could well be carrying her own grandchild. A now relieved Cecile returned to character.

"You picked the wrong one, Jane, again." Cecile taunted.

Jane was confused but Anthony knew full well what Cecile was talking about. Robert had been carrying a gun, which to the best of knowledge, had yet to be fired and would therefore still be loaded. But Jane had picked up the gun her husband had used to shoot himself. Cecile and Anthony both looked at each other, uneasy smiles on both of their faces. This was a standoff, whoever reached the loaded gun in Robert's dead hand would be the victor in this dangerous game.

Suddenly, the door to the drawing room was flung open and in burst Stevens, a look of terrified bravery on his white face. He had been below stairs with the other servants, all of whom were frightened beyond contemplation. None of them had wanted him to come upstairs to find out what was happening, but Stevens had a great sense of duty, and he had told cook and the others to stay put, but he was going to find the master and help if he could.

Anthony and Cecile spun around at the sound of the door being opened and at the same time, the taut silence was shattered by two loud bangs and the sound of bullets ricocheting off the wall. Harry fired another shot, meant for Cecile, who leapt towards Robert's body, but Anthony was too fast for her, he rugby tackled her to the ground, just as Stevens fell to the floor, blood spurting from the wound in his chest caused by the last shot Harry had fired.

Harry collapsed to the ground in horror, overcome by emotion at the sight of Stevens' body. Anthony forgot all about

Cecile, and sprang forward towards the footman, in the hope that he was still alive. Jane had taken hold of Robert's gun, and this was the moment Cecile saw her chance. Struggling to her feet, she turned and fled as fast as she could, leaving the stunned mother and son, and Anthony's best friend to pick up the pieces and face the consequences.

"I never meant to kill Stevens," Harry cried, gun still in his hand. "It was Cecile I wanted. The head had to come off the serpent. It was her I wanted dead."

He looked at his best friend. "What happens now?"

Anthony shook his head. *"I haven't a bloody clue,"* he thought. What did happen now?

"You were never here," said Jane, decisively. "Hand Anthony your gun and go."

Anthony nodded at his best friend, taking the gun off him, and watching Harry as he stepped over Stevens' body, and disappeared silently into the hallway and from thereon, who knew? The police were coming, Anthony was sure that someone would have alerted the authorities, one of the guests perhaps, who had left the party after the first shots had been fired, and his mother and he were surrounded by three dead bodies. Their stories needed to be straight. Harry was a weak link, so having him out of the picture made sense. Anthony also felt better about it; he'd let his best friend down of late, pretending Harry was never here would be redemption for himself in his own eyes. Anthony would deal with the fact that he was aiding his friend to get away with murder, later. Whether or not those who died had deserved it was not for Anthony to decide, but he needed to ensure the safety of both he and his mother. Jane had taken a life in defence of her son; it was only Soames and Harry who'd taken life in cold blood on this evening.

Inspector Naden didn't take a lot of convincing and seemed more disgusted with the details of Philip and Robert's relationship than the multiple shootings that had taken place. Philip had taken his own life rather than admit to the world who he truly was, whilst Soames had been slaughtered by Robert, who had learnt of the butler planning to cut him out of the threesome's gruesome deal. Stevens had come into the drawing room as Robert had fired the second shot, which had killed him instantly. Robert had then turned the gun on himself. Anthony had placed the empty gun by Robert and was relying on the fact that the infancy of forensics would hinder any police contradiction to their story. Thankfully, Naden saw a cut-and-dried case. The two homosexuals would make perfect scapegoats for these crimes and a positive and fast result would be another step on the greasy pole of promotion, not to mention another foot in the door of high society the corrupt inspector desperately craved.

Jane had instructed Anthony to hide the gun Harry had used to shoot Stevens. Naden hadn't even searched the house when he had arrived at the crime scene. He'd spent a considerable amount of time taking statements, whilst conveying his condolences and rudely ordering his subordinates to secure the scene and let no one in. His promise to keep the scandal out of the newspapers suited both Jane and Anthony, who both expressed their appreciation most robustly. Naden bought their story, and Jane knew she would now be treated with sympathy as the widowed wife who had known nothing of her husband's true self.

Naden's snobbery meant that the other servants, who had taken refuge in the kitchen, were questioned only briefly, not that they had much to say. Anthony wondered what would become of them, indeed, what would happen to himself and his mother. So many futures were uncertain.

Once the police and the undertakers had left, Anthony had dismissed the servants for the night, telling them all to go to bed, and instructing Dennehy to assume command of the staff. The house quietened again, lights were extinguished, and rooms tidied just as dawn brought a cold, winter sunrise and the sound of a cock crowing carried along the valley on the morning breeze, the stormy, almost gale force wind of the previous night having died out.

Sighing heavily and watching his mother climb wearily up the stairs, Anthony realised he needed to get out of the house.

Donning an overcoat over his blood-stained shirt and waistcoat, he headed for the area where the barn once stood. The fire brigade had done an admirable job in extinguishing the flames that had so nearly engulfed Anthony, who stared blankly at the charred remains of his childhood memories.

He stood alone staring at the world before him and wondered what would become of him. With his stepfather dead, Anthony had no idea what the legal ramifications for the Crawford business would entail, and the house, and his allowance. What would happen? Would Anthony be thrust back into the life of depravation and poverty from which he had been plucked when his mother married Philip? He let out a sigh and his breath made a cloud in the chill of the early morning air.

Anthony hadn't known how much he had come to appreciate all that he had until he was faced with the stark reality of it all being taken away from him. The sigh of regret became a roar of frustration. Why? Why had this had to happen? It had spoilt everything. No. Cecile had spoilt everything. The taste of bile rose sharp in Anthony's throat as he recalled the passion he thought he felt for her, and she for him, when he was no more than the next meal ticket, the next victim to be duped and drained in order to feed her greed for the high life. But wasn't that very greed apparent in him too? Had he not fed off Philip's hand, enjoyed more than the proverbial crust Philip had been sure he was able to eat? Oh, yes! In some ways, that made him no better than Cecile, the only difference being that Anthony had not resorted to murder in order to partake of the delicious meal constantly enjoyed by those entitled to eat it.

He thought of his 'best friend', Harry, a man he didn't know anymore. A man Anthony had let down, whose veiled warnings of getting involved with Cecile he had ignored whilst Harry had risked his own life, in order to save Anthony's. And for what? To have the 'future' he had anticipated walking into cruelly taken away from him by the crash of a pewter candlestick on the forehead of a man he had neither respected nor loved, in the true sense of the word. Now Harry was embroiled in all this, possibly still addicted to the cocaine he had been so willingly supplied with by Cecile, and whose life may well now be in danger at the hands of a woman whose greed and ambition would not let anyone stand in her way until she got what she wanted. He knew Harry would not answer for his crimes in this life – the rich never seemed to – but he had to live with his own demons in a world nowhere near ready enough to accept them. Anthony questioned if he would ever see his best friend again.

The sun was now a fiery orange disc in an otherwise colourless sky. The world was awakening to the new day, a day without Philip Crawford going to the office. A day without Soames quietly serving the house. A day without Stevens, the footman who was perhaps not that much younger than Anthony, no longer able to further his ambitions of becoming under butler. His ambitions had been killed, as he had, all because someone else felt their ambitions mattered more. What was he to do, Anthony wondered. What would his mother do?

Thinking of his mother made his heart hurt. She was a woman Anthony now knew was capable of murder; a woman who would have pulled the trigger on another woman, reputedly pregnant with Anthony's child. A woman who would have potentially killed her own grandchild. How had marriage to Philip Crawford resulted in his mother becoming a cold-blooded killer? Anthony knew he would never have the answer, the only thing he could possibly blame was their lifestyle. The wealth, the privilege, the absolute conviction that they deserved more than anyone else had led to four deaths, several attempted murders and the disappearance of the woman he had once loved, who may or may not be pregnant with his child, not to mention the fact that his best friend was also a candidate for potential fatherhood and Cecile and Robert Ford had also ordered Soames to kill their chauffer. Five deaths. For the love of money. Anthony shook his head and then put his head in his hands as if to try to obliterate the past few hours from his memory, although he knew he would live the last twenty-four hours for the rest of his life.

Straightening up, Anthony grimaced as he felt his wounds. Superficial cuts and a bruised groin and jaw would probably be judged as him getting off lightly. The marks on his neck had been questioned by Naden, with Anthony blaming Alfonse when the two had scuffled in *Sherry's*. It was as weak a story as could be, but the inspector was more than willing to accept it.

The mental scars, however, would not be so easy to get over, thought Anthony. How would he ever be able to come to terms with his part in the whole, sad story? For he had played a part, he had been playing a part ever since he had become part of the Crawford family. The rich, good-looking, playboy stepson of the incredibly wealthy entrepreneur who had married his mother. The cold air bit his face like guilt, he could not deny he had become part of the hypocrisy and double standards that he professed to despise. The thought made Anthony hate himself and he shivered, despite his thick, expensive overcoat. He wondered if he would ever feel warm again.

If this was the big screen production, Anthony was not a fan. His selfish ways and childish pipe dreams had contributed to much heartache. He'd forgotten who he really was as he pursued a hedonistic life of film, sex, and adventure. He'd risen from the slums by luck, and now that luck seemed to have deserted him.

"What on earth am I going to do?" he said aloud, his words dissipating into the gossamer misty morning.

"You'll carry on, Anthony," Jane uttered in a tired, weary voice. "You'll carry on, and so will I. We'll be fine and who knows what the future holds and where we are going?"

"I do, Mum," replied Anthony, as he took a big step to the left. His focus was different now, but his sorrow and doubt were perhaps too much to do anything. And was this world even able to be fixed, had society gone too far? He still had the gun in his pocket, was this the end that his story was meant to have?

He drew the .38 revolver from his coat and raised it to the right side of his head.

"No, Anthony!" screamed Jane.

About the Author

When he's not writing, or working, John helps his wife bring up their daughter, Daisy-Mae and supporting Everton Football Club, who he says need all the help they can get!

John lives in Blackpool and not surprisingly, given the mentions of the silver screen and boxing in his debut novel, he loves the cinema and boxing!

John currently works within the care and mental health industry and is a keen advocate of improving mental health care and support for young adults.

At the time of this book going to press, John has already started writing the second book in the Crawford Chronicles.

More from Provoco Publishing

THE WATCHTOWER

BY D.C. CUMMINGS

PROLOGUE

Squinting against the blackness, the old woman waited until her eyes could focus. She could see the harsh outline of the building, which stood senatorial as if it were on guard from whatever was out there. Further afield, she knew there was the sea, and the quick, iridescent sparks of light that flew, almost unnoticed, above it. She could see them. She knew they were there. And so did the tower. Why else had it been built there, upon its lonely escarpment? This stretch of coastline spans out for miles until the sea became a mere inlet to the river Watten. Hence, the name of the town, Bourne – upon – Watten. But who had been born here, upon the river Watten, Ginny wondered. Or more precisely, *what* had been born here? And why could she feel it, acknowledge it? The deeply unsettling feeling of nervous anticipation threatened to engulf her as the darkness became thick, cloying and she found it hard to breathe.

'Ginny! Ginny, you tiresome woman! Come in from the cold. There be trouble if t'maister finds you gone!'

Ezekiel! Ginny startled and drew her cloak around her, half turning away from the dancing sparks above the fretful waves.

Something was wrong out there, and although he wouldn't confess it, Ginny knew that Ezekiel felt it, too.

'I be a-comin' Ezekiel Worrall, don't be a-frettin'. Maister won't know. Why would he?'

Why indeed, she thought, with a swift, uncertain glance back at the sea. The sparks had disappeared, and, in their place, the waves roared upwards, black, malevolent, filling her with a sense of dread. She turned and ran as quickly as the darkness allowed her, in the direction of Ezekiel's voice.

*

Vinny Prease was out of breath by the time she had climbed up several flights of stairs in order to arrive at the top floor of the building. Gasping theatrically and grinning to herself at her own lack of fitness, she made a mental note to renew her gym membership, then her imagination ripped the note into tiny fragments. As if she had time to go to the gym, as if she actually *wanted* to go to the gym. So far as she could gather on the few occasions she had actually stepped over the threshold of *Gym & Tonic*, it seemed to be populated entirely by slim, over made-up women who never broke into a sweat by doing anything that constituted exercise. Her turning up there had turned a few heads at her oversized tee shirt, cotton jersey joggers, and – the shame – a pair of Puma training shoes. The heads had taken note of Vinny's lack of make-up, her round, moon-like face framed by untidy dark curls that matched the dark circles underneath her blue eyes and they had turned away from her with a dismissive shake of their own perfectly coiffured, bleached, and trendily cut hairstyles.

Now, Vinny shook her own still untidy dark head and turned her attention to the view, which was what she had taken such pains to come to see. Her thigh and calf muscles would probably never forgive her – she could feel them tensing and burning now, but she didn't care, she thought, as she swept towards the window seat and greedily drank in the vista before her. Out there, in the bleakness of a dark, wintery afternoon, she knew the view wasn't as spectacular as it could be. Yet despite the thin, whisp like mist that shrouded the treetops as they tumbled towards a restless sea, she could still make out the huge, foamy waves as they struck against the rocky inlet which formed part of the peninsular upon which, stood the building she was standing in. Along the blurred coastline, she could see for miles, undisturbed by houses and the built-up environs of modern life. Here it was more ethereal, somehow closer to the past than the present. There was no hint to modernity, no huge electricity pylons, no controversial 5G masts, no electrical substations. All she was aware of was the fractious waves and the elemental coastline, stretching for untold miles as it wrapped around the landscape like a protective hand. Narrowing her eyes, concentrating her vision, she could just make out the boggy, marsh beds which gave way to the dull, gold sand of Bourne Bay. She considered. Yes, she liked it. With a final glance out to the sea, she caught a shimmer of sparks above the bay, dancing about aloft the tumult of the waves. She frowned, wishing it was a clearer day so she could see better.

'That view is quite something, isn't it?' the estate agent who was conducting the viewing asked, as she joined Vinny next to the window. Behind the agent, Howard came up the stairs, puffing laboriously.

'When I can breathe and see again,' he grinned, 'I'm sure it is.' Making his way behind Vinny, he placed a hand on her hips. 'Like it?'

Vinny nodded, listening to her husband's breathing become steadier.

'We'll both have to do something about our fitness, though. I was as knackered as you were, coming up those stairs.'

'I don't need to worry about my fitness,' Howard told his wife, smugly. 'I'll just let you have this room and I'll have that small snug on the ground floor.'

Listening to the buying signals the couple were making, the estate agent asked, 'So, you like the place?'

Vinny and Howard remained silent, each tuning into the other telepathically, the way you were able to do, when you had been married over twenty years and knew each other just as well as you knew yourself. An imperceptible nod. A quiet smile.

Howard turned to the estate agent, as she waited, holding her breath for the couple's decision which, if favourable, would mean that she had gotten the most aged listing and the most awkward instruction off the company's sales register at last. Plus, of course, there was the hefty commission.

'We like it,' he told the woman, who visibly sighed with relief. 'Subject to survey and contract, of course, and provided the place isn't haunted.'

Outside, above the swirl of angry waves, the sparks seemed to oscillate wildly; twisting and turning around each other until they merged into an unseen brightness which flew towards the building, as if trying to protect it from the obsidian darkness which threatened to engulf it.

CHAPTER ONE

'Are we doing the right thing?' Vinny asked, as Howard ushered her onto the pavement outside the estate agency from where they had just collected the keys to their new home.

'It's a bit bloody late in the day to tell me it's the wrong thing!' laughed Howard, as he gave her a quick hug and then strode towards the car. 'Come on, Virginia Prease, we need to get there before the removal lorry gets lost, or worse, stuck on that dreadful single-track road to the house!'

Following her husband towards the car, Vinny tried to shrug off the elements of doubt that had crept into her being of late and, putting the keys to the new house in her shoulder bag, she eased herself into the passenger seat whilst giving her husband a playful smile.

'You might need to think of a new car, darling, Baby won't like the ruts and the stones on that track,' she was half teasing; Baby was Howard's low slung, perfectly preserved classic TR7 car and his pride and joy. She couldn't imagine him parting with it, but at the same time, she couldn't picture the suspension lasting very long on their newly acquired private road to the house. She had sold her own zippy little Fiat 500, because she was a slightly nervous driver, and didn't want to tackle the journey from Surrey to Yorkshire, worried about her own abilities to cope with such a distance. So, the little jaunty, yellow town car had been sold and she was considering buying something more substantial to tackle the country roads and the rocky, dirt track to the house. Something like a tank, she thought now.

'I suppose this could be my weekend car, couldn't it?' Howard replied, smiling at her as he indicated to turn onto the busy main road which lead towards Bourne – upon – Watten, and their new home. 'I could get a Range Rover, or something similar for the weekday commute.'

The reminder that Howard was now going to be office and factory based, as opposed to working from home, as he had been for the past two years since the start of the pandemic, caused Vinny further unease and she fell silent. Howard, concentrating on the unfamiliar roads and the sat nav, let the silence develop and Vinny turned her head to look out of the window at the landscape which unfurled before her.

Where they had lived previously, a stone's throw away from the Surrey Hills, the surrounding countryside had been lush, thick, and somehow uniform in comparison to the wild unkemptness of Yorkshire. The fields looked harsh, the rock formations jagged and threatening. It was more open than Surrey, she thought, which enfolded you and somehow protected you; here, there was no such protection. The greenness was mean and gave way here and there to the silvery rocks where Bourne - upon – Watten rose up and then swooped away towards the ever-present sea, tempestuous, wild.

Did she like it? When they had viewed the house that was now their home, she had been swept along on a wave of romanticism, feeling very Heathcliff and Cathy. Her torrid imagination had poured images into her head that fed her desire to grasp the opportunity which had presented itself to Howard, to reach the pinnacle of his career in engineering but had required removing, as the company had demanded of them. A relocation north, to this part of the country she had never even heard of before. Now they were actually here, and about to embark upon their new life, the sense of adventure she thought she had felt was somewhat absent. All she felt was apprehension. She realised she'd never answered her own question, did she like it?

'You'll get used to it, Vinny. We all will,' Howard's voice cut into her ruminations.

'How do you know what I'm thinking?' she asked, abandoning her unanswered question for another time, and turning to look at her husband, who had a tension about him, suddenly. Perhaps it was because the roads were unfamiliar, she thought.

'You've got your "making the best of a bad job" face on.' His own face relaxed momentarily to poke fun at his wife before his shoulders tensed again and he turned back to the road. The sat nav announced he needed to turn off to the left in four hundred yards and he weaved the car over into the left-hand lane, slowing a little.

'I wonder what the children will think of it,' Vinny mused, not falling into the trap of self-defence her husband had set for her.

'They don't have a say in it,' Howard replied, quite sharply, as he swung Baby to the left and into a country lane. 'This move is part of my job, which pays their expensive school fees, so even if they don't like it, they'll have to lump it!'

Vinny blinked in surprise. He sounded unlike himself; taciturn and unyielding. Frowning, she was about to voice her defence of their absent offspring when the car suddenly jolted and Howard let out a rarely heard, 'Fuck!' as they both heard a loud scraping of metal against stone. The tarmacked road had petered and narrowed into the single tracked, stone and shingle lane that led to their home.

'Jesus!' Vinny replied, grabbing hold of the dashboard to try to brace herself against the bumping and lurching of the car over the uneven surface. 'That sounded like a "this might possibly be expensive" noise.'

Howard winced. 'I bloody hope not,' he retorted. 'Getting parts and someone to repair Baby won't be cheap, or easy in a place like this!' It was the first time he had acknowledged the remoteness of their surroundings.

The track suddenly widened, the hedgerows on either side giving way to a large, flat expanse of stubbly green grass on one side and what looked like a sand and shingle mixture on the other. Facing them, the huge, four storey tower seemed omnificent, dark, and forbidding almost, its honey-coloured traditional Yorkshire stone exterior weathered to black, making the huge edifice seem hawklike and uninviting. Stretching out to its right was a single storey extension, which the estate agent had said dated from the early nineteenth century, although the tower itself was thought to have been built in the late fifteen hundreds.

'Spooky looking, isn't it?' Howard murmured into the silence which had developed since he had switched off Baby's engine.

Vinny said nothing, she simply nodded and climbed out of the car, its lime green paintwork and dark green roof looking very out of place within such close proximity to the ancient building. Her eyes swept around the forecourt, to the wide expanse of rough headland that was theirs also, to where the cliff dropped away dramatically and tumbled down to the boggy marsh that led, eventually, to the beach and the sea. The only sound she could hear was the insistent crashing of the waves against the headland and the pitiful caw, caw, caw of the seagulls, swooping and diving above, caught on the ever-present sea breeze that whipped around the tower almost angrily. Brushing her hair to one side, she tucked it into the collar of her denim jacket to stop it flying energetically around her face and she looked at Howard, who was wearing an inscrutable expression. The look made her feel very nervous.

'I suppose we'd better go in,' she said, rather reluctantly.

Why was she so reticent about crossing the threshold? For God's sake, the last time she had been here, she had loved the place, the remoteness, the sense of history, the bleak openness. She looked around, feeling a tightening of her stomach muscles. The air seemed to hiss, then recoil. She had no idea why she was feeling like this. Like what? she thought. Wretched. She felt as though her soul was being wrenched out of her being and all that was left was an empty shell of a life she wasn't meant to live. Panicking, she turned around to find Howard sighing exasperatedly.

'The keys, Vinny?' his voice sounded tired and irritable again.

'Gosh, sorry, Howard,' she said, suddenly flustered, hot. She pulled the keys out of her handbag, almost dropping them to the ground in her haste. Howard snatched them out of her trembling hands, muttering something about dithering women as he strode towards the huge wooden door of the tower.

Inside, it was cold despite the brightness of the spring day outside. Any light that poured in through the tall, mullioned windows quickly evaporated into a pall of what Vinny could only describe as a rancorous gloom. The vast, empty space with its flagstone floors and impossibly high ceilings seemed to wear darkness like a shroud. Vinny shivered, listening to their footsteps as they echoed in the emptiness.

'This will make one hell of a reception hall, Vinny,' Howard marvelled, his head bent upwards as he took in the ornate, coved ceiling with its magnificent chandelier. His eyes swept around the room, resting upon the large, cast-iron fireplace. 'Can you imagine this, lit? With a drinks cabinet to the left beneath the window and the lamp table to the right? We'll need more sofas. The piano can go over there.' He pointed to another large, arched mullioned window on the other side of a huge oak panelled door. Vinny recalled it led to an inner hallway, the first of many flights of stairs to the upper floors and a skinny, tall corridor off which was the kitchen, dining room, and sitting room. The snug that Howard had decided he would use as his home office was located in an arched recess off the sitting room.

'We'll need some bloody huge logs, for firewood,' she pointed out to Howard, who was standing with his back to her, staring out of the window by the fireplace. 'And kindling. Have you thought of that?'

Another look of impatience. Vinny sighed. The move seemed to have made him irritable and lacking in patience. She supposed it was because of the workload he would take on once the new factory became operational. He would commence commuting next week, leaving Vinny to do the unpacking and to get used to the new house and its remote location. There were lots of walks along the coastal path and the inland track which led, eventually, to Bourne-upon-Watten, the small townlet which had grown as a result of its geography and its proximity to the river Watten. Vinny was happy enough that there was a lot to see and discover, what she was going to lack were people. Neighbours. Humans. Apart from Howard, who would be at work most days, for many hours, she would be alone. She shivered, and not just because of the cold.

'You're right,' said Howard, turning and catching her involuntary shaking. 'It is rather cold. Let me go to the cellar, crank up the boiler. We'll need to source a local supplier for oil,' he continued, 'although the agent assures me that the tank is half full and that should last till the end of the year. Shan't be long, look out for the removals wagon!'

His footsteps receded down the corridor and Vinny became aware of the heaviness of the atmosphere once more. Glancing around nervously at the immense fireplace and the vast emptiness of the reception hall, she scurried after Howard and headed for the sitting room, at the back of the house. This room, at least, had smaller proportions that Vinny felt she could deal with. There was a set of large French doors that led to a garden terrace and sunlight streamed through them, pouring crepuscular rays onto the honeyed wooden floor. The brightness galvanised her and she let out the breath she realised she had been holding, shaking her head at her own stupidity. With a new spring in her step, she trotted over to the French doors and stared out at the flagged terrace, which housed an ancient wrought iron bench and table. She thought they could be removed, scrapped, and that the seven-seater rattan corner suite and low table would be perfect there, imagining summer evenings with a balmy sea breeze and drinks with friends. This brought her mind back to the isolated location. There were not many friends close to hand, she thought.

Still focussing on the garden, she felt a movement behind her. The boiler must have cranked quite easily, she thought, if Howard was back already.

'Well, that wasn't too onerous a job, was it?'

She turned around to greet her husband and the rest of what she was about to say died on her tongue as her eyes darted around the empty room. Again, she felt a restlessness, an unexplained frisson of anxiety.

'Howard?'

Her voice sounded very small and nervous. Hell, she was nervous, she thought, realising she was wringing her hands and that they felt damp with cold sweat. She became aware that the brightness had faded, and the room seemed dark, oppressive.

'Howard do stop messing around!'

There was a plaintive edge to her voice now, as she hurried out of the living room. The corridor also seemed much darker that it had five minutes ago. The narrowness bore down upon her as fitful shadows danced around. Fumbling for a light switch, she eventually managed to flick on the lights and as she did so, she caught sight of two figures in the doorway which led back into the reception hallway. Perhaps the removal lorry had arrived, and Howard had let the loaders in, she wondered, increasing the pace of her footsteps down the flagstone corridor. Where had they gone, was her first thought, as she reached the staircase on her left. Glancing upwards, she saw unformed shapes on the first half landing, and gasped as she heard a mournful shriek, which pierced the stillness of the air around her.

She let out her own involuntary cry and wrenched open the door to the reception hall where she was confronted by a solid, black shape of a man. Her cry became a scream as she felt strong arms clasp around her and then, there was nothing.

*

'Feeling better?'

Howard's voice was laced with concern as Vinny opened her eyes and became aware she was laid on the floor, being supported by his arms. She registered the cold hardness of the flagstones, permeating her jeans and shivered, despite her check shirt and Arran knit jersey. Heaving herself upwards, and passing a clammy hand over her forehead, she grinned ruefully at her husband as he tried to hide his annoyance at her collapse on such a busy day. When she'd cannoned into him, in her rush down the corridor, the removal lorry had just pulled up on the forecourt and the loaders were keen, champing at the bit to get the couple's possessions unloaded so that they could make a head start on the laborious journey back southwards. They had no time for and did not appreciate fainting clients.

'I'm okay,' she ventured, taking a swift look around the reception hall which, now that the front door was flung open in readiness for the unload to begin, didn't look so dark and foreboding. Maybe she was just overwrought with the journey, and the move itself. By the time she struggled to her feet, she had convinced herself that she was just being silly, and Howard had already disappeared outside to begin barking instructions at the removal people.

The feeling of light calmness she had felt in the house with Howard bent over her solicitously began to evaporate as she became aware of the oppressive darkness settling around her once more. Glancing at the front door, it was open; outside was a vague sunlight, there was no reason for this room to be so dark. Yet it was.

She became overwhelmed with a need to be outside and nearly body slammed one of the loaders who was coming through the door laden with heavy boxes. Muttering a multitude of apologies, near to tears, Vinny pelted towards the car, breathing heavily, her heart beating wildly in her chest.

'Howard!' she screamed, desperately wrenching at the passenger door of the little bright green car. 'Open the car!'

Her husband came striding over to the car, a look of considerable annoyance on his set features.

'Virginia, what the hell are you playing at, for fuck's sake?' Angrily, he snapped the key into the lock and opened the car. Vinny almost fell inside.

'I'm sorry, Howard. I needed a drink,' she grabbed the bottle of water she had put into the car at the start of their journey northward, grateful to have been able to supply him with an excuse for her behaviour.

'Is there any need to be quite so dramatic about being thirsty?' his tone was one of suppressed irritability.

'I'm sorry,' she said, again. 'Perhaps I'm tired. The journey, or the excitement, or something,' she paused. 'I'll come inside in a minute. I just need some fresh air.'

Howard had already stalked away, and Vinny was left standing by the car with a half empty bottle of water in her hand and a bunch of misgivings keeping her company.

In the far distance, out over the relentless sea, where a diaphanous mist hung like a shroud, the shimmering sparkles appeared.

The Watchtower will be available late 2024 on Amazon and in all good bookstores.

Printed in Great Britain
by Amazon

35749482R10160